THE DRIFT WOOD

PRATIMA SRIVASTAVA

olive turtle

NIYOGI BOOKS

Published by
NIYOGI BOOKS
D-78, Okhla Industrial Area, Phase-I
New Delhi-110 020, INDIA
Tel: 91-11-26816301, 49327000
Fax: 91-11-26810483, 26813830
email: niyogibooks@gmail.com
website: www.niyogibooksindia.com

Editor: Gita Rajan
Design: Shashi Bhushan Prasad
Cover Design: Misha Oberoi

ISBN: 978-93-85285-74-5
Publication: 2017

Printed at: Niyogi Offset Pvt. Ltd., New Delhi, India.

To my parents

The rain had picked up again after a next to nil lull! So had the wind whooshing wildly through the tall ashokas and palms of Shashank's house. His young daughter Shweta, sitting in the veranda with the radio in her lap, had to hurriedly wheel her chair in to protect herself from the big droplets pattering down thick and fast.

It had been pouring, virtually nonstop, the whole of last week. Nothing had changed; glowering clouds, flashes of lightning, thunderous downpours—without respite. It seemed as if the heavens had opened up, ready to empty all their pent-up fury on earth. Roads, flooded with rain water, had turned into rivers. The diffused headlights of vehicles perforating the shroud of darkness seemed to be crawling along surreptitiously as if not to offend the scourge of Nature. Moments back, there had been a noisy squall, soon to be replaced by a thick curtain of rain marching down the streets, heavy and remorseless, trumpeting along every lane of the city. The wrath of the rain god had sent all life forms—human as well as animal, scurrying into their shelters; only those with no means of protection were standing hapless—bearing the brunt of Nature's fury and praying for some sanity to return to earth.

The holy city had come to a virtual standstill. Fallen trees, disrupted electricity and communication lines, water logging in low lying areas—all these had thrown normal life out of gear. The district administration had dutifully shut down all schools and colleges *sine die*. The government offices, though open, registered thin attendance with skeletal staff.

Cloudbursts and continuous rains far away in the mountains had raised the water level in the catchments of Ganga and Yamuna, causing them to appear swollen, scary and turbulent. The elevated sandy banks on either side of the rivers had been fast diminishing with every passing hour, indicating the bulging underbellies of the rivers rising to dangerous levels. No longer did they flow quietly, passing by the city, attracting devotees to come and wash off their sins. The earthy brown colour of Ganga and the turquoise blue of Yamuna were now donning a single uniform hue of foaming white, a single tone of roaring waves, sweeping off whatever came in their way; entire trees, sheets of hyacinth, logs, boats—in short, any object that could float.

The flotsam rushing past reminded Shashank of someone long lost: *Where has he been drifting? Like lost driftwood? Would he not return home?* Imprisoned within the four walls of his house, having nothing worthwhile to do, Shashank found it hard to kill the free time he suddenly found at his disposal. He went around from one room to another, inspecting, checking to see if anything anywhere warranted his immediate attention. Soon enough, he found himself inside the store; where he had not stepped in for ages.

There was a dusty haphazard pile right in front of him, consisting of miscellaneous items that had ceased to be of use over the years. A pedestal fan, cricket bats of different sizes, a black and white television set, an old lawn mower, plastic pipes, empty cartons, deflated footballs, a pram, a tricycle — all piled up on top of something that was on top of something else. Shashank smiled vaguely, as a few bubbles of excitement rose to the surface, from his pool of memories. But was he not supposed to banish these memories from his mind? Was he not supposed to keep distance from these swirling waves of pain that he had shut, locked and sunk to the bottom of the pool, so that they lay in a dormant state until they were dead and fossilised? No, Shashank did not want to remember anything.

With lightning speed, he stepped back and was just about to pull the door shut, when he discovered that all this while he had been standing in a pool of black liquid that was being fed by a pencil thin stream meandering from the shelf on the left. He quickly set about finding the source and climbed up the mound. Hah! So this was it! It was the kadahi containing gooseberry and henna mix that Bina had soaked overnight for conditioning her hair, but had not been able to use the next morning due to her asthma attack. The rain water getting in through the skylight had filled it up and was overflowing and trickling down the shelf. Probably, Chandan, their domestic help, had placed it in the safety of the store to ward off Buzo, the Pomeranian pup, from carrying out his misadventures. Last week it had jumped into a bagful of wheat flour in the kitchen and came out white-washed from tip to toe. In this case, with the gooseberry and henna mix, chances were that Buzo would come out dyed jet black. Chandan was becoming wiser with each of Buzo's mischief, Shashank thought with a smile. He removed the erring kadahi away from the skylight and bolted the store behind him.

There was at last a brief lull. Shashank looked up and scanned the skies. He was delighted that after a long time, blue dominated the isolated patches of grey. His watch showed three minutes past ten. He peered over the balcony and craned his neck to survey the neighbourhood, exploring the possibility of a quick stroll outside. Everything around looked soaking wet. Every perceptible depression was filled to the brim. But Shashank could not care less. He had to venture out of the confines of his home for a while and breathe in some fresh air. Dashing straight into his room, he picked up his wallet from the shelf, thrust it in his pocket and took the umbrella hung on the nail behind the main door. He thought of changing into rubber pumps, decided against it and walked out in his slippers itself.

He must have walked not more than a furlong, when he realised the scale of devastation the incessant rains had brought about. The road was expectedly deserted, with people preferring to stay in the comfort of their homes. Only the neighbourhood boys roamed around aimlessly, whistling and shrieking amongst themselves as they waded through the waters in glee.

'Hi Boys! Enjoying the rains?' Shashank waved and called out as he passed them. One of the boys waved back, 'Yes Sir! We are enjoying our extended Rainy Day!'

'Enjoy it while it lasts!' he laughed and moved ahead.

Beyond the market, where the pavements had been eaten up in the last widening, the manifestation of the fury of nature was most glaringly evident. The upright telegraph poles now lay on the ground. The battered streetlights clung precariously to the edges of their grey frames and guaranteed that that night too the road was going to be bathed in darkness. The Ramlila Park, beyond the vegetable market, had turned into a muddy pool with floating filth, torn and tattered footwear bobbing like ships without sail. The little hutment at the corner of the park, which had been made of discarded plywood nailed together with some rusted tin sheets, had been totally razed to the ground. Shashank recollected the cheerful and ever-smiling faces of its occupants, Raj and his wife and hoped that they had moved into a safer haven, way before this devastation. Heaving a deep sigh, he moved ahead.

A small crowd of customers had gathered at the local dairy. Shashank hurried up and purchased whatever he thought would be needed, if the weather continued to remain intemperate. The stock stacked at the front counter of the dairy disappeared in no time. The van which brought fresh supplies every morning had not shown up since the day before. On top of that, the dairy owner himself was in a hurry to shut down and leave; his own home, in Bagadha area, was under waist-deep water. Shashank quickly picked up a few essentials like bread, butter and eggs and hastened towards home. In the slush outside the dairy, his left slipper got stuck and the strap gave way. He kicked it away like a football, followed by the other a minute later. Then like a soul-liberated or more precisely, sole-liberated man, he walked home making sure that his feet explored each and every puddle and pool. He felt as happy as a clam, enjoying the moment, carrying no encumbrance of age, profession or even of what others around thought about him. Deep inside, he was connecting with his self at ten years of age, walking back home with a bagful of fallen mangoes, collected from the orchard, in his native village Bindki, after a dust storm.

It was more than an hour since Shashank had been gone. Bina obviously had reasons enough to be anxious. A visit to the local market and back ordinarily took no more than thirty minutes, inclusive of some allowance for quick gossip. Bina could not afford to sit back and twiddle her thumbs! She had to get out for a search. She changed into a sari quickly and went towards the door opening into the rear veranda. She had to bolt it before leaving, as both Shweta and Sonam were still asleep. As she was shutting the door, a faint sound of water flowing out of the backyard tap reached her ears.

'Will this incorrigible Chandan never mend his ways? He knows the timings of the water supply, then why does he have to leave the tap open? What's the grand idea?!' Bina muttered to herself in exasperation. Her bone of contention, however, was not Chandan, but Shashank whose habit of slipping out of the house without informing anyone always sent a chill down her spine. *Every time it reminded her of someone who slipped away like that, never to return!*

Bina took a few steps towards the edge of the veranda to close the tap. Lo and behold, it was Shashank at the tap, hurriedly washing his feet! Like a missile launch having to abort at the last count, she stepped back, banged the door hard and went in.

Two minutes later, she was back in the veranda, armed with a volley of questions. But a bulging bag, languidly resting on the cane chair, changed her volcanic mood. She inspected it and found a few loaves of bread, a pack of butter partially melted within its packing and packets of toned milk, resting above potatoes and onions. She had not expected him to be so thoughtful as far as such mundane day-to-day affairs of the house were concerned. The things he had fetched on his own without carrying a little chit in his pocket were sure to last a week, in case the weather returned to its previous mood of continuous downpour. Bina was touched!

Not far away, just six doors away to be precise, the Johris, Dr Arvind and his wife Yashoda, had been up the whole night. The incessant rains had widened the hairline crack in their bedroom roof, which was caused by a peepul that had taken roots into the plaster, an year and a half ago. When it had first sprung up as a tiny green thing, Moolchand, their gardener, had sought permission to chop it off. But Yashoda had been too superstitious to lend her approval. As a result, it had now become a well-entrenched tree, with branches and leaves spreading out in all directions, giving abode to many a chattering sparrow and bulbul.

Last monsoon, underneath that very corner of the ceiling, there had been an oblong damp spot, where spores of green fungi accumulated; but this year, with the rains pouring down week after week, the soil accumulated in the crevice got washed away, causing a steady stream to trickle down the wall. Yashoda placed a bucket underneath, but to little avail. Gradually, a mini pool began to form there. Initially, Yashoda had managed to cause the thin stream to be absorbed in the empty gunny bags that she had spread out, but when the rains worsened, even piles of rugs and sacks put together were of no help.

Yashoda's irritation at the damp weather stemmed more from the fact that her arthritic knees made simple chores of mopping and wiping a near impossible task. Arvind on the other hand, had been a valiant trier, trying hard to wield the broom and the mop with the same precision and expertise with which he once wielded his surgical blade, knife and hammer. In fact, a day earlier, he had experimented with a new technique of mopping the floor in standing position, moving the rag under his foot in quick, oval, to and fro motion. But lady luck had no appreciation for his innovation and for all his concerted efforts, rewarded him with a slightly drier floor, *and a severely twisted ankle* along with a stern reprimand from his wife for attempting tasks that were seemingly outrageous at his age.

As rightly predicted by Yashoda, Arvind was left with a swollen ankle which he had to nurse the whole afternoon, fomenting it alternately with packs of ice and hot water.

'When Moolchand is in tomorrow, let him move out all furniture and empty that room,' Arvind said decisively, but cautiously, avoiding eye contact with his wife. After all, the furniture were gifted as dowry by Yashoda's father, at the time of their marriage.

Yashoda was quick to retort. 'Not a bad idea! Let us use the room as a swimming pool in which you could swim the whole day. I have heard swimming is a very good exercise, especially during the rains when people are unable to go out for walks.'

'Brilliant! Excellent idea! We can even start a swimming class for kids and charge some money! I don't think there is an indoor swimming pool in the near vicinity, is there?' Arvind quipped.

'Oh, of course we can! The Sheikh Chili that you are, such pie in the sky ideas can come only from you!' she was acerbic but concealed it with a laugh.

'Oh, thanks for the compliment, Mrs Sheikh! I can see that some of my extraordinary qualities have rubbed off on you as well. You see, one can't remain uninfluenced by one's company for long.'

Arvind's quick wit and sense of humour always diffused situations like these swiftly and easily.

The stream running down the wall had strengthened by then and the pool was getting bigger and bigger, swelling every moment.

'Let me see what I can do about this,' Yashoda said to herself as she limped towards the door.

The horizon was still not a cheerful swathe of blue, but then it was not expected to be either. After all, it was the month of August, which had always been a month when the monsoon was expected to be at its bountiful best. Farmers across the country eagerly awaited this season that showered the parched earth with cool drizzles that gradually turned into heavy downpours, filling up lakes, ponds and dams and recharging the water tables once again. Only this year, there had been an excess and the repercussions had already been devastating. What next?

Chandan had been tossing and turning in his bed, worrying incessantly. Over the years, he had found it difficult to sleep when it rained heavily, more so if the rains were accompanied by thunder and lightning. During the rains, he would wake up every morning and habitually inspect the ceiling first and then glance around his room to make sure that it was not flooded, that his cot was not floating. And till date he had been lucky; for every morning he had woken up to intact ceilings and dry floors.

Thanks to the restless night, Chandan had overslept that day. The entire household had woken up already. So he made a dash towards the kitchen to prepare breakfast.

'Run Chandan Kaka run, today you are late,' teased Shweta, who was sitting in the veranda indulging in her favourite pastime of sky watching. The threatening grey had mercifully beaten a retreat, exposing big and small patches of blues and oranges. Shweta was thrilled at the sight! The sky was her dynamic canvas on which she would let her imagination run wild to derive ethereal pleasure. On a sunny day, she would have easily located a vast expanse of Arctic, complete with a group of polar bears waiting to catch some fish among the craters in the snow. But for now, the view on the ground around her was no less spectacular. The innocuous steel wire clothesline running across the garden had transformed itself into an elongated necklace of pearls, courtesy the overnight rains; the spectacle however, was visible only to those who had that eye, the one that could see beyond the mundane.

Shweta sat at the edge of the veranda, comfortably in the high cane recline, draped in a bright red and black shawl. She rested against a fluffy cushion, sipping piping hot tea. This had been her favourite spot, a virtual gazebo, where she would sneak out, often in the morning, in the evening and during those golden winter afternoons. When others in the house would be busy with their daily routines, she would cherish her moments of solitude. The Murphy radio on the stool played on. Buzo sat under her chair, all curled up into a ball of wool. The tiny creature had been witnessing the first monsoon of his life. The previous night, he had been so scared that he had climbed on Shweta's bed and lay nestled between her feet, burying his head a little deeper every time the skies roared.

The mild breeze had picked up a little in the last ten minutes, rattling the wind chime above Shweta's head. The adolescent murraya, whose branches always danced with gay abandon in the slightest of breeze, stood unusually glum and still. Right then, a stiff breeze blew and in a sudden motion, the canopy drifted towards Shweta, like an umbrella whipped inside out in a gust of wind. Soon, Shweta was drenched with droplets of love. The murraya sapling had discovered this unique way of showing gratitude towards its saviour, one who had given it a second life. Such moments had always been of pure bliss, a feeling that Shweta had never been able to put into words.

It had been five years ago, on a hot May morning, when Shweta had located a tiny seedling, dry and wilted, inside the kitchen dustbin. On a momentary impulse, she had picked it up and ran to the garden. Using an old toothbrush, she dug a hole and planted the seedling. Its size was so small that it was sure to go unnoticed by everyone and trampled underneath careless steps. Moreover, there was that army of snails that raided the garden every night. Shweta had to ensure the safety of the seedling. So she had erected an insurmountable fence, by fixing empty shuttlecock boxes around. But having known Paltu, their gardener, well, she issued a stern warning to him, on the following day, not to dare uproot that little form of life nor fiddle with the seedling guard that she had erected.

In the days that followed, Shweta became a loving caregiver, watering it thrice, caressing its tiny velvety leaves, patting its scanty roots to grasp the soil quickly and whispering words of encouragement into the imaginary ears of the pencil thin stem to stand erect quickly. When the sun became too harsh, Shweta shaded its delicate frame with her little blue umbrella. Paltu, of course, had been cynical about Shweta's efforts all the way and even laughed under his breath. But one day, her efforts bore fruit and the discarded seedling struck roots.

The wind subsided a little and the playful murraya came to a standstill. The garden in front had become a deep pool in which the fallen bell shaped nerium flowers floated like ships in a harbour, waiting to set sail. A pair of babblers sat on the thin cane fencing by the side of the flooded flower beds, probably discussing the difficulty they would now face in collecting their food for the day.

Having removed the wet shawl from herself, Shweta felt cold and requested Chandan to get her another shawl.

'Could you please put this out to dry?' she said handing him the wet shawl.

Meanwhile, her mother Bina, in her peach and purple housecoat, hurried to the clothesline with a blue bucket overflowing with washed laundry. She had been harrowed and harried the whole of last week, devising ways and means of drying an ever increasing mound of wet and damp clothes.

Bina had a spring in her step today. Her excitement was understandable. Determined to make the most of every minute of the dry and drizzle free hour, she hung all the clothes on the line, meticulously clipping them in a way that ensured they caught the maximum wind. Shweta watched her activities with a resigned look. Every time a garment kissed the line, it caused a few of the pearl drops to fly off and disappear. And once the dreamy pearls disappeared, their retrieval was impossible. They were so delicate and magical, emerging out of nowhere on a hanging wire! The spectacle had an otherworldly feel that defied description! Shweta was dumbstruck.

Just then, All India Radio (AIR) interrupted its ongoing programme to relay a special weather forecast. There would be more rain; and more rain to Shweta meant a few more such spectacles in the offing.

Bina in the meantime had come to the veranda, carrying the empty bucket in her hand. Shweta, in a playful mood, asked her if she had noticed the many pearls she had spilled on the ground and crushed under her slippers. Bina's face crumpled in horror. She lifted her left leg and examined the muddied blue sole and then swiftly did the same with her right.

'Daydreaming, sweetheart?' She then rubbed the sole of her slippers on the coir doormat, taking care not to soil the word 'Welcome' embossed in deep red. Shweta gave a faint smile and muttered, 'I knew it, you will not find the necklace.'

Shashank was away on a three-day educational trip with the BSc Part I students. They were touring parts of Chakrata and Dehradun. Although he had nothing to do with the subject, Botany, the tour being a field trip for species familiarisation and identification, he was a willing last minute replacement for Dr Shiv Verma. His responsibility was to take care of the logistics and travel aspects. He had called up in the morning to inform that on the last leg of the trip, the group had arrived in Mussoorie and were enjoying a fun outing that day. They would be boarding the train back home in the evening, from Doon.

The information left Bina perturbed and distracted for a few minutes, forcing Shashank to ask, 'Are you there, Bina?'

'Yes, Shashank. Tell me …' Bina shook herself.

'I have stayed back in Dehradun and am right now calling from my hotel room. It has been raining here since yesterday evening and so I preferred not to go out with them,' Shashank added.

'Okay, take care. And please remember to get some besan ladoos from Kumar Sweets,' she cooed into the receiver, at the very thought of the ladoos. Shashank disconnected the call and Bina rushed back to the kitchen.

Sipping a cup of tea, in the veranda, Shweta chuckled gleefully as she located a golden flame-back woodpecker, gorgeous with the rain-washed red and yellow, pecking away merrily at the wet and soggy bole of one of the Ashok trees. It was literally the early bird looking to catch a few worms before it rained again. For a few minutes, Shweta allowed herself to be transported back into time, journeying to Bindki, with her entire gang of cousins. She could picture the 'teams' sitting on string cots in the elongated veranda, in the safety of their bedsheet tents, eagerly waiting for the rain to stop. The reason for their excitement was their impending mission to collect red velvety beetles that they believed fell from the skies, during rains.

The preparation for the same had begun the moment a dust storm had begun to gather. The skies changed colour and Granny's *itr* bottles disappeared from her dressing table. 'When did these simple pleasures of life become a thing of the past?' Shweta wondered, overcome with nostalgia.

She was still wandering around in her bubble of fantasy when Chandan's throaty voice rang in her ears. 'Come baby, let's go inside,' he said as he stood in readiness to push her chair in.

The decibel pricked the bubble.

'Kaka, you always manage to come at the wrong time!'

She gave him a fleeting frown, but Chandan, the affable fatherly self that he was, always took things sportingly, whenever Shweta was in a grumpy mood. Chandan had been particularly fond of Shweta right from the time he cradled her to sleep in his arms as a cherubic six-months-old. He always took her tantrums lightly; laughing them away, particularly from that time a few years back, when twin terrible tragedies hit the family.

He had been with the family for almost eighteen years now. He would proudly proclaim that he had come to the household of the Joshis in that very same year when Shashank and the entire Joshi family came to the city. Shashank had come to join as a senior lecturer in the Physics Department of the prestigious University of Allahabad.

Life was sailing smooth for Shweta, until an unexpected bolt from the blue, two and a half years ago, had turned her little world upside down. The accident left her wheelchair bound. The prolonged uphill journey of two years towards rehabilitation had matured her beyond her years. She learnt how to battle the demons within herself, those that would unsettle her and kick her into a state where she would hate, berate, deride and denounce her destiny. She learnt to come to terms with reality and now, on the verge of her eighteenth birthday, she had matured to the extent that many could not achieve even at eighty. Nonetheless, at times, her frustration at her misfortune did draw her into a shell where the languid stillness of her life reigned supreme. A reluctant prisoner of the wheelchair initially, she remained slouched in her chair for long hours with a book in her lap taking care to turn the pages periodically. Soon she realised what a wonderful, alive and vascular companion a book could be! Not only did it shut out the world and its miseries, but it also temporarily shut her out from her inner world of miseries. She would bury her head into the yellowing pages and create a hideout, inside which all the chasms and crevices of her sufferings would be hidden. At times, she would shut her eyes and resting her head over the soft leather edge, grimace, wince and pine all at the same time, letting out her emotions more like a bunch of entangled centipedes wriggling over each other if one attempted to separate one from the other.

Gradually, with the passage of time her trauma reduced, her wounds healed and the scars lightened. With extraordinary will power and determination, she began to put the splintered pieces of her life together and along the way, learnt how to transform her loneliness into solitude.

As requested by her, Chandan pushed the chair towards the drawing room and placed it by the side of the velvety sofa, where her elder sister Sonam was going through the morning newspaper. Buzo, whom Chandan had absentmindedly shut outside, barked as loudly as he could, attracting Shweta's immediate attention.

'Kaka you have to mess up one job or the other,' Shweta reprimanded mildly, turning the reprimand into a jest, as he started leaving the room, carrying the empty cups lying on the table, not hearing the whimpering of the pup outside the door. Chandan scampered to the door, pushed it open and stood aside, bowing slightly as he gestured to the dog to come in. Buzo in turn lifted his neck and barked a little more, conveying his displeasure. He leapt up and snuggled into Shweta's lap—the safest place he had discovered in the last few days.

Sonam was fiddling with the newspaper, finding it difficult to go beyond the first page, as the wet pages clung to each other, forming translucent semi-circles at the right corners, making it difficult to turn them over.

Shashank had returned home the evening before. Tired due to continuous travelling and in considerable discomfort due to a painful throat infection, he had applied for a day's leave. Despite Bina asking him to remain in bed, he was up and was now reclining on the drawing room sofa with a cup of tea and newspapers. As he finished his tea, the sound of Bina's anklets alerted him. He began fidgeting with the grey scarf that Bina had insisted he wrap around his throat, something he always claimed 'made him feel like tying a hangman's noose!'

Bina appeared, barefooted, with a small brass plate in her hand. A strong scent of camphor lingered on her clothes and her palms still smelled of sandal. From the ends of her long hair, left loose, drops of water trickled down. The green climber print in the lemon yellow coloured cotton sari appeared freshly watered. To Shashank, she looked fresh and pristine, even though she had had a patchy sleep the night before hit by an unexpected bout of nostalgia.

She extended a handful of raisins towards Shashank and Sonam, the day's prasad. Moving on to Shweta, she thrust a fistful into her mouth, not forgetting to move her fist above her temple, a customary prelude signifying reverence to the Almighty. Shweta was always fond of raisins—swollen and bursting with sweetness when soaked, pale and wrinkled when left alone. The mood in the room was sombre, when Buzo silently came in, with his small canines dug into a ball of red wool that he held in his mouth. He stood on his hind legs and attempted to deposit the red ball into Shweta's lap.

'Poor fellow, he is bored,' Shashank smiled.

'He wants to go out for a walk.' Sonam added.

'He will have to swim not walk,' Shashank quipped.

'Don't worry dad, by next monsoon he will be an expert swimmer,' Shweta added.

The atmosphere in the room lightened, thanks to Buzo's antics.

'So, how are the preparations for the party going on?' Shashank asked, as a startled Bina kept the wool and knitting needles aside. Shashank's memory in the matter of remembering birthdays and anniversaries had not been too reliable. But in this case, he did. After all, the apple of his eye was turning eighteen within two days and the calendar on the wall proclaimed 23 August, 1990.

'Shweta what do you want for your birthday?' He asked rather excitedly.

'A scooty daddy,' she blurted out before he could finish. That she was turning a major and was entitled to a driving license, coupled with her continued fascination for sleek two wheelers had been playing in her subconscious mind since long. Today in this moment of unguarded joy and excitement, she made a huge faux pas, which she realised instantaneously and promptly rectified.

'No Daddy, I was joking. You choose; a guitar or a cassette player will be fine,' she added with a forced smile.

Bina looked towards the dull white ceiling of the room, trying to hide her emotions. She immediately got up and went out of the room. Shashank knew that for the rest of the day she would retreat into an impenetrable shell, inside which neither he nor his girls would be allowed entry. All he could do now was to wait for just the opportune moment when he could even attempt any kind of cajoling to draw her out of that saturnine state. This exercise required the skill of a nature photographer who had to wait for hours on end to get just that right angle, that perfect light, so as to get that perfect shot, Shashank thought to himself.

From a toddler possessing a great fascination for wheels, right from her pram to her walker, to the wooden push tricycle that Granny had gifted her, to the bicycle with balancing wheels that her Nana had gifted on her seventh birthday — wheels had been a source of perennial passion for Shweta. She had never shown any inclination to possess Barbies and soft toys as girls of her age did. Shashank and Bina realised that her passion for wheels had still remained, though her circumstances had brutally changed.

The reasons for a scooty catching the fancy of Shweta, however, were not far to seek. Lately, Bina had been watching Arjun, the nineteen year old boy of their neighbourhood, zooming past their gate on his bright red two-wheeler, returning from his coaching classes. He would zip off proudly on the uneven brick-lined lane showing off his newly acquired driving skills. However, the little bump on his forehead and the scratches and minor dents in the scooty were ample proof that his initial rides had not been without hiccups.

That day, the two sisters had planned to watch a late night movie on their cable TV. Half way through the movie, the telecast was disturbed due to a power breakdown at one of the houses where the relay booster had been installed. While they waited in anticipation for the connection to resume, their thoughts wandered towards Udit, their elder brother. Had he been around, he would have by now made some alternate arrangements; the easiest being getting a temporary '*kundi connection*' by hitching their own cable wire onto another of a different network via the cable box dangling from the telephone pole; in that intricate maze of emerging cable wires, nobody would have made out.

Once the sensitive topic had been raised, the discussion continued well into the wee hours. Their punch bowl of why, when, where and how remained as immiscible as it had been at the time he had left home. While they groped for answers, coming to terms with the loss had been a collective failure for the entire family. What haunted them still was the fact that a person as affectionate and compassionate as him could gather the strength to cut off all ties and snap all bonds in a split second decision. *How could he? More importantly why did he?*

An emotional Sonam disclosed to her younger sister how she had been scanning newspapers every night before sleep, looking at all lost and found columns, excruciatingly going through notices of unidentified dead bodies found or preserved in morgues in different hospitals, a routine she dreaded each single day, but had carried out with trembling hands and teary eyes like a daily ritual.

Shweta was still in a state of mild shock when Sonam picked up another painful nerve to discuss. It was their mother's belief that had evidently become her lifeline now. A distraught Bina had taken her astrologer father's prediction to heart that 'the boy was destined to return home any time in the near future because his exile was ordained for a period not exceeding five years.'

Back then, Sonam and Shweta had questioned the old man whether he was aware of the implications of his proclamation. A sobbing grandfather had explained to them how he had arrived at the conclusion after examining his daughter's fate line, heart line, her life line, the various pyramids, mounds and islands in her palms; his sixty years of palm reading could not betray him, he was more than sure. Almost five years passed by since then.

And all these years there had been no news about him. He had never called, not even dropped a line. About a couple of days after his escape, the family had derived solace from stray news about him. One of Shashank's friends, Dr Samar, claimed that he had seen Udit at the railway platform and the two had exchanged pleasantries, but not knowing that Udit had already left home, he had refrained from asking the boy where he was headed to.

Shashank, however, was not convinced. Knowing his friend's nature fully well, he doubted the veracity of Dr Samar's story, but chose not to say anything to the family. At that instant, the story was the only straw they could cling on to. And that was the last that they had heard of Udit.

After five years the sisters were united in their belief that they had only one option before them; that is to remain optimistic and do whatever they could to find him. Living in a zone of persistent pessimism redefining Murphy's Law would help nobody's cause, least of all their parents. By the time they went to sleep, it was already 2:30 am.

An early morning dream, Granny always said, was bound to come true; and that very thought left Shweta upbeat, as she awoke. In her dreams, Udit had taken her on a little gastronomical trip, zipping around on a bright red scooty, relishing the butter textured dahi vadas of Alopibagh Chat Corner, to some mouth-watering gulab jamuns at Netram Sweets in Katra market.

In their family, birthdays were always an occasion to celebrate. A pooja in the morning followed by a party for friends and family in the evening, had been the norm, always. The whole afternoon, Shashank and Bina had been shopping, in the congested bylanes behind the Alopi Devi temple and then in the overcrowded Katra market bursting with haggling buyers, greedy cattle and lazy dogs.

Dead tired, on returning home Bina went to bed early. An hour into sleep, she woke up, all bathed in sweat, haunted by a nightmare, in which she was repeatedly losing her way home, on a rainy night. Wetting her parched throat with a sip of water she lay down again, but kept her eyes wide open. Under no circumstances did she want the dream to resurface. Her mind filled with unpleasant memories, coiling around her like a python, strangulating her in the wrap of its enormous twitching muscles.

Destiny had been unduly harsh to the family considering the quantum of pain and sufferings inflicted on them time after time; Bina rued. First it was her son Udit who chose to slip out of home one evening, leaving the family shattered in 1985. The pain and trauma of losing a son was still fresh when destiny delivered a stinging second blow in October, 1987 in the form of a road accident involving their vehicle up on the serpentine slopes leading to Mussoorie. This time the family was on a holiday to Haridwar, Dehradun and Mussoorie. She always wished to delete the twin events from her memory store, but the more she tried the more difficult it became to erase. The sequence of events till the two incidents were terribly similar, the family had no premonitions about them. Udit and Shashank shared a cordial father-son relationship and Bina in her wildest dreams had never imagined that her son could rebel against the family and would one day decide that enough was enough, the world outside was a better place for him. The Mussoorie tragedy similarly struck in a fraction of a second and before they could realise, their taxi had been knocked down just ahead of one of those infamous hairpin bends by a drunk truck driver coming from the opposite side. The vehicle, a robust Sumo, had turned turtle and had somersaulted twice before landing at the edge of the road below. All those who saw the condition of their vehicle later on could scarcely believe that all the occupants had survived. Shashank, Bina and Sonam had escaped with minor injuries, bruises and compression fractures. Granny had a fibular fracture, but Shweta had been injured so badly that even her chances of survival at that time looked bleak.

After two back to back surgeries, the worried doctors had gone into an emergency huddle, only to emerge with a cool advice for the family: *to resort to prayers*. After all, modern medical science too had its limitations. For three days, Shweta had lain lifeless on the hospital bed, her body wired to complicated instruments, where masked doctors and nurses spoke in whispers and ward boys rolled heavy oxygen cylinders in and out throughout the nights. All that the family could do was watch from the little circle of glass in the door, beyond which entry was forbidden. With his hands folded, Shashank had almost fallen at the feet of the man emerging from the ICU clothed in a green apron, faceless behind a blue mask and a surgeon's cap. Pulling away the rubber gloves from his left hand, all that the man could mumble was, 'We are trying our level best. The rest is in His hands!' The family could only wait in the corridors day after day. For them, life was at its useless indolent best, defined only in the four letters of the word—WAIT.

And it was eighty long hours of tortuous wait at the end of which the doctor came rushing to Shashank, as he sat on the red chair outside the ward, shaking him by the shoulder so violently that he thought his shoulder would be dislocated. The occasion of course was reason enough. After being in coma for three days, the patient at bed number 5, ICU-1, had suddenly woken up and had almost pulled down one of her life support equipments. The doctors who had been treating her had begun celebrating this development. The Doon Hospital had never witnessed such joy in the recent past. The Joshis wept with joy at the miracle that had unfolded before them.

At that time the grave news of Shweta's spinal injury rendering her mildly paralysed in the legs, with the likelihood of lifetime confinement to a wheelchair was not a big enough reason to dampen their celebration.

Bina normally never expressed her feelings; but today, when her daughter was touching another milestone of her life, she could not help but hurtle down the rugged slopes of her painful memories and feel sorrowful.

Shweta's morning tea tray had a birthday card by its side. As she opened the card, petals of a pink rose unfolded with the birthday song being played by an almost invisible device attached at the base. A lovely start to a special day, set the tone for the celebrations. Shortly after breakfast, it was the turn of the courier to deliver another surprise—a battery operated wheelchair had been sent by Ajit Mama from London. This was the best gift she could have asked for. It was literally the day of her independence. Her reliance on Sonam and others could now be drastically cut.

The pooja which began around noon was a time-consuming affair. The priest took more than an hour, reciting the katha and translating the Sanskrit verses into Hindi. The dozen and a half ladies seated on the floor listened to him as attentively as possible in between bouts of whispering sessions. The end of the katha was followed by a recital of arti and curiously the ladies who were the busiest during the gossip session were the most vocal in the recital. Distribution of prasad in sal leaf containers ended the first half of the birthday celebrations.

Immediately after the pooja, Shashank and Sonam were off to the market as the new dress that Shweta would wear for the evening party needed an alteration. Chandan had been running high temperature since yesterday evening and a worried Bina had forced him to visit the family doctor and get some medicines. She knew that the queue at the clinic would be long and it would be some time before he would return.

A little anxious she stood at the gate waiting for her domestic help to arrive. And she was relieved when she saw her getting down the staircase of the neighbour's home.

'You take the dishes out and clean them at the tap in the backyard. I am going to chop the vegetables in here,' she said taking out the vegetable tray from the fridge.

She was now done with the vegetables and was peeling cloves of garlic when Shweta joined her to lend a helping hand.

'Ma, why don't you rest for a while?' She asked.

'No, I am not tired. As it is I was sitting for the last two hours in the pooja,' she said and quickly took out the bowl containing mashed potatoes and corn.

'First let me stuff these kachoris and then I will do the cutlets,' she said keeping the bowl back.

'Ma, let me make the cutlets,' Shweta said pulling the bowl containing the potato-corn mix towards her. With the expertise of an accomplished cook, she stuffed *chironji* and raisins into the potato dough and shaped it into little hearts.

'Beta leave it, it's your birthday. I will manage,' said Bina.

'There is still time Ma, let me finish these cutlets.'

'No, no, dear, this much is enough. Savita must be on her way. She has promised me that she will be here by four, and will stay on till the party is over.'

'Ma, how will she go home alone?'

'Kishan has promised to come and pick her up.'

The menu for snacks consisted of samosas, corn cutlets, aloo tikkis stuffed with green peas, crisp jalebis in sugar syrup, butter fried popcorns and frothy hot coffee. In keeping with the momentous occasion, dinner too was to be an elaborate affair, with cumin flavoured baby potatoes, chana-makhana curry garnished with fresh coriander, paneer rolls in Mughlai sauce, fried rice with cashewnuts and raisins to accompany deep fried, golden brown kachoris. Bina had also prepared saffron flavoured malpuas, a dessert Shweta always joked that she 'could consume by the kilo ton.'

By evening, everything was ready and an exhausted Bina left the kitchen asking Chandan to take over. Soon after, Chandan sat by the side of a separate stove in the veranda and rolled out kachoris and puris, carefully spreading them on newspaper sheets, taking care that their edges did not overlap, lest at the time of frying, they stick to each other and not fluff.

After helping Shweta get inside the washroom to get ready, Bina sat on the wooden chair facing the door resting her bones, while waiting for Shweta to call. She pulled up her tired legs, but was restless and ill at ease. She sat listless, but her mind wandered and a steady stream of thoughts rolled by in front of her closed eyes. It was Shweta's tenth birthday, the first in this newly built house of theirs, into which they had shifted barely a week before. It was the housewarming and birthday party clubbed together. Shweta had emerged from the same washroom, pretty in a white and red polka dot frock with her wet shampooed hair falling on her slim shoulders. Bina had pulled her close, and almost dragged her towards the dressing table to put a little smudge of kohl, behind her ears, before she ran to take a test ride on her new bicycle. Since then, eight long years had rolled by.

'Ma, please help me.'

Shweta's call brought Bina back to the present. She rushed towards the washroom door. Shweta looked pretty in a lemon yellow skirt and a matching floral top with lacy sleeves. She had pulled her silky tresses into a high pony tail and wore gold tops in her ears, the one that Granny had presented her on scoring ninety percent in her Tenth Board Examination. Bina gazed at her for a few seconds and said to herself, 'Daughters grow up so fast, indeed,' and proceeded to take out the kohl box.

Sonam had bought a set of books of Shweta's favourite writer Ruskin Bond to gift to her dear sister. In fact she was surprised that this year Dad had still not purchased anything to gift to Shweta. But she had overheard him telling someone over the phone, 'Please ensure that it is delivered on time.' When she had asked him he had evaded a reply, telling her, 'It was a set of question papers for an examination.'

The guests arrived shortly and the Joshis spent a wonderful evening with the families of Dr Arvind, Dr Samar and Dr Gagan. This year Shweta had insisted on this sort of a get together and not a formal birthday celebration with cake cutting and blowing candles as she thought she was no more a 'child'. However, she wondered if her dad had forgotten the gift he had been so excitedly asking her about. The gold plated watch he had gifted her last birthday adorned her wrist today. Dinner was almost over when the doorbell rang. Bina was surprised as no other guest was expected. But it was a surprise from Shashank. A delivery boy stood at the door with a Black forest cake from Bushy's Bakery and a guitar that Shashank had left at the bakery to be delivered with the cake!

'How can there be a birthday without a cake?' Shashank smiled as he lighted a candle on the cake, 'However grown-up one might feel one is!'

Dr Samar played, 'Happy Birthday to you,' on the guitar as Shweta cut the cake. Chandan Kaka then distributed the cake to all the guests before the party ended. Needless to say Shweta was thrilled both at the cake and the gift.

It was the time of the Navratras and Durga Puja. The city wore a festive look. In the park near the Joshi home, a yellow and maroon pandal had been erected by the newly constituted Allapur Durga Puja Committee. In one half of the pandal, the idols of Goddess Durga and the other gods of the pantheon had been arranged artistically. The other half had a makeshift stage for cultural programmes. The committee had taken great pains to mark an impressive beginning, inviting some celebrity artists and priests from Bengal to guide them with the decor and the rituals, as most of the members were non-Bengalis. The chanting of the mantras during the early morning *pushpanjali*, an offering of flowers and prayers to gods and the evening arti, sung in the praise of the gods, accompanied with the assorted sounds of chiming *ghanta*, gonging *kanshi*, booming *dhak* and the 'Om' sound of *shankh,* reverberated through the entire neighbourhood. A zesty fusion of the fragrance of jasmine incense sticks and sambrani, wafting out of the puja pandal, lingered in the air all day long, making the atmosphere all the more spiritual.

It was Mahashtami that day, the eighth day of the holy Navratras; a day when Bina observed the ritual of *kanya pujan* or the worshipping of the girl-child as Goddess Durga. Shashank's mother had already arrived from their ancestral village to participate in the ceremony. Little girls not older than twelve by age and not less than nine in number, had to be invited home for the ceremony and worshipped as the nine incarnations of Goddess Durga, followed by offerings of feast and gifts. This year, however, the number had swelled to fourteen, as none of the little Durgas, staying in the neighbourhood, could be left out!

The girls lined up to wash their feet at the backyard tap. They were experienced little Durgas, who had enjoyed these moments of glory even before and therefore knew what was to follow.

One by one, they took off their sandals and shoes, exposed their little feet and giggled in glee, as Bina Auntie washed their feet, with an affectionate smile on her face. Their topic of discussion was why their mothers did not bathe them with the same affection every day before they were packed off to school! Auntie's touch was so different; it was gentle and caressing, compared to the hurried and careless scrubbing that their mothers normally gave them with their eyes transfixed on the clock and their ears alert to catch the horn of the school bus or the bell of the cycle-rickshaw!

Akash, the six year old boy, was the lone male member among the bevy of giggling girls. Feeling somewhat out of place, he asked Shashank's mother if he could come back after a little while.

'No sweetheart! How can you leave, when you are the most important guest of the day? Come, I will wash your feet first because you are so special!'

She picked up a new brass tumbler full of water and slowly poured it over his feet; then she bent down for a quick scrub of his little feet.

There was a mild resentment in his voice, as he withdrew his little feet and said, 'Granny, I had a bath with soap and water before coming here!'

'I am sure, darling you had! But this is a compulsory ritual that I have to do, you see!' she assured him, smiling from ear to ear.

Making him sit on the cot lying in the lawn, she wiped his feet with a new towel, showering blessings on him and ending with a faint murmur, '*Jai Ma Durga, please be merciful! Bring him back home! Let him not drift any longer …*'

Shweta watched as her mother carried out the rituals. One by one, the girls sat crosslegged on the neatly spread bed sheet, folded in an elongated strip on the floor. Two sheets arranged perpendicular to each other accommodated all of them and allowed Bina to serve them freely. Sonam had worn a light orange chiffon sari with delicate gold leaf embroidery. In a silver plate she had a diya, placed in the centre along with petals of rose and marigolds heaped around. In a small bowl, kumkum had been mixed into a paste with a little ghee and sprinkled with a few grains of rice. All set, Bina now worshipped each of the tiny Durgas individually; a quick arti, followed by a tika on their foreheads and a fragrant shower of rose and marigold petals on their head, was enough to turn them crimson.

New plates full of fluffed puris, chana and halwa garnished with raisins, cashew, almonds and pistachios were served. The Durgas had been in much demand today and had been to several other households already. Most of them stopped eating after having half a puri or a spoonful of chana, while exchanging expert comments on the culinary skills of the aunties of the neighbourhood: in which auntie's home were the puris softest and where the chana was tastier and even more serious issues like why the girls were given such importance only twice in one whole year! At that point, a little girl of seven made a conclusive statement to Granny, 'But my own granny says that my dad is unlucky being a father to three girls!' and therefore shouldn't Granny come with her to her home and reassure her father that girls were precious because they were incarnations of Goddess Durga! Bina, sitting behind her, was stunned at the child's observation and perception on gender discrimination and how that could wound her self-worth, even if she was just all of seven!

Meanwhile, Bina added some more puris, chana and halwa to each of their plates and covered it with another plate. When the girls were about to leave, Bina handed over each set of plates to them, along with a pair of fancy hairclips and hairbands as gifts and a crisp ten rupee note as dakshina to the representative goddess.

Yashoda had brought the entire kitchen down. All the jars, cans, bottles and boxes were made to crawl out of their shelters. Every shelf, drawer and rack was denuded. On that morning, she had opened a jar of cashewnuts and had been horrified to find some hundreds of tiny red beetles having the time of their lives, feasting away at the nuts. Even the air tight jar of urad dal had been inhabited by many similar creatures, having chewed and powdered away half the stock. Being jolted out of her complacence and smarting at the daredevilry of the crawlies, she immediately set out on a mission to air and sun out all the stuff that had survived the monsoon blues.

The central courtyard of the Johris was quite spacious and she preferred utilising this space for her *Operation Crawlies*. First, she strategised her war zone positioning—lining and aligning the jars and containers and then realigning her lead weapons—the broom, the mop and the newly purchased vacuum cleaner. Arvind had been observing General Yashoda and her moves from afar. With feigned innocence, he came forward and asked why Yashoda's Lieutenant General Savita, who also happened to be the bona fide cook of the household, had been missing from the war zone. Had the General fired her Lieutenant General already over her habitual late comings? Yashoda, was in no mood to listen to his barbs. Armed with a broom tied to a stick she concentrated on removing the oldest cobwebs from the remotest corners of the kitchen.

Arvind quietly sneaked out and pulled a chair into the courtyard. He looked up and saw the sky which had suddenly turned pewter.

'You have chosen the wrong day for your operation, General,' he observed raising his voice. Not expecting any response, he pulled the cane table near him and stretched his legs, reclining a little into his chair. He then started reading his *India Today*. Suddenly, a loud sound of a tin can falling from a height distracted his attention. He stood up and to make sure that the casualty was only a vessel, rushed towards the kitchen almost bumping into Yashoda who was coming out, brandishing the broom in her hand like a sword. This time she broke into a smile and threw away the broom. In the meantime, Savita had quietly entered the house. She had been expecting an encounter with a hollering Yashoda standing at the door, but her silence seemed to be strategic and that worried Savita all the more.

On being asked to bring out and lay the three cots standing by the side of the store, she was quick to jump to the task and ran towards the store with a childlike glee at having escaped punishment. Arvind moved to one of the cots and sat on the edge, waiting for Yashoda to reappear on the door.

The mild rays of the sun had fleetingly broken through, forming complex patterns in gold on the cemented floor, touching the ground through the holes in the loosening strings of the cots.

Yashoda then appeared with a plastic tub carrying transparent jars full of spices and lentils, a white bedsheet thrown across her right shoulder. She spread the sheet on the cot, causing the interesting patterns on the ground to disappear and breaking Arvind's trance.

Then she emptied the contents of the jars on the bedsheet, generating a new and colourful pattern. The yellow kabuli chana, the orange masoor, the green moong and the black urad each was spread in thin separate adjacent circles. On the second cot, she repeated the exercise with coriander, cumin, cardamom, whole red chillies and a mix of pepper and cloves.

'Now, what is this third cot for?' quizzed Arvind harmlessly.

'It is for you to take REST!' She disappeared into the kitchen again, leaving the word 'rest' to hang in the air.

Arvind chuckled and reopened his magazine. Even in broad daylight, he had to strain his eyes to read the letters in smaller font. Perhaps, a new pair of spectacles with slightly increased power or even a readjustment of axis was needed. On that day itself, he decided to get his eyesight checked. He tried to remember the last time that he had visited Dr Singh, so that he could look for his prescription. He remembered that it was when his son, Madhur, had come home.

He could not believe that four long years had passed since Madhur and his family had left for the UK. The realisation that Madhur was going far away from their lives hit them only when a truckload of their belongings arrived from Bangalore. Gradually, the homecoming of Madhur and their younger son, Mayank, along with their families, became infrequent; even during the festivals of Dusshera, Diwali or Holi they could not turn up. Madhur, however, was not expected to take a flight home so soon, but Mayank quite uncharacteristically excused himself every time, citing his younger child's ill health as the reason. Slowly, Arvind and Yashoda resigned to their fate and learnt to celebrate the festival days without the children and their families.

Arvind put the magazine down on the cot and walked towards the kitchen.

'Hmm … now, please may I taste one, of course, with the lady's due permission?' he asked poker-faced seeing the row of mathis, the crispy teatime snack that Yashoda had freshly fried and lined up on a tray.

This had been Arvind's habit, all through. While pleading to have those goodies that particularly topped his prohibited list, he would ask so inoffensively that Yashoda would not have the heart to say, no. Was she raising not two but three children at home? Yashoda would often wonder.

Today, seeing him hanging around the white marble platform, she was transported back in time, when her early mornings were sheer madness. One moment she would be rolling out paranthas in the kitchen, the next moment she would be in the bedroom joining Madhur in his frantic search to locate a missing sock or tie Mayank's shoelaces, while the school bus honked at the stop.

It was only when Arvind had settled on the stool with a plateful and begun enjoying the snack did she realise that ten long years had passed by since his retirement from the local Moti Lal Nehru Medical College, where he had served as Head of the Department of Orthopaedics.

'Amazing! The magic in your hands still goes uncontested!' he said quirking his eyebrows in appreciation, 'only if I could get to munch on these goodies a bit more often …' he trailed off impishly.

'Our lady, Savita, of course is an automaton of a cook, a cooking machine to be precise; you put the same ingredients, and it churns up the same dish with the same taste. Even a machine shows up a minor variation once in a while, but Sa …'

'Arvind, have a heart! Savita has to do it for seven odd families, day in and day out! No wonder her culinary art has turned mechanical!' Yashoda defended her cook, as she took out the mathis from the simmering oil in the kadahi on the gas stove.

'Good Heavens!! Another minute inside and they would have burnt to coal!' she gasped as she lowered the flame and hurriedly spread them in a steel plate.

It was just two days to Diwali, the festival of lights. The Johri home had been illuminated with strings of tiny bulbs in multiple colours. Arvind had called up the fellow at the electric shop to do the needful.

In the evening, Mayank, his wife Smriti and their little son, Anant arrived. Arvind had asked Mayank to bring along their older son, 9-year-old Adarsh, as well but the boy supposedly had preferred to stay back at his nana's place, where he lived since his infancy. What had been a purely temporary arrangement initially to devote attention towards Anant who suffered from Down's Syndrome had become a pain as Adarsh now could not adjust with his little brother. He could not understand that his brother had difficulty in speech and that a child as old as him could depend on milk for survival. The short time that the parents tried to keep the two together turned out to be a nightmare as the younger one wanted him to be far away from his mom. Arvind still remembered how Mayank had then decided to leave behind the little boy with his parents for love and care but then his wife began crying inconsolably when they were ready to leave and go home. At that time Yashoda had insisted that Anant be taken along for no mother in the world could bear the separation from her child and live in peace, whether the child was normal or differently abled.

Today Arvind was as excited as he used to be twenty-seven years ago. Back then he and his young sons would begin planning, a week in advance. They would fix the day of visit to the wholesale cracker market in Mau Aima, to buy crackers. The crackers would then be sun dried for three days to make them moisture-free.

Anant had always been a quiet boy, given to occasional giggling, whenever in high spirits. Most of the times Smriti had to run behind him feeding him the bottle of milk that remained his staple food even at five. His inability to communicate verbally was a major barrier, but not for Arvind. He knew that his milestones had been delayed but there was nothing wrong with his brain. He always dealt with him as a normal child and could easily talk to him with signs and words spoken slowly. The doting grandfather would gladly become the horse on which Anant would canter from room to room, he would be a willing sparring partner for a bout of boxing and the two would love to play a game of blowing bubbles, the one who blew the biggest bubble won! The grandfather and the grandson had planned to buy a quadcopter from the market which they would fly on the roof. In the market, Arvind and Anant purchased a bagful of crackers, consisting of sparklers, chakris, snake tablets, anars and rockets. The quadcopter was then bought from the new Archies toy shop before they took a rickshaw home. On their return, Anant dragged his mother to the place where the packet of crackers lay, pointed at them and giggled happily. The expression on his face said it all—he was excited and happy, even though he could not express his feelings with a single string of words put together. Smriti quietly soaked in her son's happiness.

At Shashank's place, Diwali meant worshipping Lord Ganesh and Laxmi with elaborate rituals. Bina and Sonam made intricate rangoli designs, embellishing the house with decorations with marigold flowers, rose petals and mango and ashoka leaf torans at the main gate, in the pooja room and especially in the rear veranda, Lakshmi's favourite point of entry.

Shashank had summoned a taxi after lunch and had taken Sonam and Shweta out for Diwali shopping. Expectedly, the roads were crowded with eager shoppers. Makeshift stalls had sprung up at every available space in the market, selling crackers and fireworks, decorative items like paper lanterns, torans or door hangings, wax-filled earthen diyas, idols of Lord Ganesh and Laxmi, flowers, perfumed candles in assorted shapes and colour, cotton wicks and cheap oil for burning the diyas, as well as earthen kitchen sets for little girls, which was a Diwali special item made by potters only for this special occasion.

Shashank left the girls in the parked car and ran errands to buy churmura, a kind of puffed rice, poha or flattened parboiled rice, gattas, a dry sweet made of sugar and particularly *chini ke khilone*, which were Bina's favourite. Unlike the earthen kitchen sets, *chini ke khilone* were toys that were edible being made of molten sugar moulded in various forms—Taj Mahal, car, cart, lollipop—virtually anything that caught the craftsman's fancy. He returned to the waiting vehicle and joked with the girls if they wanted a kitchen set each. Sonam laughed at his offer but Shweta insisted that she did want one for herself.

'Are you sure?' Shashank was puzzled.

'Oh, yes I am! And you have already offered to buy me a set, right?' smiled Shweta.

'Okay then, I shall get you one right away.' he walked away carrying the cloth bag Bina had given for shopping.

After a while, Shashank returned with a 40 piece assortment, comprising of a chulha, a fuelwood stove, a tava, a kadahi, pots, pans, plates, spoons, ladles, buckets, rolling pins all brightly coloured in red, yellow, blue and pink. …

'Anything else girls? Any crackers?'

Sonam and Shweta looked at each other and then shook their heads. A considered and thoughtful 'No.' Their Diwalis had been a quiet affair ever since their brother had left home and now with the arrival of Buzo amidst them, crackers were a strict no-no.

Back home, Bina could not believe that Shweta and Sonam could have purchased a 'kitchen set' for themselves. Shweta remained mum when confronted with a quizzical look and responded only with a naughty smile.

'Why? Can't I play with one?' she quipped in passing as Bina left the room.

The celebrations continued late into the night and ended with a game of cards, a compulsory ritual to usher in Goddess Laxmi, the goddess of wealth and prosperity. But before retiring to bed, Shweta and Sonam did not forget to open the new pack of kitchen set and take out two little earthen pots. They filled the pots with sweets, grains of gram, a betel nut and some cotton for the Bhai Dooj pooja that they would perform silently in their bedroom two days later, something they had been doing every year without fail, even though their brother Udit had left home.

They folded their hands and prayed. *Bhaiya, wherever you are, we pray that you stay well and stay happy.*

Three days later, the Johris were alone again. Mayank had left in the morning and the house was silent. Anant's toys lay scattered from the drawing room to the bedroom; the yellow tortoise, the red plastic car with a rear wheel missing, the saxophone that he so enthusiastically held in his lap and played and then clapped in delight at its spectrum of sounds.

Arvind had insisted that Savita leave the toys in a corner and not dump them inside the box bed, until instructed. The smell of Johnson's baby oil still lingered on the pillows and cushions, now neatly arranged on the beds, but were all over the place the week before.

The winter this year had knocked in early. It was mid-November and the chilly mornings had now become foggier. The crowd of morning walkers in the park behind the Joshi home had thinned considerably over the week.

The bell in the old church rang five times to signify the hour of the day. Shweta's granny had been up much earlier though. An early riser all her life, here at Shashank's place, she found it difficult to lie in bed after five. Nonetheless, she forced herself to be under the bright maroon quilt, keeping her eyes closed, as she knew that if she switched on the light, Shashank, sleeping in the adjacent room, would be up as his sleep would be disturbed by the light.

But Shashank had been awake long since. For an hour after midnight, he had been sitting in his bed gazing outside. The silhouette of the trees against the dimming sky had been swaying to and fro. A little afar, an uneasy silence brooded over the cluster of shanties beyond the road. Night never fully descended on the haphazard row of a dozen odd houses sprung over a piece of wasteland. With the nights becoming longer and cooler, some of the inhabitants preferred to sit by the fire and gossip the cold night away. Harsher the weather, greater the buzz; such was the norm. For Shashank, however, sleep was at a premium that night. During such hours of profound aloofness, he would become restless and feel as if he had been invaded, torched and shelled by an army of memories. They descended upon him from all sides, coiling around him, like a famished python, tightening its hold if the prey twitched even a muscle.

Memories of Udit were not letting Shashank sleep. Udit was lurking in his mind, playing hide and seek, a game that he so enjoyed as an infant. Shashank could almost see him—a lean figure, brushing his teeth, not caring to close the tap; leaving his wet, crumpled towel in a heap on the bed after a bath; one slipper lying upturned here and the other flung away no one knew where. Shashank could almost hear the faint sound of the refrigerator door being opened. Stealing goodies from the fridge in the still of the night was a habit that stayed on with Udit, till the day he left home, maybe even now, who knows….

Since that fateful day, it had been five painstakingly long years. The minutes had led to hours, the hours into days, the days into weeks, the weeks into months, the months into years. Shashank could never even imagine in his wildest dreams how a boy who had the fear of darkness and who always slept with a 20-watt incandescent bulb lit throughout the night, could one fine day shrug off all his fears, discard his cloak of timidity, pick up his satchel and slip into the shroud of darkness!

'Perhaps, I ought not to have scolded him so badly; after all he had only failed an examination.' He often said in those moments when words were privy to none, when drops of sweat trickled down his brow, no matter what the weather was. The danger of him being drowned in a deep pool of guilt was imminent and the only escape was to divert his attention. Shashank decided to leave the bed and go out for a walk. His body and mind were craving for some fresh air to cool his burning thoughts.

He rushed into the bathroom and splashed some cold water on his face. The water was icy cold and he gasped loud. His gaze still transfixed on the mirror he reached out for the hand towel as he moved his left hand through the salt and pepper stubble. The towel was missing! In his home, using *his* towel was sacrilege and to top it, misplacing it was double sacrilege! Only Udit could get away with such blasphemy, each time, every time, without a single reprimand from his doting father.

Just then, a muscle in his leg cramped and all of a sudden, he slipped on the floor. The sound of the iron bucket that he had inadvertently upturned alarmed Granny.

'What happened, dear?'

'Nothing Ma, just slipped a little.'

'But beta that's nothing negligible, more so at your age and in this weather,' Granny remonstrated as she gently massaged his back and legs, feeling each and every bone and muscle to ensure that everything was intact.

Shashank smiled at his mother indulgently. 'Ma, there's nothing to worry! I didn't fall … just slipped on the floor and grabbed the tap.' He was up soon, all wet from emotions. The bathroom floor was dry.

Soon enough, Shashank rushed out. His walk today was anything but brisk. He just went through the motions and completed four rounds on the concrete track. Sitting on the bench under the sole mango tree that had grown amidst the cluster of tall palms and waiting for Lallu the tea-seller, to appear, he gazed at the three neem trees that stood in the centre of the park. The canopies were thin and open and the branches had begun shedding leaves to survive the harsh winter. Lying low and dormant when the conditions were hostile was the golden rule of life, be that among plants or animals he observed. He must continue to lie low, lie dormant.

Far away in a distant land, Udit's day had begun. His routine had been monotonously similar for the last three years. The only difference he could remember was that from a strapping assistant and an errand boy to a general dogsbody, he had now graduated to the respectable post of a chef.

Vishnu, his young assistant, nineteen as per records, less than sixteen in physique and above twenty-five as far as wisdom went, had been super quick that day, finishing his work well before time. A shy fellow, who would stammer through a sentence, stopping many a times for want of appropriate words, he preferred to speak in shorter sentences, stringing together a maximum of five to six words—short and crisp, like the rotis he took out from the earthen tandoor, in a batch of four, strung together at the end of a metre long iron rod.

Still only a fortnight old to the hill town, Vishnu had been a quick learner. He had become an expert in rolling out tandooris, deftly lowering them inside the red hot ovens, his hands going in and out within the blink of an eye. He would take out the rotis just in time, as efficiently as a computerised machine, allowing them to be in for just the right time so that they stayed fresh, soft and fluffy. His younger brother would then carry them towards the serving area, to be served by waiters purposefully moving around in crisp ironed shirts and smart ties.

Vishnu's diligence had been a pleasant surprise for Udit who had seen him wandering with a group of street urchins all day. In the group he was the ringleader, always cheerful, chattering and laughing as well as devising new ways and means to keep others entertained. One of his favourite pastimes was balancing a rolling bicycle tyre on the roads and pavements, using a twig to control its direction and acceleration, deriving pleasure unlimited.

Udit used to watch him from the dining hall French window and be secretly envious of his little pleasures, his uncomplicated life, his transient joys and non-existent sorrows. But ever since Vishnu had been employed against a paltry sum of eight hundred rupees per month, he had transformed into a serious worker. Gone was his carefree attitude! At the crack of dawn, every morning, he would regimentally be at the tandoor, clearing off the unburnt coal, ash and twigs, the residue that sometimes continued to smoulder hours after the hotel restaurant shut down. He would devotedly give the tandoor a fresh coat of paint, made from clay soaked overnight in water, using a piece of rag like a painter's brush, giving each of his movements a defined and controlled stroke, like a bona fide artist busy at his canvas. The fresh earthy smell that he would impart it would remain intact till another of his colleagues descended with a box of matchsticks and a bottle of kerosene. He would then fetch some of the drier pieces of fuel wood from the pile under the green shed and stare at the hissing sound of the fire accompanied with the smell of burning resin. Udit's work would begin when Vishnu's ended. Udit had been serving as the Chief Chef at the Hotel Mussoorie Grand, located at the tri-junction off the Mall Road in Mussoorie.

Shashank was getting ready for the University, putting his papers in the green and white jhola that he always carried. Picking up the lunch box from the dining table, he rushed towards the drawing room wall. Plucking the keys of the scooter from the nail on the wall had become a conditioned reflex; but on that day his fingers touched a bare nail. How could the keys disappear from there?

He hurriedly searched his study table, the bedside table and the bookshelf, but to no avail.

'Bina, I am leaving, it's getting late. If you happen to find the key, hang it on the nail.' Shashank walked out in a huff. He looked around for a rickshaw but it was office time and he knew he would have to wait before an empty rickshaw came his way.

There was a crow, sitting on one of the overhead power lines, cawing away furiously. In his childhood days at Bindki he remembered his mother saying that whenever a crow cawed on one's rooftop, it was an indication of guests or good news coming one's way.

He quickly crossed the road and waited at the T-junction, beyond which most of the rickshaw and tonga wallas stood. 'Sahib, want to go somewhere?' a voice called out.

'Oh yes!' he said and leapt on to the seat.

'Physics department,' he said and the rickshaw sped off right away.

The crow and the guest travelled with him. '*Could it be Udit?*' he soon brushed the thought aside, '*But, he is not a guest!*' Feeling anxious for no particular reason, he tried to suppress his angst by recollecting the guests who had visited his home whenever the ominous signs had been delivered by a cawing crow. He had very faint recollection of Balram Uncle visiting them from far away Bangalore, of his many aunts, who regularly came unannounced, but his most pleasant but fleeting memory was that of his maternal uncle, who had suddenly arrived from Nepal with his family, on the occasion of Diwali when he was in Class Six. Lost in his thoughts, he did not realise when the rickshaw stopped in front of the department and a group of students came around and wished him a good morning.

'Good morning,' he wished back and went to his office.

He glanced at his watch and checked the time table in his diary; he had highlighted a rectangle written BSc, Part II, Lecture Hall 3 in green ink. He still had a good ten minutes. Just then Lal Bahadur the peon barged in. He was taken aback, 'Is anything the matter?'

'Sir, I have been blessed with a grandson,' he said, opening a box of sweets. 'Please take some.'

'Oh, heartiest congratulations!' He picked up a whole laddoo. A bite into his favourite sweet, right at the beginning of the day, he thought, would do his mood a world of good and help him gather his wandering thoughts.

'Sir, there is still time for class, should I bring you some tea?'

'Hmm ... Yes, please,' he said. A cup of tea was always welcome. With each sip, he felt the turmoil within settling down. As he finished, the bell rang and he sauntered towards the lecture hall. His mind was relaxed and he quickly brought to mind the Laws of Thermodynamics that he had to teach that day.

The Johris had found that living alone was a painfully difficult proposition. Dr Arvind still remembered how he had tendered his resignation soon after joining the Medical college and returned home bag and baggage. To his bewildered parents he had a simple answer, 'It's too lonely there, I can't stay alone.' His senior professor had thankfully kept back the letter and given him a week's time, to have a re-think and inform about his decision through a telegram. Some of his friends and relatives had laughed it off saying that he was behaving like a homesick schoolboy not wanting to go to hostel. That was way back, far too many years ago. Moved by his adamant stand of not leaving his family, his parents tried to save his new and promising career opportunity by relocating to the city and staying there, providing him emotional support. Their decision to shift to the city along with him had had been his motivation for withdrawing the resignation, not the charm of a hassle-free city life or the prestige of being a faculty at one of the most reputed medical colleges. However, Arvind could not complain since over the years his parents, sisters, nephews and nieces continued to stay over with him from time to time, either for education or for medical treatment, giving him the taste of home away from home. But again, as time passed by, his cousins and nephews and nieces finished their education and had moved on and settled in their lives. His parents were no more and the guests had reduced to a trickle, mainly people dropping in for medical treatment or for appearing in a competitive examination.

His own sons Madhur and Mayank were settled and had their own families to look after. The couple's wish that at least one of their sons stay with them could have been fulfilled had the younger son Mayank continued with his job in the telephone factory in Naini. But after the initial years in the factory he chose to switch over to a better paid job and moved out even when Arvind tried to reason out with him the economics of the switch. Taking a house on rent, hiring maids and part time domestic helps along with conveyance charges he would shell out from his new place of posting was sure to offset the increase in his monthly pay. But Mayank had insisted that he wanted growth in his career and had walked away without shedding a tear, unaffected by the sight of his own mother crying and choking with emotions. That she had been spending sleepless nights for almost a month was also something he could easily ignore, saying, 'All mothers are like this, she will soon come to terms with it.'

Since then the couple had been trying to settle down but the pangs of the empty nest syndrome had cost them dear; with a cascading effect, the emotional emptiness had accelerated their old age blues. Their ageing minds no longer had the cushion effect of guffaws, giggles, echoing laughter, meaningless gossip or of those one-off petty fights to energise and rejuvenate the everyday humdrum of life. Their monotonous routine had been made all the more dull though trouble-free by a friendly milkman and a vegetable vendor, who religiously dropped their rations at the doorstep, while Savita, their maid of many years, made sure that they need not lift a finger. This collective assistance ensured that the mundane affairs of everyday life did not bother Arvind and Yashoda. Every today was like yesterday. The only saving grace was that every evening Arvind devoted a few hours to his clinic, where even now patients turned up habitually. His consultation fee of ₹ 100 was more of a formality to keep things a little serious for the satisfaction of his patients. He didn't need the money now, he wanted company, wanted people, wanted visits from friends and relatives. He longed for those gossip sessions over chai-pakora. He wished he could again spend an evening making litti-chokha over an open chulha in the backyard or a barbecue grill during a get-together with friends and relatives. 'When you don't get what you like, you have to like what you get,' he would often tell Yashoda, when she became too depressed.

At times he would also joke, 'Let's go to a movie today' and she would respond with a wry smile, 'Are you ill or something?'

That night, Arvind was surprised to find his wife falling asleep immediately after taking her sleeping pills, compared to other days when a second dose was usually required to ensure that she got some sound sleep. Arvind had with great deal of effort managed to keep Diazepam at bay; by making books his companion till sleep engulfed him for a few hours. Their bedroom walls had no clock, the one Madhur had couriered from London had also been dumped in the store. It was not the passing hours that they dreaded; it was the ticking of the clock that they were averse to, as it served no real purpose other than increasing their anxiety that life was passing by. Lost in these thoughts, Arvind fell asleep with the book resting open on his chest.

When the first rays of the sun peeped through the skylight of the bedroom etching golden petal patterns on the opposite wall of the room, Arvind woke up. He looked around and was surprised to see the reading lamp still on and the book he had been reading lying on the floor, near his slippers; upturned with the title in bold 'How to Cope with Loneliness' glaring at him. He picked up the book and wiped its cover with the edge of the bed sheet, trying to absolve himself of the sin of letting a book fall; he had always revered a book as a form of Goddess Saraswati. He glanced at Yashoda, who was still in deep slumber as he could see the movement beneath her eyelids; perhaps she was into a dream and her radiant countenance and occasionally twitching lips conveyed that it was a wonderful one.

'Let her dream be over, before I wake her up,' he said to himself, as he walked towards the washroom. As he came out, he saw that Yashoda had left the bed and the sound of clanking pots and pans meant that she was already in the kitchen, preparing bed tea for him; a habit he had developed after marriage and which had continued ever since.

'Your tea,' said Yashoda, keeping the off white cup with intricate floral design etched with a golden border, on the table.

'Why didn't you wake me up? There's so much work pending …' she mildly remonstrated before disappearing into the kitchen once again.

At his neighbour Shashank's home, anxiety and worry were palpable. Old granny had been feeling homesick and wanting to return to Bindki but had stayed put due to Bina's health issues. Bina herself could not understand why suddenly her health had become problematic. In addition to her troubles due to asthma, some ailment or the other would flare up suddenly complicating matters. More than half a dozen doctors had been consulted and they unanimously agreed that stress and anxiety were the root causes, that her problems were psycho-somatic. On some days things would be so bad that she would be unable to get up from her bed in the morning. Shashank's quota of paid leave had been dwindling rapidly.

With Bina unable to take care of the house and his mother wanting to go back to Bindki, he could foresee that things would be difficult to manage. Sonam would be overburdened; The maid Chunni was least expected to mend her ways, her frequent French leaves would not lessen. A full time maid Vishambhar uncle had brought six months ago went away after three months as she felt homesick. He often wondered why mother had to go away so soon! If she could stay back, Chunni's husband could be employed as a part-timer to take care of some of the chores such as ironing clothes, shopping for groceries and vegetables, getting milk, medicines and running errands.

Every night after dinner, he had a habit of reading for an hour before going to bed. But these days he would hardly open a book. Instead, he would often sit in his study and brood over his myriad problems. The books lined on racks in his study, remained untouched.

His study table today was cluttered with receipts of purchases, doctor's prescriptions and a bunch of envelopes containing newsletters which he had not even opened. He sat on his chair and tried arranging the papers; perhaps that was the place from where he could begin reorganising his life. To his horror, he discovered that beneath the pile lay two envelopes which he should have posted long back! They were important official correspondence addressed to a professor in Oxford University. He made up his mind that the first task he would make Chandan do the next morning would be to rush to the post office at the stroke of ten. He kept the envelope underneath his pillow, not taking a chance with his memory which had been betraying him, much to his chagrin, of late.

The faithful Chandan had been his errand boy since his early days in the city. His had been a case of total reliance, to the extent that none of the trivial issues dealing with the mundane ever got to bother Shashank. Chandan had been fully competent in all types of household chores. Fixing up LPG bookings, replacing leaking taps and fused bulbs had been as routine and easy for him as rolling out chapattis day in and day out. Shashank had found in him his Man Friday, upon whom he could rely for anything and everything that could be delegated. Even in his absence, Chandan had provided respite to his hassled master, who had comforted himself with the thought that he was around, little realising that he had gone to his village months back.

Engulfed in his silky cocoon of oblivion, he felt a little better. He filed all the important prescriptions in a folder. Removal of the scattered papers revealed a thick layer of dust settled on the tabletop. He lightly brushed the tip of his index finger against the teak polished surface and then examined it, in a fashion he often did in his school. He would then rush to his class teacher, taking care that the dust remained on the finger and request for the ayah to be summoned to clean their desks, so that while the ayah took a good fifteen minutes wiping the thirty desks and chairs again, he could enjoy some free time with his friends.

Here, he immediately took out a white hanky from his pocket and wiped the table, inspecting it after wiping each time, but the feelings were far different from that childhood pleasure he derived while doing so in class with his fingers. He also remembered how he had imposed a blanket ban, a prohibitory order completely barring any maid's entry into his study since a bank cheque book was misplaced. An order he had then reluctantly modified when he had discovered Bina having to carry out the cleaning and dusting work by herself; and dust being a notorious trigger for her asthma.

Caught in a quagmire, he shut his eyes and pulled his legs up on the chair. He found himself unable to put the pieces of the jigsaw puzzle of his life together. His mind during times such as these would drift and wander, searching for escape routes. The far and few routes that would appear in front of his loosely shut eyes were those he would never tread. He had been a teetotaller all along to the extent that he could not even bear the smell of alcohol, which he found to be too pungent and nauseating. Even during his three month long stay at Oxford University a few years back, he had steadfastly refused to consume any beer in the weekend parties where he was invited to by his Indian origin friends. He had been stubborn in the face of all ridicule and fun. When he was back home from England, he had even stopped taking the occasional paan. He wanted to brave life as it is, with all its foibles.

A temporary escape to Bindki was something he always found tempting; but even that he felt would be tantamount to running away from his life and its challenges, riding on a horse straddled with guilt. Burdened with responsibilities on the professional front also, today he realised that for the last four to five years, his only connect with his homeland had been his mother, who had been visiting him rather frequently to lend him emotional support.

Vishambhar Chacha had arrived from the village the day before with the welcome news that Gauri, the cow, had delivered a healthy calf three days back. He had been a regular visitor to their place for the last twelve years, courtesy an on-going court case over some land dispute in his family in the Allahabad High Court. The outcome of the hearing the following day was the last thing on his mind. It was a routine for him now as the result would have hardly any bearing on his life. Had a judgement come in his favour some decades ago, his financial status would have been different, his life would have been a little easier, but it was irrelevant now. He was in high spirits being the harbinger of this news as well as of all that had been transpiring in the village in the last three months that Granny was not around. Granny was ecstatic to see him and the good news that he had brought added to her joy.

Chacha brought with him an oversized bag that looked like Santa's sack. It contained some files and papers of his case but most of it was filled with goodies that he had brought for Shashank's family. A can of rabri, fresh green peas, baby potatoes, homemade carrot halwa, fresh jaggery, mango and jackfruit pickles and a jar of cane vinegar looking appetising with floating red chillies, garlic and mango shavings.

His unexpected arrival had cheered Granny all the more because she had been wanting to return home lately but had not been able to broach the subject with Shashank due to Bina's indifferent health. Like every year, she was here for the navratri poojas and had planned to stay for a month or so and be back in the village in time for the sowing of the potato and wheat crops. The family still owned a lot of land in the village and granny had been shouldering the responsibility to ensure that the tiller of their land did sow the crops timely. In her absence, her younger son Pranav had been looking after the same but somehow she was not sure that everything would be in order. Now that Chacha was there she thought that she could go back with him, without bothering Shashank. The mere prospect of going home soon had infused a new lease of life in her.

'Chunni, make some ginger tea. You just keep the water to boil. I will make the tea myself with the jaggery Vishambhar has brought.'

Ten minutes later, she appeared from the kitchen carrying the tray, 'Now taste this tea, it's very different from the regular tea, the one made with sugar.'

Chacha gave a broad smile, 'So, today I get to relish Bhabhi's special tea!' he said, returning back after spitting the betel juice.

Shashank looked at his mother who was folding the blanket Chacha had left on the cot.

'So Ma, now that Vishambhar Chacha says that everything is fine in Bindki you must be relieved.'

'Yes, but I need to go back for a few days. I will return after settling a few things. Beta, if you don't mind, can I return with Vishambhar tomorrow?'

'But Ma why so soon? You stay here this winter. Your knees will be much better.'

'You know son, that caretaker Maddi is so careless. If I don't keep a strict eye on him, he will not look after the wheat and potato crops properly. And he doesn't listen to Pranav.'

'But Ma, give Pranav a chance, he too can get the work done. If you want I can also visit Bindki for a couple of days and help out.'

Ma looked a little downcast. 'Okay, I won't go if you don't want me to, beta,' she said in a small voice.

'Ma, I will never force you to stay here if you don't want to. But if you can stay on for a week more, I can accompany you, as there are two continuous holidays next week,' he hastened to add.

'No, no, you shouldn't take the trouble. After all, Bina is not keeping good health. You need to take care of her.'

Now that it was clear that Ma would be going home Shashank was a bit ruffled. And to add to his troubles Chandan had left for his hometown a week earlier, to be with his ailing wife Saha. Saha had been juggling between India and Nepal, spending a few months here and then a few there as she didn't want to lose her connections with her native place. Two months back she had left for Nepal to be with her son's family to help raise the triplets the daughter-in-law had given birth to. But now she herself had fallen ill, a bout of malaria had been lingering leading to some other complications. This apart, about six months back floods in river Kosi had washed away his home, forcing his family to live in the flood relief camp that the district administration had set up to offer food and shelter to those affected. Just a fortnight ago the camp had been shut down and his family had to stay under the sky, on the outskirts of a forest area. Shashank had been very helpful. He had given Chandan enough money to rebuild his house but the area was still inundated. Finding a new piece of land was a tough job when hundreds of thousands had been affected by the flood. Chandan had to rush home. Though he had promised to return in a month's time, Shashank knew that it was highly unlikely considering his circumstances. The maid, Chunni, was a stopgap arrangement; she was neither efficient nor regular. Besides, she would feign weird illnesses and take strings of French leaves on the pretext of family emergencies and the like.

That evening, after dinner, Shashank joined Sonam in the kitchen and gave her a hand in washing the utensils. Shashank arranged the dinner plates on the steel stand right above the kitchen sink and wondered, 'Why did I never think about a small geyser in the kitchen?' He looked at the empty wall above the tap. 'Perhaps because Bina never complained,' he consoled himself. For a moment, he stood and examined the shelves. Jars were all arranged in rows; neatly lined up according to their sizes, the bigger ones at the back, the smaller ones in the front and the smallest forming the third layer.

He then cleaned the gas stove, while Sonam readied a bed for Vishambhar Chacha.

Once in his study, he lay on his bed keeping a book by his side. From the drawing room, the rumbling roar of Vishambhar Chacha's snores could be heard. He looked at the wall in front of his bed. A poster of a cute little boy standing at a door saying, 'May I come in dad?' caught his attention. The room was Udit's and he had been using it these days so as to give greater privacy to Shweta at night. With only ladies in the room, she could easily visit the washroom or change into her night suit. Bina always preferred to sleep by the side of her daughters, an unknown fear haunted her after Udit had left home.

What will happen when Ma leaves tomorrow? Will the girls manage by themselves? What will Bina say? Who will take care of Shweta, once Sonam leaves for her classes?' Shashank thought to himself; but he knew that he ought not to be selfish. He also knew that Bina would never confront him with any uncomfortable questions till things really became unmanageable in mother's absence. The only way she would perhaps express her distress would be by saying that 'Had mother been there, things would have been easier ...' Bombarded by a billion thoughts, Shashank fell asleep.

He opened his eyes when the alarm went off at six. Immediately, he put on his shoes and went out for his daily walk. Today he took a detour and went towards the Buxi Bundh; he found that walking at a slightly higher elevation allowed him to have a refreshingly different view of the surroundings. On his left, a little far ahead, he could see the agricultural fields, sown with wheat; they resembled huge cots covered with green velvety sheets. At a few places, some mustard shoots had flowered early, providing a wonderful yellow relief. Beyond the agricultural fields, he could see the vast expanse of the banks of river Ganga, filled with an array of tents and flags of different colours fluttering atop many of them. When he concentrated and strained his ears, he could catch the faint sound of the chantings of Ganga arti drifting along with the wind.

As he readied to leave, a group of noisy mynas chirping behind him attracted his attention. He took a few steps towards the road but then returned to have a look underneath the bench he had been sitting. Close by he found a nest, fallen on the ground. He inched to have an even closer look, only to discover two of the tiniest pink baby squirrels he had ever seen, huddling among the mesh bowl of cotton, blades of grass and bits of sponge. Like an inquisitive child, he squatted on the ground to inspect if the two babies were alive. He looked around to see if the mother squirrel was anywhere but found a crow waiting in anticipation, fancying his chances for an early morning feast. Now he understood the reason for the mynas vocalising in unison; they were trying their best to scare away the crow. He thought of picking the nest up and putting it in the little depression where the mango bole had forked into a Y, but he was not too sure if this act of his would not cause the mother squirrel to disown her babies. So he crossed the road and waited in front of the temple, keeping an eye on the crow all the time. He located a mongoose crossing the road but thankfully it was headed in a different direction. Barely had it gone, the mother squirrel came scampering down the mango bole chittering and flicking its tail. Then, one by one, it carried the babies in its mouth and sheltered them in the relative safety of a hole, somewhere in the nearby tamarind tree, across the boundary of the palatial bungalow. Relieved of his duty, Shashank made his way back home.

Back home he found his mother and Vishambhar Chacha gossiping in the drawing room. She looked cheerful and happy, though a bit sleep deprived. Changing into his slippers, he joined them by the fire in the iron wok. He took off his gloves and extended his palms above the fire.

Despite the gloves, his hands had become stiff. The warmth of the bed of red charcoals was comforting. He looked at his mother's face glowing in the mild orange of the fire. The forehead had prominent furrows, the crow's feet had deepened, the cheek looked sunken and her hands trembled faintly as she held them above the flames. She was only seventy, he reiterated to himself, estimating her age with his own and the year of her marriage. She would definitely live longer. After all, age is just a number, he consoled himself, thinking of the 90-year-old mother of the temple priest, whom he had met the other day, walking towards the temple, leaning on a sturdy walking stick.

'Huh …' he nudged those foolish thoughts away and stole a glance at his mother's face once again and from her cheerful countenance as she soaked the warmth by the side of the fire, a little sanity returned to his labyrinth of thoughts. Vishambhar Chacha was in the middle of his story, telling how a portion of his own house had suddenly crumbled in the rain one night, leaving him precariously placed under the rubble and how he had wriggled out with the help of a rope thrown towards him.

'How is Chachi?' Shashank asked trying to initiate a conversation with his uncle. He had last seen her six years ago when she had come to take a dip in sangam during the Kumbh mela.

'She is fine, but age catches up with everyone, you see. Despite her cataract operation last year she has almost nil vision in her right eye. And you are well aware that she has always been anaemic. And to add to her misery, last week she was stung by a scorpion,' he informed.

'Oh, no!' Ma's eyes widened in surprise as Chacha had not shared the story with her, yet.

'Oh, it had rained that day. All afternoon it had been a heavy downpour and in the evening she was in the kitchen—cooking. The firewood was damp and not burning properly, so she asked me to get some dry cow-dung cakes from the outer store. But I was busy enjoying my hookah, so I selfishly asked her to get a few herself. She had hardly opened the door of the store and picked up two, when she was stung! Oh, that plump scorpion which raced away before I could get the shovel and …..' the last words got stuck in his mouth.

A collective sigh and the story continued till everyone had almost finished tea.

'At what time is the bus beta?' asked Chacha.

'There is a bus every hour. You can take the one after lunch at two. And Ma, do you want to go today itself? Have you decided? Is it final?' Shashank asked.

'It's been a long time, dear. Let me go, stay there a month. If needed, I can always come back.'

'Surely, Ma. I won't stop you. One does miss one's home, after all,' Shashank said almost apologetically, as Chacha smiled, displaying his betel-stained teeth with the upper left canine missing.

'I will be back for the Maghi purnima snan with Chachi in a month's time. If Bhabhi wants she can return with me then,' Vishambhar Chacha said trying to sympathise with Shashank.

The old man had not ever set foot beyond the boundaries of his state and Granny had spent more than five decades of her life in the village. She had been a witness to years passing by, as Bindki had grown from a non-descript village dotted with clusters of hutments at the time of her marriage, to one having baked brick houses, erratic electricity and piped water. Could anyone fault the two elderly souls then, when they were craving to go back to their own nest? For her, village life was something she was accustomed to since early years. In fact the first time she came to a city was when Shashank had joined the University and he insisted that she visit him for a week. And Shashank still recounted how she was stupefied when the milk cooker had whistled in the kitchen. Brushing teeth with a freshly broken twig from the neem tree in front of the house, taking a bath at the family well, visiting the Ma Chaura Devi temple at a stone's throw for her daily pooja, feeding the cow Gauri and then taking breakfast sitting on a cot outside was a routine she missed here. Here outings meant going to the temple daily and visiting the market once in a while. She also missed the conversations she would have daily with Kali, the woman who always brought fresh vegetables for her. Others like Munni, the woman who came to make cow-dung cakes, Maddi's daughter Bindia who brought grass for the cows and buffaloes were also her daily companions in the village.

The house looked empty that evening. Ma and Vishambar Chacha had left for Bindki. Shashank visited the room where Ma slept and sat on her bed. He could still smell the fragrance of the til oil she used in her hair from her pillow. 'Maybe she will come for the Maghi Purnima snan in coming January with Chacha,' he said to cheer himself up. The ringing telephone at this moment was a welcome diversion.

Once back in the village Granny had settled into her usual routine. Things she had been worried about had been taken care of. Maddi had been summoned on the day of her return itself. And it was a pleasant surprise that he had been sincere in sowing the crops timely and had looked after them well in her absence.

It was a cold January evening and she was sitting by the side of a fire with Vishambhar Chacha, Munni and Maddi with a glass of tea in her hand. Her little grandson was loitering around wanting to sit in her lap.

'Don't come too close to the fire,' she was warning him again and again.

'How many times have you watered the wheat and potato?' she asked Maddi sitting crosslegged on the floor by the fire.

'Come with me tomorrow and see for yourself,' he said pushing the burning log a bit deeper into the fire.

'Right, but remember watering helps protect the crop when there is dense fog, so better be alert,' she cautioned.

The fire blazed a bright orange and Granny's face glowed in the reflecting embers. Happiness and serenity was evident in the glow.

Thousands of kilometres away, in a posh London home, Madhur and his wife Shelly were also sitting by a fire in their drawing-room discussing the timing of their forthcoming visit to India.

'Are you sure we need to go this month itself?' Shelly asked.

'What do you mean? I have already booked the tickets long back. At that time you agreed with the dates, didn't you?'

'Oh yes. But then my school had not fixed up the dates for this educational trip to China. I don't want to miss it,' she said with a frown.

'That's alright but I can't waste so much money. You know how much the tickets cost. If you want to attend this China trip, better stay back. One cancellation I can still afford. In March I won't be able to make it, you know that. Besides, we need to finalise a small flat somewhere, maybe in Delhi so that we have an asset and a home of our own.'

'Why in Delhi?' she asked.

'Because I can't afford one in Mumbai.'

'I mean, why not Bangalore?'

'Why at all in Bangalore, I have no intention of settling down there. Delhi is centrally located and closer to home. Moreover I can only afford something around Delhi, maybe Noida or Ghaziabad.'

'Now don't use that as an excuse to force me to visit India. If you ask me I wish to settle down here itself. See how my brother

Sameer has purchased a house and his kids are studying in the best schools of UK.'

'Shelly you know I am not that ambitious and I wish to settle in my homeland, not in a foreign country. We should not be selfish, I think old parents should not be left alone. Being close to them makes a world of a difference. But I will not stop you in case the two boys wish to settle here. You can always be with them.'

'I don't know how one can be so adamant,' muttered Shelly walking out in a huff.

Madhur stretched out his legs on the table in front and reclined in the chair. He closed his eyes for a while. A stream of thoughts about his homeland wandered across his mind.

It had been four years since he had last been home. Even when he had visited India two years ago for a short business trip he had returned from Bangalore and could neither visit his city nor meet his parents. Suddenly he thought of his colleague Samrat. He couldn't even fly back for the last rites of his father who had died a fortnight ago. And it was only yesterday he had taken a week off and flown home.

What if? He just panicked at the thought and came to the window. Long queues of vehicles zipping past on the road was the only thing he could see. People were hardly visible.

He was reminded of his own city, a city he loved despite its cracks and crevices, foibles and faults. During his stay here in London, he often remembered his days, that joy of taking a rickshaw ride to Civil Lines on a hot afternoon only to visit Softy Corner for some ice cream with his friends, a dip in Sangam on a lazy Sunday afternoon or sneaking off to Company Bagh to enjoy the special guavas sold by vendors there.

A mute homesickness brewed within him for these years that he had been in London.

The tickets for the January 20th flight to India had been booked long back but Madhur had kept it a secret and not informed his dad about the visit. He now picked up the phone and called home.

The phone kept ringing but there was no response. He checked the time; 4:30 pm in London meant that it was 9.30 pm back home in India. 'Maybe Dad is in the washroom,' he said to himself as he waited by the side of the phone. An agonising five minute wait followed, during which he paced up and down the room, only to call again. With his ears glued to the receiver, he waited, but the phone kept on ringing.

'Maybe the phone is dead and it's a false ring,' he consoled himself.

A friend came to see him. He couldn't call his parents again that evening as the guests stayed back for dinner.

Next morning he was up early. He waited for some time, preferring to call at the time he was sure his dad would be free from his morning routine. Anxious and worried, he went to the window and peeped out. On the road below, the vehicular traffic was as disciplined as always. Red signal meant a car would halt even if there was no other vehicle visible on the road. In the neighbourhood park children played. He could see his son Arin sitting on a red bench with Shelly, having an animated discussion on something.

The morning rains had given the city a wash. The trees around looked fresh, the roads sparkled; and images of the buildings in the thin film of water on the roads, periodically swaying in the puddles as a result of eddies, created a wonderful illusion. To him, nothing was familiar; the species of trees, the architecture of the buildings, the people, the language. Quiet, muted and refined modes of celebration seemed bland to him, when compared to the loud and boisterous revelry so common in his homeland, be it Dussehra, Diwali or Holi. This coupled with absolute order and perfection around always increased his craving for his homeland. In his initial days in the city, a strange homesickness had crippled him for days. He missed his familiar land and his people to the point where tears filled his eyes whenever he got a phone call or a letter from home. He often sought traces of his parent's faces and voices by frequenting neighbourhoods having predominantly Indian population. There he would sit in the parks and other public places for long hours, feigning obvious unconcern to the happenings around, his head buried deep into a book, but in reality all he would do was overhear people conversing in a language that was his own, discussing issues which sounded so very familiar to him.

Over the weekend dinners and pool parties with Indian families, he would relish the mustard flavoured fish, the stuffed bhindi, or deep fried paneer curries, staying far away from the pancakes and the turkeys and the lambs. He would push the cutlery aside and eat with his hands, knowing fully well that Shelly would have a lot to say when they returned home. Those evenings, he would allow himself to be fooled for a short while imagining that his mother was there somewhere in the kitchen cooking his favourite stuff and once the dinner was over she would come, her sari full of greasy patches, smelling of spices and wiping the sweat on her forehead she would say, 'You didn't eat properly beta, you hardly ate anything.'

He often remembered his congested neighbourhood and the roads where each user followed his own set of rules; where, other than humans, fellow users could be as diverse as a pair of cows, who would plonk themselves right in the middle of the road, a herd of buffaloes would sleepwalk towards their destination, or even a file of donkeys would saunter their way to the washing ghats.

He ran to the phone and called again. The line remained busy and he couldn't connect. It was only after trying for twenty odd minutes that the call was through.

'Hello, Madhur!' The two words that he had been longing to listen finally reached his ears.

'Hello Papa, where were you? And where has Ma gone? I've been trying to call for the last hour or so … why don't you buy a cordless phone?'

'I am sorry, son. Savita must have had reduced the volume while dusting … right now I was passing through this room and hence heard the ring. I am so sorry …'

The conversation continued for twenty minutes, during which Yashoda came in.

Replacing the receiver, Arvind thundered, 'Don't let Savita touch the phone! Foolish lady! She fiddles with everything.'

'What happened? Why do you have to shout?' Yashoda was astounded at his sudden rage.

'Savita had reduced the volume of the phone! Madhur had been trying for an hour or so and we could not hear a thing! He was so worried,' he thundered.

'Anyway, forget it, good news!' Smiling from ear to ear, Arvind announced, 'They are coming home, in a fortnight!'

'Don't joke!' Yashoda virtually jumped up from the sofa.

'I AM NOT joking!'

'Oh really! I can't believe this!' Yashoda almost broke down.

Since that long distance call, the house had suddenly acquired a new lease of life. A flurry of activities began, keeping both the occupants of the big house busy for a change. The dull yellow coat of paint on the walls, which had been peeling off at many places revealing fancy shapes beneath, had been whitewashed. An army of twelve had been hired to finish the job in time. The layers of moss that had inhabited the terrace walls for quite sometime had suddenly been scraped off without even a notice being served on them. The first floor rooms had been redone, with the doors and windows getting new curtains, the sofas getting new cushions and the floors laid up with new carpets. The creaky doors of the ground floor master bedroom and the termite-infested kitchen door were replaced. The rusted latches and handles on the doors and windows had been replaced by shining brass ones. The unmistakable smell of fresh paint still lingered in the air.

Arvind found Yashoda busy in the kitchen, frying something in the kadahi.

'Smells good!' he said leaning towards the kadahi. 'Oh the recipe you were noting down yesterday from that cookery show on television.'

'These are doughnuts for my grandsons. I know this is something all English kids like,' she had a twinkle in her eye as the wonderful aroma dominated the resinous smell of paint. The previous evening, she had also made Madhur's favourite besan laddoos and had kept the jars on the dining table. A caveat had also been issued to Arvind that he should not take more than one at a time and stoke up his diabetes.

'Don't overstress yourself, Yashoda; after all, they are coming back to their own home. They are not our guests!' Arvind raised his voice from the living room, where he was making a list of purchases he had to make from Civil Lines market. As he sipped his tea, sitting on the big teak chair, he began imagining life after a day; how much would Madhur have changed? Would his grandsons Aryan and Arin recognise him and would his daughter-in-law Shelly, still be the shy bahu that she had once been? He kept the cup on the table and muttered to himself, 'It's just one more day to go ...' and walked towards the drawing room. The watch on the drawing room wall showed 10:30 am. He began to make a mental note of the residual work he had planned for the day but somehow the aromas from the kitchen distracted him and he moved towards the kitchen.

The harsh sound of the grinder blades welcomed him. Yashoda was getting ready to stuff the freshly ground roasted spices into those bright red chillies. The pickle was another of Madhur's favourites, which she was sure he would not have tasted for long. She remembered the jar-full that she had packed for them when they were leaving for London last time had to be thrown away at the Delhi airport as the aviation authorities did not allow food items to pass through security.

Yashoda hummed an old song as she was stuffing the red chillies with the spices, gently pushing the filling inside with her thin wrinkled fingers and then dipping it in the smoked mustard oil before arranging them in the glass jar. The flaming red chillies signified the new found colour in the life of the lonely twosome.

'Don't you pretend to be ill from tomorrow, you know that I will have more work once they come,' she issued a mild warning to Savita.

'Have I ever done that Maaji?' she turned around from the sink and spoke in a manner of mild rebuttal, letting the water flow from the open tap as she talked.

'After all Bhaiyaji is coming home after four years,' she smiled trying to assure her employer that she would not be found wanting or would be wilfully absenting herself in order to escape the extra workload.

'Okay, now go and keep this jar in the sun and please be careful! It's made of glass,' she finished off.

Arvind was inspecting the lawn. A hired labourer hurriedly mowed the green and brown grass which had been run over by weeds. Time was too short to plant the neglected flower beds with any plants; hence he had purchased a dozen potted plants having flowers in full bloom. For a change, today the weather was pleasant with warm sunshine scattered everywhere compared to last week when it was all foggy and dull.

Two days before they were to take the flight to Delhi, at Madhur's London apartment, the excitement in the air was palpable. Shelly was the only one who was packing her stuff reluctantly. Madhur had taken out two suitcases and two bags and put them out to air them. He had also been to Harrods and purchased gifts and mementoes for his mom and dad and also for some friends. Their own stuff, varying from clothes, woollens, caps, chocolates, packs of ready-to-eat cereals, shoes and other accessories had also been separated and readied for packing. Madhur had been wondering at the increasing pile of stuff Shelly had been gathering at the corner table but had decided against any interference. Shelly always hated advice or counselling from anyone in any form, particularly in matters she considered personal. Once before, they had a serious argument over an issue similar to this, at the end of which both had decided not to interfere in each other's packing as long as the suitcases could be carried in flight without having to pay extra for excess baggage.

On the day of the travel, Arin had the heaviest cabin bag, full of his own stuff and those that he had collected for presenting to his *dadu.* He had been very secretive too, locking one of the compartments of the bag with a number lock. Shelly tried persuading him to discard the bag and use a portion of her own handbag instead, but to no avail. He had been adamant, reminding her that Papa had promised him that he would be allowed to carry his own cabin bag. A little chastened, Shelly decided to give up.

Finally the family was on board the Air India flight from Heathrow to New Delhi. An hour or so into the flight, the co-passengers had settled but Aryan and Arin were still exchanging their seats. Out of the four, Shelly had closed her eyes during the takeoff and was still in that state, disinterested. The two boys, however, were very excited. They repeatedly enquired from Madhur about the number of hours the flight was expected to take, repeating the question every half an hour. The fourth time they had asked the question, Shelly had opened her eyes and literally pounced upon them, telling them how foolish they had been and how they had made themselves a laughing stock in front of other passengers. Little Arin had interrupted her telling her that he could see most passengers were asleep and if that was not enough they had been conversing in Hindi. Aryan had made a tongue-in-cheek comment. 'Bro you are wrong, didn't you see even Mom has woken up from sleep?' Not one ready to lose an argument, an infuriated Shelly had turned her back towards them and pulled the blanket over her face muttering, 'Do, as you please.'

The rest of the journey was expectedly quiet and uneventful, with the boys preferring to keep mum.

Madhur, on the aisle seat, remained fidgety, adjusting his blanket, taking a sip of water, going to the washroom in between some fitful sleep. He could see Shelly in deep sleep in her seat across the aisle. For a moment he wondered if she could have stayed back and attended the China tour with her fellow teachers. He also knew that his in-laws were in London now for the house-warming ceremony of his brother in law Sameer's new home. Was Shelly interested in staying back due to this reason? he thought. But then she had otherwise also never shown interest when it came to visiting his parents. She had been staying in London for a year when their marriage was fixed. Initially she had also tried to convince Madhur that once he got a chance of visiting England, he should think of taking British citizenship by all means, a proposition he had refused to even consider. But now after being in London for almost five years, he was also not totally averse to the idea, allowing Shelly to be happy with his indecisiveness. Their periodic tiffs over the issue had still continued. But deep in his heart he wanted to be back home in India. The diverse thoughts agitated him and he popped a Disprin tablet into his mouth, hoping to get relief from a throbbing headache that he thought would subside on its own. It was only when most of the lights in the plane were switched off except the dimly glowing night lamps in the aisle that he fell asleep.

When the plane entered the Indian skies, he awoke, some invisible clock within him ringing a silent alarm. He looked at the boys, they were in deep sleep. He lifted the screen on the window just a bit to steal a glance. Outside it was all dark. The break of dawn was imminent; he could make out, even though the watch on his left wrist still remained in Greenwich Meridian zone. He slowly nudged Aryan, whispering 'India' into his ears, but he pulled his blanket up after a big yawn. He tried to sleep again, Delhi was still far.

An announcement startled him out of sleep. He only heard, 'Thank you' and waited for the repeat announcement. But instead of the expected one, came the co-pilot's voice, 'Dear passengers, the flight is being diverted to Bombay, due to heavy fog. We regret the inconvenience caused. Thank you.' He quickly glanced out through the window, unwilling to believe the co-pilot. Down below, the image of flickering lights of the city, hazy and dimmed due to heavy fog shimmered. Delhi was so near, yet so far.

'Oh God!' he sighed; but there was nothing that he could do, except secretly pray that the aircraft head back to Delhi as soon as the weather conditions became a little friendly. As they deplaned at Bombay airport for the unscheduled stopover, he headed straight towards the phone booth and dialled home.

'Hello Papa, we are in Bombay right now as the flight could not land in Delhi due to a dense fog.'

'Madhur, it's Ma on the line, beta.'

'Oh! Ma how are you?'

The receiver had by that time gone into Arvind's hands.

'This fog had to come today of all days,' came the voice from the other end; 'But don't worry, in an hour or two, it will clear.'

'My only worry is that we don't miss our train from Delhi tonight.'

'No ... no ... the fog clears once the sun rises; I am sure you will catch the train.'

'Ok Papa, bye for now. I'll call you again.'

'I'll be there at the station tomorrow,' the voice quivered with choked emotion before it was disconnected.

'What happened?' asked Yashoda, unsure if she had heard correctly what Madhur had to say, sitting down on the sofa in the bedroom.

'Hmm ... the flight could not land at Delhi due to heavy fog. So now they have been diverted to Bombay.'

'Great, they're home, at last! Bombay isn't too far.'

She rose from the sofa and laboriously walked towards the window. She opened the window and peeped outside. It was still pretty dark and foggy. A puff of icy cold wind entered the warm and cosy bedroom. Out of reflex, she shut it immediately. 'It's only 6.30, by 10:00 it should clear,' she sounded hopeful.

At the airport, Madhur next dialled two of his friends Tanmaya and Vidya in Bangalore. Shelly who was standing by his side prompted him, 'Ask if that fellow is ready to sell now, we can go and have a look.'

Madhur gestured her to stop.

Once he was finished with the call, he turned towards her and said, 'What is the hurry? We are here for a month. I will first speak to Latha in Delhi. Please don't pressurise me for Bangalore. This is secondary, I want to be with my people, I want to relax and enjoy.'

Arvind meanwhile was searching for the phone number of Shiva Taxi Service for going to the station the day after, frantically turning over the pages of his old diary.

Yashoda had plenty of work at hand. For now, she sat in the second bedroom, with a new bed sheet – a red and blue cotton print, still with the price tag intact – in a little dilemma thinking whether, she should tuck away the edges beneath the mattress or forego the effort. Arvind had always questioned her over the futility of the exercise, asking her what purpose it served whenever he saw her exerting herself to lift the heavy Dunlop mattresses in order to push the edges in. He would then gently remind her that their home had no kids who would use the bed as a trampoline, causing the sheet to gather and crumple in the centre. But she would remain silent unable to kick a habit she had carried since childhood. Till date, she could not bear the sight of a messy bed with crumpled sheet and scattered pillows.

She had aired and sunned the fluffy quilts for three days and now was pretty sure that there was no smell of the naphthalene balls within its folds. She folded them and arranged them on the bed. Then she changed the covers to a bright yellow velvet, thinking of Aryan's favourite colour.

The room had hardly been used in the last four years. Two months back, some guests of Mr Verma, their next-door neighbour, had occupied it for three days on the occasion of his daughter's marriage. For those three days, the Johris had been a cheerful host, treating the Vermas as their own guests, gossiping till late in the night and offering tea and snacks from their own kitchen. That had been a welcome change, providing them respite from the overpowering loneliness they felt most of the times.

The phone in the bedroom rang again. Arvind was waiting on the sofa nearby. This time it was good news. The British Airways aircraft was taking off for New Delhi after getting clearance from the ATC. The dormant enthusiasm had taken wings again.

The aircraft hovered over the orange peppered blue Delhi skies before its turn came to land. The airport authorities were having a torrid time, re-scheduling take offs and managing landings of hundreds of aircrafts with all schedules thrown out of gear by the freaky weather. As the plane taxied down to land, with the landing gears in readiness, a strange sensation tingled Madhur. Finally, when the heavy tyres kissed the tar of the runway, causing a screech and a thud, his heart began to pound faster. He was ready, his hand on the buckle of the seat belt, wanting to break free. The feeling was so very familiar to what he had experienced many years ago as a schoolboy, when he returned from school, throwing his bag on the drawing room sofa, flinging his shoes out, not bothering to see where they landed and then running to his waiting mother to be embraced in her slender arms. Madhur felt a lump in his throat as he fought back his tears.

All these years, he felt like a cutting, severed from its parent plant and dumped in an alien soil to strike roots.

Madhur adjusted his watch, tuning it with the Indian Standard Time. It was 5.45 pm. Taking into consideration the traffic snarls expected in the Capital in the rush hour, it would take at the most an hour and a half to reach the railway station, Madhur had calculated. In addition, a fifteen minute stoppage at Abdul Biryani shop in Connaught Place was something he had considered mandatory in the schedule. His trips to Delhi always included a visit to this famous eatery. 'This guy serves the best biryani in the world, the flavours are gentle, perfectly the way I like' he would say. Most starred restaurants served pulav in the name of biryani, he had always felt. He took a pre-paid taxi from the booth, wanting to avoid any haggling over fares, but was careful to let the driver know about the envisaged journey via the biryani shop. The luggage was loaded on the carrier at the top of the car and soon they were a part of the endless sea of traffic on the road.

The road journey to the railway station was a bit of a letdown, the vehicle moving as a tiny particle constituting a giant wave. Every few minutes the wave moved, sweeping a small stretch of road, before coming to a halt again. Just before the bus terminal at ISBT, there was a road block as a DTC city bus had broken down right in the middle of the road, creating a severe bottleneck for the heavy traffic. But thankfully the traffic cops managed to pull it aside.

Aryan sat clutching the front seat of the car. He had tried putting the seat belt but the buckle was broken and the driver had nonchalantly informed that it was compulsory only for those occupying the front seat. A bit perplexed, he held on to the seat in front, swaying from side to side at each bend of the road. The sight of cars, honking madly, changing lanes like a snake running away from its enemy, the monstrous buses almost overflowing with humans, vehicles with flashing red beacons zipping off, jumping traffic signals with glee, the daredevil two wheeler riders snaking in between the slim interspaces of two vehicles had unnerved him already.

'Dad, how far is the station?' he asked, almost petrified at the roller coaster ride.

'Not far, dear, just another ten minutes or so.'

Madhur remained cheerful; the sight to him was all too familiar. Finally, the taxi screeched to a halt in the station parking lot. They got down from the taxi only to be mobbed by half a dozen coolies. The taxi driver came to their rescue, bargaining and settling the deal with two of them for rupees two hundred.

The station was overcrowded. Madhur asked one of the coolies the reason.

'Oh sahibji for the last few days most of the long distance trains are running late by 12-16 hours. Some have even been cancelled, hence the passengers are stranded. You will see the rush in the train.'

And true to what he said, the train was full to capacity. People stranded at the railway stations for long hours after missing their connecting trains were willing to travel even without confirmed berths. Therefore it was not surprising to see a family of five insist on travelling even if he gave them a single berth and were ready to pay the penalty for the other four, for them it was that urgent.

Fortunately, Madhur had four confirmed berths. Shelly had insisted on travelling in first AC but only two tickets were available forcing them to settle for second AC. Luggage adjusted beneath the seat, she pulled the curtains to shut out the world—of haggling people, bargaining coolies and quarrelling passengers over luggage positions—from her London-bred sons.

'Dad I'm hungry,' said Aryan, unable to resist the aroma of the packed chicken biryani.

'You had a full burger in the flight I suppose,' Shelly intervened.

'Just wait for a few more minutes. Let the train move. You can have your dinner then,' said Madhur, looking at his watch.

The train finally moved out of the station and the commotion reduced, with people settling down—some on their allotted berths, some on their suitcases while some did not mind crouching in the space between the two adjacent lower berths.

'Hasn't he paid for his ticket, Dad?' Little Arin was curious, pointing out to a young man seated on his bright red suitcase.

'Of course he has, dear,' Madhur tried to dissuade him from making personal comments.

'Then why is he sitting there, on his luggage?' he innocently added.

'Because there are no vacant berths available!'

'All you mean to say is the train is going choc-a-bloc?'

'Oh yes, it is!'

'From where do so many people come, all travelling at the same time?'

'Shall we have dinner first?' Madhur suggested.

Shelly opened the handbag and handed a pack to Aryan and another to Arin who was tired but busy peeping through the curtains at two children getting up and down the side upper berth, the three step steel ladder having caught their fancy.

'Hey! Finish your meal fast Arin and don't you use your hand for eating!' she had a volley of instructions.

'But mom, I just rubbed this much of sanitiser on my hands,' he protested.

Shelly's accented English attracted the attention of some passengers passing by in the aisle. Arin, a highly sensitive child, was taken aback by his mother's behaviour and he immediately began nibbling at the succulent chicken from the biryani, avoiding meeting her eye at all costs.

Madhur pulled out his pack too and without saying anything, began eating. Shelly's cold stare was a mild reprimand but he was too engrossed in gorging on his biryani to even bother. He had already surrendered himself to the mild flavours of saffron, cinnamon, cardamom and black cumin laced with the aroma of the aged basmati rice, to take note of her.

For Madhur, a foodie, it was a perfect start to a month long holiday he had planned.

The coach attendant for a change was very hospitable. He arrived after they had finished their dinner and made their beds. Jet lag ensured they were soon deep into sleep.

Madhur had set an alarm in his watch for 6:00 am, as he had been a victim of jet lag many a time earlier. Jet lag apart, most of his overnight train journeys back home in India were replete with hilarious incidents that his friends mockingly attributed to sleepwalking. Twice over on his way back home from his hostel in Gorakhpur he had to be woken up by the cleaning and maintenance staff in the Chauri Chaura express and that too hours after all the passengers had disembarked and the train had been parked in the railway yards. That is why, even though his hometown, Allahabad, was the final destination and the train did not go any further beyond, he had set the alarm. He sometimes wondered if his sons carried a similar trait. Aryan once had slept off while returning from a school trip and had been luckily discovered when the bus driver had gone to the backseat to check for his tools and a routine inspection looking for anything precious the kids might have left, before going home, two hours after the other children had gone home.

The alarm rang and Madhur sprang out of his brown blanket. He eagerly looked outside through the window, before waking up the others. It was foggy and the agricultural fields on both sides of the track were wrapped in a veil of white. Unable to recognise any familiar landmarks that should have been visible around this time he checked his ticket. Departure time 9:30 pm, arrival 6:45 am was clearly printed. Getting into his slippers he came out of the coupe and looked for the attendant. 'Where have we reached?'

'Kanpur, in another hour or so hopefully,' he said. 'The whole of this fortnight it has been like this … the fog has been pretty thick,' he sounded apologetic.

'Take rest *Sirji*, I will come and get you tea once the train reaches there.'

Back at his berth, he prepared to lie down again. The excited child within him had to wait. Shelly and Aryan were fast asleep and Arin was the only one who was awake but surprisingly quiet as his eyes caught his father's.

'Do you want to come down?' Madhur asked.

'Yeah, getting bored up here.' He mumbled.

A thumbs up sign from dad, implied a go ahead. He was down in a flash. Both father and son then lay on the same berth, covered in a blanket and peeping out through the hazy window, watching the agricultural fields and the electricity and telegraph lines passing by, at times being interrupted by a cluster of mud and hay houses indicating a village. There was no sight of any humans or animals except a few stray dogs barking not very far from the rail track. Two pairs of sarus cranes wandering in the agricultural fields made him sit up. Before he could take out the camera, they had disappeared from view.

Unending slums full of shanties, garbage dumps overflowing with polythene and an occasional nullah full of stagnating blackish polluted water indicated that Kanpur was approaching.

'Hey, dad, there is so much of dirt around!'Arin suddenly blurted out.

'Yeah son, this is an industrial town, very old, which has unfortunately developed a bit haphazardly.' He left his remark hanging in the air.

Kanpur arrived and the scheduled stoppage was for twenty minutes. Shelly woke up and enquired if it was Allahabad. On being told it was still Kanpur, she went to sleep again. Aryan meanwhile was up.

'Dad, can't we get down here?' asked Arin.

'You want to see the station?'

'I am tired of sleeping, dad.'

Madhur and the two sons stepped out of their compartment on to the platform.

A young boy with a toothy smile came up to them and asked, 'Sirji, some tea for you?'

Aryan and Arin gazed at him for a few seconds, the continuous gaze unnerving him and making him conscious of his appearance and outfit. He looked a little gawky, around twelve-thirteen years of age, dressed in over-sized sneakers and a thin sweater. He carried an aluminium kettle, the base coated with thick soot, resting on a tiny portable *angeethi*, an indigenous brazier of sorts. The semicircular handle of the *angeethi* and the handle of the kettle had been clubbed and tied together with a rag to facilitate easy carriage.

Madhur asked him smilingly, 'Ginger or cardamom flavour, what do you have?'

'Ginger, Sirji; green cardamom is very costly, I prepare only ginger flavoured tea,' He wanted to impress.

'Ok, we will take three.'

Madhur knew that his sons had never tasted tea. He looked towards the coach to check if Shelly was at the door. Instead, there stood the coach attendant, biting into bread pakoras and holding on to a cup of tea.

The kids were enthusiastic at the unexpected slice of luck coming their way. Back home, their mom had been very strict, never compromising with the healthy food regime she had charted for them right from their infant years. Weekly menu, printed on a white sheet of paper, duly stuck at the door of the fridge, was a constant reminder to everyone in the house about the supreme importance of diet and health. Even the schedule of different flavours of milk for different days of the week was pre-decided, and strictly adhered to. Tea was totally out of question at the place where Shelly's verdicts on such petty issues were final. Aryan considered himself lucky, because the last time they had visited Dadu's place, Dadi had regularly given him ginger and tulsi flavoured tea to cure his cold, when allopathic medicines had proved ineffective.

'Anything else you want?' Madhur asked his boys casually as he passed by a kiosk selling hot samosas.

'Dad, we have not brushed, otherwise the samosas look quite inviting.' Aryan quipped as he breathed hard to inhale the aroma.

'Arre Bhaiya … eight samosas, please,' Madhur handed out a hundred rupee note to the shopkeeper. Clutching on to the samosas in a paper bag, he paid the bill and quickly boarded the train along with his boys.

The boys hurriedly brushed at the coach basin, ignoring the overflowing dustbin underneath. All they could think of at that moment was the pack of samosas waiting for them.

'I hope all this does not wreak havoc with your bellies,' Shelly said as she took up a bottle of mineral water and proceeded towards the basin, unwilling to use the train water for even brushing her teeth. They were too delighted at having been left alone to gorge on their dear samosas.

Back at the railway station in Allahabad, sitting on a steel bench, Arvind was getting fidgety. The wait had been tediously long and tortuous in that bone-chilling cold. The platform shed blocked out the sun completely making it much colder underneath and the announcements over the public address system kept on repeating that the train had been delayed by four hours.

Finally at 12.30 pm the Prayag Raj Express rolled on into the platform. Madhur was at the compartment door for the last one hour to feast his eyes on the familiar landmarks, the guava and mango orchards, the Yamuna river and the sandy banks teeming with the tentage township for the Magh Mela and finally the stations of Bamrauli, Manauri signalling the arrival of his own station, Allahabad. As his own coach rushed forward, leaving the main platform behind, he saw his father standing near the Wheeler Bookshop and then starting to run towards his coach.

As they alighted from the train, half a dozen coolies surrounded them as their branded suitcases with fluttering stickers of the airline cargo and security checks were indicators that they were potentially good payers. Arvind had to jostle through them to reach his son. The father and the son hugged each other; as Aryan and Arin caught up to touch their dadu's feet. Shelly had a quick greeting, a formal *pranam*, with hands folded and a half smile. She felt a bit embarrassed by the public display of affection between father and son, muttering under her breath, 'Do you think we can now make a move?'

Their taxi screeched to a halt in front of the house. Yashoda had been waiting in the porch, pacing up and down for the last forty odd minutes. She rushed to the gate, tossing away her slippers in the porch, running barefooted for speed. She was almost in tears, at the sight of her son after four long years, appearing thin and weak, the face dominated by bony jaws and his cheeks no more chubby. The bear hug led to an overflow of the droplets of emotions from her eyes, trickling down on her wrinkled cheeks, clouding the crescent in her glasses, momentarily blinding her in love. The two boys were overwhelmed by the welcome! They looked at their father's face and then their grandparents, unable to understand, how excess of joy could bring tears to one's eyes!

Yashoda had readied breakfast assuming the train would be on time. It was almost lunch time but the items she had prepared with generous doses of love could not wait for the evening to fall. They had to be savoured by the visitors, like a multi-coursed meal. Everyone was in agreement; lunch would be delayed.

At sunset, the boys ventured to the terrace, with their dad in tow, wanting to have a closer look at the bright kites hovering over their rooftop. Arvind and Yashoda had also joined them. While everyone was busy, Shelly took a round of the first floor of the house, the rooms where her own goods from Bangalore had been dumped, right after they had left for London.

She inspected each and every item like a cunning buyer, tapping the furniture, checking the chests and the drawers, quickly running her index finger over the surfaces to see if a layer of dust had settled. Finding everything clean and spotless and aesthetically arranged was something she had not expected. The two rooms were as well maintained as the three on the ground floor. Had it been Bangalore, Shelly for a moment could have assumed that Arvind's parents had rented those rooms to paying guests, earning a handsome profit in the bargain. But she had known the city well, here it was virtually impossible. Another wicked thought crossed her mind. Had they put it up as a furnished accommodation and gathered good money behind their back? She also remembered that Madhur had requested his dad at the time of leaving that once his things came from Bangalore, he should sell them off and deposit the cash received in his account.

She rushed to the kitchen to gather any evidence that could be proof of the first floor having being used by a family in the recent past. Disappointment awaited her as she discovered that the brown cartons containing the kitchen appliances, along with the cooking range, lay packed, the Welcome Movers and Packers logo still intact on the covers.

Neither did she ask, nor could anyone tell her the reality, how the aged couple had made it a point to get up to the first floor, daily, no matter how the knees ached or the back stiffened, an hour in the morning, hovering around the maid. For them, spending time in the company of these inanimate articles every day, getting them dusted and polished, gave them an unexplained comfort, a reassuring feeling of their kith and kin being somewhere around, who would come back to them sooner than later.

Time continued to moved on with invisible wings.

Bina's health had improved slightly. It had been more than six months that she had been on medication for some ailment or the other. A battery of tests conducted on her had all been normal. The doctors had then finally concluded that the root cause of her problems was hormonal imbalance, triggered by constant stress and anxiety. A heavy dose of stress busters along with anti-depressants had been prescribed.

For Shashank, time crawled on leaden feet, but thankfully it never came to a standstill. His diary had more scribbles than ever, noting down appointments with doctors, groceries purchased and needed, monthly payments to the paperboy, maids, gardener, LPG refills and all sundry issues he had never bothered about. And above all, taking Shweta thrice a week to Dr Arvind's clinic for her physiotherapy sessions in the evening between five and seven. These sessions were the only hope Shashank had of seeing Shweta on her feet again. Years back, when Shweta had survived the accident, he had been delirious with ecstasy; but, as she started to regain her health, Shashank set for himself another milestone. He now began to dream about the day when Shweta would stand on her feet, run, cycle and swim.

Shashank was particularly worried that day. In his diary, he had put a big question mark over the second and third week of January, encircling the fortnight in red ink. Though he knew that worry could offer him no solution, he was under tremendous stress, unable to foresee how the situation would turn out in the next few days. Ever since he had settled in the city, every single year had seen not less than a dozen people arriving from Bindki to take a holy dip. He was worried that with Bina's fragile health, things would be difficult for him. He thought of asking mother to come again but she had left only recently. He spoke to Bina and found her to be surprisingly upbeat.

'I am looking forward to their visit, why are you so worried?'

'How will we manage?'

'The only thing we need to provide them is some living space and bedding to sleep. The other things they themselves can take care off. I remember, Vishambhar Chacha's wife cooks the tastiest kamal kakdi ki sabji that I have ever come across and your masi's kadhi, not even a chef would be able to replicate it! Other than eating, gossiping and more eating, more gossiping, what else do you think I would do?'

This flexibility and inclusive mentality of Bina had been a huge pillar of strength for Shashank, right from the beginning. How fortunate he had been having married such a positive person like Bina, thought Shashank to himself as he left the room.

A week later the contingent arrived. A group of sixteen, out of which a few faces were familiar to him, while a few were those he had never seen in his lifetime. For each of them, it was an opportunity that they could not let go.

Fortunately, the main bathing day was just two days away.

Shashank liked the air of expectancy and cheer in the house. All the rooms were occupied, the gas was hardly switched off as the guests always welcomed the many rounds of hot tea being served in the bitter cold.

The five ladies in the group were busy shelling peas and chopping vegetables and all Bina was made to do was to sit on the cot in the melting afternoon sun and gossip while she was given a head massage by one of the elderly ladies.

Udit had been secretively following the news of the ongoing mela in the city that had been his hometown not long ago, though he liked to believe that he had resolutely discarded from his mind all memories relating to the city and his own past self, like a piece of old clothing. A new haircut, a switchover to a moustached face and proficiency in the local dialect had given him a brand new identity. Besides, with his fair complexion and chiselled features along with the typical Garhwali accent that he had consciously cultivated, he easily passed for one.

Nonetheless, despite all his efforts to wipe clean his past, he could not tame his defiant curiosity, much as he would have wanted to. His curiosity would always pique him to listen to the vernacular news on the state television network, much to his chagrin. He would slip out of his cabin at 7:30 pm daily, to get the latest updates of the city and the ongoing fair. He had even subscribed to an edition of a Hindi newspaper that had been issuing a special two page 'Mela News' supplement every day.

Udit had been sitting in front of a small but roaring fire in the fireplace of his room and extending his hands to gather some warmth. One thing which never ceased to amaze him was the little fireplaces which seemed to be a mandatory feature in most of the buildings and houses he had seen in that hill town. The one in his room was to the left of his bed and had ample space to accommodate a fire that could keep his room warm compared to some he had seen in newly constructed hotels, designed more to add to the decor than to serve any real purpose.

His life revolved around the little fireplace in the evenings, when he would be all by himself after returning to his room from the hotel. The fire would be the only dynamic feature around him. The leaping flames, in different hues of blue, ochre and amber, with their crackling and hissing sounds, would keep him in good spirits. Sitting by that fire he would recollect what his school teacher who taught them Value Education in Class VI had once said, 'If you do not have a family to go back to, you would float in life like a flotsam, like driftwood.'

Udit saw in himself a driftwood, wandering aimlessly in the turbulent waters of destiny, which for that moment had deposited him in Mussoorie. Skimming through the newspapers every night to cut out some interesting facts, articles or even pictures which caught his fancy before going to bed was a routine he never missed, no matter how late or how early he was to bed. For all these peculiar habits, he preferred staying alone, steadfastly refusing any offers to share a room with his fellow staffers. Absence of any prying eyes and any wagging tongues close to him had allowed him independence where he could indulge in his eccentricities throwing caution to the wind. He loved his life this way, living inside this uninformed bubble, with its rainbow colours of happiness, sadness, delight and distress all bunched together in no particular order.

The morning was beautiful. He sat on the broken chair in his balcony, listening to a whistling thrush singing on the spruce across the road. The mountain ranges covered in molten gold glowed and changed hues rapidly. Around him, the boughs of deodars were burdened with snow. The balcony had been his window to the world right from the beginning. A group of langurs had discovered the oak that stood just beyond the railings, as a perfect hideout where they chose to rest and relish the stuff they would steal from unguarded shops and vendors, snatching from unsuspecting people or even picking up from the garbage, littered down in the narrow gorges cutting the hill slopes. Every morning he sat here, sipping his glass of tea, peering down at the school children clothed in woollens, chattering their way to school. Since it had snowed of late and it was also the time of the winter vacations, schools had closed, leaving the roads to horses and mules, delivering goods to various shops in the market uphill. A few of those pickup vans would also be visible, overloaded with firewood or sacks of potatoes and onions traversing up and down the slopes with the engines denied regular servicing and maintenance crying hoarse. A few of the people earning their living by carrying load up the narrow winding roads and barely existent tracks, where no motorised vehicle could ply, were also visible. Rain or snow, they would always be trudging up the slopes, the load precariously balanced on their backs aligned at an angle of forty five degrees to the road, varying from a gas cylinder, to a cot, to a box bed, a cupboard or even a Godrej steel almirah! Watching them, Udit began to realise that fate, after all, had not been as cruel to him as he sometimes thought it to be.

Madhur had got two luxury tents booked in the mela township, courtesy an old friend of his. This friend, working in the Department of Tourism, had called him up, way back in November, asking him if any of his NRI friends were interested in availing the spiritual package. When Madhur showed no keenness for the offer, the friend sounded so despondent on the phone over the probable failure of his own project and its possible repercussions over his career prospects that he volunteered to get the first two bookings himself. That had allowed him to partially return a few of the long list of favours he had enjoyed during his bachelor years in Delhi. Then perhaps as a result of some belated wisdom, he had enthusiastically spread word among his circle of friends, marketing the package as if it had been a project of his own firm. It was just a day before flying home that he had received a call from his friend confirming his bookings and thanking him profusely for the windfall of customers the firm had, a quantum they had not expected to cater to.

'Papa, I have got tents booked for all of us in the mela for three days. Wouldn't Ma and you come along with us?' Madhur asked.

'Oh, beta, why did you take the trouble? We have been seeing it for the last thirty years! It is just that our bodies don't permit us to walk those long distances …' Arvind sighed.

Shelly meanwhile emerged from her room, with her battery operated hair drier in hand, drying her hair, a few curlers still on her head. She had overheard part of the conversation and was curious to know the other part.

'You mean to say all of us are going to stay in those tents?'

'Yeah, let's try something new. A surprise for you, isn't it?'

'A surprise undoubtedly! I hope the facilities will be at least three-star? If not then please do book us in the real Taj, at least for a night's stay.' Shelly stated conclusively.

Madhur for a moment was completely befuddled. He preferred to keep mum.

'Moreover, I feel your mom and dad will not feel comfortable there ... let's not pressurise them to come along with us.' Her words pierced Madhur and Arvind like sharp crystals of acid rain.

Madhur, highly embarrassed, tried hard to laugh it off. 'But, I am not taking them to a hospital for a surgery, Shelly! It's just for fun's sake ...!' he shrugged off. Fourteen years of marriage, could not bring out of her, even fourteen words of love for him. Even Gizzy, their dog back in London was more sensitive; she had at least shed a few tears while Madhur had been leaving her in the dog hostel, before their India trip.

'Dad, if Dadu and Dadi are not coming along, then you better count me out too.' Little Arin pronounced his verdict even though nobody had asked him yet.

'Me too Dad,' came the voice from the other room. Aryan was in agreement with his little brother.

'Ok, let's see.' Arvind said, trying to end the conversation before it offended anyone. It would also keep their son optimistic for the night at least, he thought.

The next two days were uneventful as Shelly and Madhur did not discuss the tent bookings and the stay. But when the boys had slept Shelly had reminded Madhur of some other things he needed to think about and pay attention to apart from his present focus on good food, good entertainment and meeting up with old friends. This reminder had put Madhur in a spot of bother but he chose his words carefully. 'Don't worry, I remember. I've spoken to some of my friends about it.'

Two days before *Mauni Amavasya*, a landmark day for ceremonial ablution in the holy rivers, Madhur had brought home a taxi to ferry everyone to the tents. Shelly had packed a big suitcase along with a bag and a sleeping bag. After ensuring that all her stuff had been loaded in the taxi, she stood at the back of the taxi. The senior Johris occupied the rear seat. The boys were mindful of leaving a space for their mother, quickly shifting onto the laps of their grandparents. Shelly waited outside for a split second and then occupied the front seat next to the driver.

The driver looked amused.

'Are you sure you are comfortable?' Madhur peeped through the window and asked her in a hushed voice.

'Please don't bother. You can sit at the back with your parents,' she said emphasising the last four words.

'Right, suit yourself.' And he came and sat next to his mother.

Shelly pulled her woollen scarf close to her ears and rolled up the glass. In the rear view mirror Madhur could make out that she was gathering her bitterness; the little strings of upheaval she was trying hard to conceal.

The taxi was off, but before long, the traffic was such that it moved in short bursts; a few metres at a go and then a laboured crawl. Amidst the surging, tremulous, wilful and laughing river of humanity, Madhur felt a bit lonely and lost. The little boys had never seen so many people at a place ever.

'Dadu, why are they crowding the road?' asked Arin innocently.

'No they aren't crowding, they are walking towards the mela.'

'On foot you mean to say?'

'Oh yes, not everyone here moves in a taxi, you see.'

'And how far do they have to go?'

'A minimum of six miles.'

After the initial chatter, an uneasy silence prevailed through the rest of the journey lasting about an hour.

In the luxury tent, Arvind lay on the teak and rosewood bed, while the kids watched TV. Yashoda was busy talking to a lady, the occupant of the neighbouring tent, who had come all the way from Guwahati. She spoke in broken Hindi but was quite garrulous. During the course of her conversation, she had revealed that this was the first time that she had crossed the borders of her state. Her husband, a wealthy businessman having a lot of tea estates to look after, had decided to take a week off for this holy sojourn.

Arvind, who had been lying with a newspaper in his hands, suddenly sprang up and reached the peg where he had hung his trousers. He searched the two front pockets and the one at the back.

'Looks like you forgot your wallet back home as usual!' said Yashoda walking in and closing the door behind her.

'No, no, no, the wallet is here.'

'Some tickets or important receipts I suppose. Don't worry, you will not need anything here for the next two days,' she proclaimed and cuddled up on the bed, pulling the blanket right up to her face.

'Dadu, do you need something? Should I fetch it for you?' Aryan was distracted by his search.

'No, no, you won't be able to. It's something important,' he said as he continued unzipping pockets of his carry bag. He pulled out a bulging medicine bag and brought out all the foils on the table.

'If you have forgotten some medicine, there is a dispensary on Kali Sadak, but you will have to walk a kilometre, if they don't allow the vehicles.'

Just then a small white envelope came to his hand and the twinkle in his eyes returned. Relief was writ large on his face. The envelope contained an old yellowing family photo, a black and white stuff that was moth-eaten at the edges.

'Dadu, whose photo is this? Doesn't look like ours,' Aryan wanted to know.

'Child, I am looking for someone. I have promised to do this till my last breath to someone very dear to me.'

'Please may I know who is it?' came Yashoda's spanner, her voice emerging from underneath the blue velvet blanket, in a manner similar to the hundreds of fishes jumping out from the blue waters, her eyes catching the pattern of the blanket.

'Oh I thought you were sleeping! Yesterday Shweta gave me this, when she had come for the physiotherapy. She is optimistic that I will find Udit here in the three days that we are here, poor girl!'

'I hope you are lucky this time. However, till date I have not heard of any lost person being found in a fair.'

'It is not for nothing that I have been christened Sheikh Chilli, you see,' he laughed loudly and then wiped his face with his hands.

The announcement on the public address system repeated 'A boy named Udyan, from Bahraich, aged fourteen, dressed in blue pants, light brown shirt and white sports shoes, with sharp features and fair complexion had gone missing, four hours ago. His parents are waiting in the Lost and Found booth at Kali Sadak and any person finding him or bringing any information about him would be suitably rewarded.'

Arvind got up and shut the door of his tent and asked his grandsons to increase the volume of the television. But try as hard as he might, he could not shut out the chain of thoughts that crowded his mind. That sultry September evening in 1985 Udit had gone missing, in very similar blue pants, brown striped shirt and white sports shoes. That unfortunate evening, sitting beside a sobbing Bina, he had scribbled an advertisement below a photo of the boy and sent to all newspaper offices in the city to be published for the next ten days, every day without fail. However nothing much had happened except a few useless calls on his phone, a few postcards vaguely informing him of Udit's last whereabouts, an exercise undertaken by some more out of greed for the reward offered than with any intention of providing any genuine help.

The whole of the next day, the kids, Madhur, and the senior Johris roamed around in the mela. Their day had started early, beginning with a boat ride from Arail towards the sangam, the confluence of Ganga and Yamuna. Though the main bathing day was still a day away, it seemed like the whole of India had descended on the city. Every inch of land had been swamped by human feet. Their boat made its way through the crowd of other boats, with the oars slapping against the blue waters of the Yamuna, quick and sharp, along with groups of gulls, gliding on the waters, feeding on something that was being thrown towards them by the devotees from the boats. A motor boat belonging to the police, christened 'jal police' passed by, leaving behind waves in a 'V', creating a mild turbulence in the waters, causing their boat to wobble a bit.

'Dadu, we will drown now and no life jackets either,' Aryan, screamed.

'Nothing to worry sahib, don't worry, nothing will happen,' the boatman reassured them.

'But Aryan, why are you so scared? You know how to swim, right?' Arvind asked.

'Sirji, I can cross the river, in forty minutes flat. Even when Ma Ganga is in spate, I have crossed many times, please relax and trust me.'

Thereafter, when things settled, Madhur watched the spectacle as excited as his sons, staring at the devotees taking dips, closing their eyes and chanting in unison, *Ganga ma ki jai*, then holding their nose and disappearing in the chilly waters, only to reappear after ten odd seconds, with washed and purified conscience, body and soul. After the first dip, the following four only served to add to the bliss they must have experienced, as was evident by their glowing countenances among the glowering posse of policeman, trying hard to regulate the crowd.

Shelly had chosen to stay back preferring to spend time with a book. She was allergic to dust and could not risk falling sick in India. After all, it was a pleasure trip and moreover, her own parents and friends were awaiting her in Bombay.

Arvind was keenly looking at the people passing by. He particularly gazed at all those boys, who were lean and thin, sharp featured and appeared to be around twenty-five years of age.

Even while visiting the pandals to undertake darshan of the holy sadhus, his eyes followed and scanned the young men around, trying to find resemblance of Udit in the ash covered bare bodies and sandal smeared faces.

At last the day that every devout pilgrim had been waiting for arrived. It was the auspicious *Mauni Amavasya.* Even before sun had peeped through the grey skies, the snan had begun. Thousands of devotees had arrived in the area the night before and had spent the night in the pandals, listening to the holy discourses, so that they could beat the early morning rush, take a dip and head back home.

The guests from Bindki had proceeded to the tented township on the banks of Ganga the previous night itself, to avoid the huge rush. The whole city had been taken over by hordes of crowds, the railway stations, the bus stands, the hotels, the dharamshalas were all overflowing with people. The roads and lanes had been clogged by people and vehicles. Normal city life had come to a standstill. Despite the arrangements, it was very difficult to restrain the surging crowds, all of whom were desperate to reach the mela. Behind the main pandal, was a dining area where the queue was becoming unmanageable. Hot tea in earthen cups was being served to all who sat, waiting for the auspicious bathing time to begin. '3:28 am,' the announcements repeated every now and then.

At the sangam, the boats carrying devotees had started gathering a little after midnight. People waited in boats parked in haphazard queues, creating a traffic jam on the waterways.

On the land, people waited in never ending queues that snaked towards the bathing *ghats*, the crowd being regulated by heavy barricading. The police control rooms buzzed with activity as there was no room for complacency, particularly when there were millions of devotees all around. The different *akharas* were on their way as per the sequence allotted to them by the district administration. Their processions were a curious attraction for many in the crowd. While the devout covered from head to toe, shivered and huffed and puffed their way towards the banks, panting, the sadhus romped around in joy and fervour, despite being scantily clad, at times, only in their bare skin, with long braided hair falling down their ashen backs.

In a queue, next to the pandal of Shri Shankaracharya, the Johris snaked along. Yashoda's knees for a change, looked good; the night before, they had been pampered by a professional masseur with gels, hot packs and sprays. Shelly had her face covered with a hanky, she had carried a surgical mask for the purpose but when Aryan had laughed at her in the tent, asking her to stay back and watch the live streaming on TV, she decided to replace it with a white hanky.

At the sangam ghat, it was all slippery and wet. Yashoda had spread a bed sheet over a relatively drier patch and settled down, asking the boys to remove their clothes and get ready for a dip. The boys were not exposed to taking a bath at a public place and were shy to take off their clothes. However, seeing their dad and dadu doing the same and everyone around doing the same too, they followed suit.

Shelly asked Yashoda, if she had come prepared to take a dip.

'Oh yes, when I have come this far, how can I go back without a holy dip?' replied Yashoda, as she safely kept Arvind's watch and wallet inside her black purse.

'Why don't you two take the dip first, we can go once you both are back and keep a vigil on our clothes?' said Madhur.

Shelly tightened her scarf again. 'Me and dip? No way. The water is too muddy and there is no place to change. I will sit and watch.'

'As you wish.' Yashoda smiled faintly. She had nothing much to say as she folded her cardigan and kept it over the pile of clothes that had gathered.

Shelly kept guard as the others went for a dip. Madhur held his mother's hand and escorted her into the waters.

'Ooh! Dad, the water is so cold!' Arin shouted as he stood shivering in waist deep water.

'You will feel better after a minute or so. It happens in the beginning,' Arvind said.

With chattering teeth and shivering forms, drenched by faith, they immersed their frames in the holy waters of the sangam. Shelly looked around bemused, how men, women and children of all ages were bathing and worshiping, unmindful of their bare bodies. At the banks of the holy river, all life forms found themselves clothed with an invisible cloak of faith, impenetrable to any eye that was full of lust or thoughts laced with sinful intent. Shelly felt ill at ease, wondering if her decision not to take a dip had exposed her to the multitude around her.

The words 'Mama please hand me that towel,' broke her tangled thoughts. She saw a wet Aryan standing in front of her, his fair body still wet, with some patches of sand glistening near his neck.

'Mom, I think, you shouldn't miss this. It's an out of the world experience,' he said as he took the towel and turned his back towards her.

Not far from them, a strapping young lad stood selling plastic gallons, around twenty of them strewn in a wire. Though, outwardly they were containers meant to carry some holy water back home, but on their white surfaces were sure to be stuck memories, memories of having been to the place where a mere dip had the capacity to purge the body of all sins and the souls of all guilt. Arvind beckoned him to come near. He bought a pair and gave him a ten rupee tip as he mentally went through the photo in his wallet; the features were similar and the age was around twenty-five.

'Where are you from?' he asked, tightening his belt over the trousers.

'Udai … from …' he muttered something that was lost in the din around and the next instant he had slipped away. There were hundreds waiting for his gallons and it was a day of brisk business for him. He could not afford to waste time.

Far away in Mussoorie, the weather had been unpredictable for the last fortnight. It would rain for two days and then snow and then two relatively hot sunny days would follow, pursuing a conspicuous new pattern. Locals, however, were happy as early snow would mean an increase in the tourist influx, boosting the tourism industry, which was the backbone of their economy.

During the day, Udit hardly had anytime free for himself as the hotel at this season, was always full of tourists, rushing from all parts of the country to enjoy the snow. Otherwise, for him all months of the year were the same, having nothing to do once he went to his room late in the night from the hotel. A Rubik cube, a Walkman and a chess board were the three things that gave him company till he fell asleep. The chess board remained on his bed always, as he had no opponent to play with other than himself. So he played against himself, changing his seat after each move, to overcome any temptation of underplaying on the opponent's behalf. He knew that by doing so he would win the game on the board but a pinch of guilt would trouble him for the rest of the day.

His room on the second floor of the old building adjacent to the hotel gave him a bird's eye view of the area. He considered it a strategic location, a perch from where he could see all he wanted to see. In the mornings, he would see the hills wrapped in mist, all cloudy and white, till the sun would slowly emerge causing a breathtaking array of lights changing quickly from red to orange to golden and in the same way, the distant hills changing colours from black to purple to green. He could also keep an eye on the hotel staff whose work preceded the others—the boys working at the tandoor, the cleaning and the housekeeping brigade, whose duty it was to sweep away the fallen leaves, the pine cones, the litter of plastic packs and dust from the surroundings.

Shortly after lunch time, Udit began to feel unwell. He requested the manager for an off, promising to do an extra night shift next week to compensate. The leave granted, he was back in his room and lay on his bed. An hour of rest he thought would help him overcome the fatigue he had been experiencing of late. But when he got up after an hour, he was running a high temperature. He came out to the balcony and called Vishnu up. He was then helping a driver to park his car. When Vishnu was there in his room two minutes later, Udit was just barely conscious.

'Please get me two tablets of Crocin and a packet of fruit buns.' he said thrusting a twenty rupee note in the boy's hands. Vishnu ran down the stairs at once.

Feeling restless, he peeped through the little window across his bed and he could see most of the roads, tracks and roofs covered with a layer of white. He remembered that when he had returned to his room, it had only been drizzling. Perhaps he had slept for long as the sleet must have been heavy to cause such a thick cover. His watch showed 5:15 pm. On the road leading to his hotel were dozens of tourists, enjoying the 'snow,' first timers to a hill station, mistaking the layer of sleet for the fluffy and cottony snow. Udit wondered what attracted the tourists so much to the hill town even in winters, when the residents had so many hardships to face and survival became a struggle for one and all.

Arvind in his luxury tent in the mela area was preoccupied with memories he could never forget. He could not sleep that night. He lay quietly on the bed, listening to the various sounds that were drifting into his tent. He was gazing at the flowery patterns forming the slanting roof of his tent in the dim night lamp. At times he turned over to gaze at the stars wriggling through the curtained windows. He remembered Shashank, Shweta, Bina, Sonam and for a moment felt sorry for no particular reason. For the last five years, he had been trying his best to bring some happiness in their lives. They had been neighbours for almost ten years now, but had become good friends only after the family had met with that horrific Mussoorie accident. At that time he had found it impossible to believe that fate could be so stubbornly selective, choosing to shower all her curses on a particular family for no apparent reason. Not one to leave things to Destiny and Fate, he took in his hands the responsibility of supervising Shweta's rehabilitation; and more so because he himself was an orthopaedic surgeon by profession. He had also voluntarily slipped into the role of the medical advisor for the family, helping them fix their appointments and selecting the best doctors for them.

However, in the mela, he had donned a different role. Here, he had been a man on a mission. This year, again, he had come prepared to carry out his search for Udit, armed with a new photograph. Finding Udit out in a crowd of a million people was like searching for a needle in a million haystacks, he knew, but a miracle could happen anytime and Arvind had been optimistic about that. In that year, he had been even more optimistic because he was staying within the mela arena for three continuous days. He lay down again only to allow a stream of memories of Udit, that exceptionally good looking boy, pass by the screen of his mind like a film.

Under that tinned sloping roof, Udit was wide awake, when the world outside slept. A little past midnight it was and the star studded sky above had stiff competition from the lights twinkling in the hill town, creating a spectacular continuum. He had slept early due to a headache and now surprisingly with the headache gone, sleep was a casualty. Adversity he knew had strange companions, but pain and sleep had never been compatible. Having nothing to do and having no one around, he felt tired and lonely. He looked around for something to eat. Vishnu had dutifully brought his dinner, and finding him asleep, kept it on the plastic chair and covered it with a newspaper, carefully tucking the ends of the paper under the plate to secure it from the insects that appeared every night. He removed the paper and saw that chapattis had hardened into round pieces of leather, embroidered with patterns of black and the curry had almost frozen.

'Better not to eat this,' he said to himself and turned over the paper to cover it again. A picture of a sea of humanity, a congregation, at his birthplace, by the side of a news item in a column, caught his eyes. He wanted to read but the letters danced in front of his eyes forcing him to shut them. He had been one of them, many years ago, bathing similarly at the silver banks of the Ganga and Yamuna, holding his father's hands, almost climbing onto him to escape the cold waters. He remembered his umpteen boat rides on the river, just the five of them, having a full boat to themselves, where he and Shweta would keep changing their positions, competing in attracting the most gulls while offering the puffed rice they carried from home.

Then one day, a sudden moment of extreme rage compounded by a quirky twirl of fate uprooted him from his home and hearth. It seemed that some invisible force had pulled him up and thrust him onto the winding roads to Hotel Mussoorie Grand.

His stomach churned and he slumped in the chair with acute nausea. A series of hiccups followed and he searched for a spoonful of sugar in his room, a remedy he had known since childhood.

His granny always said that hiccups meant that 'someone dear was thinking about you and remembering you.'

Who on earth would remember him and that too in the dead of the night, he wondered. His home had ceased to exist. His virtual contact with his home, through the wires and receiver of a telephone at the Sharma PCO booth had snapped without a warning, when one fine evening being ditched by memory, he dialled a wrong number three times back to back, enraging an old lady at the other end, whose asperity had increased with each of his succeeding calls, finally ending with a gibberish curse. In a state of shock he had returned to his room to check where another blow awaited him. He had been utterly careless, by scribbling his home phone number at the back cover page of a magazine that had been feasted upon by some rats. His pathetic pleadings to his rudderless memory then had remained unanswered, no matter how hard he tried, scribbling permutations and combinations of digits which began correctly but got jumbled up midway.

Narayan had been his schoolmate since Class IV, at St George, and the two had studied together all along except for an year when Narayan had dropped out of college due to his father's illness. He was the only one Udit had called before leaving his home, but had been secretive about his escape. In the aftermath of his consciously solicited 'independence', he had bobbed many a times in the sea of repentance and longed to go back; but some people around him, perhaps sent by some supreme power, had ensured that he stayed afloat. The Manager Sahib was one such person. Initially, Udit had dreaded and hated him in equal measure, but later he donned the mantle of Udit's friend, philosopher and guide as well as his pillar of strength.

The weather began to change with the stars disappearing from the sky. A stiff wind blew, carrying some heavy clouds. Through the rest of the night, rain pattered the tin roof in rhythmic beats at first and then in unstructured disoriented strokes. Standing by his window, Udit could hold the branches of walnut tree that grew nearby, if he extended his hand. The raindrops were helpless, swaying and swinging with the fierce wind before gravity pulled them down. The weather outside struck a chord with his melancholic mood and the two resulted in his drifting back to sleep around daybreak.

When Vishnu knocked at the door, Udit woke up to find him standing with a glass of tea. Beyond Vishnu, Udit could see the snow falling in disorderly swirls. He waited at the door for a few seconds and saw Vishnu, retracing his steps to the hotel kitchen, walking through the slush in his slippers while the tourist all around struggled in their crampons.

Shweta was tense since morning because she would meet Dr Arvind during her physiotherapy session at his clinic in the evening. She was anxious, knowing fully well that had something positive emerged from the search in mela, Arvind Uncle would have been the first person to barge into her house to share the good news. Overcome with lassitude, she looked for an excuse to evade the session that day.

She wheeled herself out into the veranda. Buzo followed her. The soft rays of the afternoon sun had filled the veranda and the murraya seedling which had now grown into a handsome adolescent, suddenly allowed itself a little jig. The bole of the leafless neem in the park behind had two squirrels scampering up and down. A shikra came and settled on the lower branches; perhaps it had eyed a little prey on the ground but was unaware that the camouflage of the canopy was missing. The babblers, a group of seven, resting on the hibiscus shrub near the corner were quick to spot the enemy and began a loud chatter, issuing a sign of imminent danger to friends in the animal kingdom.

Watching these little creatures always soothed her nerves and whenever she was in a state similar to the one which had entombed her today, they were a source of much succour. Near her chair, a group of ants had decided to steal away some crumbs of bread that Chunni had swept away underneath the shoe rack. Buzo protested meekly at their daredevil act as a live theft right under his nose was an insult to his prowess, but then decided it was too trivial an issue to intervene. He turned around and circled over to the other side to catch a nap. The crumbs were many times bigger than the ants but whenever they fell, a few more of the group joined and carried it a little further. In the half hour that Shweta sat there, not a single crumb remained on the floor; with the mission successfully accomplished, even the group disappeared. Feeling much better, she closed her eyes and relaxed as a cuckoo cooed somewhere in the distance.

A positive mood swing had lifted her spirit and suddenly the physiotherapy session looked less cumbersome. So what if she had been utterly naive and emotional in handing over a photo of her brother to Dr Arvind. As a human being she was entitled to her share of mistakes, she said to herself. That evening, Sonam accompanied her to the clinic, but Dr Arvind was not at home. He had gone to Civil Lines for an ice cream party with his grandsons. Her heart was not in the session as she just went through the exercises.

The week passed by and Shweta and Arvind could not meet. Next week, when they finally met, her gloominess had evaporated. No questions were asked; Shweta remained calm and uncharacteristically quiet. Meanwhile, Arvind insisted on getting an X-ray done and called up the technician.

'My darling the day is not far when I will see you running across the garden.' Arvind said as he held the wet X-ray film in his hands, moving it back and forth against the light of the 100 watt bulb and smiling broadly. 'You can take the plate home tomorrow.'

That night as she lay in bed, Dr Arvind's words echoed in her ears. The mere thought of a normal life excited her, taking her sleep away. She also thought that if that happened, how much of happiness it would bring to her parents for whom, life had become an endless cycle of days and months just passing by. They had nothing to look forward to, no hopes nor happiness descending into their drab, dreary and monotonous routine life. That night, a speck of hope and excitement had begun to rise in the dormant seed of her life that had lay shrunk and shrivelled for long.

The next day, on her return from the physiotherapy session, she held the X-ray plate in her hands and tried examining it holding it against the bulb in her room. She could not make out anything, particularly the change that had excited Dr Arvind so much. Days passed by thick and fast.

Both the Johri and Joshi homes were quiet again. With the end of the mela, the guests had gone back to their respective homes.

Ten months had passed by. It was December, 1991. A decent marriage proposal for Sonam had put Shashank in a fix. He had not been preparing himself for her marriage so early. Though Granny had been throwing subtle hints when she was home last time, he had chosen to ignore, laughing off the matter by telling her that she should continue receiving proposals, filtering and shortlisting them so that he could decide as and when he thought the time was right.

Bina on the other hand, kept on prodding Shashank on the issue telling him that that the proposal merited a serious thought. Shashank promised to think over the issue but even after a fortnight could not arrive at a decision. Finally, Bina suggested that if he thought it was too early, the formal engagement could be done and the marriage delayed by a year or so with the consent of the groom's family. Surprisingly, the boy agreed to this proposal and the engagement function was hastily conducted in the third week of the month. A small function was arranged at home, attended by Granny along with the groom and his family. The date of the marriage was to be decided later.

At the Johris' home, there was a surprise in store. There was a phone call from Madhur informing them that Shelly would be in India for a week, precisely from 28th December to 4th January, for some urgent work. The senior Johris were puzzled. Why on earth would Shelly be visiting them so soon and that too alone? By now they had understood that she was a reluctant visitor to India and that too only when it was absolutely unavoidable.

'Are you sure, she is visiting us and not her parents in Bombay?' Yashoda asked Arvind who was warming his hands over the embers of charcoal lighted in an *angeethi*. 'I suppose, Shelly's father has to undergo a heart surgery. Maybe that is the reason she is coming.' Yashoda speculated further.

'Can't say for sure; the last time I spoke to Madhur, he told me that his father-in-law was fine and that the operation had been indefinitely postponed.' Arvind added some more coals in the fire.

Yashoda had planned to cook Arvind's favourite fish curry in mustard gravy today and had left the fish marinated in the kitchen.

'People say that fish is a good omen, I hope this news of Shelly coming home will bring some good luck for us,' she said.

'Oh, I thought fishes when alive were good omens, not spiced and fried. Anyway, now I will get some fish every day, whether you cook or not,' he signed off in his inimitable way.

'Why not buy an aquarium instead?' She added with a chuckle. By then Arvind had gone out to attend a phone call.

Later in the night Yashoda was somewhat perturbed over the news of Shelly visiting them.

'I don't know why, but my heart says this visit may not bring good news,' she said as she searched for her bed socks kept under the pillow.

'Don't think too much. She may have something on her agenda which is confidential. As long as it doesn't affect us, why should we worry? Now let me switch off the light.'

Far away in Mussoorie, Udit's health showed no signs of improvement. He felt weak and groggy. On that morning, he had fainted in the kitchen, while demonstrating to his chefs the right way of chopping onions for some stew, for a particularly fussy foreign guest. So sudden had been his fall that the other cook in the kitchen frying cutlets for breakfast had rushed towards him, leaving the gas stove on a high flame. He was unconscious, when he was dragged outside and made to lie on a wooden bench, with the knife still clutched in his right hand.

It was during times like these when he stole a few seconds to ruminate over his life. It seemed as if a few silent prayers for his wellbeing and safety still reached the ears of the supreme Almighty. But why he could never muster courage to cast off that incident from his mind and go back to the ones he knew still loved him, he could never fathom. When his anger had ebbed, he had been swallowed by self-pity, only to be replaced by shame and guilt. The realisation had dawned on him that in the coming years, issues as petty as the ones that had triggered his escape, would be no more than little specks in the map of his life. Then he would be haunted by an overpowering repentance, that had he allowed them to fizzle out and be self-consumed, his life would have taken a different course.

Twice he had called home, all packed and prepared to pick up his bag and catch the first train back home, but destiny willed otherwise. At the other end, his grandmother had picked up, and responded with a string of burly hellos …. Hallo … hallo, without waiting to hear his muffled voice at the other end. Some technical disturbance in the line had altered his voice such that Granny was unable to recognise him. After an agonising three minutes of this electronic communication, a flustered Granny had disconnected the call, saying, '*Beta*, why did you call if you had nothing to say?' blissfully unaware of the identity of the beta who had called.

That night, he had cried in bed, stifling his tears, choking as he had dwelt upon the fact whether his granny had developed some hearing issues or was it that his own voice never emerged from his mouth loud enough to travel to the tiny receptors screwed inside the phone. To add to his misfortune, after an year, the telecom department informed him, 'This number does not exist.' Since then, there had been no connection between him and his family.

Even though it was very cold that day, Udit had kept his door open. The sun was mellow and he could see the shadows lengthening on the ground. If he craned his neck a bit, not too far from his room he could see the majestic deodars, standing erect and upright even though their branches were overburdened with snow.

Udit could hear Manager Sahib coming, his brown shoes making a distinct click-clack sound on the parquet floor as he climbed the flight of steps that led to his room. This was something Udit dreaded because whenever he came, he had some unpleasant news to convey.

'Today evening, you will be going to Dr Bhasin. Don't kill yourself like this. I have asked Ajay to take you to the clinic.' He instructed as he settled on the faded red plastic chair near his bed.

'I am taking the medicines, but my weakness …' he paused and left his words hanging in the air, like his life that he had left dangling on the thin thread of destiny.

He sat at the edge of the bed, staring more at the polished shoes, than looking him in the eye. Feeling drained and depressed, he neither had the strength nor the will to raise his gaze.

'You can't be your own doctor always,' the manager said, 'and you can't be always right, you see. When you are unable to decide things for yourself, let others decide for you.'

Udit could sense genuine concern in his voice. Over the years, he had almost forgotten the emotion of care and concern. So, when these words came unexpectedly from the hotel manager, from whom he always maintained a cultivated distance, he had difficulty registering them.

In fact, Udit read more than what was said, the unsaid words pointing a finger at the reckless decision that he took years back.

Shelly had landed in Delhi and was on her way to Allahabad. Arvind had taken a taxi and was at the station to receive her. The train had been delayed by two hours.

With a rolled newspaper in his lap, he waited on the platform and drank tea in a kulhar. The dominant flavour of baked mud made the tea all the more relishing. Although he was suitably dressed, in an overcoat, to brave the cold, the chilly winds were troubling him. The cap on his head provided little relief as the wind hummed in his ears. He felt for his ears and found that they had stiffened and resembled those of Buzo, Shweta's constant companion, sitting patiently by her side through her strenuous sessions.

On Yashoda's insistence he had carried a shawl. He decided to unfold and wrap himself much like his wife, covering his head, dropping over his shoulders and then into a wrap. His nose and spectacles were left protruding out. He dozed off. It was only when the engine of the train roared towards the platform and the concrete floor under his legs vibrated under the impact of the hollering wheels that he got up.

'*Hmm, this sleep, no one knows when it will come.*' He stood up and pulled himself towards the AC compartments which were rushing away from him. A2, seat no.12, he remembered and continued.

Up against the milling crowd and dragged by painful knees, it took a while before he could reach the coach. Shelly had disembarked and was waiting with her luggage, a bright red strolley suitcase and a gold vanity bag.

'Papa, I thought you forgot,' she had to comment, as she bent down and reached for his feet.

'How could I?' was all that Arvind said.

There was no conversation between them in the taxi. Through his half shut eyes, Arvind could see a bank of cloud in the sky being carried away by a boisterous breeze.

At home, pleasantries were exchanged more out of formality than otherwise. Something seemed amiss. The cold winter morning had showered its coldness over their relationship, indulgently. As an upshot, Shelly retired for the day after having an early brunch citing the excuse of jetlag. The door of her room was shut to the other two members of the house.

Next morning she slept till 9:00 am. Yashoda was worried when the door of her room did not open. Is there something wrong, she asked Arvind.

Arvind knocked softly at her door. She did not open but he could make out that she was speaking to someone on the phone. He knocked again, this time loudly.

She came out ten minutes later and asked, 'Who was at the door?'

'I knocked,' said Arvind.

Shelly remained quiet.

'I hope your father is fine?' asked Arvind.

'Oh yes, Papa has found a new cardiologist and he is quite good. He says there is no need of surgery in the near future.'

'That's good.'

Arvind wanted to say something but he could not.

Shelly had to convey something but she held herself back, looking for the opportune moment.

The conversation broke off.

Yashoda had appeared in the meantime. She switched on the heater; it was still half an hour before the scheduled power cut.

'How are my grandsons? Do they remember me?' She asked.

'They are good. But both of them fell sick when we went back to London. Perhaps some infection they picked up here. The city is so dirty,' she added as a matter of fact.

A few minutes of silence followed.

'How many more years in London?' Yashoda dared to ask.

'Can't say, all our relatives want us to be in India and we face the same question wherever we go,' she was slightly annoyed.

'Maybe we'll be forced to come back, by next March itself. The company is winding up its business in some countries. Who knows what is in store for us! We have to keep some backup ready in case we are the unlucky ones.'

Before her soliloquy could extend further, Arvind snapped, 'What do you want to convey?' The magazine in his hand trembled, the crisp and glossy cover producing a faint but audible sound. 'Madhur occupies such a senior position, how can the company just lay him off?' he asked in disbelief.

'Can't say anything for now, many of his friends have left and joined other companies.'

The conversation seemed like a laboured chore among the three of them.

It was early morning. Arvind was slowly lumbering towards the gate, looking for a genuine excuse to skip his routine today. It had been a week since he had ventured out of his home for a walk. On that day, he was adequately dressed, fully covered from head to toe in an overcoat, a monkey cap and knee length woollen socks that Yashoda had knitted two years ago. At the gate, he met Mr Oberoi, who offered him a lift in his Fiat. He accepted the offer gladly and the two were off; the heater in the car made him feel comfortable.

Yashoda had seen Arvind off and had bolted the door securely, behind him. She knew it would be around an hour before he would return and with the fog continuing to engulf the city, it was better not to take chances. She was not in deep sleep as a backache had been troubling her, the whole of last week. So she dragged herself towards the sofa in the drawing room. Within minutes, Shelly came and sat on the diwan next to the sofa, covering herself with the blanket that was lying there.

'Ma, Madhur had called up last night.'

'Oh, dear, the boys must be missing you.'

'No, no, they are grown up. In fact, I'm planning to put Aryan in hostel this year.'

A bewildered Yashoda looked at Shelly's face trying to catch some emotion, but she looked as poker-faced as always.

'Ma, he has given a message that I need to tell you. We need to buy a flat, so that we have a place to live when we are back. You know how the rents have shot up these days.'

'That's a wonderful piece of news to get early in the morning! We will have a nice housewarming party then. But . . .' she said, as if struck by belated wisdom, then chose to be mum, the words unable to break through her chords.

Shelly had been so abrupt and sudden that Yashoda was unable to find the context of her carefully and thoughtfully worded sentence.

A knock at the door broke her trance.

Yashoda waited for Shelly to open the door, but she was too busy filing her nails.

Yashoda, still in her grey night gown and off white angora cardigan, laboured towards the door and opened it. Through the open door she could not see anything beyond the porch. Arvind took a few seconds to get in as he was picking up the newspaper. The few seconds of exposure that she had while waiting for Arvind to get in, had caused a momentary shiver in her body. Her palms had become a bit numb, she felt. She tried to hurry and reach the bed, but only managed to limp a few paces, wobbled and then slumped on the blue sofa nearby.

'It is killingly chill outside,' Arvind said as he untied his shoe laces.

'I made a mistake … no more walks this week. It will cause me more harm than good.'

Savita, meanwhile had dropped in early, carrying a bright mink blanket pack on her back. Before Yashoda could ask anything, she spoke apologetically, about having to attend a party that day.

'Do you have to go out of town?' Yashoda asked.

'No, no, Memsahib, it is the Rais, in the back lane. They are completing fifty years of their marriage today and their entire family has gathered,' she said.

'They are hosting a big party at a hotel in the evening and they have invited me too. Lots of guests have come, Memsahib; the families of their two sons have flown in from America and their two daughters are also here,' she continued, smiling broadly.

'And see they have gifted me this blanket on the occasion.' She proudly kept the pack on the table near Yashoda.

'Memsahib, I want half-day off in the afternoon. Tomorrow morning, I will be here on time.'

The conversation had been totally one sided. Savita was so excited that Arvind and Yashoda couldn't help but listen.

Without waiting for any reply, she hurried to the kitchen. The elderly couple smiled indulgently.

Hardly five minutes had passed, when she was back in the room with tea, in bright green cups. 'Today it is Savita superfast, otherwise it is mostly the passenger train, merrily chugging along the track,' Yashoda chuckled.

She reciprocated with a half-smile and disappeared into the kitchen once again.

Two cold days passed by. It was slightly sunny that day.

Shelly sat in the living room with her head buried inside the morning newspaper. Arvind was sipping his tea quietly after he had drawn the curtains on the windows. Natural light filtering into his room always did wonders to his mood.

Two hours later all three of them were having breakfast sitting at the round glass topped dining table. This was an addition to the family furniture last year when Arvind had insisted that they no longer needed such a big one. 'Papa, Madhur says we need to arrange for some money as we have to buy a flat in Bangalore,' Shelly suddenly said out of the blue.

'A flat in Bangalore? Why?' Arvind was totally surprised.

'When we come back, we would need a house,' she said casually.

'But last January Madhur was telling me that he wanted to switch over to a new firm and settle in Delhi?'

'In Delhi? Never. It's so polluted. Better we stay in London,' she continued, a little shocked after hearing that Madhur had plans of settling in Delhi.

'Anyway, even if it is Bangalore, why is he worried? I can help if there is a shortage. Take 7-8 lakhs from me.'

'But Dad we need more, lots more.'

'Ok I will give you ten. As it is the rate of interest in the bank is less. Let it be put to some good use.'

'No, but he doesn't want to take your savings.'

'Then what?'

'He says selling a part of this house, at least our share, will give us a handsome amount.'

'What do you mean, Shelly? What is your share and my share? We are one family. This is our house, I have made this with my blood and sweat.' Arivind's face was full of angst, shock and unbridled fury.

'Moreover what makes him think that I am bound to bequeath this property to my sons? I may want to hand it over to a charitable trust to open a school for poor kids. It is not something I have inherited, I hope he remembers.'

'But dad, normally in India don't the boys inherit their parental property,' Shelly said, matter of factly.

'You are mightily mistaken Shelly, please ...'

House ... sell ... flat ... share ... savings ... money ... Arvind suddenly felt as if his senses had been numbed and no it was not due to the cold this time. Words had left his mouth. He felt as if he had gulped down something so acidic and strong that his vocal cords had been scalded along with his throat. He glanced at the remaining tea in his mug.

'But Madhur did not talk about any such plans when he was here last January. Certainly he has not finalised a flat sitting so far away in London?' Yashoda blurted and then limped away to the kitchen. Savita had left the milk boiling on the stove. It had to be switched off before it overflowed.

She turned off the gas and then limped out in immense pain towards her bed. Her back pain had surged again.

Shelly followed her to the kitchen.

'Ma why are you both getting so sentimental? After all this is a structure made of bricks and cement and mortar. We also have a legal right to this property. And why do we make property? Is it not an asset to help you when you need money?'

Yashoda meanwhile had somehow pulled herself towards the guest room and onto the bed wincing in pain. As she managed to lie on bed, the power went off.

In the darkness, she said, 'Madhur, as a man, might not understand the attachment we have with this place. I thought, as a woman, you would.'

'But Ma, we are planning to sell only a part. You and dad will have enough space to live. In London, old people prefer to shift to old age homes, you know,' she walked out almost stamping her feet in disapproval.

The dark blue curtains on the windows had not been drawn. She lay in darkness for half an hour, praying for the pain to subside.

'I am going out and will be back by evening,' Shelly announced from the dining area. Yashoda could hear the clacking sound of the gate being closed.

Arvind entered the room.

'Where has Shelly gone?' He asked quietly as if nothing had happened on the breakfast table.

'I could not hear properly which place she said. My back has been hurting so badly,' she said, grimacing.

'Wait, I will get a hot water bottle for you. First you swallow this.' Arvind handed her a painkiller and a glass of water.

After keeping the glass back on the table, he went to the kitchen.

Yashoda often wondered how her husband managed to stay calm and composed in all situations.

The hot water fomentation did provide some relief to Yashoda. She could then sit in her bed with her back supported by the wall at the back.

Arvind sat by her side.

'Shelly would be back for lunch?'

'Don't think so.'

'Don't worry. I know Madhur well. It's Shelly's idea. He will never agree to this.'

'But what do we sell if they insist? Which part?' She suddenly asked.

'I don't believe this. They can't force me to sell. Let me talk to Madhur.'

In Shelly's absence, Arvind booked an ISD call. He knew it would take a minimum of two hours before the operator would get back to him.

He waited, both for the maid to turn up and for the operator to revert to him. Neither did by lunch time. His watch showed 1:30 pm.

He loitered around in the house for a while. Went out and paced the lawn and returned. He then went to the kitchen and wondered if he could cook anything for lunch as Yashoda was in terrible pain.

'What should I cook for lunch Memsahib?' He jocularly asked Yashoda, bowing his head.

Yashoda managed to laugh, but stopped short of saying anything. Lunch was nowhere in her mind.

He went and inspected the fridge. He found some left over yam curry and rice in two tiffin boxes.

Let me do something with this, he said to himself as he opened that plastic container. It contained some atta Savita had left after making chappatis yesterday evening. He warmed the leftover rice, adding a spoonful of ghee and sprinkling a little salt. To the stale curry, he added freshly chopped coriander and drops of lime. Remade and redone with the two, he tried rolling a few chapattis. Five he managed somehow, one partially round, one a big oval, three in the shape of amoebae on the move. He then put everything in a tray and came to Yashoda's bed.

'Lunch is here, come on get up,' he said pulling away her blanket.

The warm food brought in sunshine to her face, pulling away the pall of gloom that Shelly's negativities had cloaked it with.

Half way through lunch, the telephone rang. The trunk call was through.

'Hello Madhur?' Arvind almost mumbled into the receiver, his mouth still full of rice.

'Papa, what happened? Is everything fine?' The voice from the other end was loud and clear.

'Son, Shelly says you want me to sell a portion of the house, are you aware? Who has tutored her?' He stammered through the sentence, completing it with a lot of effort.

Yashoda watched, holding a piece of chapatti, soaked in gravy of the curry, in her hand. The conversation continued for full ten minutes in which most of the times, the person at the other end spoke. Like a hapless observer, she watched from her bed, the rapidly changing facial expressions.

'But why?'

'You take ten from me.'

'Take a loan, you have long years of service ahead.'

'If that was, the case, why did you not tell me anything during your last visit?'

Yashoda could listen to only a few bits of the conversation from Madhur's side when he raised his voice. And she had heard him say, 'Dad I thought money and materialistic things were not for you. At this age you need people around you not money or property?'

'I hope you understand that if I am unable to buy this flat, I may be forced to rely upon a backup plan. And Shelly says we stay back in UK and take up British citizenship. I did not want to do that but now I may need to rethink.' he continued as Arvind listened in disbelief.

With her eyes transfixed on Arvind's face, she could make out a very rapid progression, from anxiety to anguish to helplessness to that of indignation followed by the now so evident resignation. At this end, only a string of negatives, no ... never .... not possible ... impossible ... rang in Yashoda's ears till the line was disconnected. With his fingers still coated in the orange red gravy of the curry and grains of rice, the frugal meal he was relishing a few moments ago, he rushed towards the washroom.

Yashoda waited for him to come back and finish his food. He came after ten minutes.

'You didn't finish the food? Why have you washed your hands?' she asked.

'Hmm ... I am full,' he said pulling on his overcoat.

'Then put these away,' Yashoda said washing her fingers in the bowl itself as she was in no position to walk to the wash basin. Arvind picked up the tray and carried it to the kitchen.

He then stuffed the leftover chapattis from the plates into a polybag by the side of the kitchen sink. Food was never to be thrown in a garbage bin, Yashoda had always insisted. Leftovers, were meant to satiate some hungry stomachs, be it a street dog rummaging through a garbage mound, a squirrel on the lookout for a few chunks, or even a hungry crow cawing by the side of the kitchen window.

Then sitting by Yashoda's side he suddenly said, 'Do you think Mayank will also ask for his share now itself?'

'I can't say, times have changed now. I never expected that my boy Madhur, whom you also teased as mama's boy would one day talk like this. Remember how often he said that he would open a shop here and not take a job because he could not live without his mom,' her eyes were now full of tears.

Shelly returned late in the evening after Arvind and Yashoda had retired for the day. Dinner had been just bread and milk.

'Madhur was never like this,' Yashoda said as Arvind switched off the light.

'Don't worry. He can't force me. I will find a way out.'

Next day, early morning Shelly was all packed and ready.

'Where are you going? You said you were here till the weekend?' asked Arvind.

'Of course I am here in India but I wish to meet a few friends who are waiting for me. Sometimes friends are more understanding and helpful than one's own blood relations.'

'What are you saying Shelly?' Yashoda tried to intervene.

'Ma, next time I come here, I may find a school here. At least I keep my friends informed and updated. They will offer me a place to stay. Well I am off to Dehradun. My friend's sister is getting married tomorrow.'

It was only after she had left that the Johris brooded over the unpleasant situation they were in.

'I thought that she wanted to sell some old furniture that had been dumped up there,' Yashoda said.

'This boy, what has he been doing in London? He couldn't save enough there for all this. And I think Mayank will also not agree, what do you say?'

'You ask Mayank to speak to him. After all it is not only Madhur who has a share in this,' he continued.

The Johris would have readily agreed to part with furniture and all other miscellaneous stuff that had arrived, a day before they had been on their flight to London. The message to Arvind and Yashoda was simple; dispose off the items and deposit the cash in their account. Madhur and Shelly would have done that themselves but since their journey to London had to be brought ahead by a week, they were left with no time to do these odd chores.

Nonetheless, the Johris retained them. Inanimate objects of wood, steel, iron, plastic along with some mattresses and multicoloured kitchen jars in different shapes and sizes had managed to keep them happy and fooled for days together. They had taken pains and had managed to arrange each and every item in the three rooms on the first floor, repairing them, cleaning them, and polishing them, as if they were waiting for the family to shift in any day, any time. Disposing them off, altogether, in lieu of some currency notes was an option they had never even dreamt in their wildest dreams.

Memories provided them pretty company. They could still recognise the red and black bed sheet Madhur had carried from home, once when he had come for Diwali. The top shelf of the book rack had caught Yashoda's attention; it had Madhur's books, majority of which had been gifted to him by Arvind and the first page of each bore the same four lines,

To,
My dear son Madhur,
With love,
Papa.

The words appeared stencilled in Arvind's beautiful cursive handwriting, in blue ink. *How could Madhur even think of selling away his memories?* Yashoda wondered.

A fortnight after reaching London, Madhur had called up to inform that they had reached safely and had been in the process of settling down. He had also told them how they had managed to rent a furnished apartment, saving them the botheration of collecting furniture, upholstery and other household gadgets. He had been excited describing the central heating system the houses there had, allowing them to remain in casuals inside, when outside it had been freezing. The only trouble they had been facing was devising ways and means of drying clothes as they were still unfamiliar with the public laundry etiquettes, the laundry being in the basement of the same building. At the end of every conversation he would gently remind them to sell whatever could be sold and put the money in the bank, confirming that his father had not misplaced the slip bearing his account number, the one, he had handed him over outside the New Delhi airport.

Now, four years down the line, much water had flown down the Ganga and the Thames, eroding some banks, creating some new ones, sharp and unstable. Erosion, corrosion, dilution and pollution of feelings, emotions and bonds now threatened to show up in not too pleasant frames.

The ageing couple, in the twilight of their lives, had been asked to sell their home and put a price tag on something that the next generation thought had become worthless with the passage of time. Madhur and Shelly belonged to the use and throw generation that believed in frequent buying, using and throwing away and then again buying, using and throwing away. Sentiments and emotions were non-tangible and therefore of little value. In contrast to their thinking was that of Arvind and Yashoda, who did not know how to arrive at a price for a home, whose four walls had coats of human affection, whose windows and doors were porous to love, whose vacuous spaces still lingered with the fragrance of those who lived there once, whose minutest interstices had been permeated by unshakable faith and blind trust. It was the result of the deep chasm of generation gap in the thinking of the first generation and the next, thought Arvind.

'This house cannot be divided into two usable portions in any way,' Yashoda observed after being quiet for a long time.

'But I think if we don't agree to what they want, these boys will leave us for good. Sometimes children can be so heartless. See, Oberoi's eldest son is not on talking terms with them over some property dispute. And, oh Lord, they are so rich. I never thought you or I will live to see this day,' Arvind sighed as he uttered the last sentence in a whisper.

'Now I understand why people say the toughest battle to win is against your own bloodline,' Yashoda said throwing up her arms in despair.

That day Savita had prepared paranthas and fried fresh green peas for breakfast. Arvind and Yashoda were there in the lawn, sitting on the string cot, enjoying the sun when she arrived with two plates in her hands and announced, 'Breakfast!'

'Get me some tea too, please,' Yashoda said and waited, putting aside the plate. She noticed that the grass in the lawn had yellowed and thinned, exposing patches of earth in many places. The pots were still full of marigolds. Opposite the kitchen window, the square bed had spinach, fresh and succulent. Suddenly something flashed across her mind. 'Now I know,' she exclaimed, 'what they were doing that day …'

'Who, what? Are you dreaming about the mystery serial you watched yesterday on TV?'

'The reality of life these days is more mysterious than all those serials put together,' said Yashoda.

'Hmm … lessons in philosophy. Oh, I had forgotten that you are a graduate in the subject.'

'Look I am serious. I had seen Madhur and Shelly pacing the lawn, discussing something agitatedly. At that time I could not guess what they were up to.'

'Oh, really?'

A male and a female cuckoo fought on the neem tree nearby.

That night, they held a long discussion over the feasibility, if any, of slicing their home into two. The garden beyond the porch that Madhur must have eyed was as much a part of the home as the covered area.

'No way! Impossible!!' he cried and broke down.

It had been raining and snowing in Mussoorie for the last three days. The afternoon snow had been unusually heavy today. The slush on the road meant that there were not many vehicles plying on it that day. Those who had any urgency, preferred to walk. Udit was looking for an excuse not to visit the doctor. He had been like that since childhood. Somebody had to nudge and push him to consult a doctor if ever the need arose. His mind was in chaos, unable to decide what was best for him, till Vishnu came to his room and informed that the hotel car, a white ambassador, was waiting at the gate.

He had to go.

Dr Bhasin suspected it to be typhoid and promptly advised some tests. Plenty of rest, simple home food and prescribed medication, needed to be followed compulsorily if Udit wanted to get well soon. Early next morning the Manager was back in his room.

'You don't worry. Take rest and don't forget to take the medicines. I will ensure that nothing is deducted from your salary this month,' he said.

'If you wish you can go home ... but then that would be a long journey, it would worsen your condition. Better that you stay here.'

Udit had always thought that the Manager had polite words only for his clients, who in his scheme of things were there to contribute in causing the hotel's coffers to swell. He had never seen him in any kind of conversation with the other hotel employees other than snapping; 'Do this!' 'Now, get this done by today evening!' 'No, I can't wait!'

'Udit, if you need anything, please just send me a message through Vishnu and I'll promptly arrange for it.' He got up and then casually put down the paper bag that he had brought.

The bag contained bright red apples. Udit was speechless.

For the next few minutes he was buried under an avalanche of memories. Years ago whenever he would fall ill, his mother would always remain around him. She would walk into the room, feel his pulse, touch his forehead, cover him with a sheet all this even when he would be in deep sleep. He also remembered how she would softly cry while sponging him when he was down with typhoid years ago as a ten-year-old.

He took out the apples from the bag and put them in a plate. And then he took one in his hand. Had mom been around she would have peeled it and offered him thin slices after sprinkling a little salt and pepper, he thought, as he took a bite.

April 1992. The skies roared and thundered all through the night and strong winds howled through the branches of the trees. There were three quaint but clear sounds audible in the silence of the night, one of the leaves rustling against each other, the other of the chowkidar tapping his wooden lathi on the concrete walking track in the park behind and the steady pitter-patter of raindrops falling on the window awning of Shweta's room. Sitting on her bed, Shweta wondered why the weather turned freaky just at the time the mangoes and the litchis were in full bloom. Buzo as always, had occupied his place underneath Shweta's bed. The first thing she did in the morning was sneak out in the veranda to survey the impact of the storm. But the backyard presented a pretty picture. It was thickly carpeted with the light purple drek flowers from the adjoining tree in the park. She was thankful that the mango tree in the park had been lucky, with flowers still visible in ample numbers. The fact that it was nestled between the amaltash and the drek, saved it, while the brunt of the impact was borne by its companions.

Shashank was in a great dilemma that day. There was a message from Sonam's would be in-laws that they could no longer wait for the marriage as the boy was leaving for the US in June for an year on an in-service assignment. They preferred the marriage to be solemnised early so that the formalities for Sonam's travel could be completed in time. A conversation with the boy had not been of much help either. He had politely conveyed that he had absolutely no issues with Sonam staying back in India if they wanted the marriage to be delayed till June first week, but his only concern was that it would be at least a year before he could come back and take her along or even more in case the assignment was extended, which was quite probable. He had also dropped subtle hints that they could even wait for his return and plan things thereafter.

Shashank was agreeable to this proposition but Bina was reluctant. She was afraid that once the boy went to a 'foreign' country, there was no guarantee that on his return, he would remain committed to the girl he had been engaged to. Sonam had no opinion on the issue, agreeing to abide by any decision her parents took for her. Ultimately, Shashank agreed for the marriage ceremony in the beginning of May. Later in the evening, a visit by the family priest confirmed that the wedding card would bear the date, 6th May 1992.

With a little over a month to go and a hundred things to take care of, Shashank was nervous like an examinee having to take a surprise test. He realised that before anything else, the house needed renovation. Next day, early morning, more than half a dozen labourers were put on the job, scraping the old coat of paint from the walls and filling the crevices with putty and fevicol mixture. Bina knew that the dust and dirt could be a potential trigger for her asthmatic troubles. So she decided to go shopping for Sonam's trousseau while the painting job was on.

The moment the painters entered their house the next day, she and Sonam left for the market. Their first stop was at Sukhbasi Lal, the famous sari shop in Katra. The shop had just opened and the saris were being arranged in the showcase, hurriedly being wrapped around the blonde mannequins. The platform on which the customers were expected to sit and select had been swept and mopped clean.

The mother and daughter waited outside the shop as they had come too early. A young boy appeared and offered them tea.

Seeing the puzzled look on their faces, he hurried to add, 'Don't worry madam, I work in the shop itself. Sethji has asked me to provide tea to you; after all you are our first customers for the day!'

Once inside the shop, the salesmen were eager, treating them like royalty, showing saris of the entire range from Banarasi silk to Kanjivaram to crisp chiffons to moonga silk from Assam. Within half an hour, they were drowned in the river of saris that had suddenly appeared before them, waves of bright, shimmering red, blue, pink, yellow, magenta, fuchsia fabrics with intricate designs and patterns. The process of selecting twenty-one of them was not easy. One by one they began picking up, choosing from the pile, sorting out for a primary selection and then keeping them aside for the final decision to be taken later on.

The shop owner offered them soft drinks and pakoras, because it was near lunch time. Then the final selection began from the thirty-two they had segregated earlier. By the time they were finished, they had five heavy bags to carry home. The time was 3:45 pm and Bina calculated that they had another half an hour to go. So they crossed the road and entered the cosmetics and bangle shop, across the road.

The next few weeks passed in a whirlwind of activities. Shashank and Bina hurried around, sending the invites, making the bookings for the caterers, fixing the cooks both for the actual function as well as for the guests who were expected at home at least three days in advance of the wedding. Pranav and his family had arrived and so had Granny along with a few relatives from Bindki. Other guests, including Bina's sisters, cousins, Shashank's uncles and aunts, had also arrived. The house was full of people, just two days before the ceremony.

Shweta's maternal uncle, whom she fondly addressed as Ajit Mama, had specially flown in from London. In their childhood, Sonam and Shweta addressed him as 'Toffeewale Mama' a term coined especially for him because whenever he visited them, he brought big packs of toffees and chocolates. This time he had brought a special suitcase, with a 'Handle with Care' sticker prominently displayed.

The ladies remained a busy lot. Other than packing and wrapping all the gifts, they had to help in the decoration of the house, carry out the preliminary ceremonies and rituals, and also take part in the song and dance. Sonam's trousseau packing had been done by Bina herself and the other gifts were given to aunts and cousins to pack. So while the big brown coconut had taken the form of a dancing peacock, the dry fruits had been aesthetically packed inside sheets of cellophane, each given the shape of the nut it contained. The steel utensils that were to be used in the ceremony had been painted with designs and images of Lord Ganesh along with elephants, horses and fishes, all said to be harbingers of good luck.

A shamiana had been erected in the neighbourhood park for the jaimala to be followed by dinner. The pheras and the other marriage rituals were to be held later in the night in the courtyard of the house in a beautifully decorated mandap.

Two days to go for the wedding, Ajit Mama sat with his sister in the courtyard, overseeing the halwai making sweets and savouries. The aroma of pure ghee filled the air as the expert halwais were on the job frying mathis, roasting nuts and boiling sugar syrup in huge iron kadahis.

'Bina, I don't see balushahis being made, don't they know how to make them?' Ajit Mama suddenly asked.

'Bhaiya not everyone here is a foodie like you. People have become calorie conscious these days. Hence we thought of having only these besan laddoos, dry fruit laddoos and shakarpaares with less sugar you see. If you want to have some, I will ask Shweta's daddy to get some from the market. But I think you should be careful with your diabetes.'

'But, I thought once in a while it is not bad to indulge a little. As for me I'd still love to gobble a few. As it is how many more years do I have left, at the sunset of my life? An year more, an year less how does it matter. Let me at least enjoy my balushahis before I depart,' he said dryly.

Bina realised she had been rude to her brother. She looked at him fondly with tears welling up in her eyes thinking if she could have told him the truth. As he sat a bit downcast with his gaze lowered on his feet, she could see how much he had changed, how his age was so visible now. The head had silvery strands of hair clumped towards the margins. His face was the same, round with a barely discernible chin, but the wrinkles caused the skin around his cheek to sag. His eyes had huge bags underneath and the lashes and the brows had turned an ashen silver. His hands trembled a little as he sipped tea from the kulhar. He was nearing seventy-five.

A streak of guilt passed through her body, similar to flashes of lightning in the sky she often saw from the window of her room, when it thundered.

'Bina, where are you?' Shashank's voice boomed from the far end of the courtyard. Relieved, she left abruptly, in silence, wiping the tear that had welled up in her eyes.

Shweta had overheard the conversation, as she was sitting barely a few feet away, directing people decorating the mandap with strings of marigolds and ashoka leaves. She came over. 'Mamaji, I'm sorry for Ma's rudeness, she has indeed become quite irritable of late. Truth is, Udit Bhaiya was very fond of balushahis. Hence Dad decided not to include it in the wedding sweets list. Ma would have been very upset and emotional. Maybe that's why ...' she trailed off.

'Don't you think that they need to put a strand of red roses there?' he deftly changed the topic, understanding the underlying pain the family was silently bearing, pointing to the elongated strands of fresh marigolds and wavy ashoka leaves strewn together, 'It will add colour and fragrance.'

After a pause he continued, 'That day at the airport I saw Narayan. He was probably on the same flight as mine. Do you think he would have any information?'

There was a twinkle in her eyes.

'Really Mama! You could recognise him?'

'Oh yes, how I can I forget him! He was the one, who took your mami to Dr Arvind, literally on his shoulder, when she had fractured her pelvic girdle way back during my India visit, sometime in 1982 I think … that bow shaped scar above his right eye, his fair complexion and extra-large ears. I had fondly called him "Pilot sahib" then and he took it so sportingly. I could have spoken to him, but he was so far away. I could only catch a fleeting glimpse of him, rushing out of the airport.'

'Mamaji, I don't know why we are so unlucky.'

The conversation came to an abrupt end as Chandan appeared asking for a hundred rupees. The money had to be paid as fare to the vegetable vendor who had come with an auto laden with sacks of vegetables. Chandan was a special invitee to the ceremony and had come all the way from his village in Nepal only to attend the ceremony. A man with a heart of gold, he had turned up for the wedding, hiding his own pain of having lost his wife.

A day before the wedding, sangeet was held in the evening. A function where all the ladies of the neighbourhood along with Sonam's and Shweta's friends gathered for song and dance to the beat of the traditional dholak. A lively affair set the tone for the festivities to follow. Later in the night Sonam's mehndi ceremony was held. Two of Sonam's best friends Tina and Disha had stayed back for the night. It was quite late after dinner but they insisted on putting mehndi on the palms of all the ladies of the house. Bina refused saying that she had a lot of work to do and she could not sit idle for long with the mehndi in her palms.

'Auntie, we will make such patterns that you will still be able to use your fingers,' Disha insisted.

'Auntie don't worry, we will do it when you lie down to sleep,' Tina said.

Bina relented and as the two girls began making patterns on her palms, a tinge of sadness crept in. The thought that it was just a day to go for the wedding and her darling daughter Sonam would be leaving home soon trubled her.

Next morning the henna on Sonam's palms had turned a beautiful red. Today the celebrations had begun early with the haldi ceremony. The ladies of the house, friends and Shweta applied haldi and chandan paste on the would be bride and sang traditional wedding songs. This was followed by patri ceremony in which Sonam and seven other girls had to partake a special lunch in the mandap itself, said to be the last food for the bride in her parental home. The ceremony became poignant and hugely emotional as the sound of shehnai being played at the door by two ustads could be heard within the house.

In an atmosphere of joy mixed with a little sadness at the prospect of having to live without Sonam, Bina carried on bravely overseeing all the arrangements and taking care of the relatives and guests. However at every ring of the doorbell, she would rush towards the door hoping that someone she had been waiting for, for so many years, might just turn up. But it was not fated to happen. Her wait was destined to be a prolonged one.

Late in the evening, when the barat arrived, Sonam looked a stunning bride in her red and gold lehenga. Jaimala was followed by dinner and after a break of an hour or so, the marriage ceremony began in the mandap. The kanyadan was performed by Shashank and Bina as also by Ajit Mama, Pranav and his wife. Later it was a very poignant moment when the 'lava parchan' had to be performed by the bride's brother. Thankfully Ajit Mama immediately called Pranav's elder son to perform the rituals and sent both Bina and Shashank away from the mandap to see if the pooja room was ready to receive the newly married couple for the customary arti that would follow . However, Granny made it a point, that he keep a passport sized old photo of Udit in his pocket, while performing the rituals. While the photo was old and faded, his memories were as fresh as ever. Over the years, they had been swept under the proverbial carpet, to be smothered and killed. But, there they had multiplied in astronomical proportions and had been alive and kicking. Normally they lay dormant and inactive, but whenever they gained entry into a human brain, fed by the call of blood, they would cause tremendous upheaval, till they were forcibly evicted by either a stronger pleasant memory or a thought focusing on something urgent and demanding.

Sonam had left for her in-laws place, early in the morning. The same house that wore a festive look for the last month or so looked deserted, despite the presence of so many guests still there.

The guests left, one by one, rushing back to their own lives. Deep down they knew, perhaps, another event which necessitated a family gathering could alone bring them together again, more out of social compulsion than otherwise. Till then, absorbed in the nitty-gritty of their own lives, they would remain in touch, conveying their love and affection through a letter, a greeting card or at best a phone call where they could hear each other's voices across the two ends of a cord.

Ajit Mama had stayed back for a month. He had planned to return after a fortnight but then he cancelled his ticket as his sister's condition worried him. He could see how she was struggling with another vacuum in her life. A week after the marriage, Bina had broken down, in the middle of the night. She had woken up upset and crying and it was only after a prolonged and gentle prodding by her elder brother that she recounted her nightmare. In her dream, she had been crossing a river on a boat, when the boat had capsized mid-stream and she had watched in horror, her son Udit, being washed away by the strong currents of the river in spate.

Ajit had consoled her. And it had not been easy. He emphatically told her that it was impossible that her dream could ever be true, for it was only a fortnight ago, that he had met Udit's friend Narayan at the Delhi airport. Narayan had told that Udit was there at Delhi railway station just a week ago, taking a train to Bombay for some work.

A lie had been helpful.

Granny, who was still there after the marriage, was, however, sure that a dream of a river in spate did not bode well for the family. But Ajit Mama had managed to convince her that though she was right in her interpretation, as per his knowledge of the symbolism of dreams, if a person who had not been physically close, had been carried away by the currents, the dream conveyed a reverse meaning. Something good was about to happen and very soon. In the next twenty days, he kept everyone in good spirits recounting anecdotes of his early years in the foreign land. His stories had a wide range, beginning with his troubles when he was new to England and the problems he faced due to his heavily accented English. He recalled how he carried a pocket diary in which he would scribble down what he wanted to ask, pretending to be a rich businessman from Dubai. But his ploy would sometimes misfire, when passersby would offer him money, mistaking him to be a deaf and dumb beggar.

Amidst all the mirth and laughter, Mama would not forget to counsel his younger niece. He had understood that beneath Shweta's tough exterior lay a crestfallen heart. Physically she had adjusted to her post accident life, but something continued to torment her. After many such sessions, Ajit Mama managed to convince Shweta into believing that her present physical condition was the result of an accident and purely temporary. He had many stories to tell of people he had known who had recovered fully only due to their willpower and their extraordinary belief that it was a passing phase. He showed her an album with photos of Sudha Chandran performing in London, the iron willed dancer who had continued with her dance despite the loss of a limb. In the initial days, after Sonam had left, Shweta had found it difficult to live all by herself. Over the years, it had been Sonam who had been her true companion, eating, sleeping, singing, laughing and crying with her. She had been a soul mate, taking care of Shweta's needs without having to be told. Whether it was helping her with her morning routine or deciding the kind of haircut she was always with her, boosting her confidence and encouraging her to live a normal life.

After Sonam's departure, Bina had tried hard to step into Sonam's shoes, but failed. Her own fragile health meant that neither she had the time nor the strength to be able to take care of her daughter, the way Sonam had been doing, making it appear deceptively easy.

Then one day the unthinkable happened. It was a Saturday morning and Shweta was at the gate in her wheelchair buying vegetables from the vendor who was passing by. As she turned to go inside, she saw a rickshaw stop at the end of the lane. Whose guest, he could be? she thought as she paused a few seconds to have a look. A young boy, not more than nineteen or twenty got down from it. She was surprised that while the boy appeared quite tall on the seat, once he had got down, he was scarcely visible. Curious to find out the reason, she asked the vendor to move aside to get a better view and saw that beneath the waist, the boy had only two stumps in the form of thighs. After getting down from the seat, he transferred himself to a little wooden cart with wheels, which he pushed with his hands. He took out a wallet, from his olive green backpack, handed over money to the rickshaw puller and then wheeled himself into the other lane, swiftly. She came in, shaking her head in disbelief. She glanced at her legs and pinched her knees.

Thank God, she mumbled.

The next hour Shweta was speechless and a tornado of ifs, buts, how, why, can, can't almost blew her away. She steeled herself, and allowed the storm to subside. At the end of it, she told herself that she had had enough of her lugworm existence; she would now begin *to live*, once again. A resurrection had begun.

A change in attitude began to dawn and that shell of aloofness and indifference crumbled fast. Her mind became active, devising ways to emerge out of the burrow that she had dug herself into, after that fateful accident in Mussoorie.

Fortunately, an opportunity came her way. Shashank had summoned a carpenter to replace the door frame of the small room, adjacent to the washroom that was attached to Shweta's room. The room served no purpose, it was only eight feet by eight feet where some books, files and old papers had been dumped. That door frame had become totally hollow because of termite infestation and the carpenter had said that replacing the entire frame with a metallic one was a good option, to prevent any future termite troubles. An idea struck her and she took permission from Shashank to let her design the room especially for herself. Once she had got the green signal, she caught hold of the carpenter and a plumber to carry out some structural engineering. The wall separating the washroom and that little room was removed and a broad sliding fabricated metal door was installed. This enabled her to enter into the bathroom, still seated on her wheelchair. This way she could ea ily approach the new washbasin, bigger in size with taps and hand held faucets for greater convenience. The mirror on the wall behind was fixed at a height that allowed her to brush her teeth, wash her face, shampoo her hair sitting on the chair itself. An improvised WC had been fixed on a new platform that allowed her easy access and gave her independence to manage her daily routine all by herself. Her bathing area allowed her to transfer herself from the chair on to the steel platform, effortlessly, with hot and cold showers within easy reach. Her wardrobe cupboards were shifted to the newly created space providing her more privacy and better accessibility. She herself was surprised that the little bit of engineering that she had done in that room, disturbing the little ecosystem of spiders, moths, and termites had brought such a tremendous change in her life. No longer did she need anyone to help her with her daily chores. Life had become easy.

Weeks passed by. For Ajit Mama, the time to return had come too soon. Two days to go, he asked Shweta to help him with his packing. On that afternoon, when he saw Bina sitting beside his suitcase, her eyes moist, he made a promise, holding her hand that he would come back from London soon and then the only mission in his life would be find out Udit and unite him with them. Three months was all that he needed to wind up his work, transfer all his assets and liabilities of his flourishing business of carpets and the chain of home decor stores throughout England, to his sons and grandsons.

As the taxi waited that Sunday afternoon, to reach him to the railway station, he went over to Shweta and whispered in her ears, 'Track Narayan in the meantime. We can get vital clues from him, when we begin the actual search.'

A mission had begun.

It was a scorching hot day in mid-June. The streets had been deserted even before the clock struck ten. The office timings had been revised since early June. The schools were already shut for the summer vacations and the sandy banks of the Ganga and Yamuna had donned an emerald green with luxurious growth of cucurbits, popularly known as the gourd family. The vendors sold more of iced water, lemonade and soda. The pavements by the sides of the roads were full of temporary shops, where watermelons rolled over one another and competed with musk melon for strategic space, with some half-sliced ones on prominent display, their red juicy flesh aimed to attract potential customers. By their sides had popped up ice kiosks, selling large blocks of ice laid on brown jute sacks and covered with a few more jute bags to prevent them from melting away before a customer arrived.

Giving them ample company were the potters, who had descended on these pavements not only with their stock of earthen pots, surahis and containers but also with their wives and kids, cooking and playing in makeshift tents, a little away from the road. Arvind and Yashoda, had given up sulking after the initial phase of anger and repentance for having done all that they could to enable Madhur reach the position of affluence he was currently in. In hindsight, self- criticism was not too difficult, but that was making matters worse for them. They had concluded that whatever was destined to happen would happen and they would not resist it. So they adopted the stance of wait and watch. The previous six months they had been quiet, mingling only with a few families and friends, with whom they had wanted to share their predicament but had not succeeded in bringing words up their throats in a manner they would have liked.

Meanwhile, the ISD calls which invariably came every Sunday had stopped and the old couple no more looked forward to the calls. In fact if their phone per chance rang about the time those calls often came, between 5:00 to 6:00 pm in the evenings, they would dread lifting up the receiver.

In the evenings, when the sun showed some mercy, they would water the lawn, lovingly ensuring that each blade of grass was showered and each leaf of the plants washed and sufficient water filled in the pots to last till they were watered again. No matter how hot and uncomfortable it was, they made it a point to sit for an hour or so on those grey plastic chairs. The table fan would whir behind them blowing air laden with the smell of wet earth mixed with the mild fragrance of white flowers of cestrum that bloomed in the farthest corner.

One such evening, they had hardly settled in the lawn with Yashoda bringing a bunch of deep red amaranth, separating the tender leaves and stem from the little weeds and blades of grass that had inadvertently come along, when somebody at the gate distracted her. At the gate stood the colony postman, impeccably dressed in his khaki uniform. Well past the office hours, this was no time for him to deliver mail, but sincere fellow that he was, he would wait for the heat to reduce and then reach the mail to their destination.

'A letter for you, Doctor sahib,' he said as he put the letter in the bright red letter box at the gate. Arvind waved to him, acknowledging that he had heard. Ten minutes passed, but he showed no intention of retrieving the letter from the box. He was busy fiddling with the radio on the table, trying to tune in to BBC news service.

Yashoda too kept on cleaning the amaranth, unfazed, while a pile of weeds began to accumulate near her feet.

There was no urgency in either of them to find out the message that had arrived resting inside the folds of that envelope.

Savita meanwhile was there at the gate, hurrying inside. In the evenings she was always in a hurry, preferring to roll out chapattis first and dumping them inside the casseroles when they were still hot. Next she would make the salad and then leave the curry simmering on the stove, telling Yashoda to check and switch off the stove in time. The chapattis would become limp with the steam condensing under the cover, inevitably requiring Yashoda to warm them on the iron tava before serving dinner. But then she never complained; Savita had her own family to look after, a husband who worked as a construction worker and five children in the age group of two to fourteen years.

'Savita, please get that letter from the box,' Arvind finally asked for it.

Their hearts pounded as Savita handed over the white envelope, with that monogram in the top left corner confirming that it was an aerogram from London, with the sender's name substituted by initials M.J. and an address different from the last that he remembered Madhur mentioning.

Aerograms these days arrived only from London and from Madhur and that too very rarely. Gone were the days when his post box in the medical college would be flooded with mails from countries across the world, inviting him to deliver a lecture, a talk or at times even offers to join those super speciality health care centres, at a salary he could decide. But he had persistently and doggedly resisted all the temptations and peer pressures and those pictures of a wonderful life across the seven seas. He had consciously chosen and stayed back in the land of his birth, to be in the company of those he loved. He had always firmly believed that success had to be savoured and for that matter what better company could he wish than that of his near and dear ones, those with whom he had laughed and cried all along?

He grabbed the knife and slit the envelope open. The next instant he paused. The envelope was still in his numbed hands, when his face turned a deep red, with deep ridges appearing on his forehead; his teeth clenched as if he had just slit open a throat. Rarely had he been nervous like this. Even in operation theatres, he had been much calmer and relaxed, cutting through layers of human skin and flesh with his scalpel, with the effortless ease of a sculptor, chiselling away at his creation. The typical smell of human blood, gushing out, on to his hands, over his surgical gloves, never evoked the kind of nauseating feeling he experienced right then.

Madhur had sent a letter. The contents seem to have been hurriedly put together, sentences beginning with something and ending with something totally unrelated like an incoherent man babbling away in an inebriated state. The customary greetings were there at the beginning but the end was abrupt, informing him that he had two months by which the money had to be paid to get the flat. He had also meticulously drafted an advertisement on his father's behalf, which was to go in the newspapers just in case he could not find a buyer by word of mouth.

That night Mayank called up.

'Dad, I spoke to Madhur Bhaiya yesterday.'

'What did he say?' Arvind asked.

'He says he has no other resources and he would need a house once he came back to Bangalore. That could be in six months or at the most in two years.'

'What is your opinion then?' he asked.

'Dad, if I had enough, I would have helped him. But you know my financial status.'

'Is he sure of settling in Bangalore?' Arvind asked.

'No, right now he says maybe, but he says that in any case it would be a good investment.'

'But that's being very selfish,' Arvind said, his voice livid with anger.

'Dad, don't worry. Even if he takes his share, you and Ma can continue living in my portion. I will come back to settle there once I retire. I have no plans of building a house here.' Mayank added.

Arvind kept the phone down even when Mayank was saying something. Mayank called up again immediately but no one picked up the phone.

Arvind and Yashoda spent a sleepless night. A division and a sale appeared inevitable now.

So, if they agreed to Madhur's plan, the Johri home would be split up into two, with the senior Johris set to retain one half and the other half up for sale. The sale money would then go to Madhur and Shelly, their share. An hour later, a tense Yashoda had taken two more diazepams and was asleep as Arvind took a piece of paper and a pencil and began sketching something on it. Purchasing that 1000 square yard of land had not been easy for Arvind. The requisite money had eaten into his entire savings and had even made Yashoda part with her jewellery. Madhur was in primary school and Mayank had just started school. The property had a great sentimental value for the elderly couple because it was hard earned.

How insensitive could Madhur be not to realise that? Did he not understand that Arvind could bequeath his property to anyone? Arvind wondered. He had taken it for granted that the property would be divided between him and his brother. While he could be forgiven for possessing such selfish thoughts, right now he was just bent upon snatching his share from the hands of his old parents; Arvind wondered.

He took out Madhur's letter from the drawer. At the back he drew a rectangle. This was not a corner house and therefore there was no way this house can be laterally bisected into two; he said to himself. The land was a roughly rectangular plot facing the road. A longitudinal slicing therefore, was out of question and a latitudinal one, though theoretically possible would imply that the Johris build a staircase in the air to have access to their own house! *I never imagined that this day would ever come in my life*, Arvind scribbled as he folded the letter and threw it inside the drawer. He wished he could shut up his reality inside the drawer, likewise. A solution had to emerge from somewhere.

That evening when Shweta came for the physiotherapy session, accompanied by Shashank, Arvind asked him if he had some time at his disposal.

Over a cup of tea, the two discussed the issue.

One of the ideas that emerged was that the back portion could be sold, after a new two room portion was constructed in the front for the two of them, with a common ten feet passage from the front gate, to be commonly used by occupants of both the parts.

'But then what about Mayank's share?' wondered Arvind.

Yashoda, who was listening to their conversation from the kitchen came with tea and said, 'Let's go to an ashram, maybe one in Haridwar will be good. Let the two of them take their shares now itself and be done with it.'

'No, why should we? We are not dependent on them in any way,' Arvind snapped.

Continuing his discussion with Shashank, he then asked, 'How much time do you think a contractor will take to build a new portion?'

'Not less than four to five months, I suppose,' Shashank said.

At this age, it was impossible for the two of them to get it done in the way they had done, many years ago. Besides he knew that hiring a contractor had its own hassles. Selling a floor was ruled out as there were not many interested in buying a floor by itself. A pie after all was always attractive when it was whole, not sliced.

An anxious and painful fortnight went by. Then one fine morning, Madhur was at the door unannounced. The Johris were conspicuously bereft of any joy; there was no trace of either happiness or surprise at his unexpected arrival. If anything was discernible, it was a twinge of sadness on their faces, as if a juror had arrived to finalise a will.

That afternoon, Yashoda overheard him speaking on the phone, 'It takes a little time, but I'm sure I'll do it.'

Over lunch, Arvind confronted him.

'What brings you here Madhur?'

'Dad I came for a conference in Ahmedabad. I thought I should come home and see you both.'

'Good that you thought about us. We are old. You never know, anything might happen,' he said tears welling up his eyes. 'What about your plan then?'

'Which plan dad?'

'The flat thing I mean?'

'Dad I thought you would understand. Anyway what will you do with such a big house? The two of you need two rooms at the most. Maintenance is also not easy, you know.'

'But then going by your logic …' Arvind stopped midway.

'Dad, you know that Shelly wants to settle down there in UK itself. I have managed to convince her that we will have our own flat in Bangalore with a lot of difficulty. And if this doesn't happen, I may have no reason to come back to India,' Madhur argued like a professional advocate.

'You mean to say that you have no other reasons to come back home? You have no attachment with your parents? You will not come back when we die?' Arvind was now trembling with anger.

'Finish your lunch. Your discussions can continue later,' an irritated Yashoda shouted from the kitchen.

That night Madhur skipped his dinner telling his mother, 'I had more than enough during the day.'

Over the next three days, father and son had angry animated discussions. Arvind had a simple logic; he was willing to sell the whole house if there had been a medical emergency or if Madhur had lost his job and needed money to start a business. But when there was nothing as alarming, it was absurd to sell a part of one's parental house to fund another house.

But Madhur refused to see reason. He remained adamant with his own logic that there was nothing wrong in his proposal. He remained perturbed and flustered, entering into arguments with his father even over issues not distantly related to the plot selling business. Yashoda had to intervene many times, telling him that '*this was not expected from a son like him and that raising his voice did not mean that he was right in the argument.*' The normally cool Arvind suppressed his anger, hid his emotions and bore the pain by accepting defeat at the end of every argument, locking himself up in a washroom for a few minutes to regain composure. That was important as Arvind knew that if he and his son indulged in mutual recriminations continually, as a mother and a wife Yashoda would be facing the greatest torment, selecting or siding with either of them.

He even offered to part with all the savings he had, but Madhur remained adamant that the amount would not suffice. This was a clever ploy as he knew that once he settled for the bargain, cleaning up his savings, all responsibilities and liabilities they had or those expected to arise in future would be his, and he, Madhur, would be bound to shoulder them.

Two days later, Arvind was still on his bed with a cup of tea in his hand, watching the morning news on TV, when the telephone rang. The phone ringing early morning made him sit up and run towards the phone as some real urgency could be the reason behind someone calling so early.

A person from Raipur wanted to know the details of his house vis-a-vis the plot dimensions, the number of rooms existing if any, the year of purchase et al. Unable to fathom as to how these facts were to be shared with an unknown person, he screamed into the phone, 'Wrong number!'

Five minutes later, the phone rang again and this time before Arvind could utter a word, the caller repeated the name and address of the person he wanted to speak to. Dr Arvind Johri, house number 1221 and he referred to some advertisement appearing in the newspapers that morning.

Too stunned to respond, he removed the receiver from his ears and kept it on the table, and walked away after disconnecting the call. He had kept the phone hung deliberately as he wanted to take no more calls. He opened the door and walked out. The newspaper rolled and tied with a thin brown string still lay in the porch. Today he felt no urgency to pick it up and quickly glance through the headlines. He moved towards the gate.

Beyond the road, he could see a group of parents standing with their children, waiting for the school bus. While the children stood talking with each other, planning which games they would play in the evening, the parents held their school bags and water bottles, unwilling to burden the slim shoulders with any load, as long as it was possible. Leaning on the gate, he watched the bus arrive, the children running towards it, the parents handing over the bags and bottles to the attendant. As the bus passed by his gate, some children waved to him. He responded, waving back to them cheerfully, as if he had known them for long.

He spent an hour in the lawn, walking around and then headed back towards his room. The newspaper roll was missing from the porch, but he could not remember seeing Yashoda pick it up.

As he passed by the dining space, he saw Madhur cutting out something from the newspaper. Quietly he went inside his room and switched on the TV again, the volume maximum.

Madhur was to be in India for three months. Arvind had overheard him telling someone on phone during the long conversations he would have, every night. Over the next fortnight, the phone would ring all through the day, even at odd hours in the night; perhaps some NRIs located in the other time zones were interested in his property. Madhur had taken upon himself the task of attending the calls after he had found that his father was not forthcoming in providing information about the property to the prospective buyers.

That night Arvind remained restless and fidgety. He tried to sleep but could not. Around midnight he woke Yashoda up.

'I am feeling unwell, see if I am running any temperature,' he said.

Yashoda lovingly caressed his forehead. 'No, there is no fever, it's normal. I think we should agree to what these children want. After all how many more years have we to live? Let them be happy. At least we will die in peace,' she said.

'Yes, I think you are right, let's go to Haridwar for some time,' Arvind said as he popped a painkiller.

They did not consult Madhur or thought it necessary to inform him of their plans. They were sure that for now, he was in total command of his ruthless avarice; everything else had been rendered secondary.

Next day Arvind called Madhur to his room.

'I think you want this money dearly and nothing else will suffice. Do as you wish, find out a buyer,' he said without any emotion.

Madhur nodded and went out of the room.

In the evening Arvind spoke on the phone after a long time, calling up Raju Taxi Service, to arrange for a taxi to drop them at the railway station.

These days Madhur had begun to have late dinner, long after his parents had retired for the day. Yashoda would call him, plead with him to join them for dinner at the table but he always found one excuse or the other, to avoid them. Yashoda would then leave the food in neatly arranged casseroles, along with plates, cutlery and a glass, all covered with crisp tissues, with a bottle of water, sometimes leaving little chits, 'Your favourite paneer sabji,' or 'mutton curry with potatoes' above the casserole. Madhur on his part would be peeved at these gestures and he would secretly think that these were indicators of 'senility and old age.'

Early next morning, as the Johris were all packed and ready, Madhur walked in and asked them, how long the trip would be.

On being told that it was still uncertain, he said something which Arvind couldn't hear.

'What did you say?'

'Dad, if you can give me a power of attorney.'

Arvind stared at him mutely, anger writ large on his face.

'Just in case, it's needed Dad, don't you worry, I won't do anything without your consent,' he added with a hesitant smile.

'But why on earth do you need that? I have already agreed to your proposal. You fix up your customer and inform me. I will be back the same day,' Arvind was angry.

'Dad, you should trust me. I promise I will not use it. Just it will be with me to lure the would be buyers.'

'Don't try to fool me Madhur. I don't trust you. And it is clear you don't trust me either.'

'I do, but …'

'What do you mean by but?' Arvind was livid, his anger red-hot.

'Ok. I'll give it to you. Yashoda let us delay our departure by a few hours. I will go to Mr Oberoi and get the attorney for him. Otherwise he won't let me live in peace in Haridwar also, selfish fellow that he is.'

He banged the door hard and walked out. Yashoda took off her shoes and lay on the bed again.

At Oberoi's chamber he poured his heart out. In front of someone who had been a very close friend of the Johris, he could keep no secret.

'I have an idea but it's not too great, Oberoi's eyes sparkled for a moment.

'What is it, let me know,' Arvind said.

'Let the land be sold. You don't say anything to your son …'

'Then what do we do with the idea?'

'See, the buyer will put the land to some use. The moment he begins building something, a guy comes and puts a case in the court saying that the land was his originally and the sale was illegal.

Then the case would go on for long. Ultimately the buyer will be so fed up that he will leave and go …. Or better still, I will buy in someone else's name …'

'No, no … no … we are old people. Let's not think of all this Oberoi. What is destined to happen will happen,' Arvind blushed with guilt at the mere discussion.

Arvind returned in an hour.

'Now let's go Yashoda,' he said.

'These sons … can be so heartless …. I never imagined,' she sighed.

'I hope when we return, we will at least have a room to live for the rest of our lives or do you plan to swallow it all leaving nothing for us or your brother?' Arvind said, handing over that green legal paper to Madhur as he got into the taxi to head to the station.

'When you leave, hand over the keys to Shashank Uncle,' he added as an afterthought.

'Dad, I wish you would understand,' was all Madhur had to say. Arvind and Yashoda did not even look at him. Madhur realised he had gained his share, but lost the love of his parents. But his short-sighted selfishness did not let him dwell on the loss.

'To the railway station, beta,' Arvind told the driver.

With the power of attorney handed over, there remained no reason for the old couple to think of returning home soon. If they could not bear to see something happen in front of their own eyes, it was better they stayed away. 'Out of sight, out of mind' Arvind would often say and then break out in laughter.

It was August now. The stay in the dharamshala at Haridwar had stretched to a month and the couple had no reasons to complain. The rent per day was meagre, just ₹ 50. And along with three meals it came to ₹ 250 per day. At the end of the month, they had paid all their dues and were discussing that it was not a bad proposition to continue. But that very night, after dinner, the manager of the dharamshala came to their room and enquired about the approximate duration of their stay. Although he did not reveal the reason behind his enquiries, casually telling them that the local police station had to be informed about all occupants who stayed for more than a month, Arvind was jolted out of his complacency. Now he had to make some alternate arrangements. Next day over lunch one of the kitchen attendants told him about availability of rooms on rent nearby with good facilities.

Within three days, they had zeroed in on a single room house partly furnished, with a kitchen having a gas stove, the room having two cots, a ceiling fan, a wooden table and two chairs. It looked so familiar to the set up the couple had when they had arrived in the city of Allahabad, in 1958, thirteen years after their marriage, when Arvind had to join in the medical college. Then, the house soon changed into a home. This was their temporary shelter not only from sun, wind, rain and storm but also from avalanches of memories that could come hurtling down the slopes of emotion, any day, any time, unannounced.

The Johris had more or less a fixed routine here. During the day they would explore the city, visit the temples, take a dip in the Ganga and attend evening arti at the banks. At night, the exertions would throw up aches and pains, but still they did not bother much. A few pills popped into the mouth would reduce them to manageable limits.

This was a vagabondism the old couple had come to terms with, even welcoming it as it took them far away, so far that the shadows of the unpleasant and bitter reality of life could not follow them.

Compared to their home, this one room set up did not need much maintenance. Within the room, the floor was visible only in two rectangular patches, of three feet by two and a half each; three paces outside the kitchen door and one was sure to land on the bed. Four paces on the other side of the bed was the attached bathroom, with a western style WC to boot. Arvind often joked that he and the landlord definitely were related in their previous birth, an invisible bond that had spilled on to this birth, resulting in a house tailor-made for him, being offered on rent at a time when he needed it the most. His belief had been further strengthened when the previous Sunday, a shy coy girl wrapped in sari, had been sent by the landlord, to enquire if they needed her services for any of their chores.

Yashoda was relieved. As it is, she had been finding it difficult to handle the kitchen on her own and washing utensils at the sink aggravated her back troubles every other day.

Arvind and Yashoda at times wondered if their destiny had contrived all the unpleasantness only to lead them to this doorstep of divinity.

As long as they managed to keep themselves afloat and sailed around in the bubble of spirituality, things were smooth. But at times, the bubble got pricked, causing them to fall down on the shifting sands of reality leading to heartburn. Whenever an unsuspecting acquaintance would get homesick and start discussing familial roots and branches, they would find themselves vulnerable being hit by pangs of separation and of the scarcity of love in their lives. Days continued to roll by, with the two lonely souls managing to stand erect every time they stumbled and tripped over the sandbanks of their emotions. One day, around Diwali, Arvind mustered enough courage to call up Shashank, wanting to confirm if the 'sale' had already taken place. Deep within, he was sure, that the thing he dreaded, must have already taken place and it was only a question of how well prepared he was to handle the moment of truth.

'The front portion has been sold to someone, I have heard, a gentleman by the name of … Lid…' Shashank said hesitantly.

But for Arvind, the line had been disconnected after the word *sold* had reached his ears. He did keep the receiver glued to his ear but nothing registered in his mind. Eventually he managed to say 'Goodbye Professor' and left a hundred rupee note at the PCO counter, rushing off, not bothering to collect the change. The man on the chair behind that L shaped desk, called for him, but he had gone deaf and no sounds were able to register in his brain even if they managed to get beyond his eardrums.

Any thoughts of returning home soon, had been put to rest for the Johris.

It was the winter of 1992. With the month of December round the corner, a mild chill was discernible even during the day time. The sun was mellowing now, a shadow of its old self, packing lesser punch, dimmer in both heat and light. While day broke much later, evenings fell quite early. A little beyond tea time and it would be quite dark. Shweta had been desperately trying to track Udit's friend, Narayan, ever since Ajit Mama had confided in her that he had caught a fleeting glimpse of him at the airport last March. She had been trying to call at an old telephone number, scribbled in pencil at the back of Udit's wooden almirah, assuming that the prefix N, indicated Narayan. Luck had eluded her always, as the call was never through.

The previous Sunday Shashank was at Nazareth Hospital to undergo a minor procedure for removal of gall bladder stones. There, a quirky twist of fate had ensured that she met a distant aunt of hers, Bimla Mausi, in the hospital corridor. The two had a headlong collision as Mausi was hastily walking out of a ward but was facing sideways giving a mouthful to a wardboy. Shweta in her motorised wheelchair was going towards the surgery ward, in that same corridor. Highly embarrassed at the collision, she had burst into laughter, which had attracted more people than her comic fall. It had taken a few moments for Shweta to realise that it was none other than Bimla Mausi.

That was typical Mausi; bold, daring and willing to take on anyone who dared ill treat a suffering and weak person. Here she had heard the wardboy curse an old man as he had soiled his bedsheet.

Once they had met, Mausi's hurry had evaporated as she dutifully came over to the private ward where Shashank was recuperating and spent the next two hours talking, gossiping and laughing; the three things she enjoyed most.

Not one to mince words or be diplomatic or shrewd or even as polished as a city-bred person was expected to be, she remained rustic and blunt. 'Any progress in Udit's case?' she had whispered into Shweta's ears, taking advantage of the moments of privacy the two had, when the nurse on duty had arrived to give Shashank an injection. Her sullen pout had conveyed to her that there was no good news on that front.

The arrival of the doctor for checkup had provided them another three minutes of privacy. This she had utilised to provide some precious information, 'Narayan's parents still live in the same house, three houses away from mine, where they were once tenants.' Two years ago they had purchased the house, through Narayan's savings. Supposedly, the last time she had seen Narayan himself, was sometime around Holi. Shweta could not doubt the authenticity of her information, for Mausi was distantly related to Narayan from his father's side.

Bimala Mausi was an enigma to many. Estranged from her husband five years after marriage, she had dared to live an independent life, at a time when a single woman living by herself was unheard of in their society. Garrulous and selectively extrovert by nature, she lived life one day at a time and remained happy. With regards to her own life, she had nothing much to discuss. In a good mood she would laugh at herself, saying that she was the only one of her kind created in this world.

Brought up in an orphanage, since the age of ten, life had been more than a struggle for her. The brief period she had spent with her husband had been an aberration, which she dubbed in hindsight as a good riddance. Free of any encumbrances, she enjoyed the luxury of living her life on her own terms, never bothering what the world around had to say. In her early sixties now, she had zealously guarded that thin veil of secrecy around her persona and mockingly disdainful of the opinions that were hurled at her by wagging tongues. The only thing she appeared fleetingly possessive about was the house she had built over the years, room by room and brick by brick, transforming the minimalistic tin roofed two room set that had been bequeathed to her. Her inheritance was more by default than anything else.

She had no idea about the whereabouts of the man she had married, though people told her that legally he remained her husband even then. She had not known that there existed something called separation at the time she had been left behind, as an eighteen year old married woman. What many around her termed as a colossal loss, she was herself unsure if it was a loss at all. At the age when she was married off she had been utterly naive, believing the institution of marriage to be an extrapolation of her childhood games, with dolls and dollhouses. The seriousness dawned on her when her thin and tender frame was repeatedly exploited by that man, more in lust than in love. Her days were more comfortable when the crowd of her in-laws ensured that she stayed away from the clutches of that man. Every morning at the call of the rooster she would begin the tedious household chores—cooking, washing, mopping, bathing the dozen odd kids of varying sizes—dutifully shouldering everyone's burden to appease and gain acceptance in the new family. Whether the family had indeed accepted her or not, she never got to know, for the man who had accepted her, by putting vermillion on her forehead in front of the sacred fire, surrounded by so many witnesses, had broken free of her life one fine morning.

This was all that people knew of her.

It was the first week of December. Late into the night, around 1:30 am the phone in the Joshi home started ringing. Shashank initially thought that it was a false ring and remained in bed but when the ringing was persistent he picked it up. His brother Pranav calling from Bindki at this unearthly hour worried him.

'Everything fine Pranav?' he asked before he could hear anything.

'No, I rang because Ma is not well. Her condition is critical.' Before Pranav could complete the sentence or Shashank could ask anything further, the phone got disconnected.

Shashank had still been recuperating at home, the stitches in his abdomen were still painful. But, the message from the village made him forget all his discomfort. Nervous, he thought of calling Pranav again, to confirm, but could not move. His legs trembled and the muscles numbed due to fear. He knew that critical had no meaning. In a place like Bindki only basic medical facilities were available and that too at the PHC at block headquarters, which was ten kilometres away. Here the doctors were found only on pay days or when some VVIP came visiting. For the rest of the period, two nurses, a mid-wife and a junior doctor remained on duty.

The junior doctor, though highly respected for his devotion towards duty, could only treat minor ailments like fever, cough and cold, stomach aches or diarrhoea. In a primary health centre such as this, proper treatment meted out to a patient who had been admitted in a critical state was unthinkable.

Shashank was ready to take the first bus to Bindki. Bina knew that the matter was serious and wanted to accompany Shashank. They thought of taking Shweta along but Bina realised that it would be difficult for Shweta to manage in the village home particularly because the washroom was located quite far away in the courtyard and that too with an Indian style lavatory. In the crowd of relatives that were expected to be there at this time, it would be very difficult for her to take care of Shweta's special needs. Moreover, leaving the house locked, without a caretaker, was not very advisable either.

'Let Shweta be here, she would have difficulty in the village as the rituals will require us to bathe at the family well daily and also frequently go here and there.' Shashank said.

'But how will she stay here alone? Had Sonam and Anup been in Calcutta, we could have called them over but they are so far away, in America,' he added as he wiped his spectacles on his shirt sleeves.

'Don't worry, I will call Mrs Dev and request her to come and stay with Shweta.' She immediately picked up the phone and called her.

A known nightworm, Mrs Dev was awake and active, creating poems and stories about beautiful sunrises and sunsets and silver sea beaches in the dead of the night. She readily agreed to come over and stay with Shweta during the period of their absence.

'Beta, don't tell anything to Sonam if she calls. She will start worrying,' Shashank told Shweta as he gave her a hug and an affectionate pat on the back.

As Shashank and Bina shut the gate behind them, they found Savita hurriedly walking towards them. She didn't ask anything but gave them a quizzical look.

'Mrs Rai in the lane behind had asked me to come early but their house is locked. Probably they have not returned from the marriage party they went to attend yesterday night,' she clarified on her own trying to justify her early arrival.

'Ma is serious, we are going home. Please take care of Shweta,' Bina said as she adjusted her suitcase on the rickshaw's footrest.

'Memsahib, don't worry, I'll take care of Didi.'

'Mrs Dev will be here with her. If you take care of the cooking and other chores, it would be of huge help. Just see that she is not burdened.' Bina pleaded.

'Don't worry, I am here and in case Mrs Dev doesn't come, I will stay on, for sure, till you return,' she assured.

'And yes, Shweta, Ajit Mama is also expected this week, I think. I'm forgetting the exact date,' she said, hoisting the grey bag on to her shoulder.

Feeling relieved at Savita's presence, Shashank and Bina left for the bus stand.

Shweta felt lonely and upset at the sudden turn of events in Bindki. It was around 10:00 am when the phone rang again. It was Mrs Dev on the line. She had called to inform that her sister's family had turned up from Mumbai, unannounced, to surprise her on her birthday, the day after and that she would not mind if Shweta joined her at her place instead. She also said that she would send her car to pick her up and that Shweta should pack up and be ready. Politely refusing the offer, Shweta told her that she would let her know after sometime.

Savita overheard the conversation. Seeing that Shweta looked worried she immediately said, 'Didi, I will get my kids here and stay with you.'

'Will your husband agree?'

'Why not? I will convince him, Didi.'

Savita left in a few minutes, promising to return in an hour. Not knowing what to do alone, Shweta wandered into her father's study. Adversity sometimes threw up strange opportunities; she knew. She stared at the book rack overflowing with books and old diaries. She had been looking for something that she knew lay hidden amongst his vast collection of books, an elusive diary.

Why not look for the diary now she thought.

Knowing her dad's possessive nature, she had never dared to fiddle with his books. Even when he was not around, Shweta was sure that if she removed even a single book from its place and replaced it at the same place, Shashank on his return would immediately come to know that someone had tampered with his books. But today she was determined to go ahead.

An hour and a half later Savita returned, with her baby daughter and son in tow. A handbag stuffed with clothes, a bed sheet and a tube of tooth paste was all they had brought along. She settled both the kids on the carpet in the living room and switched on the TV, asking them not to move while she did her work.

Meanwhile Shweta had shuffled all the books on the two lower shelves and unable to reach the ones above, called out to Savita who rushed out from the bathroom, her hands still coated with soap.

'Please get those books down for me,' Shweta said.

Savita looked at her wet hands and then wiping them with the end of her sari, she climbed on a stool to bring down all the books from the two top shelves.

'When Sahib returns you better not take my name,' she smiled and went out.

'I need to do something to kill time. Let me wipe these books clean. Please get me a rag, Savita,' she implored.

Shweta wiped each book and then holding each by its spine, dusted off the dirt that had accumulated at the margins. Books were always an attraction for her; the peculiar smell of print always fascinated her. A little later, the hillocks of books had been flattened to manageable plateaus, each carefully labelled with the shelf and the sequence arranged from front to back. However, the treasure trove had not yet thrown up the thing she was looking for. Having decided to make the most of the opportunity, she called Savita again.

'Should I now keep them back?' she enquired.

'Oh yes!' Shweta hurriedly began handing over the books, checking the order for each shelf. This exercise consumed two hours of their time.

'Didi, should I now get you something to eat?' Savita asked.

'A little later maybe. Right now I don't feel like eating,' Shweta said.

'Can you get that carton down?' She asked, pointing to the brown cardboard carton stacked at the top of the Godrej Almirah on the opposite side.

'But, Didi, it's too high for me! Anyway, let me see.' Savita pulled the stool, stood on it and tried reaching it, but it was still a hand span away.

She then called her son and hoisted him up on the almirah. 'Now give me the books inside that carton, one by one.'

The little one sat down on his haunches and began placing the books one by one into his mother's outstretched hands. At last, Shweta found the elusive little gem which had she had been searching for a long time. 'Everything that the Lord Almighty does, has a hidden design' she remembered Granny saying, whenever she came across an unpleasant situation. Shweta now held her prized possession in her hands and peered into it as Savita prepared to leave the room with her son.

'Tomorrow morning we will hoist the carton up again,' she declared and left for the kitchen.

It was late evening when Savita ran to pick up the phone in the drawing room. There could be some important message from Memsahib, she thought.

But the lady on the phone was someone else. 'Some Bimla Mausi is there on the phone, Didi. She wants to speak to you,' she said.

'Hello! Shweta dear, I saw Narayan at the grocery shop yesterday. I thought I should share the news with you,' she said without any preamble.

'Mausi, did you speak to him?' Shweta asked.

'No, he does not recognise me.' That was a very polite way of telling her that Narayan perhaps was unwilling to acknowledge her publicly.

'Doesn't matter mausi,' she almost whispered into the phone, her voice choking. Rest of the conversation she could not remember as she kept the receiver back.

She was overcome by a wave of conflicting emotions, a strange mix of happiness, anxiety, thrill and fear. She was saddened at her physical limitation, but she could not wish it away. Half an hour of turmoil was followed by a relative calm, during which she thought what she could do with the information that Bimla Mausi had provided. Could she wait for Shashank to return or would it be too late then? What if Narayan left? Maybe this was her only chance and looking at the complete absence of luck in their lives, she made up her mind to do something right now. She rang up Sushil Taxi Service immediately and booked a taxi for the following day.

Sleep was a far cry when she went to bed. On a folding cot in the same room, lay Savita with her kids.

She switched on the reading lamp by her bedside and took out her hidden treasure. It was a blue coloured hard bound diary, with the year 1982 inscribed in gold.

Her hands trembled as she opened the first page. Udit Joshi, in black ink, was the only entry among all the columns printed on the first page; there was no address nor details, absolutely nothing else. The whole of January had no entry. February onwards, had some hurried scribbles. Books to be purchased, notes to be made, birthdays of some friends, schedule of some cricket matches were visible, but almost illegible. However, the details of pocket money received every month were entered quite lucidly.

March … amount received ₹ 250 only, was circled in red pen, with the date 3 March, 1982, Wednesday, underlined.

Under the expenses column, he had written:

Cold drinks party at school – ₹ 35

Wallet from Shiv leathers – ₹ 55

Birthday gift for Narayan – ₹ 120
A woollen scarf for Granny – ₹ 45
Total exp = ₹ 255

And the total expenses had been highlighted with a fluorescent yellow, flanked by two question marks in red.

More or less similar entries filled the other pages, with some entries restricted to single or twin words, written in a stylish and calligraphic hand; the words themselves 'oh why', 'as always,' 'no never', 'really great', 'how mean'.... were quite puzzling.

Perplexed by the nature of the entries, Shweta drifted into sleep and the diary lay open on the bed beside her.

Next morning, it was only when the taxi had arrived at the gate that Shweta realised that it was going to be difficult for her to manage the trip alone. She mulled over the options available to her and then asked Savita, 'Would you like to come along with me?'

'Why not? I will drop my kids at home on the way,' she said and started adjusting the pleats of her sari.

'But who will look after them at home?'

'My mother-in-law is there.'

As the taxi sped away towards the congested lanes of Rambagh, Shweta chewed at her finger nails, worried what would happen next. She was going in search of the first link that could help her put together some other pieces of the puzzle that could lead to her brother one day.

Not too far away, in the city of Lucknow, there were many chewing their nails in the corridors of power. Something unprecedented was happening in the holy city of Ayodhya, an event that would have immediate repercussions in terms of law and order in the state, many had begun to predict.

The taxi stopped on the road, supposedly in front of Narayan's house, as Shweta remembered the house number Bimla Mausi had told that day. The name plate at the gate read J.P. Singh. Shweta had faint memories of Narayan's parents having seen them during her visits to attend Narayan's younger sister's birthday. As she waited at the gate, she was nervous and acutely self-conscious. She knew that now nobody would recognise her here. Unsure if they would let her in, she remembered God, steeled herself and decided to give it a try. She adjusted herself in the chair, clipped the hair pin, tied her hair again and took a deep breath, ready to face the moment of truth as Savita rang the doorbell.

It had been a full ten minutes, since the two had been waiting.

Finally she could see that someone had removed the curtains just a wee bit and had peeped through the drawing room window. A little later a strapping young boy of around nineteen or twenty emerged.

With a baffled expression, he asked, 'Whom do you want to meet? If you are here for some survey, there is no one here to answer your questions.' He was as blunt as a gawky teenager could be.

'I am here to meet Narayan Bhaiya's mother,' Shweta managed to say despite the cold reception. The boy now looked a little relaxed and smiled a bit, trying hard to be polite after hearing his brother's name.

'Please come in,' he showed them the way and turned to open the door for the chair to be wheeled in.

'Tell Auntie that Udit's sister Shweta has come.'

The boy returned in two minutes but this time he looked more bewildered than he was earlier.

Sensing his discomfort Shweta, said, 'If Auntie is busy, we can always come later.'

'No, she is confined to bed right now. If you don't mind, you can come inside and meet her.'

They were ushered inside a dimly lit room. A frail lady lay on the bed, looking weak but not ill. The expression on her face changed as she turned over to face the guests.

'Oh Shweta, so good to see you after so many years. You came for Nidhi's birthday always, I remember. Narayan always talked about how you ran way with their books and pens and hid them all over the place, when they studied together during examination days,' she continued.

Shweta prepared herself to ask the most important question but suddenly Narayan's mother said, 'I had a fall in the bathroom, three days ago and there is a fracture in my back. The doctors say it can't be put into a cast, so I have to lie still like this on the bed for three weeks and allow it to heal.' Shweta wondered if she needed to tell her own story, how that little girl and her pranks she was so fondly recollecting had been pranked by destiny one fine day. But for the time being, she preferred to keep mum.

'Narayan Bhaiya ...' she had just uttered, when Narayan walked in, a bag slung across his shoulder.

'May you have a long life!' his mother looked relieved and happy, 'Shweta was just taking your name.'

He looked around, flummoxed; he could not recognise Shweta. He tried hard to smile and appear friendly, using the moments to recollect, who she could be? Maybe someone distantly related dropping in to see his mother, he thought. Then he picked up a magazine from the table.

'Narayan Bhaiya are you in contact with Udit Bhaiya?' Shweta suddenly asked.

The mere mention of the name had startled him. The magazine in his hand fell down. He stared at the lady in the wheelchair, a bit awkwardly. He had known that Udit had two sisters and though there had not been much interaction, he had seen them in the house and had fond memories of the younger one wanting the same pen, the same eraser, even note books of the same colour and make as Udit possessed. But could that lady in the wheelchair be one of the sisters, he wondered.

'I am sorry, my memory fails me,' he said rather apologetically; trying to justify the rather cold vibes he had till then shown towards the two visitors to his house.

'In the beginning he had called me a few times, but he never gave his contact number. I asked him so many times and tried to convince him, but he was then in no mood to listen. I thought that it was his initial anger that was blinding him to reality and once that subsided he would realise his fault and return home.'

His expression had totally changed in the last few seconds.

'He sent me a letter once ….' he then got up and went inside, leaving the sentence unfinished.

A few minutes of uneasy silence followed during which they could clearly hear the news on television in the other room with the newsreader saying 'parts of the state are tense; adequate forces are being rushed to take care of any eventuality. There is an apprehension that riots could break out in some parts of old Lucknow and …'

They waited for Narayan to return.

Narayan's mother looked tense. Narayan reappeared holding an old inland in his hand, the blue margins had faded to a dirty yellow, and silverfish had also feasted upon it generously. He handed it over to Shweta. She held it in her hand for a minute, unable to read anything. It was filled with his beautiful handwriting, a right slanted running hand in black ink filled the two adjacent sides. The last page was empty.

'Ma, I will get your medicines from the market and also fruits and vegetables, you never know,' the younger brother said and went away, the urgency clearly visible both in his voice as well as his steps.

'Didi, let's go home, anything might happen anytime, we will be stranded,' Savita almost begged. Shweta looked at her watch. It was 5:45 pm and the sun had set. It was getting dark.

'Just a few minutes, we have a vehicle, don't worry,' Shweta said.

She quickly glanced at the postage on the inland. The name of the district was illegible, the print had faded. But the state was clear, it was from Madhya Pradesh.

She sighed. *Of all the states, this letter had to come from such a big state! We would get no clue from this. Even the CID will take a decade to track someone hiding in such a big state.*

Narayan nodded his head in agreement. The younger brother meanwhile had returned.

'Bhaiya people in the bazaar say curfew has been imposed in some parts of the city. The streets are full of policemen.'

'Ok then we too need to hurry home. We will meet sometime again.' Shweta took their leave and beckoned Savita to move out.

'Feel free to call me any time.' Narayan added and followed the two to the gate.

As they came out and walked into the market ahead the people looked hassled and panicky. The shopkeepers were downing their shutters even as customers stood around to make purchases. Fear was palpable in the atmosphere. And there was no trace of the taxi and the driver that had brought Shweta and Savita.

'Didi, looks like the taxi driver has run away. What will we do?' Savita was terrified. They waited by the side of the road, just a furlong away from Narayan's home in the hope that a rickshaw or an auto would pass and they would soon be home.

Shweta was tense A few drops of sweat appeared on her forehead even in that cold evening.

Minutes turned into an hour, they did not know what to do and where to go. The sole PCO across the road had a long queue of people making calls. Shweta thought of calling the taxi service, but she had left her diary at home and did not remember the number. While they were mulling over the options, the PCO owner hurriedly downed his shutter and vanished into the crowd.

The watch on Shweta's wrist showed 7.30 pm and the road was completely deserted. They both knew that they were in for real trouble.

'Should we go and ask Narayan Bhaiya for help?' Savita asked.

'What help can he offer?'

'Perhaps, he will allow us to spend the night in the safety of his home.' Savita was now really scared, but before they could move ahead, out of the darkness, there sprang out a swarm of people running, shrieking and falling over one another.

Savita showed some quick presence of mind. She opened the gate of the house just behind them and pushing the wheelchair inside, frantically shut it behind her. A power breakdown followed, plunging the entire area into darkness. The compound within which Shweta and Savita had taken shelter was unusually quiet. They waited in a dark corner by the gate hiding behind the mango tree. Ten minutes passed by. Shweta was scared, though outwardly she put up a brave face.

Suddenly a door sprung open and they could see a lean figure wrapped in a shawl, walk towards the gate. Perhaps she had come to lock her gate, Shweta thought.

From a distance, she asked, 'What are you both doing here in this darkness?'

Words were stuck in Shweta's throat. Her heart pounded heavily. She wondered if Savita could hear her hammering beats. Savita, standing behind her, shivered in fear.

'Sorry by mistake we entered the wrong house in the darkness,' Shweta somehow managed to say and began wheeling towards the gate.

Savita was already at the gate and was out in a flash. Shweta had followed her out and was about to get on to the road, when one of the wheels of her chair got stuck on the uneven pavement. The chair turned turtle, hurtling her down on the road. The loud thud made Savita turn with a scream, 'Oh Didi! What will we do now'?

The lady who was still at the gate, struggling to put the right key in the lock heard the loud thud and came out.

She suddenly exclaimed, 'Oh no! I can't believe this! It's you, Shweta!' Her tone changed in a flash.

'Come in, quick! I am so sorry, dear …' she repeated as she gently pushed Shweta's chair from behind. Savita followed them, unable to understand the reason for the turnaround.

A candle flickered inside a glass in the drawing room. It was only when they had settled down and Shweta addressed her as Bimla Mausi, that Savita realised that the lady was known to Shweta. A new lease of life had been injected into the two figures who had stood petrified underneath the mango tree till a few minutes ago.

'Strange are the ways of Almighty!' Mausi's voice reverberated across the room.

Looking upwards towards the ceiling, she continued, 'What a quirk of fate! You were destined to arrive at my home like this, Shweta! And what a welcome I had for you!' she sighed deeply, as expressions of repentance appeared on her face.

'Both of you please stay back here for the night. It's unsafe to go out.'

'Who else stays with you, Mausi?' Shweta asked trying to initiate some conversation after she returned with some tea and snacks.

Getting a bit uncomfortable, she picked up her thick plait and tied a bun at the top of the head. 'I don't have any blood relatives as you know, whom I can call mine, you see …' A long pause followed. 'Or I should say that I'm a unique creation of God. …. When my own left me at the mercy of this society, I found so many like me that with the passage of time they have all become mine.' Mausi continued after a brief pause. 'The rooms above are occupied by girls who have come here to study or those who arrive in the city for work, interviews and exams and have no money to stay in dharamshalas or hotels. I don't charge them a rupee but they are free to donate if they have enough,' she pointed to a wooden box on the table.

'But, nobody believes what I say,' a strange impish smile lurked on her face. Shweta was unsuspecting.

By dinner time, she could hear the chattering of many girls. The kitchen was just behind the drawing room.

A young girl brought food in two white melamine plates for Shweta and Savita.

It was way past midnight. The sound of silence filled the room. The candle in the glass had blown out long back and the room was pretty dark.

'Didi, we will go home early in the morning,' Savita said.

'Yes we will, don't worry.'

Suddenly a clanging sound of the gate caught their attention

Savita got up and peeped through the curtains. Two young men were getting inside, with a young girl.

'Some people are coming in!' Savita was scared. 'Didi, who are these people, coming and going in the darkness of the night?' she whispered.

'Didn't Mausi say that many girls stay here. Just a few hours and we will go home.'

The whole night people kept coming and going in that house.

It was still pretty dark. Savita, an early riser, sat on a chair near the window, impatiently waiting for the day to break. The wall clock showed 6:00 am.

Finishing off with the morning ablutions, they waited for Bimla Mausi to emerge. An hour had passed and it was 7.30. Buttery rays of the sun were peeping in from the space in between the curtains.

'I think, we should leave,' said Savita as she hurried towards the kitchen to find out if Mausi was around.

'Mausi is not here, she has gone for some important work,' a girl looking somewhat upset, informed Savita.

'Didi, please let's go from here, now,' Savita pleaded.

'Right. Please convey my regards to Mausi,' Shweta told the girl.

Out on the street, the shops were still closed. The tiny hole-in-the-wall tea shops which would normally be crowded with tea seekers by now, were also shut. Only street dogs roamed around, puzzled at the unusually quiet morning. Savita was excited on spotting two rickshaws parked near one of the shops, chained to the telephone pole on the road but the rickshaw pullers were missing. Their normal abodes, the front platforms and verandas of the closed shops were all vacant. They waited in a corner of the market.

The nervous wait seemed to have no end in sight.

'Didi, let's go to Narayan Bhaiya and ask for help. Let's not delay any more. If things get worse we will be in a soup, yet again. It's not good for us to roam around like this,' Savita was firm.

Reluctantly, they again went to Narayan's house and knocked.

'Please come in,' Narayan said, opening the door..

Sensing that their early arrival had put the family in discomfort, Shweta immediately said, 'Bhaiya we are stuck up here since yesterday. Please help us get home.'

'Oh! is it? Where were you in the night? Don't worry, you are safe now.'

Narayan called up three taxi services, but to no avail. No drivers had reported for duty that day. Public transport always became a casualty whenever a curfew was clamped in the old city.

Narayan was in a dilemma. He knew that now it was his responsibility to escort his friend's sister home safely.

'Relax both of you, I will drop you home. Let me get some tea for everyone,' he said and went in.

His mother was surprised to see them again.

Shweta herself began, 'Auntie, we couldn't go home yesterday as the taxiwala ran away. We were lucky that we found shelter at Bimla Mausi's place otherwise God knows what was in store for us.'

Auntie's jaw dropped, 'You mean, *there*?!'

Shweta wondered at the emphasis she laid on the word there.

Narayan standing with the tea tray looked at the surprised faces.

'No problem have tea first.'

His mother remained quiet. Narayan then picked up his helmet and asked Savita to help Shweta on to the scooter behind him before she herself rode pillion. The wheelchair would occupy a corner of the house for the time being and he promised that he would ensure that it reached her as early as possible.

As planned, Ajit Mama landed in Delhi around noon. Booked in the Prayag Raj express at 9:30 in the evening, he had decided not to get into a hotel but wait at the station, in the waiting room itself.

In the waiting room, he found company. The gentleman who came and occupied the chair next to him had also landed in Delhi early morning that day, when it was still dark and foggy. He too had to board the same train and de-board at the same station!

He was there to have a look at a plot of land he had bought a few months back, rather one his son had bought for him through a power of attorney. His name was K. Liddle.

The two gossiped for an hour or so. Then keeping their luggage in the cloak room they took an auto to Connaught Place to have lunch and just stroll around to kill time.

The two got along really well and the hours passed by quickly. Mr Liddle and Ajit Mama were now on board the Prayag Raj Express. Though it had started from New Delhi at the scheduled time of 9:30 pm the previous day, it had been delayed by two hours for some unknown reason.

Mr Liddle and Ajit Mama walked towards the canteen at the platform, wanting to have a cup of tea together before heading towards their destinations. Mr Liddle had booked a hotel for himself. They were still waiting for tea to arrive when the announcements on the public address system caught their attention. The areas of the city that had been placed under curfew were being repeated again and again. Hotel Sanskar was located in one such area. The succeeding announcements listed out the timings when the curfew was to be relaxed in each of the areas to facilitate the residents fetch essential commodities like milk, vegetables, etc. By his watch, he had to wait for an hour and a half, till 10:30, after which he could easily make it to the hotel in a fully reserved taxi, plying now at exorbitant rates. A worried Liddle gulped down his tea and waited for Ajit Mama to finish his.

Once out of the canteen, the two men were surrounded by a bunch of taxi drivers, trying to persuade them to take a ride. Liddle was a little edgy and nervous, trying to call at the hotel to get some information about the situation there. He had no engagement at the hotel itself and he saw no point in getting to the hotel to remain trapped within its four walls. He called up another hotel located in the curfew free Civil Lines area but the rooms there were full, a marriage party being stuck there for two days. Ajit Mama had sensed his discomfort and offered him a stay at his sister's place, till the situation improved. Liddle politely refused and decided to take the evening train back to Delhi, if he managed to book a return ticket. Ajit then waited at the platform, taking care of his own and Liddle's luggage, as he waited in the queue. Half an hour of wait was futile as no tickets were available in any of the AC coaches for the evening train.

'Now, you please come with me,' Mama was assertive.

'Okay. Let's go, then.'

All three of them, Ajit Mama, Liddle and the taxi driver who was sure to earn some quick bucks, early in the morning, set out for the destination.

Shweta meanwhile had put her 'Operation Search' in suspended animation for the time being. Savita had rushed home after returning. In fact her husband was there outside the gate and was seen agitatedly pacing up and down the road. Seeing the two of them return with Narayan, he was relieved and had walked over to lend a helping hand. Savita had immediately taken leave, citing her little children back home, but Shweta knew that it was her husband who was the root cause of her angst, for he did not seem to take their night out quite sportingly.

'You forgot that you have little kids to look after. I came looking for you in the night and found the house locked. You didn't tell me that you might have to stay for the night.'

Shweta had heard him say as Savita had settled on the backseat of the bicycle, pleading, 'Hear me out first, don't be angry, I was …'

Shweta, knew that now there was a next to nil chance of her returning soon. The thought of staying alone in the house had alarmed her, but there was nothing else she could do. She thought of calling Mrs Dev, but then decided otherwise.

That diary meanwhile came back to haunt her. She lay on her bed and flipped through the pages once again. The entries had a similar trend. One of the entries read-

Monthly pocket money – 00.00

Expenses

Books – ₹ 135.00

Bicycle repair – ₹ 25.00

Cough syrup – ₹ 15.50

Total – ₹ 175.50

And by the side of a great circle drawn around the total figure, stood a 'PS. No thanks to my dearest G.'

The entries made Shweta read between the lines as the unspoken message was loud and clear. There was something that tormented him deeply. Outwardly, one could find no reason for his despondency or the subtle trauma that his writings reflected. However, deep within him, there existed a multitude of reasons, a tangle of resentment and anguish that had forced him to take the decision to escape from life. Beneath his cheerful exterior, there lay a hardened crust of melancholy that might have been punctured on that day. She continued with the reading, her eyes filled with tears at some of the heart breaking entries. In two hours, she had almost reached the year end.

Just then, some faint noise at the door distracted her. A little scared, she peeped through the window.

Two men with their backs towards her, were animatedly discussing something.

Since her motorised chair had been left behind and her old manual one had rusted and was not moving smoothly, she had asked Savita to lock the front door from outside and hand her the keys from the window. In case some close acquaintance knocked, she would hand over the key from the window, letting the person in. This was her plan.

'Wonder who has come at this time of the day!' she said to herself and pulled the rusted wheelchair close to her bed.

Before she could shift onto the chair, sound of luggage being stacked near the door made her nervous and she again peeped through the window.

'Oh, my God!'

How could she forget that it was December 7 and Ajit Mama was expected to arrive?

'Mamaji,' she shouted like a child, from across the window. 'Here are the keys. Please open the door and come in.'

Shweta struggled to pull her chair towards the drawing room. Ajit Mama had come inside her room.

'Where has everyone gone?' he asked.

He never expected to find Shweta alone in the house.

'Daddy and Ma have gone out for some urgent work, Mama.'

'What is so urgent that they had to leave you alone and go?' he asked in disbelief.

'Mama I will let you know everything by and by. Please sit down and be comfortable first.'

'Shweta, meet my friend, Mr Liddle from US. We met at Delhi railway station, and found out that we were heading to the same place. By the way where is the chair you were using earlier?'

'Oh Mama! Please hold your questions for a while,' she smiled and diverted the topic.

Mr Liddle, at 65, looked very fit and agile for his age. Dressed in a navy blue suit with a purple and gold cravat and a stylish hat, he looked regal and aristocratic. When he opened his mouth, the first words that sprung out were, 'Hello, young lady, how do you do?' He then extended his hand towards Shweta for a handshake. The warmth he exuded with his words and the accent he was blessed with had blown away any thoughts that were creeping into Shweta's mind about an unknown guest landing at her place.

'I hope you don't mind if I help myself to some water?' he asked, moving towards the dining table.

Shweta rued that her sharp memory had ditched her on the most important day. This little slip on her part could have landed Mama in a soup, had she not been awake and sitting near the window. The events of the day before, had tired her both physically and mentally and had it not been Udit's diary that she had been reading, she would have slept off and then even a bomb going off in the vicinity would not have awakened her, leave alone the ring of a doorbell!

Her initial euphoria at Mama's arrival vanished as she realised that she had no helping hands. Savita was not there, Chandan Kaka was not there. Cooking was not impossible but it was definitely inconvenient. Had it been only Mama, she could have managed with bread, butter, eggs, Maggi noodles and the fruits that she had stocked at home. She did not have much time in hand and she had to lay breakfast on the table with whatever she had. The electric kettle and egg boiler that Bina had set on the table in the dining area came to her rescue.

Without much fuss and to her pleasant surprise, she found that she had managed to serve a decent breakfast to the guests! While

Mama and Liddle enjoyed the meal, she sipped her tea slowly, thinking about lunch.

'Dear lady, don't worry, I am your mama number two, not a guest and I don't feel like a guest too. I feel as if I have known Mr Ajit for years, perhaps we were related in some other birth?' he said sounding typically like her granny, whom Shweta had recently lost.

Suddenly, she could picture her granny sitting on the chair in front of her, telling her that whatever happens in life is predestined. Man is a mere puppet in the hands of destiny. The lines ingrained in our palms, carry the minute pieces of the great puzzle of life, which we try and put together with our actions and deeds. We all succeed in solving the puzzle ultimately, when we look back and connect the dots. Her eyes welled up remembering Granny, but the time was not yet right for divulging the news to Ajit Mama, she thought to herself.

The ring of the doorbell broke Shweta's trance. It was Savita's elder sister, Sunita, at the door.

'Savita has sent me here to help you out with cooking and household chores for the next couple of days.'

Sunita, a thin figure, wrapped in a bright green printed sari, with the *pallu* around her head, was stunningly similar to Savita, in appearance. Shweta heaved a sigh of relief. Sunita could not have come at a better time.

It was only after lunch that Shweta broke the sad news of Granny's demise to Mama. Mama immediately picked up the phone and called up Bina not only to offer his condolences but also to assure her that he was there to take care of everything and she should not worry. 'Certain things in life are predestined,' he observed and concluded with, 'see how my journey to India has taken place in such turbulent times!'

Over evening tea, Mr Liddle laid bare his plans. He had planned a trip to the city to have a look at the small plot of land he had purchased recently. The purchase was by instinct, as at that time he had neither any need nor any plans. Seeing an advertisement in a newspaper that his son had casually carried in his travel bag from India, he had taken this impulsive decision to buy the land. His youngest son and he had been frequent visitors to India and the son always carried a power of attorney. So the initiation of the legal formalities did not take too much effort on their behalf. His friends often labelled him whimsical for taking such impulsive decisions, but till date he had never had to repent over any of the decisions taken, however hasty they might have been.

A taxi had arrived after breakfast the next morning. Mr Liddle was ready. His style of dressing was immaculate and suited to the occasion; this Shweta had marked since his arrival the day before. Today he was dressed in a grey suit with a midnight blue tie, complete with a matching hat on his head.

He pulled out a diary from his burgundy briefcase and after going through a few pages, paused, put the red marker in and handed over the diary to Shweta.

'My dear, could you please direct me to the address at serial number 6? I hope it's not too far?'

A smiling Shweta took over the diary from his hands to read the address. 'Mama, you said number six?' she confirmed.

'Yes dear, the one at six.'

Shweta's smile faded away the very next moment when she read the name of the owner and the house number as Dr Arvind Johri, House number 1221!!

'It's very close, Mama, very very close.' she said.

'I am an old man, can't walk much you see and I am scared of these street dogs.'

The senior Johris had returned from Haridwar a week ago, depressed and disillusioned. They had tried hard to make a home away from home, a nest where they could pass the remainder of their years in peace, but that was not to be. Their depleting cash reserves worried them no end as much as their loneliness. The initial euphoria of living in a holy city had died down once they completed taking rounds of each and every temple and shrine; thereafter, it became more of a monotonous chore that they had to undertake only to survive and only to kill some hours of the day. Besides, living in a single room house came with its own share of disadvantages. The same four walls, which looked friendly on a happy day, seemed claustrophobic, cold and bereft of any warmth on a dull and gloomy day.

They realised that they could not run away from their reality for long. They needed to go back sooner or later and confront whatever life had in store for them. Caught in a web of myriad emotions, one evening they abruptly wound up their establishment and took a taxi to the railway station, giving away all that they possessed to their domestic help. Arvind was in such a hurry to move that he did not even wait for the landlord to return, preferring to leave a slip with an envelope containing his dues.

When they alighted from the taxi, the house that was once their own, appeared alien. A few metres from their porch, a feet wide and a feet deep trench had been dug which continued towards the front gate, leaving a six feet passageway. The beautiful lawn they once tended to with so much of love was now someone else's plot.

For two days, they had been so overwhelmed with emotions that tears would keep welling up their eyes every now and then. Arvind had even called up Madhur and requested him to reconsider his decision if the legal formalities were still remaining; but Madhur callously told them that the deal had been finalised and the financial transactions had been done, the papers had been signed and there was no way that the sale could be aborted at this stage. With that piece of news, the Johris had come to realise the finality of the proceedings.

Coping up with the new situation was not at all easy. An uneasy feeling of betrayal kept pricking their heart.

Within a few days, heartbreak awaited them. Madhur called from London, telling them that the buyer of that 'little chunk of useless land' was already in town and was about to come that day to have a first look at his property. It was supposedly Arvind and Yashoda's 'bounden duty' to give the buyer a conducted tour of the property.

Madhur's words had reopened wounds that had begun to gather some skin, though healing was never expected.

'Is Madhur really our own bloodline?' Yashoda wondered with a wry smile hanging on her lips. 'All his concerns lie only with the buyer? His parent's feelings … their sentiments have no value for him?' she remarked with resigned acceptance.

'Money makes strange bedfellows, Yashoda!' Arvind said.

'Yes, it does … I am learning life's lessons, learning them the hard way,' Yashoda muttered to herself.

In the afternoon, they locked the house and went to the Hanuman temple in Civil Lines. Though they had been regular visitors to this temple, today the visit was more to escape the sight of an unknown businessman, measuring their land, calculating the area, haggling with them over the width of the common passageway that Madhur had so thoughtfully designed. The Johris knew that once a new building came in the front portion, the older one would be relegated to a position of less importance. To the occupants of the new building, it would be an outhouse in their backyard, meant to shelter the unwanted and unwelcome.

Mr Liddle stood in front of the plot. The main gate was locked and hence he could not get inside and take any actual measurements. Annoyed at the lack of cooperation from the seller, he had turned around to have a look at his name. The nameplate read Dr Arvind Johri, ex. Prof & Head, Dept. of Orthopaedics, Motilal Nehru

Medical College, Allahabad. Something struck him and he just returned, neither happy nor sad.

He repeated the name many times in his head, but his memory refused to serve him.

Two days passed by in a jiffy. Mr Liddle surprisingly made no effort to undertake a second visit to his plot. He showed no enthusiasm to have another look at the piece of land he had bought without a second thought. Instead, he left for Dehradun the very next day. Before leaving, he took the Joshis landline number and promised to remain in touch with Ajit and his niece.

The city was fast returning to normal. Curfew was relaxed from dawn to dusk. The initial fears and misgivings had settled down. Shashank and Bina had still not returned from Bindki. A major fault in the telephone line in their village had made any communication impossible since the last call Ajit Mama had made to them.

A telegram had arrived the day before informing them that it would be another ten days before they would be back. With some improvement in the situation, Savita was back and now that Ajit Mama was there, she could go home at night, after finishing off all the chores.

Reading Udit's diaries had become an obsession with Shweta. For the years 1983 and 1984, he had kept a single spiral bound note book of not more than hundred pages. The entries were irregular and short and mostly pertaining to his pocket money and expenses made. Some entries were very terse one liners which were his own compositions or borrowed quotes, Shweta could not fathom. Some of them read-

'So what, not everyone is equally lucky?'
'This too shall pass.'
'Fight, fight, fight till the end…'
'Saddened, so much, is there no escape?'

'Cool it, man, cool it!'

'Humans have seven births, they say, maybe in the next ...' The only one slightly positive streak in June 1983 entry was a mention of India's World Cup win at Lord's Cricket Ground, 'Wow! What *A* match!! Today, I'm proud to be an Indian!'

'*A confused and lost soul dithering at emotional crossroads*' was a rough inference that Shweta begun to deduce as she flipped through her prodigal brother's diary.

One afternoon, Shweta and Ajit mama were out in the garden, after lunch; soaking the sun. Mama lay on a bamboo reed mat spread over the grass, munching warm peanuts with green coriander chutney. The warmth of the sun was quite pleasant. As always, the murraya swayed noisily seeing Shweta in the vicinity. A grey hornbill pecked at a fruit on the upper branches of the nerium.

'You know Shweta, what I missed the most in the UK? This kind of leisure, sitting in the sun, the night sky with the moon and the twinkling stars and the joy of munching warm peanuts like this. Nothing can match this. What happened to your battery operated chair, Sweetie?' Mama asked suddenly.

Shweta was caught off guard. Now she had to recount how inauspicious had been the start to their secret operation. The unfortunate events that had culminated with that providential escape and return back home surprisingly did not cause the same roiling within her, now that she recollected them, for Mama.

Narayan had been the first piece of the puzzle that she had failed to put in place, a fact that caused a fleeting spasm of pain to contort her face.

'I should not preach, but you know, all we can do is try. The result is not in our hands. So let us not waver from our resolve that come what may, we will definitely hunt out Udit. But first let us go and recover your chair; it will make your life simpler,' he said as he helped her onto her old wheelchair and wheeled her inside. They could not wait to book a taxi for another visit to the Narayan home. It was scheduled for the next day.

That night Shweta was nervous. Though this visit was primarily to get back her wheelchair, her mind was full of thoughts, some vague, some optimistic, some scary as if she had been summoned by Narayan to reveal something. Unable to sleep, she continued reading his diaries. A diary entry made Shweta sit up. Quite unlike the previous ones, which ranged from his accountings, to a twin word phrase to crabby one-liners and monologues, it extended to a full page.

My Life's Rugged Terrain

Laugh and the world laughs with you,
Weep and you weep alone, they say,
Alas, I laugh alone,
I weep alone,
Come on my world,
Give me a shoulder to cry upon.
Is it my fault then,
That I want to be loved?
That I want to be hugged?
Come on, it's not too late,
I promise,
I will forgive you.
Let your affection overflow,
Let me be drenched with emotions,
Let me swim in hope,
Let my fears drown,
Before it is too late!
How long will I ride on Granny's plough?
Hoping that some seeds of love,
Lying buried,
Will spring to life?
How long?
How long?

The poem had been left incomplete but the essence was not too difficult to grasp. Shweta's search had provided some answers to the questions that had been distressing her for long.

This time at Narayan's place, the welcome was rather cold. His mother did not look too happy at the arrival of the two guests.

'How did you come to know that lady Bimla?' she quizzed.

'Auntie, she is from a village which is close to my mother's native place near Mau and I had met her only twice earlier. Once she had come to attend Sonam-di's marriage and the second time, in Nazareth hospital.'

'She is a lady of questionable reputation; everyone around knows that! There was a police raid two nights back and people say that a lot of objectionable stuff has been dug out from her place. They have also picked up a few girls for interrogation. Didn't you say you stayed over there that night?'

Shweta's jaw dropped for she had no clue of what Narayan's mother was talking about.

'And do you know, some people in the adjoining house saw you going out from here and then entering that gate? They also saw you going with Narayan on his scooter. God knows what they would have thought! I am so thankful to God that the police did not come here for questioning!' There was pronounced resentment in her voice.

Shweta had barely known Bimla Mausi. So she could not give any argument in her defence. At the back of her mind, she recollected the events that took place in the night and her sudden disappearance in the morning and tried to match the missing pieces of the puzzle.

The conversation was cut short abruptly when Ajit Mama went out and summoned the driver and asked him to keep the wheelchair in the dickey. Both of them left the house in a huff without saying a word, either to Narayan or his mother.

On her way back home, Shweta felt uneasy and guilty, but restrained herself from discussing anything. Ajit Mama just patted her back and quietly said, 'Cheer up! Never allow yourself to get so upset over trifling matters. You haven't done anything wrong!

People are entitled to their opinions, but that does not mean that they are always right.' He tried to pep her up. 'We will find out Udit on our own, come what may,' he announced with full confidence.

Back home, Mama also joined Shweta and the two sifted through Udit's diary entries, searching for hidden clues. This was an essential exercise they thought as that would allow them to have some insight into his state of mind just before he left home. A situation in which they tracked him down only to discover that he was in no mood to return would be the worst anticlimax to their search. That whole night they scanned the pages, sifting and sieving through all the apparently trivial stuff to read between the lines. Suddenly, they came across a mysterious comment—'On the steps of a temple, huh or underneath a lantana scrub … great people are not born … they appear … Lord Krishna … ha ha!' This was among the last few entries in that spiral bound notebook, the last being, 'The Almighty takes care of all whom He creates … it is good to be a driftwood for sometime …. if the soil is salty and roots have begun to wither … it's better to float away like driftwood … A flood or a quake will change everything one day …

There was no diary for the year 1985.

The glimmer of hope that had been flickering in the sister's heart for a moment was in danger of being blown out by the realisation that it was not a decision taken by her brother in a fit of anger. It had not been a split second consequence of a seething rage. It was instead, a simmering discontent that had one day boiled over. However, Ajit Mama sheltered the flame and allowed it to gain in strength, by coaxing her into believing that the last entries showed that Udit had then decided to take a temporary sabbatical to get rid of his self-perceived and self-created illusionary demons of pessimism. Mama laid special emphasis on his choice of words, 'sometime', 'change' and he was more than sure that it was just a temporary foray of a disturbed mind. Udit could and would be easily brought back, if traced.

The flame of resolve to hunt him out had been rekindled in Shweta. She became more determined than ever, that she would not let it extinguish, under any circumstances, come what may.

A fortnight later, Shashank and Bina returned from Bindki. Along with their own luggage, they had brought back two additional steel trunks that looked like Granny's. The unexpected and untimely demise of his mother had left Shashank quite shaken. She had passed away in sleep, during her afternoon nap. Late in the evening, it was Pranav's younger son who had discovered that she was not waking up even after he had called and shaken her many times. Though the village *vaidya* had examined and concluded that she was no more, she was rushed to the hospital at the block headquarters. The doctors there tried hard to revive her, but she could not be brought to life. The worst fears of the family had come true.

Shashank had been rattled by the loss. Outwardly he put up a brave front to all and sundry that came to offer condolences; but at night when he went to bed, all his resoluteness would crumble into a heap and he would sit up and grieve. The list of his grudges against his destiny had grown a little longer with this colossal loss. The older ones had been smudged a little with the passage of time but that of his son Udit, remained bright and bold.

Ajit Mama had been thinking of moving to his nephew's place just a kilometre and a half away. The nephew and his wife had been calling him daily wanting to know when he would join them. He had told Bina a couple of times that he was not sure if Shashank would be comfortable with his presence in the house. But she should rest assured he would be around her and he planned to share one meal daily with his sister's family. Bina had been dithering over the issue, unable to decide whether she should ask her aged brother to stay with them or let him move to his nephew's house.

Shashank and Bina's home was big and spacious. For now, the three of them had ample space to roll about like little peas in a capacious pod in the four spacious rooms. Besides, the first floor rooms lay vacant throughout the year. However, she was unsure if Shashank would be in the right frame of mind to discuss such an issue. One morning she overheard her brother talking on the phone, discussing with his son back in England that he felt a bit awkward staying in his sister's place but was not sure if leaving her and Shashank alone at this juncture would be a logical decision.

That night Bina mentally prepared herself to talk to Shashank after dinner. Normally this was the time he spent in his study preparing for lectures scheduled the next day or any other work related to academics. As she entered the room, she found that two books and a bunch of question papers were lying on his table. He had told her in the morning that he was not able to finish some important works as he was finding it difficult to concentrate on them.

Shashank stood by the window, lost in thought. He did not realise that Bina had entered the room, till she switched on the night bulb. Seeing Bina, he came towards her with a quizzical look.

'What were you doing near the window?' she asked.

'Nothing much ... just killing time. I am unable to concentrate these days. I have to hand over question papers for Lucknow University undergraduate course by tomorrow but I am stuck after four questions,' he said settling on the bed beside Bina.

'Time passes by, so quickly,' he sighed looking at the old black and white photos strewn by the side of the pillow. He had been flipping through them to get some solace from memories associated with each of them.

'See these,' he said, as he picked up the photos one by one. His mother draped in a golden yellow Banarsi at the time of his marriage, mother holding Sonam in her lap when she was born, smiling from ear to ear, holding an hour old Udit, wrapped in a white towel in Kamla Nehru Hospital, mother posing with a bald Sonam and Udit immediately after their mundan ceremony in Alopi Devi temple.

The two trunks that he had brought home from Bindki were real treasure troves, storing a lifetime of memories through items as diverse as photo albums, old coins, some jewellery, some empty cases, inlands, postcards, telegrams, school notebooks, slate and chalk, clothes of newborns, things she had kept closeted to herself, a means of comfort, an insulation against any feeling of being alone.

'Don't think too much, take a few extra classes, the distraction will help. It is natural … don't worry … time is the biggest healer,' she whispered as she patted him on his back, an affectionate pat to cheer him up. Bina had forgotten that she had come to discuss something else with him. She could see that the tragedy had left him very feeble. She sat and observed as he pulled the pillow behind him and stretched himself, closing his eyes. It had been many years since they had spent any time together. Bina could see that age had caught up with him. His right cheek was now full of black and brown moles as if someone had sprayed a generous dose of crushed pepper, the tiny pieces had stuck in some invisible glue. Underneath his eyes were bulging eye bags, silent indicators of the amount of stress that had been bubbling within. She put her hand on his head and caressed him gently. A few tears rolled down his eyes and he pulled her close to him, held her in an embrace and cried softly. Five minutes later, he was up as he plodded along to the washroom. When he emerged, he not only looked better but felt much lighter in the head. That momentary outburst had provided a vent to his emotions, which he had been holding on to himself. He picked up the glass of milk from the table and again sat by Bina's side.

Two days later, he found Ajit Mama packing his stuff in an air bag. He chose to ignore, not wanting to intrude into his privacy but the same evening when he saw him struggling in packing his sleeping bag, he offered to help. Once it was done, he tossed the bright blue thing on to the bed and turned around to ask, 'Where are you going?'

Ajit Mama paused for a moment and then said, 'My nephew insists that I spend a few months with him also.'

'But he stays nearby, why are you then packing?'

Ajit Mama remained mum.

'I know you are thinking about not staying in your sister's place for too long and hence you are planning to move out,' Shashank added.

'Bhaiya, how many years have you spent in London?' he asked a stunned Mama.

'Not less than fifty, I guess,' came the reply.

'Even half a century there could not change your thinking, come on change now. You see, you are not going anywhere. I look upon you as my elder brother and I draw so much solace from your presence in this house. I have already suffered so many losses one after the other, but this time, I will not let you go. Please have some mercy on your sister, if not me,' he said with folded hands.

'I had no control over the previous losses, but this one depends more upon you than me, and my gut feeling says that if you stay with us there would be a change in my luck. And who knows, maybe I could recover what I have lost?'

Ajit Mama's plans had been shot down with a gun loaded with bullets of love. Shashank's passionate plea had left him with no excuse where he could seek cover. 'I submit to you bhai, maybe a little change in luck is needed for all of us,' he said and slowly walked over to Shashank to hug him.

Not too far away, the Johris too were trying hard to come to terms with the new circumstances. That they had accepted the bitter truth was a first step towards their goal of reconciliation with their destiny. The trenches that had been dug along the margins of the new plot could never stop them from crossing over to the other side emotionally. Arvind had a favourite pastime these days. He would stand in the porch and scan each and every square inch of the area in front, standing like a child strictly forbidden by his mother not to venture into unfamiliar territory.

He remembered the days when he had shifted to this house, a naughty Mayank would often sneak out into the porch and beyond, to catch butterflies and beetles and moths and at times put a few in his mouth. A hassled Yashoda then had managed to control his escapades by telling Madhur that he should always keep an eye on his little brother, as on the roads roamed men who lifted and carried away infants, hiding them in their enormous robes. Taking it too seriously, he would come running, shouting, 'Ma, run, run, Mayank has wandered into the garden!' And Yashoda would break into a mock race, dashing towards the garden to save him.

Many decades ago, back home in his village, he would remember, his mother would prevent him from wandering anywhere near the family well, not more than fifty odd metres away in the right corner of their huge courtyard by whispering into his ears about the jamun tree being the permanent abode of a ghost.

On some days, he would reminisce the recent past and would be washed over with a multitude of memories of Madhur and Mayank. The boys playing holi on the lawns, their faces and bodies painted in red, blue and black, with their hair dyed in varnish silver, dancing to the beats of popular Bollywood numbers. The lawn had also been the venue of many a cricket match, involving two teams, each with a single player, with Arvind, the umpire, not only keeping count of the balls bowled and the runs scored but also keeping the rival teams as far apart as possible so that the match continued in a cordial atmosphere. Often, he would secretly wish that he could uproot the young mango and the neem trees that stood by the outer boundary wall, and transplant them by the side of the trench within his own boundary. He was deeply attached to the two trees, as Madhur had planted the mango and Mayank the neem. They had competed with each other the whole of next month over whose sapling would grow faster. In the winter that year, when the neem seedling had become leafless, there had been a big fight between the two, as Madhur had declared himself the winner of the on-going competition. The next day, the mango had been found hacked at the base while the neem had been protected under an umbrella tied to a thick stick dug into the ground nearby.

Back to the present and his mind would bring forth some blurry images, a three storied villa with its fancy doors, windows, decorated terraces overflowing with climbers and imported lamp shades and royal chandeliers, a double storied market complex or even a milk dairy, with a huge cowshed, home to mooing cows and buffaloes. Then he would glance at his own house behind, the walls with flaking plaster and unsightly patches of algal designs near the base. He would then shake his head in despondency and retreat into the confines of his drawing room, drawing all the curtains to shut out the cruel world outside.

March and April were the only months when the tourist influx to the hill station of Mussoorie was comparatively less as most schools in other parts of the country conducted their annual examinations around this time. For all those who were on the pay rolls of hotels, this was a time to pay attention to their long pending personal works. At Mussoorie Grand, half of the staff at the hotel had gone home. But for Udit, this was the time he never looked forward to. Work was the only thing that kept him busy and free from negative thoughts that would come to him sometimes in waves and sometimes in torrents and then swirl and kick at his heart and conscience and then tangle and linger within him for days.

Ever since he had joined the hotel, life had been more or less the same. The only change others pointed to him as a recent positive achievement in his life was his promotion to the post of Assistant Manager of the hotel. Though there was not much that had changed with regards to the nature of his work, except that now he was not required to cook. He would now direct and guide the new boys and then sit in a cubicle behind the Manger's room, supervising other works like the store, purchases, the maintenance and all other undefined miscellaneous works.

He and the hotel manager had become good friends. He had yet another new friend, a four-year-old, whom he had nicknamed Chhotu. Now his monotonous daily routine would be interrupted by the little one loitering around near his room, playing some pranks and evoking a rare laugh from him. These moments of joy he had begun to cherish, the sight and sound of Chhotu's innocent laughter resonating within him, even when he went back to his room at night.

Often he would pamper him with sweets, little plastic toys, balls or with anything that caught his fancy. At times, both would play cricket in the long veranda behind the hotel, and the match would end when Chhotu would hit a shot big enough for the ball to disappear to a place from where retrieval was impossible.

Chhotu was the son of Lila, a new addition to the hotel staff. She had joined in January and had been assigned the job of washing the laundry. She was around thirty, somewhat plump, with a round face and protruding eyes. She was a woman of very few words and her words were limited to a chosen few, chiefly the hotel Manager, Chhotu and an occasional greeting for Udit, whenever the two crossed path. Unlike the other female staff, she was reserved and remained closeted in her room. She would emerge from her room in the morning and disappear by lunch time, shutting herself to the world outside. Initially, little Chhotu would tag along with her, following her from one room to the other as she gathered the used sheets and pillow covers, sometimes running away with a colourful cushion, if it caught his fancy. A flight of eight steps from the left of the entry to the car parking, led to a squarish area, where surrounding a tap, lay aluminium and plastic tubs with a board, announcing 'hotel washing area.' Lila would have the entire area to herself, where she would wash the linens and then hang them on the clothesline, a string of a dozen running close to each other. Chhotu loved the area, as he could play hide and seek behind the hung clothes. On some days he preferred to wash himself along with the laundry as he would sit in one of the tubs, splashing water and blowing bubbles from the detergent mixed water.

It must have been a month after their arrival at the hotel, when Chhotu was down with severe cold, the congestion and fever resulting in febrile seizure. It was Udit who had rushed from his room to help, hearing Lila's sobs and frantic wails. Since then, she had become a bit liberal, allowing the boy to play with children of other hotel staffers who lived nearby. Chhotu on his part, had developed a particular liking for Udit.

It had only been four months that Chhotu had arrived in Udit's life, but his arrival had brought a little sparkle in Udit's otherwise drab and dreary existence. He now looked forward to his days off, when he would hold him by the finger and go for a stroll on Mall Road. En route, he would have plenty to buy, a balloon, a freshly roasted maize cob, an ice cream or pink and fluffy candy floss. An occasional horse ride lifted their spirits, but Udit would always get Chhotu tied to his belly with a muffler, not risking a fall in case the horse had a change of mood, deciding to canter or gallop to break his boredom of trotting alongside his owner.

Another thing Udit loved to do. It was blowing bubbles for the little one, who would giggle and laugh and would run behind the bubbles, jumping up with his cusped hands to hold a few. And whenever a bubble would land on his shoe or a chair near him, his joy would know no bounds! He would try hard to pick one of them, and would let out a big sigh when his touch would cause it to disappear. In the previous week, Udit had managed to blow one onto Chhotu's extended palms and the delight then on his face was such as if it was not a bubble but the whole earth that had come to rest on his little hands! Slowly, Chhotu began to exert the most potent influence in Udit's life. His negative attitude began to change. Learning to relive simple pleasures of childhood ignorance from Chhotu, he discovered a redo button in life, when all along his search for an undo button had met with consistent and constant failures.

The affection and fondness of the two was mutual. Over the months, Chhotu started following him to his cubicle. He would sit beside Udit and munch on the wafers and biscuits that he would get from him. Sometimes, he would fall asleep by his chair on that red and blue coir carpet. Udit would then take leave for a few minutes, cradle him in his lap and go to Lila's room to hand him over. Sometimes he would not find Lila in her room, then he would return to his cubicle and put him to sleep on a makeshift bed, joining two chairs front to front.

In this way, Chhotu and the Manager reinforced his belief in human relationships that sometimes those not related in flesh and blood could provide one with unexpected succour and happiness in life. He had often felt like asking Lila the whereabouts of her husband, but then he could never gather enough courage to pose innocuous questions such as these to anyone, anticipating his own discomfort if the same questions ricocheted towards him.

Lila's life, present and past, remained a riddle for the hotel people. She never bared her story to anyone. Whenever probed, she would break into a smile and find some excuse to rush to her room. The only rumour that every ear in the neighbourhood had heard was that she had worked at the home of a very rich businessman in Haridwar and he had recommended her name to the hotel manager here.

Little Chhotu was literally the opposite of his mother. Chatty, friendly, with an infectious smile he got along easily with people around him. The harsh Mussoorie winter had aggravated his susceptibility to cold and despite all the layers of woollens he wore, cough and congestion troubled him continuously. One day, Udit out of sudden impulse took out the black thread with the dangling lucky charm he wore around his neck and put it onto Chhotu's neck. His granny used to say that it was a child's primary defence against evil eyes and it also set right the planetary positions which were responsible for a child falling sick quite often.

The new found positivity in life made Udit start writing a diary again. He began to pen down his thoughts on anything that he felt was interesting or any incident that he wanted to remember later. This was something he had picked up from his dad. Now, over a period of time, it had graduated to composing short lyrics or short stories on nuances of everyday life.

It was a hot Sunday afternoon. The Johris were preparing for their afternoon siesta. Arvind was at the window of the bedroom to draw the curtains to cut out the light that was entering into the room. He had left the jumbo sized desert cooler switched on before lunch, to let the room cool in advance. Both morning and evening Arvind had the task of taking the plastic pipe from the garden tap to the tank and filling it to the brim. If he did not do the chore in the morning, then he would have to spend the whole of afternoon in the room that would be a hot air oven by then! He would often joke that Yashoda could definitely cook an omelette on the floor of the room, if she wished to save some LPG in the cylinder!

The weather and the electricity supply had been real teasers this summer. Today morning, while filling the cooler tank, the power supply had gone off resulting in the water supply going off as well. As a result, the tank could not be filled fully. Arvind went out of the room, with a towel wrapped around his head, to gauge the water level. But before he could remove one of the back iron mesh, he heard two people talking near the gate. A few steps towards the gate, he saw a truck parked very close to the compound wall.

He thought of the discomfort of the truck drivers. Poor fellows seeking some moments of respite under the shade of his neem and mango trees, he thought, as he went indoors. He headed to the bedroom to take a quick nap because a power cut in the afternoon was inevitable. The refreshing scent of the few strands of khus roots he had yesterday put in the cooler tank filled his room and he fell asleep.

In the evening, it was still quite sultry when he came out in the porch to see if his potted plants needed an extra watering. Some unfamiliar sound at the gate drew his attention. Through the narrow vertical slits of the iron gate he could see red bricks being stacked just beyond the wall. He rushed towards the gate with the cup still in his hand and half the tea still left.

The sight of the bricks filled him with sadness. With one hand he clutched the top of the gate and tried to gulp down the sadness with the sips of tea left in his cup. He beckoned one of the labourers, who came towards him, wiping the sweat streaming down his forehead and chin.

'What are the bricks for?' he asked.

'Sahib, the contractor says construction work has to begin soon.'

Puzzled at the long pause, the man asked, 'Please may I go?'

Arvind nodded absentmindedly.

But it was inevitable, wasn't it? He tried consoling himself as he walked back. And the first thing he did was to draw all the curtains, not leaving even the tiniest of chinks between them; '*out of sight, out of mind*,' he muttered to himself.

For a moment, he thought of sharing the development with Yashoda but the next instant decided against it.

Next day he was restless, peeping through the drawing room curtains many a times. He himself was unsure what he wanted.

Three days later, work had begun. An army of labourers, men and women and a few kids, wandered around, trampling his garden brutally. Two men arrived on a scooter and the one in brown safari suit quickly inspected the area, moving along the trench with a hawkish eye, scanning the boundary, noting down something on a notepad with a pen that he had securely placed above his right ear lobe. And if that was not painful enough, he chose to pass by the drawing room window, shouting that the boss or 'the Bada Sahib would be here in two three days, so you better be quick.'

The Bada Sahib, Mr Liddle, was busy, hundreds of kilometres away in Mussoorie, supervising the restoration and repair works of the building he had purchased next to a popular hotel. He had another property on the outskirts of the city, a three bedroom house, made of wood and slate and nestled between oaks and rhododendrons, with a seasonal stream running behind. This was his preferred place of stay, whenever he was in town. While work here was going on in full swing, the plot lying vacant in Allahabad was at the back of his mind and when the contractor had called up saying that work had begun, he booked the tickets for a visit, on the following Saturday.

He had also called up his new-found niece, Shweta, to inform her that he would be in the city for two days, in the last week of the month, much to her delight. At the end of the conversation, he had politely enquired if it was too hot there. 'God! I hope I will not melt away…' he said on hearing that the temperature ranged during the day time between 40-46ºC.

Normally the middle of May meant plenty of pre-monsoon showers, but for the last three years both the arrival and the retreat of the monsoon had been erratic. This year too, it was no different, third week of May it was and there had been only a few scattered and scanty drizzles.

Meanwhile Arvind would see the increasing height of the two walls that were being constructed, one running straight from the pillar of the gate to the porch and the other, right along the porch, obliterating the front view totally. He wondered what the building would be and who the owner was. Was it going to be a residential house that would soon be occupied by a family full of men, women and children or would it be just a young couple with two kids, each entitled to the luxury of a separate room with an attached bathroom.

A thunderstorm that very evening followed by a heavy shower was a welcome surprise after the soaring temperatures of the previous week. The new plot with the boundary wall, still only three feet high, had become a pool. It was still dark when Arvind woke up. Even the sleeping pill he was popping into his mouth at bedtime every night was unable to give him uninterrupted sleep for a few hours at a stretch. To top it all, before the clock struck five, he was up, his biological clock ticking away faster than he wanted it to. He came out of his room and stood in the porch staring at the newly formed pool. Ripples appeared and disappeared as a mild breeze stroked the surface of the water and then blew away only to break into soft music as it rustled through the young leaves of the mango and neem near the boundary. A group of crows quickly descended on one of the roundish boulders visible in the centre to take a hasty bath, before flying away, flapping their dark and unattractive wings.

Meanwhile, a light drizzle came along and the ripples disappeared. As the raindrops kissed the water surface, the standing water leapt up in joy giving rise to small and delightful eddies. A crow cawed on the lowermost branch of the neem and a koel sang in hurried bits before going quiet. A crow cawing early morning was the sign of a guest about to come, his good friend, Shashank, had once told him. He remembered and broke into a half smile. Then he moved away. Like a child he was delighted that the standing water would ensure that there was no construction activity possible at least for a day or two.

Mr Liddle, meanwhile, had arrived in the city. The heat of the place unnerved him a little, coming as he was from a pleasant Mussoorie. He had checked into a hotel in the morning although Ajit Mama had insisted on phone that he could straightway come home. But conscious of the fact that he had not met Shashank and Bina, he decided to stay put in a hotel and then pay them a visit when he would visit his plot.

The hotel people on knowing his impressive credentials as a businessman, were overtly friendly. They had arranged a chauffeur driven car for him for his local visits within the city. With a packet of sweet in one hand and a bag containing gifts he had brought in the other, he rang the bell outside the Joshis' home.

Since morning, Ajit had been telling his sister about a friend of his who was to visit them that day. The gentleman at the gate was tall, smart and lean with a stylish hat tilted slightly towards one side of his head. He could be none other than Mr Liddle, thought Bina.

'Good morning, I am ...'

'Mr Liddle, if I'm not mistaken,' intervened Bina.

'Oh yes, sisters recognise their brothers, they possess that sixth sense, I suppose,' Liddle laughed as he was ushered into the drawing room. Ajit Mama and Shweta who were waiting in the drawing room, greeted him warmly.

Shashank who was busy on the phone, joined them few minutes later. He was surprised to see how Mr Liddle and Mama got along like a house on fire, laughing away at the silly anecdotes they had to share.

'Have you ever been to this city earlier?' Shashank asked, still unable to believe that a person could buy land just like that, on a whim, and that too in a place where there hardly existed any business prospect!

'Oh yes, briefly. Way back in 1962. I was a scholar here, in the great Muir College, on a project from my university. Stayed here for full eight months, shared a room with a colleague, whose name I can't recollect. Only if I had a better memory,' he smiled innocuously.

Mr Liddle left after an hour and a half, promising to drop in again, if time permitted.

He had already left a message with his contractor to be there at the plot. And when his car stopped at the gate, the contractor and his assistant were there, waiting. The plot was still filled with ankle deep water. And beyond a metre, from the new gate, it was all slush and slippery.

'So what is the progress?' Mr Liddle asked.

'Sir, the boundary wall will take a day or two at the maximum; today we could not do anything because of this slush,' the contractor had an excuse ready.

Seeing Mr Liddle quiet, the contractor was encouraged to offer his suggestion. 'Sir please send the design to us early so that we can begin the actual construction soon.'

'Oh yes, it is almost ready, another week at the most it will take before I finalise the plan. Once it is ready, there would be no delay from my side,' he said and requested them to leave. 'Be in touch on phone once I get back to Mussoorie,' he added as he walked towards the car.

Mr Liddle opened the door of the taxi only to shut it again. A bemused driver saw him walk towards the main gate of the same house. He quickly peeped from the window to make sure that everything was fine within the car. Liddle rang the bell and then walked in through the open gate.

At the door of the house, he waited.

Yashoda opened the door and was surprised to see an unknown figure standing at the door.

'I wish to meet Dr Arvind, if he is free,' he said.

Yashoda for a moment did not know what to say, whether to ask him to come in, or to leave him waiting at the door while she went inside and informed Arvind.

Seeing her predicament, Mr Liddle said, 'Oh you have such lovely plants! Please can I have a look, if you don't mind?' He immediately stepped a few yards back.

Yashoda rushed in.

Arvind emerged, a minute later, curious to find out who the gentleman could be, for going by his wife's description, he could not be a patient in need of medical attention or someone with painful knees or aching back descending on his clinic for physiotherapy.

'Sir?' Mr Liddle turned back in a flash.

'Oh sorry to have bothered you at this hour, I am Liddle. I have bought this land actually … and we have not even met … I thought I would just call … He extended his hand towards Arvind, smilingly.

For a moment, Arvind was totally blank, for a person whose image he had conjectured and had so hated all these months was now standing in front of him! Realising that he had embarrassed Arvind, Liddle almost withdrew his hand. Arvind realised his mistake. He promptly grabbed Liddle's palm, shaking it with stiffened fingers and stifled emotion.

'Oh, sorry to have kept you waiting, please come in.' Arvind turned and went towards the drawing room.

Mr Liddle followed him unmindfully.

He sat on the sofa, looking down at the carpet and the carved legs of the glass topped table. Suddenly he was groping for words and regretted visiting the household on a momentary impulse.

'What was the need to meet the owner, so foolish of me' he said to himself as Arvind switched on the two tube lights in the room filling it with light. The blue and gold curtains had still been drawn.

Liddle threw a glance at the wall on the right, accidentally.

He blinked and blinked twice, thrice …

The photo frame, though now faded and dull, had the same landscape in water colours, the same strokes, the same colours …. with tiny initials K.L imprinted in the lower right corner! It could not be a coincidence. A painting could be copied, but a painter could never be so naive as to reproduce the initials too! The sequence of events came stomping across his mind, for a moment rendering him absolutely speechless! 'God! Could this be true?' he muttered under his breath.

Arvind and Yashoda had nothing to ask.

They offered him a cup of tea and some cookies for the sake of formality and to kill time.

Liddle wracked his brains. It was the same painting that he had made, the same frame he had so meticulously chosen. Could this be true?

He almost stared at Arvind and then at Yashoda.

Arvind returned the favour with a stern glare.

He controlled his emotions and his tongue. 'Are you an ortho surgeon doctor,' he asked.

'How do you know that?' Arvind was now getting irritated.

For a moment, Liddle thought of blurting out everything, but then decided against, controlling his infamous whim, this time around.

'Sorry, I need to hurry, we will meet again someday.'

He returned to his waiting car, still nodding his head at the power of destiny. The power of attorney that he had so casually handed over to his son one day, had led him to witness the power of destiny!

Back in the hotel, he had a quick wash. As he switched on the TV and sat in his bed with a glass of cold coffee in hand, he watched the news clipping showing an avalanche rushing down the mountain slopes somewhere in Europe, burying half a dozen skiers under a rubble of snow. He himself felt buried under an avalanche of memories that surged over him from all sides.

Shweta had retired for the day, and was in bed, when she remembered the gift pack Mr Liddle had brought for her. She found that her mother had kept it at the table by her bedside. She stretched herself and managed to pull the pack towards her. With a smile across her face, she pulled it open. Inside there appeared something soft and silky. As she removed the newspaper wrap, she found a light blue coloured shawl and a packet of chocolates.

'For my lovely niece,' read a pink card.

She held the silky fabric of the shawl against her face, put it on her shoulders and glanced at the mirror on the wall opposite her bed. A smile crossed her face as she kept it back, collecting the sheet of newspaper in which it had been wrapped. A split second later, she crushed it into a ball and aimed towards the dustbin, beyond her bed, near the door. She was just about to throw, when she suddenly stopped. In a flash, she opened and flattened the ball in her hands.

It was a news item, from Mussoorie, mentioning the protest meeting at Gandhi Chowk by members of a group supporting the cause of a separate hill state. But what attracted her attention was not the news item, nor even the photos of the people sitting there on the road with posters and banners. It was a long shot of a man, inadvertently caught in the frame. He was thin and lanky, with a beard and a military cut hair.

And thereafter, Shweta and Mama remained busy the whole night discussing their modus operandi.

Udit had not seen Chhotu since morning. Normally, Lila allowed him to wander around after breakfast and play with the neighbourhood kids. He wondered if something was wrong. And then he thought that he need not read too much into a break in a child's routine. Maybe today he had found something else that was keeping him busy and occupied.

At the hotel he found out that Lila had not reported for duty. The cook in the kitchen told him that on the previous evening she had gone to her room complaining of dizziness and nausea.

He thought of sending the receptionist to her room to find out if she needed any kind of help. Then he thought people might attribute some motives to his act and restrained himself. In the evening, around seven, he was free and was preparing to go to Mall Road. Some new blankets had to be purchased for the hotel. The evening was pleasant. Nonetheless, he put on the windcheater before getting out. He intentionally passed by the thin passage in front of Lila's room hoping to at least hear Chhotu's voice. There was complete silence and the room appeared bolted from inside. He knocked on the door, very lightly, but did not wait. As he walked ahead slowly, he strained his ears to catch any sound of a door being opened. Once on the road, he thought that maybe her husband had come to pay her a visit and therefore she was not in her room. Had she been ill, at least she would have sought help from someone to visit the dispensary. He mildly reprimanded himself for being too inquisitive and for poking his nose into other people's affair.

'I have my own troubles to attend to, and I foolishly bother about others,' he chided himself, promising that till the following day, he would not even think about the mother and son duo.

That day, he purchased half a dozen blankets, something he had been planning to do for the last two weeks. He returned to the hotel in a happy state of mind, accompanied by a young man who had volunteered to carry his load to the hotel on his back for a mere fifty rupees.

He was having dinner with the Manager in the hotel, as his family had left for their native village. As a bachelor, Udit had an open kitchen near his room, in which he sometimes cooked on the kerosene stove. Today the two friends were enjoying food from the hotel's kitchen.

'Do you drink?' asked the Manager.

'No I have never tried. I have never seen anyone drinking in my family, to be precise.'

'But man you did not stay at home long enough to be able to see!'

'My father was a strict teetotaller.'

The conversation was interrupted midway. A boy who supplied firewood to the hotel came running towards them.

'Lila's room has not opened since morning today and everyone can hear Chhotu crying nonstop,' he was breathless.

'Let's go,' the Manager and Udit hurried towards her room.

They knocked on the door, both of them taking turns, shouting 'Lila … Lila … Lila!' but there was no response.

Chhotu's cries had become more desperate. Udit then shouted his name. 'Chhotu … Chhotu … Chhotu!' … The cries momentarily stopped when his name was announced and then resumed.

In the meantime, somebody had informed the police. The SHO reached shortly and asked two of his constables to break open the door.

Inside, a terrified Chhotu stood near the door, sobbing wildly. The police went near the cot, where Lila lay face down, in a blue and red printed sari. A lady constable did a quick examination. She then turned her face over and felt her pulse. Her expression changed as she gestured towards the SHO with her hand indicating that she was no more.

Udit and the Manager were in a state of shock.

How could this happen, they discussed in hushed whispers by the side of the passageway as the police completed formalities before taking the body away. Chhotu bawled in Udit's lap as the room was sealed.

Next afternoon, the police came back to complete the remaining formalities and also informed them that the body would be handed over to her family the following day after the cause of death was determined.

A traumatised Chhotu was the only immediate family member she had left behind. Relatives, if any, were known to none. The Manager tried to find out if anyone even distantly related to her, stayed anywhere closeby. His telephonic calls to Haridwar failed to elicit any response from her previous employers. A domestic help stationed there informed the police that all the members of that household had gone to Canada for a vacation.

It was left to Chhotu to perform the last rites and also all other rituals that followed. And Udit volunteered to help the little boy, but in effect it was he who was doing everything, holding the boy in his arms. Chhotu at times smiled innocently, at times cried continuously and at times slept with his head resting on Udit's shoulders. For those who talked in whispers, opining that Udit would bring misfortune to himself and his family by performing rituals he should be far away from, Udit had a ready reply, 'There is no misfortune left that has not befallen on me, I don't care anymore.'

That night, his diary had a new entry, 'Life is unpredictable, never take it for granted.'

At night Udit and Chhotu slept in a corner of the hotel lobby. Udit did not know what to do. He was not related to Chhotu, even distantly. He was at best a friendly big brother, pampering the little boy with candies and lollies and occasionally a few toys. The Manager visited the two often, enquiring if he could help them in any way. Before leaving, he would not forget to assure Udit that someone would turn up soon to claim custody of the boy.

A week had passed. The post-mortem report did not have a single reason as to the cause of death. It listed many in difficult medical jargon, blood toxicity, septicaemia which was important for the police as any foul play had been ruled out.

Then one afternoon, a jeep full of policemen descended at the hotel along with three persons from an orphanage in Dehradun. They demanded that the child be handed over to them, after the completion of the formalities. Udit was puzzled to find them at the hotel unannounced. The Manager took him aside and told that the Chief General Manager had himself visited the orphanage and requested them to take custody of the boy. It took almost two hours, filling forms, pasting photographs and signing papers. Ultimately, Chhotu had to go. He cried as the lady from the orphanage pulled him away from Udit forcibly and went towards the vehicle.

Not a single pair of eyes was dry that day, when the police vehicle sped away.

The man in that crushed newsprint bore a dozen similarities to the one in the photo Shweta had in her hand, plucked out from the black and white photographs in the family album. The age difference between the two photographs was eight years, an easy inference as the protest was a recent occurrence, the date and time being mentioned clearly in other newspapers as well.

'Mama, I think this is our only chance, our only clue which might lead us to Udit Bhaiya, God willing,' Shweta said.

'We shall try our level best, the rest is in His hands,' said Mama raising his hands in supplication, invoking the Lord Almighty for help.

The next day early in the morning, the receptionist at Hotel Samrat had still not arrived and the chowkidar fumbled with the phone, as he tried hard to connect the caller to room number 305, K. Liddle. The lady on the line could not wait as the call was urgent.

The conversation was quick. A delighted Mr Liddle had agreed to come over in an hour's time. Shweta's call had also provided him with a welcome excuse to pay a second visit. He was desperate to divert his mind from the pangs of guilt that the developments by the sidelines of his own plot had caused the day before. For Liddle, a bit of friendly chit chat, a little banter always came in handy, whenever something unpleasant weighed on his mind. Throughout the previous night he had been restless with some of the weirdest dreams he ever had.

The heat outside surprisingly had not troubled him much but today morning when he was taking a shower, he was for a moment mistaken that he had switched on the hot water faucet. When he had rechecked and found the same hot water in the other taps as well, he dressed up again and called the room attendant. In a fit of anger he took him to the bathroom and asked him to put his hand under the running water from that very faucet, with the letters COLD inscribed on the beautiful gold top. The frightened chap had then clarified that it was indeed cold water directly being pumped from the overhead tanks and it was due to the extreme temperatures outside that the water appeared heated. An embarrassed Liddle had refused to buy his argument, till he fortified his truth by taking him along to a wash basin in the dining hall of the restaurant where the water was equally hot! The fellow then offered to bring for him, a bucket of water from the well in the hotel compound, insisting that it would be much cooler than the one directly piped from the tank.

He had then reluctantly agreed to his proposal and had a bucket bath, after many years. Refreshed, ready and now cheerful, he waited for his breakfast to arrive in his room. He sat on the sofa and switched on the TV, but he hardly listened to the news. His mind had wandered and strayed into the corridors of memory right into the year of 1962. His wife Jenner had accompanied him when he had arrived in Muir College, for a short stay for some data collection work; it was a research project that he had undertaken. She was in her third trimester of pregnancy and had insisted she too would come along with her husband. Liddle had wanted to leave her in Bombay with her parents but she had not agreed to it. The initial days were difficult, as they had to share a two room house inside a narrow lane in the present old Katra colony, with another colleague.

It was a cold November morning. They were still settling down for their morning tea by the side of a small fire that their domestic help had lighted for them in an iron vessel, in their back veranda.

All of a sudden, Mrs Liddle went into premature labour. Thankfully Liddle himself was at home, it being a Sunday. The onset of sudden labour, six weeks before time had caught them unawares. Their maid had called up two ladies from the neighbourhood and also a midwife and prepared to get the delivery done at home. But some complication had resulted in the baby not descending expectedly with her progressing labour. The ladies were scared and one of them ran to Liddle and asked him to either call a doctor or take Jenner to a hospital.

Liddle had rushed out of home, forgetting even to put on his shoes, to find a suitable conveyance to carry his wife to a hospital. Ultimately, he had returned with a tonga; but the vehicle could not enter the three feet lane which led to their house. Jenner had to be brought to the waiting tonga, some 60 metres away! The ladies had shown some quick presence of mind. They had wrapped her in a blanket and the three of them had almost carried her to the tonga. The baby perhaps decided that to be the right time to discover the world outside ! By the time, Jenner had been laid at the foot rest of the tonga, the baby's head was visible. But she was unable to push the child out. One of the ladies tried to pull the baby out but failed to. The hospital was quite far away and carrying her to the hospital in such a critical condition on a horse pulled carriage meant inviting further trouble. Liddle knew that both the mother and the unborn baby were in real danger. He pleaded with the ladies to accompany them to the hospital. One of them obliged but the other ran away, out of shock.

As the tonga slowly trotted on the road, with Mr Liddle cradling his wife's head, the other woman kept an eye on Jenner's tummy and her breath. Suddenly that lady yelled to the tongawala, 'Hurry up, Hurry up, the baby is in danger!' Then she turned towards Liddle and blurted, 'I don't know what is happening, the baby is half way out, his head and neck are jutting outside, while the other half, is still in!' Liddle stopped the tonga and asked her. 'What do I do? Will we reach the hospital?'

'Sahib, memsahib is getting unconscious, and the baby in this position will not survive and I am too scared to do anything!'

Liddle got down from the tonga to see if something could be done. He located a nameplate on a door, beyond the road where the tonga stood. A prefix Dr made him run into the house. He knocked at the door like a possessed man, not knowing what he was doing!

The house was occupied by one Dr Arvind Johri, MD.

He was an orthopaedic surgeon at the MLN Medical College. For the last four years, he had been plastering broken bones, adding screws and rods to joints gone astray and medicating patients with joint pains and inflammations. And there, at his door, stood a man with folded hands and flowing tears literally begging for help to save his wife.

He protested meekly, saying that he had no experience of delivering a baby. Liddle did not listen to him, but dragged him towards the tonga, a few steps away to 'see her condition.' The sight scared him but he was quick to assess that if he shut his door now, two lives were sure to be lost.

'I will try,' he had said then and had taken the lady in labour inside his home.

There, within fifteen minutes he had helped save three lives, Mrs Liddle, a baby boy and a girl! That Jenner was pregnant with twins, the Liddles had not known!

Liddle collapsed at the doctor's feet and wept with joy. The doctor heard Liddle in his delirium thanking him, terming him an angel from heaven, his God whom he would worship all through his life, a gratitude that he would never be able to repay!

Today, after three decades, life had given him a second chance, at least to thank him once again; repaying that huge emotional debt was, however, humanely impossible, said Liddle to himself. No amount of money or wealth could ever weigh equal on the scales of the doctor's goodwill and the benevolence that he showed that day!

Liddle cursed himself and his whims, when he had bought that piece of land without thinking. Dr Arvind and Yashoda's torturous mental state and their agony over having to part with half of their land, were written in bold lines on their old faces.

Was their financial condition in any way responsible for this sale? Liddle wondered.

Lost in a maze of remorse and afterthoughts, he took only a glass of juice followed by some iced tea and stepped out of the hotel. He continued analysing what he would do next, mulling over various options and did not realise that he was just two houses ahead of Shweta's.

'I have to go there to that house with that grey gate,' he almost shouted at the driver in agitation.

Shweta and Mama were excited to see Liddle. Shashank had left for University early as he had some invigilation duty. Bina was down with a mild fever and was resting in bed.

'So my niece looks excited today, what is the reason?' Mr Liddle asked after the greetings and handshakes.

'Mamaji, I need your help.'

'Oh sure, I am at your disposal, young lady,' he bowed his head in jest.

Shweta surprisingly was so overwhelmed with emotion that she could not utter a word, only managing to hand over the photos and the crushed newspaper to Liddle. Thereafter it was Ajit Mama who spoke, recounting the sequence of events he had heard and repeated so many times about what had happened that September, in 1985.

The story had stunned Liddle into complete silence. A frail old man and a twenty-one year old girl had taken it upon themselves to find a young man who had disappeared some eight years ago.

'Now, what did your dad do all these years?' he asked scratching his head in disbelief.

'He tried his best, but our destiny willed otherwise. Over the years he lost heart, totally.'

Liddle peered into the photo. The features were strikingly similar and he could not disagree on that! As it is, he had been a firm believer in destiny, ever since his twins were born in that manner, unheralded, unexpected inside an unknown home at the hands of a doctor who had delivered a child for the first time in his life.

'What a day this is turning out to be!' he smiled and thought to himself.

'Mama did you visit the plot yesterday?' Shweta asked as he prepared to leave.

'Yes I did, I did.'

'But Mama I bet you could have bought a bigger plot just behind this one. I find Arvind Uncle so depressed these days. Had Madhur Bhaiya not forced him, he would never have sold it. You could have taken the bigger plot and built a nice 5-star hotel with English … Chinese … and Thai restaurants,' Shweta said.

'Is it so? The Johris didn't want to sell? Why didn't you mention this earlier child, if you knew it,' Liddle asked, the shock clearly visible on his face.

'Mamaji, it was your first visit and I did not know you well enough to share something so private to them,' Shweta said.

'Never mind dear, what's done is done,' Liddle averred, gathered the photos quickly and kept them in his briefcase.

'Ok, then, we meet again soon. And my dear niece the manhunt begins as soon as I reach Mussoorie, don't worry. If I take on a project I don't rest till I finish it, you see.'

As his taxi passed by the road in front of his own plot, he asked the driver to stop a few metres away from the gate. He could see the assistant contractor haggling and arguing with Arvind over something. Quietly he walked towards the gate, but then stopped and waited. The argument that he overheard left a bitter taste in his mouth. Arvind was requesting the contractor to let him know the building construction plan. He was literally begging him to keep in mind the fact that there was a house behind, in which an old couple lived. The contractor was as rude and impolite as a person could be, telling him to mind his own business and not be sentimental about the land he had sold for hard cash. He also had the audacity to tell him that being as old as he was, he should now concentrate on the spiritual aspects of life, visiting temples and other religious places and not be attached to such materialistic things. Enraged, he thought of firing the man then and there, but of late he had become so conscious of his decision-making ability that he stopped himself and returned to the waiting car.

Back at the hotel, he was in a confused state of mind. While he was partly excited at the prospect of uniting a son to his family, he was troubled with the hurt that he had unknowingly caused to Arvind and his wife. He wanted to go and tell Arvind that he was not to blame for the unfortunate events that had unfolded in his life. Unwilling to be whimsical again, he wanted to be fully prepared while dealing with this delicate subject. He could not bear causing any more hurt to a person who had played God in his life.

Under normal circumstances, he would have got down from his car, approached the contractor, politely shook his hands and said, 'Thank you Sir for all you've done for me. It'll be a pleasure to invite you again,' and then sent the cheque for his dues through the driver.

The quagmire of such unpleasant thoughts and events had spun a cobweb over his mind. And his irritation at the quirky turn of events was quite palpable as he rang up the hotel reception and complained about the water jug being empty. The room attendant who came also got a mouthful for the bedsheet being dirty and the pillows being too hard. Ultimately the hotel manager came and apologised profusely, promising to take the errant boys to task.

An hour later, his anger subsided and he began to watch TV. The news item about the huge tourist influx at Mussoorie, where the weather was getting better and better did wonders to his mood. He could feel himself engulfed in the evening mist, walking down Mall Road full of children vacationing and romantic couples walking together hand in hand whispering words of love in each other's ears.

June 1993. Mussoorie was expectedly crowded. The sun was setting and the distant peaks had been rendered invisible, due to the thick bank of clouds that had just descended on the town. Most of the guests in the hotel were out and Udit was free, not having to attend to frantic calls on the phone, regarding a leaking pipe in the bathroom or an attendant not turning up for room service. He sat on the stairs leading to his room and gazed at the deodars and oaks in front. A few rhododendrons in full bloom added a little sparkle to the green and brown, painting a pretty picture. He wondered if he had been in the town in his previous birth as well, for in this birth he had spent only the last eight years of his life here and yet the attachment that he felt with the place was unlikely to be a result of such a short association.

A pair of Himalayan bulbuls had flown and settled on Chhotu's red tricycle that was parked in the balcony. The small rear view mirrors, at both the handles that Chhotu had insisted be tied had fascinated them and both anxiously pecked at them continuously shifting from one to the other. Chhotu's behaviour had been very similar, he recollected. Riding the cycle, he would intermittently gaze at himself in the mirror, adjust his hair, flash different kinds of smiles and then readjust the tilt of the mirror and begin pedalling again. The loss of Chhotu had saddened him. He wondered how such a temporary association with someone unknown could cause the kind of attraction that they had developed for each other. During such tender moments of longing for the child, his thoughts would again veer into negativity, into those unpleasant thoughts that he had harboured in his childhood and adolescence about life and its ways.

He had grown up with the belief that he was not the biological child of his parents. He had always considered his dad as one with no tender feelings of love for him and that is why, he had absolutely no memories of any father-son bond shared between them. But his bonding with Chhotu had managed to pierce a little hole in his philosophy of pessimism, through which every now and then a little bubble of optimism would sneak in. 'He had been a rigid introvert, keeping his feelings close to his heart always, but that's not the way it should be,' Udit would say as if to sum up a short story in his diary.

A strong wind came down from the hills and rattled the rooftops of the shops lining the road below. He felt cold and moved towards the room to get a shawl or a woollen. He found Vishnu standing at the door with tea.

'Why you did you not come in?' he asked him genially.

'I was about to,' Vishnu said flashing his usual smile.

Vishnu's happy go lucky disposition and his cheerful visage always reminded him of his teacher's sermons which he so hated in his moral science class. She always insisted that happiness was a state controlled by one's own mind and in the long run its primary requisite was to derive joy in what one did. For a child, reading a story should be a source of joy, for an artist indulgence in his passion should provide him joy, for a teacher, teaching should be a source of joy and for a mother, nursing and tending her baby should be a source of joy. He wondered how much joy Vishnu's work gave him that he always appeared to be so happy and content. Devoid of any social moorings, his own work at best was only an anchor which had kept him confined to a routine. The monotony of his routine coupled with the aimlessness that often enveloped him searching for those elusive moments of joy everyday, he would let open his cache of bitterness once again. Did Dad ever play a game of cricket with me? Did he ever bring a gift for me? Did he ever take me to a theatre to watch a movie? These thoughts would help him recoup and recover from his own guilt and inevitably the comparisons would follow. With his two sisters, he had been so different; soft as butter, helping Shweta with her homework, bringing beautiful dresses for both of them before a festival, dropping them to school on his scooter, accompanying them to the Wheelers Book Shop in Civil Lines to purchase their books and notebooks before the start of a new session. And then when he had confided in his school friends of Class V his best friend had advised him, 'to find out if he was their real son and not one picked up from somewhere.' He had then gone about finding the truth on his own and after sifting through all the family albums concluded that since there existed none of his photos as an infant or a toddler he could recognise, 'I must have definitely been picked up from the steps of a temple or from the roadside underneath a lantana bush.' The next day, he had gone to Shashank and posed the question to him, 'Where are my original parents?'

'Oh God. Now who has passed this great wisdom on to you boy? I never thought my own son would be so daft. Get lost!' When he had stuck to his ground, unwilling to budge, he had been slapped twice. Finally, his honour had been saved by the timely intervention of Granny.

The very next day a calm Shashank had called him to his room and made him sit in his lap. Then he had addressed him as 'young man' and had gone on to bare his heart, telling him how circumstances had forced him to send Udit away to Bindki with Granny because Bina was seriously unwell, implying her second pregnancy that had ultimately ended with a stillborn. Thereafter, the death of Udit's grandfather happened and a shattered Granny had asked him if he could leave Udit with her for some time to give her company. Thus his stay away from his 'original parents' had been prolonged, two years to be precise and Udit was brought back 'home' only when he had turned five, the age to begin schooling. At the end of the episode, a shaken Dad had pointed to a calendar on the wall behind, one with the image of Lord Hanuman baring open his heart quite literally to reveal pictures of Lord Rama and Ma Sita within him. He had then quipped softly, 'Now I can't do that, can I?'

A wind had sprung up again, bringing with it dark burdened clouds. Heavy drops of rain were followed by a lashing storm, with tiny white marble like hailstones bouncing off the narrow stony path that led to old temple atop the hill.

A call from the Manager at this instant was a huge relief and a welcome diversion.

By the time he returned to his room, it was way past midnight. A wedding reception at the hotel ball room had kept him occupied. He was tired but sleep was nowhere near. A game of chess did not extend beyond fifteen minutes. He had beaten his opponent, the invisible him, fair and square and in a pleasant mood he poured himself a glass of warm milk and stood by the window. The clouds had parted and a full moon was visible above the hills. The stillness of the night was interrupted periodically with the cicadas in the nearby forest breaking into a song, reaching a crescendo and then calming all of a sudden. A distant caterwauling caught his attention and he scanned the vast expanse of forests. But before long, he was lost in the woods of introspection, the hangover of the bout of nostalgia that had knocked him down threatening to overpower him once again.

16 September, 1985. He could recall that date even in his deepest sleep. That unfortunate day, he had come back home from college along with Narayan, sitting on the carrier of his bicycle, holding back his tears, scared and shivering from within. Both of them had spent considerable number of hours loitering around the college campus and by the row of tea shops outside the gate, gulping down cups of tea, to drown that sinking feeling that he had failed an exam. Although he knew that this failure in Physics paper could only be a temporary setback and he still had a chance, if he worked

hard enough and cleared the supplementary paper, a month later, that sickening feeling refused to leave him. The thing that rankled him, pricked him uncomfortably was how on earth could he flunk in a Physics paper, a subject taught by none other than Dad!

How would he face his father that day had been the million dollar question. Narayan was the only one who had suggested that he should tell the truth no matter what the pros and cons be. After all the worst possibility could be a transient anger that could last a day or two, at the most. Narayan that day had tried his best to convince him that he should have the courage to tell the truth, but somehow two of his other friends had managed to convince Udit that if he could utter a small lie, that would save the day for him and then he could study hard and clear the supplementary exam. The final outcome would be the same, either way.

That evening when Shashank had asked him about his results, he had concocted a story that his result had been withheld due to some confusion with another student by the same name, who had not appeared in that paper. Shashank had believed his son without question and had also asked him if he wanted him to take up the matter with the authorities. Udit had politely refused his offer of help, telling him that now that he was grown up, he could handle such petty issues on his own. The matter rested there.

A week passed by and nothing happened. His lie stood ground perfectly and he was relieved that the situation he dreaded, created no further trouble. But three more days and one evening when his father had returned home from university, all hell broke loose. Shashank had been made in charge of conducting the supplementary exams that year and while going through the forms submitted by the students, he had got the shock of his life when he had come across Udit's form, showing an embarrassing 29 marks against the Physics paper.

After that incident, eight years had gone by and Udit slowly realised his mistake that he ought not to have lied to his father not once but twice over. Shashank had been very cooperative and reassured him that if he had failed there was no reason to make a big issue out of it, for time was still on Udit's side and he would help Udit understand the concepts, yet again. He had been kind and affectionate, telling Udit that life was not only about passing or failing in an examination. Even if he failed, he would still remain his son, he would still love him the same and he would still pray for his well being and happiness every day in his prayers.

Reminiscing now, Udit felt that he had then been unreasonably adamant and inflexible so much so that no pleadings or no emotions could make him relent. He had stuck to his guns, daring to question his father, if he had doubts over his own son's integrity. Shashank could not hold himself back then. He took out the neatly folded form from his shirt pocket and threw it at Udit's face. Half an hour later, however, he had called Udit back again, this time in his own study and in total privacy tried to counsel him. Choking with emotion, he had held his hand and with eyes shut, in pain, he had said that the big issue was not that Udit had failed; he was hurt more because he had been taken for a ride by his own son, whom he had trusted so blindly since childhood, signing his reports cards without a frown no matter how he had performed. Udit had always been an average student, never as excellent or outstanding as his parents would have desired. That evening Shashank had gone out for a long walk and had only returned by 11 pm.

Udit had overheard him lamenting before Bina that it was he who had failed in the exam, the exam of life. Sharp pangs of guilt had overcome Udit. He had realised the seriousness of the blunder he had committed. He had wished that his father would scold him but sadly nothing of that sort happened. The whole night Udit remained restless. Unbearable guilt and self-doubt had gnawed away at his conscience and in the morning a visibly upset Shashank, had quipped, 'I hope you've not cheated me like this anywhere else.'

That was the proverbial last nail in the coffin. The person he loved to hate had defeated him yet again. He had kept a pair of shirt and pants in his college bag and taking away whatever pocket money he had with him, he sneaked out of the house, angry and unhappy, more with himself than with his father. He had gone towards the railway station and with anger dominating any reason he took the first train that was leaving the station. It was only when the TTE had elbowed his way into the general compartment and asked him to show his ticket that he realised his folly.

A knock at the door provided him an excuse to leave his bed. Vishnu had come with his tea and breakfast. A strong sun angled into his room. A barbet in full cry, perhaps on the walnut beyond his window, diverted his attention from the sleepless night that he had just endured.

As he walked towards the hotel, he could see a government jeep stopping in front of the hotel gate. He walked down to enquire if any official had arrived to carry out an inspection or to point out that a tax was pending with the hotel or something similar but seeing a lady carrying Chhotu, he was so excited that he blurted out, 'My Chhotu seems to have come back, I can't believe this.'

'Excuse me,' a man near the jeep beckoned him though he stood hardly a few metres away.

'I think you will not mind keeping this child with you for a few days. He has not been able to adjust there in the orphanage. Right now, he is unwell. The doctor said that he had been too shocked to cope with the trauma …'

A concerned Udit almost snatched Chhotu from her arms. All the bitterness that had accumulated in his body since yesterday evaporated instantly. He cradled him and held him tightly. The child's body was burning with fever.

Chhotu did not open his eyes despite Udit calling him a number of times. 'What's wrong with him? He looks so pale and thin! Why did you take him away at all? We could have taken much better care of him,' he said and began walking towards his room. On the adjoining wall, a baby monkey clung to his mother, as she leapt up to the oak.

'We will send you the expenses earmarked for him every month,' the lady informed. But Udit was not listening. Sailing in his bubble of bliss, cradling his bundle of joy, he was unwilling to listen to any extraneous sounds. From his room he called up Dr Raj who visited the hotel if any of the guests fell ill.

In the evening, the entire hotel staff had trooped into Udit's room. Everyone had a gift for the boy, a plastic bat and ball, a puppy nodding his head continuously, a train loaded with passengers, packets of candies. The hotel manager had come with a bag of fruits.

'Chacha, I don't like that place where they took me. My mom lives here, you know.' He cried and asked for his mother, pointing to the room where the two lived earlier. He even dragged Udit towards the room, forcing him to walk in. The little boy called out to his mother, searched for her under the bed, behind the long yellow floral curtain of the window, clung to her pile of clothes which lay folded on the only steel trunk that they had possessed.

After ten minutes of search, he finally walked around towards the door where Udit stood and holding on to his hand, again dragged him telling him that Ma had gone to the hotel to wash clothes.

The stark reality of life unnerved him. Immediately Udit took him in his lap and walked towards Mall Road.

Mr Liddle was immensely relieved to be back in the cold climes of Mussoorie. The renovation activity at his hotel was on in full swing and the three rooms on the second floor had already been refurbished. Occasionally Liddle preferred to stay in one of these rooms and watch the crowd trooping in on the mall, chatting and laughing. Mussoorie weather never ceased to amaze him. People would walk in light cottons, knee length sneakers and tees, girls would wander out in fancy skirts with noodle strapped tops and enjoy ice lollies and creamy softy and chocolate bars. An hour later, the sun would disappear, the hills in the distance would be blanked out from view, a thin veil of mist would descend and the very same people would now pull out their woollens from their bags or huddle inside shops for comfort, buy sweaters, jackets, caps and socks, put them on and come out again and enjoy. Now the vendors selling roasted corn cobs by the side of the tiniest of fires would enjoy brisk sales. Life was a continuum, always.

A passing thought distracted him. He went inside one of the rooms and made a call to one of the contractors he had hired in Allahabad.

'You need to stop the work immediately,' he roared into the receiver.

The voice at the other end quivered and trembled.

'I will let you know soon, what needs to be done, but for now, stop the work!'

It was again on a sudden impulse that he had acted. But that call had given him relief unlimited. He was still undecided what he wanted to do but for the time being he wanted to do nothing. He loved being in a state of voluntary idleness. Sometimes it gave him time to ponder over circumstances.

He then remembered the other important work he had promised to undertake. In his briefcase lay the bunch of photos Shweta had handed over to him. He studiously went through each of them, trying to construct the features that would remain unchanged with age and then matching them with that of the man in the photo shot by a newspaper journalist. He was not entirely convinced about the similarities between the two but was willing to give it a try.

How to go about it was the big question.

A week later Liddle ran into an old friend of his during his early morning walk, a retired DIG who had served in areas around Dehradun and Mussoorie for a number of years. After retirement he had come back to settle in his native village. Familiar with every nook and corner of the town he offered to help immediately after Liddle shared Udit's story with him. He was sure that he could be easily traced, for Mussoorie was a small town. His friends and former colleagues were sure to offer help even if he kept things strictly unofficial. Buoyed by the developments Liddle invited him over to his home in the evening for dinner, telling him that the occasion deserved a little celebration.

Back in the plains, complete stoppage of work at the plot surprised Arvind. It hadn't even rained. Neither the burly contractor nor his lanky assistant were to be seen in the evenings, the time they normally came for a summary inspection of work done during the day.

'Wonder why the work at the plot has been halted!' he said as Yashoda walked in with tea.

'Who knows? A miracle might be in the offing?' She said trying to be optimistic amidst all the sadness that pervaded their home these days.

'You mean to say that the buyer will leave it vacant or he will have an orchard planted here for us. Being environmentally friendly is the latest fad among the elite these days,' Arvind snapped back. Yashoda preferred to stay mum and sipped her tea.

'That businessman is very rich or so I've heard, so he can very well afford to construct, demolish, reconstruct. Wonder if he has any plans to resell? This boy Madhur could not understand what could be the consequences of selling the front portion of a house. If someone comes up with a liquor vend here, we will be doomed.'

Yashoda pretended not to hear. She had stopped lending ear to presumptions and assumptions.

Udit and Chhotu had become inseparable in the last few days. Many mistook them to be blood relations, seeing the bond they shared.

And now the pages of Udit's diary had many entries.

'A lovely stroll on the Mall with Chhotu, with ice cream and candy floss, Bliss,' read one of them.

'A flute, a dog and a big car for Chhotu today and the delight on his face; little pleasures of my life ...'

Positive developments began to happen in the Operation Search as well as in Shweta's health, infusing a new life in her. She had begun to take her physiotherapy sessions at Arvind's place more seriously. On the previous Saturday, Arvind had made her undergo a few tests and was excited with the results, pumping his fists in the air as he stared at the graphic peaks and plateaus on a paper. He had also called up Shashank to inform him that an orthopaedic surgeon of great repute would be in the city for a week and that it was a great opportunity for them to consult him and seek his advice.

'I will come along, don't worry, just fix up the appointment as per your convenience,' the excitement in his voice was palpable. For Shashank the good news could not have come at a better time.

He noted the phone number and immediately started calling to get the earliest appointment. The line remained busy and it was only after forty-five minutes that he managed to book an appointment for the next day.

Anxious about the outcome of the proposed consultation with the doctor, Bina passed a sleepless night. Her anxiety stemmed from the fact that if the outcome of the meeting turned out to be less than favourable, it could be a big setback for Shweta. For the last three years they had been depending upon physiotherapy sessions and were hopeful that one day Shweta would be able to walk on her own. The events which had now become a bit hazy in some compartments of her brain had refreshed and she could recount each and every moment of that terrible day when their world had come crashing down all of a sudden. That event had occurred two years after Udit left home and all efforts to trace him had been unsuccessful. To break the all-pervading sense of loss and overriding melancholy at home, Shashank had planned a family outing. The two daughters had remained confined to home choosing to skip family functions and weddings, apprehensive that rather than the bride or the groom, people would be more interested to know the exact reasons for Udit's disappearance. Besides, Bina's health had been anything but good and the bouts of constant depression she suffered from had made matters worse.

It was then that Shashank had decided that they would make a trip to Dehradun, Haridwar, Rishikesh and Mussoorie, a trip that would be a fun and pilgrimage outing combined. Granny had been hesitant initially but later she had a change of mind when she realised that this was a golden opportunity for her to fulfil her long standing wish of taking a dip at Har ki Paudi in Haridwar. The first half of their ten day trip had been fun. On the sixth day they had returned to Dehradun and stayed at a dharamshala near the railway station. Shweta and Sonam were eager to spend time in Mussoorie rather than in Dehradun. They insisted that the stay in Dehradun should be as short as possible. Shashank wanted that they stay at Dehradun for a day extra so that Bina and Granny got some rest.

But seeing the girls unhappy, it was decided that they would travel to Mussoorie in the early hours of the day after. The road had a lot of traffic and they were just about five kilometres away from Mussoorie and had crossed the last of those infamous hairpin bends, when a truck coming from the opposite direction rammed straight into their taxi and hurtled it down on the road below.

People who came to rescue them and pulled them out of the vehicle, bruised, battered and all soaked in blood, thanked God and proclaimed that the Joshis were lucky. Their taxi had rolled down but had landed in an upright position after hitting a trailer that had been parked at the other edge of the road The impact had been such that Granny had a major fracture though Bina escaped with only scratches and cuts on her left hand. Sonam had a deep wound in the leg and Shashank sitting in front of the vehicle had lost consciousness after his head hit the dashboard. It was Shweta's bad luck that she was the one who had sustained maximum injuries. Some good Samaritans had promptly taken them to the government hospital, ferrying them in a mini bus vacated by a group of travellers travelling to Mussoorie. At that time not many believed that she would survive.

In hindsight, now Bina believed that God had been kind to them. Had that trailer not been parked there at the wrong side of the road, their taxi would have taken a few more somersaults down the hill and then probably … she would shudder at the thought. Some of Shashank's colleagues had visited them at the hospital and offered help. A month and a half later the family had returned home to an unexpectedly warm welcome by a huge group of friends, well wishers and colleagues from the University at the railway station. Outside their house too, waited a good number of people, many unknown faces, expressing joy at their arrival. The gents shook hands, the ladies hugged and young children smiled, the overwhelming welcome lifting the family morale.

Many months later, Shweta had overheard her dad talking to her granny about how he had planned that unfortunate trip. One day, shattered and shaken, when he was sitting heartbroken on the steps of the Hanuman temple at the banks of Yamuna, a priest had come to him and consoled him, telling him that his son was fine and was somewhere around in Dehradun, Haridwar, Rishikesh region. That had propelled him to plan that trip but destiny had willed otherwise and he was almost on the verge of losing his daughter, this time perhaps, forever.

Ever since, he had compressed and wound his search into prayers, morning and evening, day in and day out, wishing for his son's wellbeing. His day always began with the secret hope that today would be the day when his son would turn up at the door, unannounced, unexpected, surprising all. No wonder as long as he was at home, every ring of the doorbell would see him scurrying towards the door, before the bell could ring a second time.

Bobbing up and down in the ocean of thoughts and memories, Bina did not realise that the day had broken. She was still in bed when Shashank walked in.

'Bina, it's 6.45 already; are you okay, do you want to sleep more?'

Buzo had followed Shashank, barking softly as he stood by the side of Bina's bed. His milk time was 6:00 am.

She sat up in bed, almost startled that the day had broken so soon. She had hardly slept. 'Oh, it was uncomfortable, I don't know why, the mosquitoes sang in my ears, the whole night.'

'But you forgot to switch on the mosquito repellent, dear,' Shashank said.

'We will have to leave for the hospital early; otherwise the queue would be very long.'

Up there in Mussoorie, Udit and Chhotu had returned from their morning walk. Chhotu was an early riser and once he was up, he always wanted to be out. The confines of a small room with a solitary window to the world outside, was too small for his inquisitiveness. He loved moving up and down the stairs, following the puppies that would come around wagging their tails and occasionally would even run behind the squirrels that would keep scampering up and down the majestic boles of the deodars and the oaks. The only thing that scared him was the sound produced by monkeys jumping on the sloping tin roof and every time a troop came jumping across, he would cling to Udit, not getting down from his lap till he was sure that the terror had subsided.

Chhotu had now developed a liking for tea, the one that the vendor near the bifurcation of the Kulri Road made. And the generous man always had a cupful ready for the boy with some extra milk and sugar. The other day while the two were sitting on the wooden bench near the tea stall, a smart old man had stopped by and offered him a chocolate. Little Chhotu had accepted it more out of curiosity for the bright gold and black pack than out of any knowledge of what it contained. When Udit had removed the wrapper for Chhotu, he had realised that it was a Swiss chocolate.

Three days later, the man Chhotu had christened Chocolate Uncle met them again carrying a new pack in one hand, a stick in the other and a cigar in his mouth. On seeing him approach, Udit covered his face with his woollen muffler that he normally kept tied around his neck. He could not withstand even a single puff of cigarette smoke as it triggered an allergic reaction in him causing him to sneeze furiously for at least an hour.

Within the span of a month, Chhotu had received imported chocolates four times. One day Udit thought of asking him who he was when they met again. But they did not meet till one Saturday afternoon, he saw him having an animated discussion with the bookstall owner at the corner shop in Kulri and the owner was respectfully referring to him as Mr Liddle.

At the Nazareth hospital, the queue was long. From the doctor's chamber in the main building housing the Orthopaedic wing, it extended till the gate. Almost a hundred and fifty odd people were waiting to consult the doctor after getting their admission slips. Getting the slip was easy because the hospital had set up four special counters anticipating the huge rush. Arvind had accompanied the two to the hospital. One of his former colleagues was kind enough to take them to his chamber, asking them to wait inside rather than stand in the unending queue. He had even offered an out of turn consultation, but Shashank had politely refused. They sat on the sofa adjoining the window and waited for their turn. The nurse on duty outside the chamber, responsible for ushering the patients in had generously offered to send the peon to the room, when it was time.

Back home, Ajit Mama and Bina tried to catch up on the lost years, journeying back into time with some smiles, some laughs and some tears. Over the years, the physical distance in terms of continents apart that they lived, their different time zones and rare meetings had resulted in almost minimal interaction between them, limited to a rare phone call or a letter. It was lately that Ajit was free of responsibilities and had craved to be in touch with his sister. His yearnings had also acquired desperate overtones, when he had received the news of his younger brother passing away, due to a massive heart attack. That was three years ago and circumstances had been so cruel that he had been unable to take a flight home, the reason being his own leg lay immobilised in a cast. Their conversations over the phone in the aftermath of the tragedy had been very brief, both not wanting to burden the other with any gloom when they knew that they could not share their pain.

The brother in an alien land thousands of miles away and the sister here had suffered in silence, sharing their grief only with their shadows. Today they had found an opportunity to compensate for a fraction of the lost years. The years gone by suddenly came alive once again. Bina steered clear of any mention of Udit, avoiding the topic and midway through the conversation walked away to pick up the phone, though Ajit had not heard it ring.

The wait in the hospital was excruciatingly long, with patients trooping in the chamber time and again seeking clarifications from the doctors. Shweta was initially nervous regarding the outcome of the meeting. But seeing the kind of patients who had turned up, the extreme complications, the excruciating pain some of them bore, the crowd of unfortunate children struggling with deformed and unformed bones, she felt that her own disability was nothing in comparison. Suddenly, see saw Bimla Mausi limping in.

As she sat on the stool, a junior doctor asked her, 'How are you Bimlaji?'

With a smile on her face and a twinkle in her eyes she said, 'I am fine, the pain is now bearable.' Then seeing the doctor bewildered, she added, 'One day everyone has to go, then why let the spectre of looming death spoil my days till I am alive.'

Shweta was shocked as well as curious to know what was wrong with Bimla Mausi.

A young girl who had accompanied Mausi, took note of the medications. Mausi was instructed to wait in the general ward. A ten membered committee of doctors was to meet, discuss her case and examine her shortly. Bimla Mausi had walked out, cool and composed, holding that young girl's hand. After she had walked out, the two doctors discussed that surgery was inevitable. One of the doctors also remarked, 'The lady is extraordinarily brave and gutsy and anyone else in her position would have given up long ago.' These words had shocked Shweta into a stunned silence. For the next fifteen minutes she did not utter a word as Shashank and Arvind tried to paint an optimistic picture about her impending meeting with the expert surgeon.

A peon came looking for them. The three waited for a minute at the door, letting another patient, a howling six year old boy with deformed knees, come out of the chamber held in the arms of his worried mother.

The consultation was long, extending to almost thirty minutes.

Dr Arvind did most of the talking, detailing the entire sequence of events since that accident, the treatment given to her then, the surgeries she had already undergone and the progress thus far. Dr Peter, the foreign expert, asked the nurse to make her lie down. Then he came with a doctor's hammer and few other equipments and examined her, tapping at a few places with the hammer, seeking her reaction and bending and lifting her legs in peculiar kinds of motion. Shweta tried to stay calm.

The team of doctors then sifted through the mountain of reports and finally arrived at a positive conclusion. They were sure that in six months Shweta could be back on her feet, provided she religiously went on a regimen of a special series of exercises and therapy sessions to strengthen her muscles which in their expert opinion had become weak due to her reliance on the wheelchair.

The three returned home ecstatic. The excitement was palpable at the Joshi home that day. Bina could not believe her ears when the news was broken to her. Six months would pass in no time, she knew. The day could be so near, that was what was unbelievable.

Amidst all the excitement, Bimla Mausi's face she had seen at the hospital refused to leave Shweta's mind. She decided to enquire more about her, but did not know how, why she knew well and was very sure. After all the kind of respect and affection she had seen for her in the doctor's chamber could never be given to a person with questionable character. But one thing that troubled her was the fact that it was highly unlikely that she would get a chance to visit her place again.

It was early morning. The sun was just peeping through the multitude of greys in the sky. The telephone at Joshi's house rang and Ajit Mama sitting close by picked up the receiver. After initially being hesitant, he had now acquired the confidence of being in a position to answer simple queries, whenever some close friends of the Joshis called.

It was Mr Liddle on the line. He had called up to say that he was on the job which had been entrusted to him. A friend of his in the police had assured him that finding 'the boy' in the small hill town would not be a big deal. The only hitch that could hamper the efforts could be if that person in that newspaper photo was also a part of the floating population of the town, being one among the many tourists.

He also added that he was also trying on his own, albeit a little foolishly, he thought and burst into a laugh. Now-a-days, he stayed in his new hotel, three days a week which allowed him greater time to interact with people. The duration of his morning walks and after dinner stroll had increased and curiously he had explored each and every shop and hotel, tasted tea from all the vendors lining the Mall Road, his sub-conscious mind had been actively on the job. He also wanted Ajit to note down the phone number of his friend, who had graciously desired to share his personal phone number with the Joshis, on which he could be contacted any time. Ajit Mama asked Shweta to come near with a paper and pen and note down the number. A jubilant Shweta then reached for the chocolate coloured pen stand behind the telephone to fetch the green sketch pen. She wanted to encircle this number in green so that it could be easily located as and when needed. As she stretched herself, the open diary in her lap fell down.

'Ma a little help is needed,' she called out.

'Just a moment,' Bina said and within a minute she was there to pick up her diary.

'What's this? Is it needed,' she asked, trying to unroll a pink paper that had fallen from the diary.

'Let me see,' Shweta said, hurriedly snatching the little cigarette like pink roll.

'Oh, mummy I had been looking for this, you're my lucky charm, always.' It was the rolled two rupee note on which Bimla Mausi had scribbled her telephone number, when the two had met in Nazareth hospital.

Some houses away, Arvind too was in a cheerful mood. The developments in Shweta's case had lifted his spirits because he had been instrumental in coaxing Shweta always to continue with the physiotherapy sessions despite the fact that no immediate relief was visible. And now his stand had been vindicated.

It was almost 11:00 pm and he was not in the least sleepy. He had switched off the tube light to let Yashoda sleep and was listening to an old musical program on the radio, his faithful companion, by his bedside. Arvind always wondered why sleep fairy ditched him whenever he was too tired or too excited. Tonight he was mildly tired, for sure, having accompanied Shweta and Shashank to the hospital. But his excitement was stoked up, when on his return from the hospital, he found that the L shaped boundary wall that had been built in front of the porch had been dismantled. He switched on the night bulb and peeped out from the window, as if he could relive those moments again. It was dark and nothing was visible, but he could hear the wind blowing against the canopy of neem and mango near the boundary wall along the road. Though it had rained very little, in the last two three days, the crickets chirped louder than normal. He went back to bed, switching off the bulb again. The radio was left on because he knew that being in a passively-active state might induce him to sleep compared to being in actively-passive state.

Yashoda slept like a log these days. She had perhaps reconciled herself to the unpleasant developments and had coped up with them with much more fortitude. She had also let go of all expectations from her sons. Not surprisingly hence, the fact that Madhur never called bothered her no more. Getting rid of the emotional baggage had not been easy. But a determined Arvind, a week after their return from Haridwar, had suddenly summoned a scrap dealer and asked him to take away all that was dumped in the two front rooms on the first floor. After all, this is what Madhur had desired, he reminded himself many times in the twenty minutes that the dealer took in emptying the two rooms. This had done a world of good to both of them. For long Arvind had been undecided and averse to the very idea of selling those household goods, primarily because he thought that he could not put a value on them in terms of rupees and paise. He had prized those possessions till now and ironically was happy to give them away for free. The very next day he had rushed to the bank, sharp at 10:00 am and deposited ₹ 35,000 in Madhur's account.

For a while they had also contemplated on having a tenant, but then decided against it. 'Who knows what new trouble we might invite!' Yashoda had said that day, shooting down Arvind's idea immediately. She had her own philosophy 'it was better to be in the solitary company of one's own shadow than to have any company that caused undue stress.' Being philosophical and spiritual had helped her immensely.

Next day it was drizzling when the clock struck five. Yashoda was up early. Arvind who was awake till a little past midnight did not hear the sound of the alarm clock. Around six, he got up and rubbing his puffed eyes, began putting on his jogging shoes.

'It's raining outside, you can sleep a bit more if you wish to,' Yashoda chuckled.

'Really!' he exclaimed flinging away his shoes and springing back to bed.

'Here's your tea,' Yashoda stood near his bed as he pulled up the bed sheet.

'Tea? No tea for now. It will deactivate the sleep mode I wish to be in,' he said covering his face with the sheet.

'As you wish.' She kept the cup on the side table and covered it with the saucer.

'Even Madhur and Mayank as kids were never happy like this when it used to rain early morning, expecting rainy day holidays. Somebody has rightly said that kids and old people are very similar in their mental makeup,' she wondered.

The drizzle was replaced by a heavy rain and the front plot was a pond again.

Shweta had called up Bimla Mausi's number twice since morning but there had been no response. The doctor's words inside that chamber in hospital that day echoed in her ears. She could feel a shiver run down her spine.

'Has something gone wrong? But, so soon …' she thought.

No, it should not, it could not. She had not had a chance to thank that lady who had sheltered her that day, who had welcomed her inside her house with open arms, when perhaps many others would have shied away on multiple pretexts.

In the evening, she called again. This time someone picked up the phone and answered, 'She is unwell. Please leave your name and number. Mausi says she will call when she can.'

Mightily relieved, but now more eager to unravel Mausi mystery, Shweta politely excused herself and promised that 'she would call again in a few days, let Mausi take rest,' and signed off.

It was September now. Six months ago an advertisement for recruitment of POs in SBI had caught Mama's attention. He had then prevailed upon Shweta to apply, asking her to put her signature on the form while he would fill the other columns. 'You never know when luck smiles at which juncture,' he had said as he left for the post office to post the application. The examination centre for the screening test was far away, in St Soldiers School near Daraganj. Since then Shweta had been preparing for this exam but was unsure as to whether she would take the test at all, given the huge inconvenience she had to face while taking her board exams at a faraway centre in Class XII. But the positive developments that had taken place during the last month had been a huge motivating factor. Now she was upbeat and optimistic that the doctors' prediction might just come true and she could be on her feet once again.

Shashank had booked a taxi to take Bina and Shweta to the examination centre. Both the sessions had a paper each. Shweta was still undecided as to whether they would wait at the centre or return home in the two hour interval. Bina waited outside the gate after the examinees had been ushered in. She sat on a concrete bench under an old banyan while the driver drove away towards the corner of the road to park and rest.

The first paper was for two hours, 10:00 am to 12:00 noon. Bina had carried a book to read but random thoughts going through her mind had made her restless after reading just a para. She looked here and there and found a group of parents huddling around a tea vendor who had come especially prepared with extra stuff expecting good business that day. She walked towards them and found three ladies busy in conversation over a cup of tea. One of them invited her to join the group.

It was only when she sat down on the large stone slab with a cup of tea in hand that she realised that one of them was Bimla Mausi.

Bimla Mausi was unable to recognise her immediately. Bina had not only lost a lot of weight, her hair had also greyed much too soon. During Shashank's hospitalisation in Nazareth, the two had not met, as Bina mostly stayed through the night and returned home early morning, to be back by tea time again.

'Bimla Di, how come you are here?' She asked.

Bimla Mausi was surprised to hear her name.

She looked up and tried to recognise the person, while Bina was now sure that it was Bimladi, the same fair face with deeply set eyes and thick eyebrows.

'Bina? You're Bina if I am not mistaken?' she said finally.

She beckoned her to come near and greeted her with a bear hug.

'How is Shweta?' She asked instantly.

Now it was Bina's turn to be baffled.

'She is fine, she is here for the exam, but how do you know her? And, how are you?' she asked.

'I am alive and kicking. As long as He wishes, you have to live in this world,' she said, pointing towards the sky.

'I'm here as a guardian of two girls known to me. They are appearing in this examination.

After a pause, Bimla Mausi continued 'I never believed in destiny but now I realise that it has a role in our lives. You see that day Shweta came to my place not even knowing that I lived in that house. Bina listened to her with disbelief. She never thought Shweta could be so bold.

When it was her turn to talk about the years gone by, Bina deliberately avoided any mention of Udit and Mausi was also careful not to raise the topic.

During the two hour interval, she convinced Shweta and Bina to come home with her as it was very close to this centre. Her home was crowded. There were many young girls, a few of them Shweta could recognise were there at the same examination centre. And this time also, the girl who served them lunch was the one whom Shweta had seen when she had stayed at her place that December night.

'Mausi's home is always crowded,' Shweta said as she dried her hands with the green towel hung on a nail over the wash basin in the veranda.

'Oh yes, I am lucky that my home is always overflowing with people,' she smiled as she settled into a chair with a lot of difficulty, almost wincing in pain.

After lunch, Shweta and four other girls got into the taxi and proceeded to the centre for the afternoon paper.

The girls had promised to take care of Shweta, leaving Bimla Mausi and Bina at home, free to gossip. 'Your house seems to be too big for you Bimla Di.' Bina remarked, genuinely concerned about the wellbeing of a woman she had always found so warm, so affectionate and so positive about life. She had always believed that the negative stories were spun about her character only because she had dared to take on the world and not looked for a compromise with her husband. She had also refused to tag along with one of her male cousins, 'telling him that "I would be a liability. And I have a very long life so it would be a long drawn responsibility to you and your wife…."'

'The house is big, but I am not alone? Now I have so many people with me. And you know Bina, I could have easily accepted Chandu's offer but then this house would have been eyed by his own brothers. So I thought, better stay away from all this being my own master. When I die, the house will be Chandu's anyway, don't tell anyone. It's there in my will. Nice chap he is, cares for me so much and every weekend he is here,' she said almost in a whisper.

Meanwhile the hours passed quickly and the girls returned and there was giggling at the door. Bina glanced at her watch, it was 5:00 pm.

Shweta could see that Bina was quite relaxed, with a twinkle in her eyes that she had not seen for a long time.

'The papers were easy,' she said.

Bina picked up her purse and readied to leave.

'Wait, let's have tea together. My doctors have asked me to live each day of my life now but my lifeline is long,' she said lifting up and showing her left palm.

Bimla Mausi was in a mood to talk today and Bina could not say no.

Sipping her tea, Mausi continued, 'My life has been an open page. I've never been secretive about my own life. If my husband left me for someone else, it was his choice. I was clear in my life, that I didn't need a male to cling on to. Why should one do that? But our society can't take that. So I stopped reacting. Let people read what they want to. How many tongues can I stop from wagging? When my husband left me, someone told me that my life was finished but I'm not a coward. I took it as a new challenge. I took upon myself to help girls in distress. These girls you see around are neither my tenants nor my relatives. They come on their own, stay here till their work is done and then leave. I don't charge a penny, neither do I ask their purpose. But over the years my faith has never been betrayed.' The words were spoken so passionately that no one with a clean conscience and clear heart could disbelieve her. They flowed straight from her heart.

'We'll take your leave please. I promise to come another day. Shweta's papa will be worried if we are late.' Bina anxiously looked at her watch. It was almost six and getting dark and the taxi driver would not wait indefinitely, Shweta was sure.

'Mausi we'll be in touch, I have your number,' was all Shweta could say as they bid goodbye.

'I will come to see Shweta on her feet and that day is not very far, the nurses in the hospital that day were very upbeat about her progress and by that time I hope my surgery for this spinal abscess would also be over.'

The mother and daughter remained quiet during the twenty minute journey home. Bina felt sad for the woman from her village for whom life had been a continuous struggle but Shweta had a seething rage in her heart as she remembered the face of Narayan's mother that day; scorn and disdain engulfed her mind for that woman. If a woman cannot understand another woman, who else would? she thought.

She wanted to reach out to her and let out all the emotions that were ravaging through her, but for now she had to remain silent. She had to let that storm pass.

For the last few days there was no activity at Liddle's plot. Arvind wondered why the construction work had suddenly stopped. He had even thought of calling up Madhur in London but then decided it would be pointless.

In the evening he came across the assistant contractor going on his scooter, when he was returning from the market. Unexpectedly, he stopped, parked the scooter on the side and came to greet him.

'Namaste Sirji,' he began with folded hands.

'No work on the plot these days? What happened? Have you been fired or taken up urgent work somewhere else?'

'No, no, no, we have not been fired, Bade sahib has a change of plan perhaps. We would be removing the debris in a day or two; that is what I was coming over to tell you.'

'A commercial building here won't have many takers, what do you think?'

Arvind in his anxiety put words in his mouth in the hope that he would unknowingly spit out if there was something in his mind.

'I can't say anything, but last time he was here he'd said that he had a design in mind which he would send us soon, but nothing came. Instead he called the other day to stop the ongoing work. These foreign returned people have a lot of money. They construct, then demolish, then construct again. What can we say?' he said.

'Hmm, you are right.'

Arvind could have danced through the passageway but then becoming conscious of the onlookers he restricted himself to a celebratory jig and walked away briskly.

On reaching the door, he pressed the bell continuously till he could see Yashoda coming through the window.

'What is the hurry? Is it raining outside? I can't see any rain and you are not wet either?' Yashoda registered a mild protest at having to hurry from the kitchen, which had almost caused the kadahi in which she was frying fish to topple over from the gas stove. In addition to the minor accident that had been averted, her unhappiness stemmed from the fact that in her haste to reach the door she had put the next batch of fish inside the wok carelessly causing the smoking hot oil to bubble up on her hands. Though there was no perceptible blister, the two round patches were definitely inflamed.

'There is something wrong with the bell, I suppose. It was ringing continuously on its own, maybe the battery is down or water has seeped inside,' Arvind tried to bail himself out as he quickly went to his room.

Yashoda's belligerent mood had caused the fuzz of excitement in him to settle down and he did not share what the contractor had just told him.

Udit had now moved back into his own room from the hotel lobby where he and Chhotu had been sleeping every night. Chhotu had become very friendly with the hotel staff. No money from the government orphanage ever came; not that it was needed nor was Udit particularly bothered. The only thing that troubled him at times was that a day would certainly come in the near future when the orphanage people would come to take him away. His fondness for the little boy was now known to all. Both shared a very deep bond. Chhotu addressed him as Chacha, which he had accepted with some initial reservations because he thought Chacha meant that he was considerably older than those who were addressed as Bhaiya or elder brother. He would tell Chhotu to pronounce Dada, another form of address for an elder brother, but the little boy would say Dadu instead, forcing Udit to break into a guffaw. Dadu meant grandfather, and that made him many times older than Dada. Seeing him laugh, Chhotu would join in and the two would laugh together, the laughter ricocheting off the high ceiling in the predominantly empty room.

The hotel manager had been a generous friend. He had offered free meals to both Udit and Chhotu from the hotel kitchen, sparing them from the trouble of cooking on their own. The hotel kitchen always fed most of the employees free of cost as the owner firmly believed that if the cooks did not eat what they cooked, they would never try to improve their skills. Udit had politely refused the offer, preferring to cook in the little open space behind his room. His makeshift kitchen boasted of a brass stove that ran on kerosene, a pressure cooker, two little pots, three plates and half a dozen spoons. In the years that he had spent in the hotel, he had developed some new habits, such as taking a heavy breakfast in the morning, a cup of tea and some fruit for lunch and a royal dinner that he always cooked for himself. Over the years, the location of his kitchen had ensured that he could appreciate the sound of forests in the dark. He could now identify and imitate the hoot of an owl, the call of a barking deer or that of a dove in mourning on a tree nearby. The song of the cicadas or a singing lark would fill him with joy. Chhotu had also begun to recognise glow-worms and would always insist that Udit collect some for him. Now that Chhotu had adjusted well and his howling had disappeared, he was at peace with himself. He now had time to do things himself. Every morning he would light the kerosene stove, make tea for himself and boil milk for Chhotu with lots of sugar. His visits to the tea vendor which had become a regular feature had now become a weekend routine. This he had done because he had noticed that they were becoming the centre of attraction. People had weird guesses, some labelled them as father and son, some thought of them as stepbrothers citing the age difference as one of the reasons, some even whispered that he was from one of the child lifter gangs.

He was also unnerved by the stares of the policemen who passed by him. And one day, a traffic cop had even asked him who he was and what was he doing in Mussoorie. Thankfully, that day the Manager who was buying vegetables in the adjoining shop came to his rescue, immediately introducing him as his cousin brother, who had joined him in the hotel to earn a living.

Chhotu had been with him for a few months only but now even the thought of the boy being taken away from him terrified him. The two had become each other's anchor. He looked at him as his own extension, a part of him which had been plucked and sown in an invisible soil, which had now grown into someone whom he could love wholeheartedly and who loved him equally in return; both were lonely in this big world. He at times wondered if ever he was this size, this age when his parents would have loved him as much. He himself had no such memories. His faint memories which he had allowed to fade quicker than they would normally have on their own, were captured in some black and white photographs of Shweta's birthday parties, with him standing in the group of other children while Sonam, Shweta, Mum and Dad would be closeted together, smiling and posing for the photographer.

Some other memories which he had allowed to lie dormant in some of his brain compartments were those of his dad, strictly enforcing rules for the children with an iron hand; not even one of them appealed to him then and he would internally rebel against them, though outwardly complied without uttering a word. Getting up early in the morning, with the alarm set for 5:00 am was the most difficult rule he had followed. He would fiddle with that steel time piece when no one was watching and would wish that someday it would go out of order. One day he had intentionally allowed his elbow to brush against it in such a way that it fell to the ground while he was lifting his book from the table. He had followed it up with a chain of sighs and self-curses which sounded so real that Shashank had intervened and said, 'It's only a clock. If it breaks, it can be repaired or replaced, but be careful with human beings.' He even had the guts to check it out, an hour later, if it still worked or not. At that time, the depth of what his father had said did not strike him.

His mother Bina always sided with Dad, he felt. Perhaps she was scared of his anger or she was timid, not having the guts to take a stand of her own. He had a set of rules for everything in life; the bathroom had to be wiped dry after each usage, the bath towels had to be compulsorily put in the sun, the last drinker had to fill the water bottles of the refrigerator, the lights and fans had to be switched off when there was no one in the room, everyone had to carry his own plate to the kitchen sink after partaking the meals. He had once become so angry that he had christened his father as 'Hitler' and made the blunder of referring to him by the new name in front of his friends. Later he had repented what he had said in a moment of uncontrolled anger but then words once spoken and arrow once shot could never be taken back. The after effect followed soon, making him realise his folly the hard way. Every time the cricket ball went into his courtyard, his friends would refuse to bring it because it was Hitler's home and that they were too scared of taking the risk of entering into his territory without permission. The result, he would keep trudging back and forth, getting the ball himself when the rule of the game proclaimed that the hitter had to bring it back. If he ever protested, the friends would mock him for going back on his words.

From an angry teenager he had graduated to an angry young man, one who would lose his temper at the drop of a hat. He remained aloof from his sisters too whom he thought had never helped his cause. Had they supported him, some of the rules they could have collectively broken and there was no way his father could have given the same punishment to the three of them. Ultimately a few things would have changed, but God had willed otherwise.

It was only after his great escape, which he had initially thought as the attainment of supreme freedom that in his moments of weakness, he silently wept over the tender side of his father that he had ignored and brushed aside as his father's duty towards those whom he had brought into this world.

These days when he slept with Chhotu clutching his belly, he found it difficult even to get up and go towards the washroom at night. He was afraid that removing his hand would wake the boy up. He would wait as long as possible and would only go if Chhotu removed his hand or loosened his grip. Sometimes Chhotu would move perpendicular to the position he initially had slept, and he would thrust his legs against his belly, landing a kick there. But all he would do was get up, pull him back, cover him with the quilt and sleep again. He had even moved his bed towards the wall so that the boy did not roll down the bed in his sleep. Sometimes sleep would suddenly evade him after a nap and he would sit in bed and wonder what life had in store for him. The more he tried to sleep, the more he would be caught in the tornado of thoughts he thought had blown far away during his days of torment and despair.

The other day, Udit had left a sleeping Chhotu to help a German tourist at the reception who had lost his passport. On his return he had found the two chair bed in his office empty. For the next five minutes he was a man possessed, shouting, searching and running from one cubicle to the other. When he had finally located him in the Manager's room, sitting in his lap, licking a red lollipop, the relief that he had experienced was an emotion he had not known in life before.

That night he had a fractured sleep as his conscience kept pricking him, how much of pain his own parents must have suffered when one day he had willingly chosen to disappear from their lives. If he could go back in time, he would have run away again, gone to his mum and dad, fallen at their feet and ... but then he steadied himself with the thought that perhaps they never looked for him, perhaps they never loved him enough.

He remembered what one of his friends had told him once when he was only ten, that if his parents did not love him enough, that meant that he had either been found near the road in the bushes or may be picked up from the steps leading to a temple. Of all the emotions, during times like these, negativity provided him the greatest succour. Being a little foolish and a little churlish allowed him to spin a life jacket clinging to which he would swim to safety away from the swirling currents in the ocean of repentance. The debris of emotions that would lay scattered within the aftermath of such tornadoes devastating him time and again would gather slowly, filling his bucket of ifs, buts, had been, would have and could have. He himself would then put a lid on them with a thought that one day he will have enough courage to pick up a peg of pleasurable liquid and gulp all of the contents down his throat.

Mr Liddle's hotel was in the final stages of renovation. He was on the lookout for some good staff. He was planning to give an advertisement for the same in newspapers but before doing so he sent an emissary to the hotel Mussoorie Grand, inviting both the Manager and the Assistant Manager for talks on a Sunday afternoon at a time suitable to them. The Manager immediately agreed, assuring that the coming Sunday they would be at the hotel by 6:00 pm. Liddle's reputation as a man of high values and principles and the fact that he was a good friend of the owner of their hotel left no room for any second thoughts on the issue in the mind of the Manager.

Come Sunday afternoon, Udit reached the Manager's room and told him that he had been suffering from severe spasmodic pains since early morning and was therefore in no position to visit Mr Liddle. 'He must have something genuine to discuss I suppose,' the Manager said firmly when he saw that Udit was looking for an excuse to avoid the meeting. 'Everyone knows Mr Liddle and he is talked about very highly in business circles here; he has a chain of hotels. He is not the one to poach staff from other hotels for his own gain. I am very sure about it. We need not be afraid of meeting him,' said the Manager, very clear and convinced.

Udit dilly dallied but then agreed to accompany him.

Chhotu had been left behind at the Manager's house as his two kids had become quite friendly with him. The two were ready and as they walked out, Chhotu came howling from behind.

'Chacha you're leaving me behind, I want to come too.'

'You stay here with Auntie and play with Bindu and Monu, I'll be back in half an hour. I'll get you a new toy. What do you want, a gun … a bat … a racket …'

'No I don't want anything, I want to come with you,' Chhotu howled.

'We can take him along, it's not a formal meeting,' the Manager said.

'No, no way Manager Sahib. What does he think? Am I his servant? Has his mother left behind a fortune with me that I am obliged to look after him? Chhotu, if you don't listen to me, tomorrow I will go and drop you in the orphanage. Understand! You better understand!'

Udit's uncharacteristic outburst shocked the Manager.

'Leave him alone. Chhotu come along, come with me. I'll tell Liddle that he's my son. No big deal.'

Udit waited as the Manager took him inside and returned in a few minutes with his face washed, clothes changed and his hair combed. But the twinkle in his eyes was missing and they were still teary. He held the Manager's hand and walked along.

At the hotel, Liddle's Inn, they waited in a room on the first floor. The renovation had been beautifully done, the old architecture had been retained but new features had been added in such a way that it looked elegant, sophisticated and unique. The lingering smell of fresh paint was subdued a little by the resinous smell emanating from the new wooden panelling. A wait always troubled Udit. Getting impatient, he asked the Manager, if he could leave.

The manager asked him to be patient.

He then glanced around. The curtains had been designed aesthetically, with each window having a double layer of rods to hold two kinds of curtains, one a see-through fabric with a flowery pattern embossed in gold, that allowed light to penetrate inside the room and the other thick and velvety which would shut out the outside existence to the occupants once they were drawn. The old fireplace had been redone with crafted sandstone tiles forming a new border, complemented with a pair of low seated chairs arranged at the sides, that gave a regal touch to the room.

'Good afternoon gentleman,' Liddle's voice broke Udit's trance.

Startled he stood up to greet Mr Liddle with folded hands.

The discussion invariably began with the question about the native place of the two. To answer questions, that would put Udit in discomfort, it was always the Manager who took the lead.

'Both of us are from the same village in Pauri Garhwal. In fact we are distant cousins. Though I came here fifteen years ago, he is a relatively new entrant, having joined me here some years ago, after completing his studies.'

His lengthy introduction always served the intended purpose. No questions would then be directed towards Udit.

'Lovely boy, I've seen you somewhere,' Liddle suddenly said, looking at Chhotu, 'but I can't remember where.'

'Mussoorie is a small place Sir. You must have seen him near the hotel, he is very friendly and known to most of the families that stay nearby,' the Manager intervened before Udit could open his mouth.

Mr Liddle then reached out towards the gold framed tray kept on the round side table and handed Chhotu another of those imported chocolates.

Chhotu's eyes widened as much in delight as due to the familiarity he had with those gold and black packets. Udit sincerely wished that he would not open his mouth.

In many ways Mr Liddle was unique, his physique so very distinct, his mannerisms aristocratic and articulation so natural and effortless that anyone who had a chance to interact with him always went back impressed. He had a certain degree of sophistication about himself. The way he spoke, the way he dressed, the way he sipped his tea, the way he fiddled with the fork and spoon, added a regal touch to him, something that could unnerve the person sitting opposite.

Udit had immediately recognised that it was the same person whom he had met often at the tea vendor and whose piercing stare had scared him during those initial meetings. His mind was far away from the issue that was being discussed. He kept on praying that Liddle did not ask too many personal questions.

The conversation expectedly veered towards the staff at other hotels nearby, the kind of facilities they were being offered at present, their expectations from the owners, the hardships they faced and the solutions they had to offer that could bring about their upliftment and empowerment. Liddle was very free and frank during the discussions, treating them at par with himself and was all ears when they said something, jotting down some points in his diary. Throughout the hour they were together Udit kept fidgeting, trying to steal a glance at his watch, every few minutes, racking his brains for an excuse that could relieve him from his prolonged agony. As a result, whatever he heard washed over without any penetration. Unfortunately his ordeal continued for another half an hour. As a gracious host, Liddle offered them coffee with muffins and cookies, insisting that he would 'mind' if they refused to accept his coffee.

Refreshed after a cup of cappuccino each, they took leave. Udit was the first to rush out, as he was fully convinced that Mr Liddle was intently staring at him again and he was stunned by his parting shot, 'You don't look a Garhwali, but your son does ...'

On their way back home, Udit asked the Manager, 'How did Liddle relate Chhotu with me, even though he sat in your lap all the time?'

The Manager had no answer, just a shrug. But a few seconds later, he hastened to add, 'Maybe he thinks that my son can't be as fair as Chhotu is and look at my age. A person with so much of grey in his hair can't have such a small child and you already know Mr Liddle is very sharp.'

'I have a feeling Mr Liddle was fascinated by you,' the Manager joked as they walked in the narrow passageway, leading to a flight of thirty odd steps, a shortcut they often took rather than walking round the winding road leading to their quarters down below.

'Let Chhotu be at my place today. You can have some rest,' said the Manager.

'Chhotu you want to sleep with Monu and Bindu tonight?'

Chhotu said nothing but held on to his hand and turned away towards the lane to the Manager's place.

Udit still agitated at having to forcibly attend the meeting with Liddle and narrowly managing to get away with his bunch of lies walked away without forcing Chhotu to come. He was also upset with his own behaviour today.

At the Manager's home, Chhotu remained quiet and slept early, missing his dinner.

That night, Udit again remained a man at emotional crossroads. As he lay on his bed, a fleeting thought crept into him that Mr Liddle had perhaps doubted the credibility of the story he had till now told so many times to so many people.

Didn't he have that probing eye, the manner in which he stared at me, with that face slightly tilted towards the right, his twitching lips, with a momentary frown? He seems to possess that sixth sense that enables him to slice through all jackets of deceit. And from what he had outwardly read of him during his brief and non interactive meetings, he did not appear to be one of those who possessed a sadistic sense of humour. Udit was ruffled and irritated.

And if that was not enough, the empty bed added to his despondent mood, deepening the emptiness he felt within. He wished he could go over to the Manager's home and bring Chhotu back but the clock showed 11:30 pm and he pulled the quilt over himself. Underneath the warm quilt he settled for some cold reasoning. Chhotu was never his liability. That day it was he who had volunteered and run away with the boy when the orphanage people were only enquiring if anyone was willing to keep him temporarily. And could he deny how much of sunshine he had brought into his life. His behaviour today had been shocking and there was no way he could justify what he had done. Had he been selfish was a question that he could not answer with an emphatic no. After all, he had gone overboard to befriend him, gently drawing him in the vacuum of aloofness that he wanted to fulfil so dearly. Then he sat down with his diary and filled half a dozen pages cursing himself, apologising to Chhotu, asking for forgiveness from the Lord Almighty. At the end of it all he felt much better and it had dawned on him that a moment of anger, a fit of rage could never ever sever or hack down a bond of love or a relation of blood.

Next day it was still dark when he began walking towards the Manager's home.

'How is Chhotu? I wish to take him back,' he said as he entered the drawing room.

'Chhotu??' The Manager gave him a quizzical look and continued, 'Yesterday late evening the orphanage staff came and took him back, poor boy.'

Udit was shell shocked. The Manager he had known was a serious man, he could never joke. He collapsed on the chair and covered his face with his hands as tears rolled down his cheeks. He began to sob. The Manager then rushed by his side and put an arm round his shoulder. Little Chhotu had meanwhile crawled towards him and he patted his back, exclaiming 'April fool, Chacha April fool.'

He caught hold of Chhotu and got up, 'I will come later.'

'Don't ever play with the emotions of angels like him,' the Manager added. 'My children really love him and I won't mind adopting him. Don't talk about the orphanage again.'

Ashamed and repentant and bowed down by guilt, he returned home.

And that night when he picked up his pen and diary, he followed his heart, writing whatever thoughts flitted through.

'Love always need not be expressed,

True love lasts forever,

Nobody in this world can love you more than your mum and dad.

And then he turned the page over to write,

I love you dad. I love you mom … so much.

I'm sorry. It was foolish of me to leave home and then stupid not to ask for your forgiveness.

Had I returned home, you would have loved me just the same.

But … now … I am not sure … If I return …

Suddenly Chhotu mumbled something in his dream and Udit kept his pen down to check if he was saying something. He tried to wake him up but he was in deep sleep. Then out of sudden instinct he checked his mouth. It was still full of the last bite of chapatti he had taken during dinner. He smiled and then took it out with his hand, fearing that it might cause choking. As he came back to bed after washing his hands, he realised that it was not necessary to be related in flesh and blood to love someone truly. Even if he assumed that he was an adopted child, a destiny's child, his father would have loved him just the same, if not more than how much he loved Chhotu now. He could now recollect that at times he slept on his study table, but in the mornings he was always found on the bed, properly covered and laid secure under a mosquito net. His school uniform was always ironed by his dad. Every Sunday, he would spread a sheet on the floor and use the charcoal iron box to iron his own clothes and Udit's saying that the electric ones were light and the trousers did not get the proper folds. He always tied the perfect knot for his school tie after a wash. And Sunday evenings he took it upon himself to polish all shoes that lay in the rack, brushing and polishing them without any hurry. Udit then would loiter around expecting that he would be summoned for a lecture, as the dirtiest shoes on the rack were always his, with lumps of mud and grass still sticking by the side of the heels or in between the spikes. Mentally he would prepare himself for a little confrontation, rehearsing the words and phrases he would throw in his defence but it never happened.

His mother whom he had come to hate equally for being a partner in his dad's crimes, was the one who would get up with the morning alarm. She would be rolling out paranthas, pumping the stove at 6:00 in the morning when others would still be dreaming under their quilts. She was the one, whom he often asked to sign test papers when he had performed poorly. And she had always obliged, the only rider being, a mild reprimand, in the nature of a hushed whisper, 'Perform better next time.' And, God, she always 'finished' his homework in case he had slept off with the notebook the previous night, at times without even telling him. In school, when the time for submission came, he would frightfully turn over the pages, only to find that it had been completed and the invisible 'hand of God' had taken great pains to be calligraphically as similar to him as possible. A sickening self loathing rose within him. Had he been plainly ungrateful or had he been blind to the simple truth and had perilously ignored it under the pile of his own imaginary grouses and grievances.

Ever since, Udit's diary entries had a certain degree of positivity that amazed him no end.

The debris at Liddle's plot was getting collected that day, with two labourers shovelling basketfuls into aluminium pans to be emptied onto a waiting tractor trolley outside. A third one was busy stacking the odd whole brick that came out from the fallen wall. The contractor had not made an appearance since morning but Arvind who was eagerly watching the progress since breakfast finally came out and told one of the labourers to hurry up.

'Finish the work by evening,' he said, commanding them as if he had himself commissioned them, and any carelessness would bring about the maximum punishment.

Next morning, when he was going for his walk, he saw that indeed all the material that had been lying there had been carried away. He jumped over the foundation that was still visible and crossed over into the plot walking along the edges like a policeman hunting for clues at a crime scene. Here he was not searching for something, but each blade of grass that had been crushed under the demolished wall, he felt was weeping at its destiny. First they had been brutally sliced apart from the rest of their own and then they had lain uncared, unwatered, unloved with hordes of people trampling over them without a bother in the world.

One of the labourers came over to him and said, 'Bade Sahib should have decided, what he wanted, all our efforts have been wasted. Now if he decides to begin something else, he would find it difficult to find even people willing to work here, so soon. Having to fell a part of a building during construction is considered a bad omen in our industry.' For Arvind, omens had ceased to hold any meaning. Whatever the future held in store would unfold, he could neither delay it nor stop it but till it actually happened, he could enjoy the state of bliss, he decided, vowing not to rail at his fate anymore. Blissful ignorance could be the only means of escape, he had come to realise. He had heard from one of his nephews settled in Bangalore that Madhur had finalised a flat in the city and was getting it registered shortly. He had no information on the matter, neither was he inclined to be in the know of developments. The only thing that he now planned to do was to withdraw the power of attorney he had given Madhur, because trust had been the biggest casualty between father and son, when the sale deed had been struck.

He secretly drafted the notice, hiding it from Yashoda, thinking that it was highly unlikely that she would locate it in the newspaper columns, hidden between advertisements. Two days later, he was utterly surprised when Yashoda summoned him from the bathroom. He rushed out, toothbrush still in hand, toothpaste foam still in his mouth, suspecting that she needed help in getting up from the sofa.

'Now what is this?' she said, her eyes widened and full of disbelief. 'You have given this?'

'Hmm …' he mumbled something that was absorbed in the toothpaste foam. He rushed to the bathroom, to try and gain a few moments, in which some excuse would pop up in his mind. A lie alone could bail him out now, he felt.

'I'm sure it's not yours,' she fired again as he reappeared, still wiping his face with the towel.

'Actually, this was legally required; I met Oberoi the other day in the market. He advised me to publish it as a safety measure. He is an advocate, you see. As it is, Madhur has taken his share, the rest is Mayank's. I haven't disowned him or anything, just withdrawn the power of attorney,' Arvind justified, stuttering through the verbal bail application in front of an unpredictable judge.

'I still can't believe that Madhur could change for the worse so suddenly. That boy was never like this, on that trip he was so loving, so caring, so concerned about our health and happiness. He took us for that tent stay in the mela! I could never make out that underneath his affection, his outpouring of emotion lay such a selfish and evil design!' Yashoda added letting her emotions flow.

'I hope that Aryan and Arin don't do the same to him,' Arvind said quietly and took the newspaper from her hand. And by a sleight of hand he retained that single page under his shirt, crushed the rest of the paper and threw it into the bin.

'Now let's forget it, let bygones be bygones,' he announced to himself.

The notice meanwhile had been quite an intelligent and in the circumstances necessary move. He had informed to whomsoever was concerned, that the POA was meant for a single transaction only and that since that transaction had been carried out, the POA was now infructuous, null and void. He had stuffed all those legal terms he could think of, because he did not want to go through something as painful as this ever again in his life.

Ajit Mama had been getting slightly impatient as there had been no call from Mr Liddle and it was almost six months since their search had begun. One afternoon he asked Shweta whether she thought that travelling all the way to Mussoorie could help expedite the search.

'It is a tourist place Mamaji, so many people come and go, it would be next to impossible for an outsider to stay in a hotel for a few days and search for a person who has voluntarily gone missing many years ago. Don't you agree?' she asked.

She then continued without pausing to listen to Mama's reply. 'We're not even sure that he ever visited that place and are banking on that hazy picture of a man clicked by a news reporter! Had he been sighted there or had he disappeared from there, things would have been different.'

'You are right. Let me put through a call to Liddle this evening,' he said and then buried his head in the newspaper he had been carrying.

Shweta knew that this was his way of dealing with emotions when he found something difficult to cope with. As his eyes moved along the words printed on those sagging sheets of paper, his brain would rejig his thoughts, pick the positive ones and realign them; Shweta knew and allowed him those moments. Mama himself was very particular that neither Shweta nor his sister ever saw him in a moment of weakness.

Shweta's own state of mind varied from being ecstatic at one instant to completely despondent the next. Her optimism gave her strength and motivation to visit Dr Arvind for physiotherapy sessions which extended to long hours both morning and evening. Though she never shared with anyone, of late she had begun to feel some tingling sensation in her spine in areas which till now were numb. She had even tried to be up on her feet by holding on to the arm rest of the sofa which lay by the side of the window but had fallen after ten seconds, but for those ten seconds, she had been on the top of the world. Those fleeting seconds had been etched in her recent memory with that stolen glance outside the window, that spot under the reetha tree, where the rain water gurgling out through the storm drains had accumulated and the pattering raindrops had created an illusion of a row of ships setting sail from a harbour.

Ajit Mama called up Mr Liddle in the evening. Liddle as usual was bubbly and chirpy. His voice came through the phone loud and clear.

'How is my niece?' He began.

'Oh she is absolutely fine and the good news is that we expect to see her on her feet in a few months,' Mama spoke excitedly.

'Oh good, that is the greatest piece of news I have heard in a while now,' the accented voice at the other end chuckled in delight.

'And how are my sister and brother-in-law?'

'Good, they're good. I've never seen them so optimistic in the recent past, hopefully things should go as expected.'

'I have some work in your city and would be visiting you very soon, not sure when,' he added. 'And my friends in the police have zeroed in on a few people. They are trying to find out but then it is a difficult job, you know. Let me assure you, once he is located, I will definitely convince him to return home,' he added.

Ajit Mama listened in silence. He knew that they were searching for the proverbial needle in the haystack, where even the position of the stack was uncertain.

'I know, I know, I'm thankful to you for all your efforts. We can only try, whether he will ever be united with us is as it was destined to be, just as was his birth in our family.' Mama tried to be philosophical, trying to justify the eagerness and urgency of their efforts.

'I'll give you a call the moment there's something positive,' Mr Liddle said, almost apologetically.

'Right then, we'll be in touch,' Mama concluded.

'It is a difficult job dear,' said Mama turning towards Shweta who was sitting by his side.

'Looks pretty difficult. What can we do Mamaji. Perhaps he has no attachment left for the family. If he had any intention of returning he would have at least tried to find out how his family was. He has never contacted even his friends. And God forbid, if we find him only to discover that he doesn't recognise us, better we don't find him at all. Then I fear, Ma and Daddy will be heartbroken. Ma might not even survive the shock.'

For the first time, Shweta and Mama were overwhelmed by the enormity of the task they had set about to accomplish. Coming to terms with the reality of having to lose someone physically and emotionally to factors other than death had been more than a struggle. After being in denial mode for the first year, the family had ultimately made peace with their queer fate, reconciled to a life without his physical proximity and had accepted it as their destiny. A loss such as this had no finality attached to it and thus it had remained a reason for greater pain for the family.

That unexpected call from Mama had jolted Liddle into action. Next morning, he was at the residence of his retired DIG friend.

'Are they doing something?' he began after the pleasantries, feasting on strawberry waffles.

'They have put half a dozen odd guys under surveillance, but they can't be interrogated you see because this is such a delicate issue. If some of them decide to move away from this place, there is nothing they would be able to do, and we would have no threads left to pursue,' said the retired DIG.

'At a personal level, I'd love to play detective. But that would probably make it more difficult, because people tend to run away even from our shadows,' he continued with an aborted laugh.

'And most people here would recognise you,' Liddle suggested with a faint smile.

'Yeah, even incognito is difficult, for people recognise my brown eyes and this mole above my lips. I can share with you the details of the chaps they are following, if you wish.'

'No, no, I trust you fully,' Liddle politely declined the offer.

Unaware of the resurgent efforts to locate him, Udit was planning to take leave for a few days. Where he wanted to go was still undecided but that he wanted to take a break from his routine was sure. Carrying Chhotu along was not at all a burden but he had not heard from the orphanage people in Dehradun for days. If they came looking for him, during the period the two were away, the legal repercussions if any, he had never been informed.

He decided to call them and enquire.

They told him that he was required to visit the police station and inform them in writing, where he was going and by what time he was likely to return.

Visiting the police station was something that did not appeal to him anytime. In order to avoid the hassle, he for a second thought of leaving Chhotu behind with the family of the Manager. At night when he slept, he thought over the options available to him, the places or the people he could visit. Surprisingly he had hardly any to choose from. He had no interest in travelling alone to a place of tourist interest.

Ever since Lila had died, a disturbing thought had wandered in his mind. Was life so unpredictable? This question haunted him sometimes. The more he tried to distance himself away from this thought, the more it troubled him. A meeting with his granny once, just once, he had been imagining, sometimes even dreaming about her but consciously he had neither agreed nor disagreed with the thought. Granny must be in her early seventies, he knew. What if something happened to her? He was no more in touch with any of his close friends, not even Narayan. New relations he had hardly forged any except for the hotel Manager who had become a good friend. With the other hotel staff, he had cordial relations but not such with whom he could share a secret or a holiday.

Ultimately he decided that he would go to the city which he once called his home. He thought even if it was impractical and outrightly foolish that he would walk into his home, but he could derive some joy, some satisfaction by having a look and by revisiting the places, the lanes, the shops, he once frequented. He could even try his luck at meeting Granny and have a glimpse of his mom and dad. Perhaps that would fill a part of the vacuum he always felt existed within him. In his recent past he had not been exactly a vagabond, but he was still struggling to strike roots. His life, now at the age of twenty-seven, was vaguely similar to the one he led at seventeen; unplanned, unsystematic, uncertain and predominantly lonely but for Chhotu. He preferred to take decisions on the spur of the moment, going by instinct, though they had all been trivial and routine. And this had stood him in good stead, providing an escape route, letting his subconscious self to relax if he messed up the things. This way he addressed the greatest fear that always rode on his shoulders, the fear of failure.

'Where are you going?' asked the hotel Manager on finding his leave application on his table.

'I don't know where, somewhere for sure,' he replied vaguely.

'But first promise that you *will* return,' he said extending his hand.

The compassion he had shown unnerved Udit again. For a second he had blanked out, not knowing, not understanding why he had uttered those words. But then he gathered his wayward emotions and composed himself to lay his palm on the one extended in front before it was too late.

'What makes you say so?' he asked.

'Nothing in particular, I need a good friend like you always, to emotionally unburden myself of all that I can't carry within. I'm selfish you see,' the Manager laughed. 'And where will the boy be?'

'Still undecided.'

'Are you sure, your trip has nothing to do with him?'

Udit was slightly bewildered by the question. 'How can that be? I'm not going in search of his near and dear ones; I've absolutely no clue about them. Next time you hire a new worker, be sure to have record of his permanent residence. And have a few of his close relatives as witnesses,' he went on to add.

The Manager gave an avuncular pat on his back and said, 'It is easier said than done, brother.' He could have carried on and cited many examples, the most easily available, sitting right next to him. But a man extraordinarily conscious of his words, he merely remarked, 'You have a point,' and left it at that.

The leave would be sanctioned, Udit knew. Completing Chhotu's formalities if he wished to take him along played on his mind for the next two days.

He was clear about one thing. That he would not end up on the wrong side of the law. But visiting the police station was something he abhorred for reasons unknown. Getting into a legal tangle with regards to Chhotu and the formalities was unthinkable. So leaving him behind was an option he seriously had to think upon. Years ago, when he was new to the town, he had picked up a pup from the street and taken it home. The pup had become his pet and when he had gone to Haridwar once and left him behind with the hotel chowkidar, the little creature had almost died due to shock and trauma. He shuddered at the thought, if a similar fate awaited Chhotu.

At night, when he went to bed, he read a story for him. At the end of the story Chhotu always had ten questions to ask. Today he did not have any.

He did not even demand to hear another story. He immediately lay down and turning towards the other side, said, 'I have come to know that you're going somewhere.'

Shocked, Udit sat up and said, 'Who told you? I've nowhere to go, where will I go?'

'I too have nowhere to go, those people who took away my Ma on their shoulders, did not take me along. I love her so much and she loved me so much always, she can't live without me. I troubled her a bit but not so much that she would leave me and go. She always said that when I grow big, we will live in a big house far away from here. How is she living without me? Chacha you please talk to those people and find out where they have kept her. I'll go and free her; and then both of us will live together. They thought that I am a little boy … Once Ma comes, you will also be free of taking care of me and then you can go and stay with your ma,' the little boy carried on and on.

Udit was shell shocked. Guilt punched him in the face. He lifted Chhotu in his lap and held him in a tight embrace as tears rolled down his eyes, wetting the boy's curly locks. He then lay against the pillow but did not let go of Chhotu, clutching his thin frame as he lay on him, chest against chest, belly against belly. He could feel his tiny heart pounding as rapidly as his own.

Any thoughts he had harboured of leaving Chhotu behind had melted away in their tears. Now if he wished to go, Chhotu was sure to tag along.

Next day morning he was there at the police station with the papers he had been given, granting temporary custody of the minor child till the authorities took a decision on his future.

The SHO made him wait for an hour as he was busy coordinating the last minute arrangements regarding some VIP movement in the city.

After he was done, a peon came and told him, 'Thanedar sab is calling you.'

He opened the door of the room where he was seated and went in, carrying Chhotu in his lap.

The munshi scanned the papers in a hurry and asked him to deposit a recent passport photo of himself and the boy. He was also asked to give the address of the likely places he was planning to visit, so that there was no prospect of any foul play with the boy. Pushed to the back foot, he tried to recollect some addresses. *Relations were easy to break and difficult to maintain*, his granny often said and very rightly so, he hadn't maintained any. Thankfully, he remembered Narayan's house number and promptly wrote it down. Then as an afterthought, scribbled that of his granny's in Bindki.

'Two are enough, you can collect your papers and go,' the SHO tried to get rid of him quickly.

From the corner of his eye, he stole a glance at the many photos that had been pinned with round edged copper pins on the board behind. He sat on the edge of his seat with a few drops of sweat appearing on his brow even in the chilling December cold.

I have committed no crime, he said to himself to soothe his racing pulse. These must be people who must have committed some gruesome murders or looted people's homes or maybe held someone to ransom, his thoughts were getting entangled.

'Any acquaintances there?' The SHO mocked with a crooked smile.

Udit chose to ignore and got up, folded his hands to take leave, repressing his anger.

'Right, you may go, but report once you're back.'

Nodding his head he came out of the police station.

The Sangam Express was ready to leave from Platform Number 2 at Dehradun railway station. Mr Liddle had settled comfortably in the second AC compartment and was busy with a book.

Udit and Chhotu had arrived at the station. At the counter, he hurriedly purchased a general ticket. It was only when he saw the rush at the compartment door, with people climbing over each other to enter that he realised how foolish he had been not to reserve a seat in the sleeper class. He had never imagined the huge rush of travellers, neither had he expected that a general compartment could be so terribly cold. Once the train left the station, the chaos plummeted to tolerable limits. The passengers in his coach had come adequately prepared, dressed in overcoats, monkey caps, gloves and carrying blankets and bedding rolls tied together with strings and ropes.

The train quickly left the habitations behind onto the scarcely populated outskirts, where a few scattered houses broke the contiguity of the agricultural greens. The smell of sugarcane being processed in the sugar mills not far away let out a distinct but not too pleasant smell and a curious Chhotu covered his nose as he asked the origin of the smell. Very soon the train rumbled through dense forests and Chhotu pulled himself towards the window, waiting for a lion or an elephant or a zebra to emerge from the thickets. All he saw was a 'big brown donkey with horns' his own term for a sambar deer. He was disappointed that the zebra and the lion remained out of sight. He went back to his seat and sat by Udit's side.

Cradling Chhotu's head in his lap, Udit closed his eyes and did not know when sleep engulfed him.

It was only around late evening when the ticket examiner called for his ticket that he awoke with a start. It was dinner time. Passengers were busy eating and talking. He had only slipped in two packets of biscuits in his hand bag and he was surprised to see how elaborately others had come prepared for dinner in the train. He woke Chhotu up and gave him the biscuits but Chhotu wanted to have 'only paranthas and nothing else.' He tried convincing him but to no avail. The family on the front seat offered him a parantha and some pickles on a paper plate and Chhotu's imminent delight brought forth the irony that allowed him a guilty chuckle. Exotic dishes he brought from the restaurant kitchen back in Mussoorie had never evoked similar delight on his face. 'Rearing a child was not child's play' he had heard his dad say many times. Years ago his parents must have been through the same phase and he must have behaved in a similar fashion, he could not imagine. Were his grievances a result of his craving for some extra attention and had he squandered something that could not be compensated; the mere thought now frightened him.

In the night, Chhotu slept, but due to the bitter cold and inadequate bedding, he could not sleep properly, getting up thrice, wanting to visit the washroom. All through the night Chhotu had been lying in his lap, telling him that, 'he would freeze to an ice cream on the bare rexine seat cover.' The lady who had offered parantha to Chhotu was kind enough to lend him a shawl. 'Wrap the child. Are you travelling for the first time with your child?' she asked. 'Where is his mother?' she fired the next question.

'Some emergency at home,' Udit said and pretended to sleep immediately afterwards so that no more questions were thrown at him.

Mr Liddle was on his way to the hotel in the taxi that had been sent to pick him up.

Udit and Chhotu had alighted at the station and had immediately proceeded to the tea stall at the exit. A cup of steaming tea and some milk for Chhotu lifted their spirits after a long journey. As the vapours from the tea cup merged into the misty and foggy morning, Udit pondered over the options available to him. A cup of tea took too little a time for him to take a decision. Another cup followed. By the time he had finished, he decided that going to Narayan's place was the best option. That would not only give them a place to stay at least till the evening, but will also provide him with some information about home.

He took a rickshaw, because he was in no hurry to reach anywhere and an auto would have taken not more than fifteen minutes to reach the place.

He looked at his watch. It was twenty minutes past ten. He calculated that by 10:45 he would be at his friend's place. On the way, he stopped and picked up a kilogram of Narayan's favourite sweet, Motichur ke laddoo from the Lucky Sweet Mart in Civil Lines.

Narayan's place he knew like his second home. A little eager he jumped down from the rickshaw before it had halted completely. As he paid the rickshaw wala the fare and waited for the change, Chhotu shouted, 'Chacha, the gate is locked, your friend has gone to market.'

He turned around to see a big brass lock on the gate.

'Oh, no, my misfortune follows me again, at least not in my hometown,' he sighed.

The tea vendor across the road came over and told him that the whole family had gone to their native village for Narayan's wedding and he had been entrusted with the task of keeping guard of the house.

'By the way, if you have come to attend his marriage I have their village address.'

'Oh yes, I have that address, I thought I would rest here and then proceed, didn't know that the house would be locked. I'd informed them that I would be coming but it looks like they did not receive my letter,' he said.

'Could be, the postman of this locality is notorious for dumping the letters by that pond behind that temple, he is a drunkard.'

'Come and have a cup of tea,' he invited.

'Chacha, where are we going?' Chhotu asked, irritated at the continuous travelling.

'Come along, we will have fun,' he tried to calm him down.

Again over a cup of tea, he had the same question to ponder yet again, where to go. In the midst of peak winter, he had to quickly decide. His return ticket was after three days, 26th December, departure at 4.45 pm he confirmed, taking the ticket out of his wallet.

He thought of going to the Hanuman temple near the sangam, the prostrate statue of the lord, he always revered, ever since he had started accompanying his grandfather every Tuesday, as a five year old. But then he was undecided because, it was sure that by the time they would return, it would be dark. Getting a place to stay then was not going to be easy particularly because he had forgotten many of the things about the city.

'Is there a place to stay nearby?' he asked the tea vendor.

'There is a hotel, Shiv Ganga, hardly a kilometre from here, and the rooms are reasonably priced. And bhai, tell me your name, when they come back I will inform them that you had come.'

'No need, we would be meeting tomorrow anyway,' he said and immediately left. He was in no mood to spend a cold and sleepless night again. Getting a room in the hotel was easy but the chap at the hotel did tell him that they were fully booked for the next month when the mela was to begin.

He had no time to listen to him. He checked in. Chhotu was excited to move into a room. And more than the warmth and the protection from the cold, a hotel room was something Chhotu was familiar with. A room with a double bed, two neatly arranged pillows, a folded blanket, a water jug on the side table with two inverted glasses and a washroom nearby.

He was super excited and chirped, 'Chacha, can I take this blanket?'

'No we will first go to the temple and then come back here,' he said going inside the washroom to wash his face.

Mr Liddle was sitting by the glass topped round table near the window of his hotel room and watching the evening descend quickly. The leafless jacarandas lining the driveway were slowly vanishing into the darkening yonder. Over a cup of his favourite coffee, he made a note of things he had planned to do in this trip.

Meeting Dr Arvind.

Visit to Ajit.

Finalisation of the jewellery show room in Civil Lines market.

Visit to the church, the Patthar Girija.

Purchase of saris for the hotel boutique.

The timing was inappropriate to go ahead with any of his itinerary items from first to fourth. The shopping however could be done in the time he had at hand. The taxi driver promptly took him to Ramjilal Ratanlal saree store in Katra. Very soon he was staring at unending yards of fabric, of textures as diverse as crisp cotton to smooth silk in red, yellow, green, purple all exquisitely designed. The sales boys tried to help him with his selection, by wrapping the saris around their waist, with the pallu deftly falling over their shoulders, sashaying down the few metres of space they had, like models on the ramp.

'Can you walk like a bride?' he joked with one of the boys who stood displaying an orange and green Banarsi sari.

'Why not?' the boy said and then covering his head and half his face like a newly married girl, he walked gingerly, seven steps, inviting a hearty laugh from Mr Liddle.

'This one is final,' he said. The sales boy was delighted; all his efforts of the last fifteen minutes had been successful.

Half an hour later, he had a pack of nine saris and bags of good cheer to carry to the hotel room.

On his way back, a visit to Netram Sweets was something he could not forget. His friends in Mussoorie had demanded, some of the special stuff he made chiefly the Mawa ki kachauri and Gajrella. After tasting a spoonful of each, he placed the order that had to be delivered at his hotel two days later.

The crowd at the temple was large. Afraid that Chhotu might be crushed, Udit picked him up and carried him in his arms. There was no queue, just a rush, with people jostling and elbowing for the most vantage space to have a darshan. He went down the steps and stood in front of the statue of the Lord. Then he put the boy down and himself folded his hands and made him bow in obeisance.

'Lord please have some mercy on me,' he mumbled under his breath. He avoided being specific because he himself was not sure what he wanted.

He then proceeded to a corner and sat down on the coir carpet, with Chhotu in his lap. He closed his eyes and folded his hands above Chhotu's tiny hands clasped together. He waited for the arti to begin.

At the appointed hour, the crowd was on its feet as the arti of Lord Hanuman, accompanied with tolling bells and ringing cymbals rent the evening air. He hummed the few lines he could still remember.

At the end, the temple priest came towards the devotees with the silver plate carrying the sacred flame, to allow people make a wish and make monetary offerings if they wanted.

'Allow me to see my loved ones at least once,' he let a fleeting thought traverse his mind, as he felt the warmth of the flickering flame in his palms and the strong scent of the camphor settled in his nostrils. He was cautious enough, not to translate his thought into words, lest its attainment became his own responsibility. A strange sense of being adrift crossed his brain.

Back in the hotel Chhotu fell asleep immediately while Udit remained awake, watching the portable black and white television in his room. He did not feel the need to order any dinner but the service boy knocked and asked if he was sure that he did not want anything.

'The kitchen closes by 10:00 pm,' he informed.

'Okay then, get a special thali,' he ordered without asking what it contained.

He asked the boy to collect the empty plate in the morning and bolted the door. He switched off the light and watched TV in the dim light of the night bulb. Around 11:45 he felt sleepy, but before retiring to bed, he lifted the plate covering the thali to see what it contained. It had a full meal but he had no appetite. He thought of having the dessert but then left it, as kheer was Chhotu's favourite sweet dish. He slept after switching off the room heater. But two hours later he was up. He sat on the bed for a few minutes and then gulped down a glass of water.

He lay in bed, turning sides; sleep had been unfaithful again, ditching him when he needed it the most. He kept on thinking what he would do the next day. He had two more days in the city before he boarded the train back to Dehradun. He had come to the city hoping to meet Narayan, catching up with some of his other mates, compensating to an extent the things he had missed and if luck permitted, manage a meeting with his dear granny.

'Tomorrow, I shall visit my granny and meet her outside if possible,' he said to himself and lay down again, covering Chhotu with the quilt.

After that, the night was relatively peaceful emotionally and he slept till the service boy knocked again.

'Who is there?' he sprang to the door at the continuous knock, rubbing his eyes.

'Would you like to have some tea?' the boy asked.

'Is this how you serve tea?' he shot back.

'Look at the clock, it's almost nine,' the boy pointed towards the clock on the wall just behind him. 'Ours is a small hotel and we do not cater to very rich tourists. It is not easy to get gas cylinders these days, we are using firewood, hence beyond 9:30 am we start preparing for lunch; so no tea or breakfast,' he explained.

'Okay, then bring tea and two bread toast with omelettes.'

'Would you be having lunch here?' he asked but then seeing Udit in a foul mood, turned back without waiting for his reply.

'No lunch, I'll be going out after breakfast,' Udit shouted.

A bad start to the day he thought but little Chhotu's antics made him smile. He was trying to put on Udit's monkey cap and jumping on the quilt mimicking a monkey.

An upbeat Liddle meanwhile was proceeding towards Shweta's place after visiting the church and wrapping up the other remaining chores. He was mentally preparing himself and rehearsing what he would tell Ajit and his niece, so that they were not disheartened.

At the Joshi home, Savita answered the bell and informed him that the family had gone out to the temple and would be back in an hour. They had left behind the message that he wait over a cup of tea, if it was not too inconvenient.

Liddle paused for a second and then decided that he could meet Dr Arvind in the meantime and return by the time they were back.

'I'll be back in an hour,' he said and got into the taxi again.

The taxi stopped in front of the gate. The road had been dug up and a water pipe line was being laid. From the window of the car he peeped through eyeing the plot. As informed by the contractor, the debris had been removed and whatever little remained had been stacked in a corner. It was 11.30 am by his watch.

Finding the main gate open, he walked in and rang the doorbell. Then he realised that the pack of sweets he had bought was left behind in the car. He immediately turned and hurried across the passageway to fetch it from the vehicle.

Hearing the bell, Arvind was at the door and not finding anyone he stood a little puzzled. He walked towards the porch to see if a cricket ball had dropped in and a child had run away before claiming it out of fear of a scolding. He was still scanning the spaces in between the flower pots when he heard Liddle's voice, 'Good morning, Dr Arvind.'

'Mr …' he tried remembering the name.

'Liddle from Mussoorie,' Liddle's answer provided him immense relief.

'Oh please come in,' Arvind extended his hand.

A few moments of awkward silence followed.

Then Liddle himself broke the ice, 'Doctor a very important work brings me …'

Arvind cut him mid sentence, 'You have pulled down the wall, change of design I suppose.'

'Oh yeah, You're absolutely right. Actually I've lately realised that what I had finalised initially is not something that I wanted. What I want would need a bigger plot. Hence the work has been stopped. I am known to be a whimsical man! I've heard that there is a bigger plot available nearby …'

'Oh, yes there's one right behind,' Arvind was excited. 'But I'm not sure if it's on sale right now. The owners were initially planning but then they have changed their mind.'

'If they're willing to shift to a flat I can buy one for them in lieu of the plot, a deal favourable to them …?'

'It's not easy to sell one's home, you see. Take my case. I needed money for something urgent. Actually we are planning to shift to Bangalore and stay with our elder son and his family. We have a flat there but now we would be needing a bigger one. My wife is finding it very difficult to live alone. In fact I would have sold the whole house but my son insisted that we retain a part. After all this is the place he has grown up, sentimental attachment is a very big thing …' Arvind rambled on.

Liddle was now hesitant.

'Is it so?' he asked. 'So nice of him.'

Yashoda walked in with tea. Settling on the sofa beside him, she began, 'It is good that you are here. Our son was very angry with us when he called up saying that we were intentionally creating hurdles for you so that you would be fed up and stop work at the plot.'

'What are you saying Yashoda?' Arvind tried to stop her feigning shock and ignorance.

'Its fine, she might have misunderstood your son's eagerness to help me. I understand Doctor,' Liddle intervened, trying to ease the tense atmosphere.

'Actually I came with a purpose. That painting there is that of a painter whose collection I absolutely love. Would you mind if I tell you that I am interested in buying it?'

'That old painting you mean to say,' Arvind was surprised.

'Yes that one, that beautiful landscape in water colour.'

'Umm … actually there is a story behind it … and I have very fond memories of that incident … These days memories are our only company, you see,' Arvind became a little emotional.

Liddle in the meantime had picked up the briefcase and opened it in his lap.

He then began fiddling with a bunch of papers. Taking out his reading glasses from his coat pocket, he rearranged the bunch as Arvind watched with bated breath. From the quick glances he could steal from his position, some two metres away, they all appeared to be some legal documents, the green paper with the stamp clearly visible at the top.

'Wonder what he wants again,' he thought, getting a trifle agitated. Had he been a young boy, perhaps he could have punched him in the face and kicked him out and thus exacted his revenge. Right now his age prevented him from attempting anything outrightly *outrageous*. And so did the realisation, that there had been a sale, a legal deal and for all the deeds or misdeeds of his own son Madhur, that gentleman could not be faulted. He found himself in the same situation that he had so consciously avoided, by fleeing to Haridwar, not too long ago. The bitter feelings he had so painfully swallowed now embittered him again. Liddle in a swift motion, put his signatures at three places, complete with the date, 24th December, 1993 and with a big smile extended them towards Arvind.

'No, I'm not selling this painting to you, everything in my house is not on sale Mr Liddle,' Arvind almost snapped at him.

'Absolutely, nothing is on sale here, nothing was on sale here earlier also but for that advertisement in that newspaper,' Liddle said softly holding Arvind by the shoulder.

'These are yours Doctor,' he said handing over those papers.

'Ah that smile, the smile of a victor, rubbing salt into the wounds of the vanquished,' Arvind thought avoiding his gaze.

Then as an afterthought, he grabbed the papers, thinking that Liddle was perhaps handing him over a copy of the sale deed, belatedly, for his records.

'What do you want Mr Liddle? That painting is not that of da Vinci. The plot and the painting exchange is impossible.'

'That painting Doctor is mine anyway ... I mean the copyright,' Liddle smiled.

'What?'

'Doctor, please give me a moment to clarify. I hope you will allow me this little atonement, though it is not commensurate with the sin I've unknowingly committed.'

For a moment Liddle's words sounded Greek and Latin to Arvind's ears. He was now pretty sure that the person in front of him had serious issues with his mental health.

'I think we can meet sometime later. In the meantime you can consult your son,' he stood up from the sofa. 'Doctor it's an irony of fate that this deal was struck in the first place. That advertisement in the newspaper had stirred something within me, some chord that I decided to cement my ties with this holy land of yours by purchasing something that would last forever, something that would keep motivating me to visit this holy land again and again. I had never ever dreamt that I would get a chance to meet you again, but probably Lord Almighty had other designs.'

Liddle had moved to Arvind's side on the sofa and holding Arvind's hands he began, 'If you remember, I am the same person, that young man who had barged into your home, some thirty years ago, pleading to be a saviour for his pregnant and dying wife and unborn twins.'

The incident then flashed in front of Arvind's eyes. He stood in the balcony of his first floor flat, sipping a cup of tea on that Sunday morning when a crazy young man came running; with a tonga in tow, he had scaled the boundary wall of his house and clambered up the stairs in a flash to reach him. So obsessed had he been that he had not bothered to find out if the 'doctor' at the name plate 'Dr Arvind Johri' stood for a physician or a 'Doctor of Philosophy.' He had fallen at his feet, begging him to help save the life of his wife and a half born child. A child who would have died half way between the womb and the world outside, a sight which still left him with goosebumps, so many decades later. A would be mother who would have perhaps survived only to live with the trauma of losing not one but two children together. Moved by Liddle's plight, he had offered to help escort them to the nearest hospital. But it was Yashoda who had then insisted that his help needed to be of a higher order if he indeed wanted to *help*. Throwing all formalities and caution to the winds, she had asked that it was time he helped the lady deliver her child. Seeing him dither as the precious seconds ticked by, Yashoda had thundered, 'That midwife who delivered Madhur in your native village, she was illiterate, if she could do it, why can't you, with your bag of medical degrees?'

Yashoda and Hippocrates had propelled him out of his hesitant state and the guest room was converted into a Labour Room. Yashoda had been his active and enthusiastic assistant, helping

Jenner deliver a pair of healthy twins. At the end of it all, he himself was on top of the world along with Mr Liddle who had then cradled both babies, one on each shoulder and run up and down the stairs in sheer ecstasy. The Liddles had then stayed put with them for three days, with the Johris taking care of them like someone they had known for ages. In the following years they had been in touch with each other even when Liddle had shifted base to the US but the contact had been lost when Johris had shifted to their own house. On the previous occasion, when he had met Liddle, he was unable to recognise him. How his memory had ditched him, he could not believe. He put the papers to a side and went and hugged him in a tight embrace. For the moment, the plot, the land, the building, the sale, Madhur's insistence; all had lost meaning.

For the next three hours, they sat and gossiped with Yashoda joining them. Yashoda had then addressed him as 'Liddle Bhai' she remembered. She also recounted how she had stitched nappies for the twin Liddles, cutting out tiny squares from her soft cotton saris as Jenner's delivery kit had remained tucked away in her cupboard that Liddle Senior could not trace. They had lunch together, Yashoda making her special mustard spiced fish curry after a long time.

Liddle was so overwhelmed with the developments that he forgot that he had to visit Shweta and Ajit too.

The exchange meanwhile was now pending as Arvind was unwilling to accept this ridiculously unbalanced exchange. He insisted that there be a re-sale.

But Liddle was adamant that this was the only way that he could wash off the coat of guilt that had enveloped him ever since he had come to know the fact that the land was his.

Ultimately Liddle won the argument.

He took leave, but vowed to remain in touch. For now the programme of visiting Shweta and Ajit had been shelved.

He got into the waiting car and asked the driver to move towards the hotel. On his journey back, Liddle was in high spirits, soaring on cloud nine.

Arvind and Yashoda were still seated in their drawing room. They were still finding it difficult to believe all that had happened.

'I still can't believe all this,' Arvind said as he shifted from the chair to sit by Yashoda's side on the sofa.

Then he lovingly put his arm around Yashoda and said, 'We in India always say that in America and England the children leave their parents early and then they seek appointment to meet .... that they lead independent lives, seldom interfering in each other affairs ... how wrong that perception is ...

'See this man Liddle. For a little help we rendered to him once upon a time, he has remained indebted and full of gratitude. And see our own son Madhur. For now he has forgotten everything except his own demand.'

'Yes, perhaps, we failed somewhere in raising our sons,' Yashoda said staring at the painting Liddle had gifted earlier.

'No, no. We did not fail. He failed to imbibe the values we taught him. Forget it now as a bad dream. I have an idea. if you support me. I think now that Madhur has already taken the money in lieu of his share, let's will this part to Liddle. I am sure he will put it to some good use,' Arvind continued.

'Absolutely, let's do this. You talk to Oberoi Bhai Sahib tomorrow itself,' she said, getting up to close the door.

Udit and Chhotu had taken a rickshaw and were going towards Civil Lines. His first stop was in front of St. Joseph's College. He stopped the rickshaw and got down to have a look. The building was the same but a new administrative block had come up adjacent to the primary section.

'See my school,' he told Chhotu.

'Will I also study here?' he asked innocently.

'No, Chhotu we'll not be staying here, we'll go back after two days, again by the train.'

Barely a few metres ahead, on the other side of the road stood the famous '*khoka rai dahi vada*' vendor, the red and yellow conical vend mounted on a four wheeled manual trolley. The fellow he knew, served mouth watering raisin and cashew nut stuffed dahi vadas, which would melt in the mouth. This was Udit's all time favourite.

Settling down on the pavement with a plateful, he asked, 'Where is your son?'

The old man smiled. A toothless sunny grin, though his cheeks almost tumbled inside his mouth. 'He has gone to Emirates, to earn a living. This profession is more of a pastime for me now.'

'You increase the rates a bit,' Udit suggested, while stuffing a spoonful in Chhotu's mouth.

'Umm … never ever thought of it … Making money holds no charm now. These days the school is closed for Christmas, hence I get less stock from home and am relatively free,' he said as he went and settled underneath the banyan for a quick smoke. Udit and Chhotu then moved inside Company Bagh and enjoyed the sun. Udit let Chhotu play on the grass which was getting a darker shade of brown, without disturbing groups of students taking down notes and studying.

As the shadows lengthened and the sunlight began to fade, when the chill became perceptible, they came out of the park and hired a rickshaw again. Labour Chauraha he told the rickshaw puller, inviting a sheepish grin.

'At the main chauraha?' the fellow wanted to be sure.

'Oh yes, you can ask your questions on the way,' Udit quipped.

In his mind, he could picture his granny getting ready, changing into a fresh sari, arranging her little pooja basket, checking for the incense sticks, the match box, the sugar cube box which she found empty most of the times. But she would never complain, laughing away the theft saying, 'It is meant to be an offering for God, so He secretly comes and empties it!' The mere thought that he would meet her, excited him. He could even feel the warmth of her body, when he would be in her embrace, the tinkle of her glass bangles as she would tighten her hold, unwilling to let him go and the tears rolling down her cheeks while she would wipe her glasses with her sari. Lost in thought he did not realise that he had reached till the rickshaw puller stopped and asked, 'Bhaiya, you did not say anything and now we have come half a kilometre ahead of the chauraha.'

'Oh, sorry I'm coming after many years, please take the left turn.'

At the T-point a police station had come up and a new row of shops in front of the old Upadhyaya home surprised him. He waited and scanned the pedestrians passing by on the road, hoping to catch a glimpse of that thin and frail figure walking towards the temple, with her trademark steel basket in her left hand. Another twenty minutes passed and a little anxiety had begun to trouble him. He thought that perhaps Granny had discontinued the practice due to the cold and old age. After all, he was returning after eight long years. For a woman as old as Granny, eight years was a long time. Thankfully Chhotu remained busy with the toy car he had purchased for him. He hurried towards the temple. Outside the temple, a dozen odd people waited, as a bride and a groom paid their obeisance inside.

Crestfallen, he then walked towards the lane where his house was located, less than a kilometre from there. Standing about 100 metres away, diagonally behind the pillar of the gate of the palatial Bhatnagar home, he waited.

'Chacha, have we come here only to stand on the road and wait? I thought we had to meet someone,' a flustered Chhotu remarked.

'Chhotu I've forgotten the house.'

'Then why don't you ask someone?'

'I will, I will.'

Nothing happened in the next ten minutes or so. A man walking his dog asked him if he was looking for someone or wanted any help.

'No, thanks so much, I'm waiting for a friend,' he was quick to answer. The colony was a pale shadow of itself, some of the older houses looked dilapidated. Perhaps most of the children of his age group had left their parents behind to take up jobs, hence this kind of silence, he said to himself.

He ambled across the road with his neck craned in the direction of his home. Someone in a wheelchair, added to all the confusing thoughts that had been crisscrossing his mind. Now he had begun to doubt if his parents still lived there. No one in his immediate or even extended family was disabled or specially abled, he was sure. Could it be Granny, he thought for a moment. But then another view revealed someone in short jet black hair, and he was again heartbroken.

'Had the house been sold?' he thought. From the place where he stood, the name plate at the gate looked familiar though he could not read the name. He could ask someone, but what would he ask, he was not sure himself. He cursed himself, but moments later gathered all his strength and went to the Gupta store, hardly a furlong. The senior Gupta he knew was not there much to his relief. But his son, whom he had always seen at the shop from afternoon till evening, still in his school uniform, was there. A man, in mid-twenties now, he looked obese but still baby faced.

He bought a packet of chips for Chhotu and a bottle of water and then asked, 'Brother, can you tell me if one Mr Shashank Joshi lives anywhere nearby?'

'You mean Professor Joshi?'

'Oh yes, Professor Joshi who teaches Physics.'

'That front house you see, the corner one,1215, the one painted in light yellow,' he pointed towards it, puzzled.

'Thanks, thanks,' Udit said. 'But are you sure they still live there?'

'Now what sort of a question is that?'

Caught unprepared, he said, 'Nothing in particular, just wanted to know. Actually their son was my best friend but we have not been in touch for the last few years.'

'Brother, how could you be in touch? That boy, Udit, ran away from home over a minor scolding he received from his dad. Professor sahib is such a genial fellow, if ever he must have said something, it must have been for his good. But what to say? There are all kinds of people in this world. Look at my daddy; he is half paralysed. I left my job in Delhi to be with him. That is the least I can do for him. My wife sometimes gets disheartened that we don't have a child. Still, I think I'm lucky. Better not to have one than to have one like their son. Today morning, Professor sahib was here, he looks so old and frail these days, poor man.'

It was an unexpected barrage, a torrent for which he was totally unprepared. 'You're right, thank you,' he said and turned around, unwilling to let another word reach his ear.

And then as an afterthought, he returned. 'Actually I had brought a small gift for Udit's old grandmother. She was very fond of me. Can you give it to Mr Joshi whenever he comes to your shop?' He took out a shawl he had brought for her, an off-white Pashmina, wrapped in golden paper.

The boy's face crumpled, 'Oh, you wouldn't know, would you, she's no more ...'

Udit's legs trembled and he fell in a heap. The world around him had come crashing down without a warning on that winter evening. He tried to gather some strength, at least as much that would enable him to stand up on his feet and walk to a spot where he could let that piece of news sink in. All his life he had never felt so weak, so frail, so feeble. It took him ten minutes, the longest ten minutes he had ever endured and only after he had gulped down two glasses of water did he manage to feel that those legs were his own. With heavy and hurried steps, he began rushing back to the T-point junction, pulled by an invisible force that allowed him to take every step on that slippery road full of memories, emotions and guilt. Intermittently, his mind would blank out and he would pinch himself and take the next step. For a moment, his chain of thoughts would adhere and attain a fledgling finality. He was ready to barge into his home immediately, without wasting a second more, but the next second he would be blank again, the links in the chain crashing and scattering far and beyond.

Emotionally wobbly, he hobbled on the edge of the road trying hard to hold on to Chhotu's hand. Never had he experienced such seismic emotions. In a state of transient hypnotism, he said, 'What will they say, after all I am their son, I have committed a mistake, I will apologise, they will also be too happy to unite with me. Perhaps they are more desperate.' The next instant though a scary thought consumed him, 'That chap in the shop did not say anything about mom. Where is she?' On the cold winter evening he found himself bathed in sweat and as he wiped his face with a hanky, a taxi coming from the opposite direction knocked him down. He lost consciousness instantly and had a gashing wound on his forehead with blood flowing out.

The taxi stopped and an enraged Mr Liddle emerged. Seeing the grievous condition of the person knocked down, his anger evaporated. He immediately felt his pulse and checked his eyes. A little relieved, he decided to shift him to a hospital and not wait for the police.

Meeting Ajit and Shweta during this trip was jinxed he thought and then rushed to their house to seek help. 'I need help. There is an emergency. A person has been knocked down by my taxi.'

'Your taxi?' Shashank said. 'Oh God, the police would be here soon.'

'Let them come. I can't leave him and run away to save myself from the hassles. How far is the nearest hospital?'

When he returned to the spot with Shashank, he found Chhotu trying hard to wake his chacha up. 'What a strange coincidence, I know this boy!' he said astonished at the turn of unfortunate events.

In the meantime, a small crowd had gathered at the spot.

'Jyoti Nursing Home is just a kilometre away, the driver must be knowing,' someone in the crowd said.

Shashank then helped Liddle put the profusely bleeding victim inside the car. Liddle held him close to his chest, even as the blood from his wound soiled the front of his coat. With his head cradled in his lap and his handkerchief pressed against the wound to stop the blood flow, he asked the driver to hurry, as Chhotu howled by his side.

'Wonder what that fellow was doing here?' Ajit wondered standing at the gate alongside Bina.

'Some people have seen a drunkard roaming around these days, but this fellow has a small child with him, who knows who he is?' Bina added.

Whoever he may be, I pray for his quick recovery! I can't forget the little boy's face! I hope even Liddle is saved from legal formalities. Shashank was genuinely worried for Liddle.

At the hospital, he was quickly admitted and the staff and the doctors had swung into action as Chhotu, Liddle and the terrified driver waited in the lobby.

The wait for the threesome, unknown to each other, was agonising.

Half an hour later, two doctors emerged and told Liddle that the patient was fine, only the wound on his forehead had required seven stitches. The rest were superficial bruises and had been treated. A day's hospitalisation was essential, more as a preventive measure. An immensely relieved Liddle thanked them.

'I wish to visit the hospital to see if that chap is fine and also to find out if Lidddle needs any help,' Shashank told Bina.

'Yes, you should, this place is new for him,' Ajit responded even before Bina did.

Shweta was saddened by the developments. All her hopes of getting some good news from Liddle had now been dashed.

It was 7:30 pm, when Shashank and Ajit reached Jyoti Nursing Home in a rickshaw.

A nurse escorted them to the private ward on the first floor. Shashank gently knocked at the door before peeping in. The patient lay on the bed, with his head and chin swathed in heavy bandage. A relaxed Liddle, dressed in a high neck beige pullover was busy playing *akkar bakkar* with Chhotu. It was evident that there was nothing to worry.

'Oh, thanks Joshi for your timely help. We were here just in the nick of time,' he extended his hand as the two visitors sat on the sofa away from the bed.

'Did the police come?' asked Ajit.

'Oh yes they were very prompt but fortunately they did not cause much trouble. They have recorded a statement of mine and this driver.'

'How is he?' Shashank asked pointing towards the patient's bed.

'Oh he's doing fine, just a mild sedation. He has lost half of his front tooth and the cut needed seven stitches. Those bruises on the face and knees must be painful, more so in this biting cold. I'm so thankful to Lord Almighty that he escaped with minor injuries. The man is lucky, isn't he?' Liddle said and continued, 'And you see, of all the fellows in the city, someone from my own place had to meet with such an accident involving my taxi. But for this Chhotu I could not have identified him. We have met each other a couple of times, business meetings you can say, but again I can't recollect his name.' The quaint circumstances and coincidence made him a bit sceptical though.

'Come here,' Ajit beckoned Chhotu who was standing near the door, feeling shy at their arrival.

'Sit here,' he said, indicating the little space by his side on the sofa.

'What is your name?'

'Chhotu.'

'What is your papa's name?' Ajit continued.

'Chacha.'

Ajit and Shashank looked at each other. A nurse came and injected some antibiotics in the saline bottle that dangled by the patient's bed.

'I've to leave tomorrow. I am sorry I could not meet sister and my beautiful niece this time,' he said and threw up his hands in despair. 'Next time I might come to your place with some real good news, who knows.'

'They wanted to come but then it was late. Tomorrow morning I will bring them here. My worry is how will you look after this child tonight?' Shashank asked.

'He will sleep with me on the attendant's bed there. He doesn't bother much. Smart boy he is.'

Next day early morning, Shweta and Bina accompanied Shashank and Ajit to the hospital. Chhotu was playing on the bed while Liddle chatted with the doctors.

Udit's sedation had been reduced but still he was sleepy and not fully conscious about the happenings around him.

'Please have your breakfast Mamaji,' Shweta said keeping the tiffin containing the breakfast they had carried from home on the side table as they settled on the sofa.

'Smells good, wow, I know sis is an excellent cook, I can't wait.' He sat down at the table and opened the box to find stuffed paranthas with pickles and some yummy malpuas doused with raisins and almonds.

'Come Chhotu, let's eat.'

'No, I want milk,' he said.

'This is a hospital, not a hotel, you must eat what is there,' he feigned mild strictness.

'Milk, milk and only milk. It has been four days and chacha has not given me even a cup of milk.'

'Let me check in the canteen,' Liddle said and pulled out a laminated card from the phone stand drawer. He called up the canteen and ordered a glass of milk along with four cups of tea and a special coffee for himself.

Milk arrived and Chhotu was delighted.

'Right, now you sit down and finish it off quickly, here, no running around with the glass otherwise, the nurse in the white coat will give you an injection.'

Afraid of getting a prick of the needle, Chhotu settled on the attendant's bed and began drinking. Suddenly he had an agitated cough and the glass slipped from his hand, spilling the milk on to his clothes and the bed.

Bina sitting by his side tried to comfort him but he had started crying, scared that an injection would follow.

'It's ok, Chhotu you get up first,' Liddle smiled a little on seeing the boy crying in fear.

'His clothes are all wet,' Bina said, feeling his wet sweater and the top of his trousers. 'The boy will catch a cold, if he doesn't change.'

'Oh boy, now where do I get clothes from?' Liddle was getting exasperated.

'Let me try in the market nearby.' Shashank moved out of the room.

Chhotu went and sat close to Shweta, staring at her brightly painted nails.

'Should I colour yours too?' she asked playfully.

The effect of waning drugs now allowed Udit to listen to other people talking but only faint whispers and murmurs reached his ears.

Half an hour later, Shashank returned with a pack containing a dress for Chhotu.

'Come, let me change your wet clothes, or you'll fall sick,' Bina cajoled Chhotu.

'We will play after you change, Chhotu,' Shweta was quick to add.

'Promise?' he asked.

'Hundred per cent,' Shweta replied.

A black woollen tee shirt, blue trousers and a fluffy jacket attracted the little boy.

'Quick Auntie, quick,' he said.

One by one, Bina took off his wet clothes and the skinny boy shivered. Shading him with her shawl, she put on the shirt and buttoned it at the collar. As she zipped up the jacket, a dangling charm in his neck caught her attention. She held it in her palm and examined it briefly.

Something about that locket struck her. 'So very similar! I wonder if these are also recycled!' the words popped out of her mouth automatically.

'Bina put it in, don't investigate, let it be there. Just change his wet clothes so that he doesn't catch a cold.' Shashank said.

Her eyes wide with surprise, she beckoned Shashank, 'Come here.'

'You carry your superstitions everywhere, don't you,' he said, sitting beside Chhotu now.

'You remember this?' she held that lucky charm in her palm in front of Shashank's face.

'Oh really, he had that in his neck?'

'No, I have brought it from home and put it around his neck.' A mildly irritated Bina immediately zipped the jacket and let the boy go.

'This only goes on to show that there are many parents like us, who still believe in the power of these little things,' Shashank tried to mollify her.

Though outwardly calm, Bina's stomach rumbled and roared in anxiety. The boy was too small to tell anything. Even then she dared to ask, 'Chhotu, who has given you this, it is so nice?'

He pointed to the patient lying on the bed and said, 'Chacha.'

As Shashank readied to return home, the little boy wanted to go to the washroom. Liddle picked up the intercom to call a nurse.

But Chhotu could not wait and Bina took him to the washroom. He sat on the toilet seat and began to sing.

'So young man, feeling better now?' asked the senior doctor who had come on a round.

Shashank tried to look away as the sight of a hospital, the rooms with those terrifying equipments, the smell of medicines still left Shashank in a daze of sorts, interfering with his thought process.

A nurse came to feed some juice to the patient. Lifting his head slightly up, she said, 'Come on open your mouth boy, you are a brave young man, you don't look good lying down.' After taking four tea spoons, he said, 'Enough for now.'

'Right I'll be back in twenty minutes; you will have to finish this off.' She then kept the remaining juice on the table and covered it with a china plate.

'And you can now open your eyes and talk, see your parents are sitting there, worried, at least say a few words to them.'

The elderly nurse, patted his cheek and turned to leave. 'I can't open my eyes,' he mumbled, 'but I can hear voices.'

'Voices?' She asked.

'I mean people talking.'

'Good, good. By evening you can go home.'

'He's doing fine and is perfectly coherent. That rules out any internal injury in the brain,' she said turning towards Liddle and walked out.

The nurse's words had stirred up the patient from his sedation. He shut his eyes tight again. Half an hour later, the nurse was back and fed him the remaining juice.

'Sister please get his discharge card ready and complete the other formalities,' Liddle requested her as she prepared to leave.

'Ok, I will send someone,' she said and went out.

A junior nurse appeared and asked for an ID proof of the patient for preparing an admission card and a discharge card. Mr Liddle volunteered to sign in the attendant's and guardian column but she wanted some document for identification and for hospital records since he was a major.

She started walking towards the patient's bed, probably to ask him to provide one.

Liddle stopped her, 'Please come after five minutes.'

'Shweta please have a look inside this bag, maybe you will find some card, some document, even a ticket;' and he handed the bag the victim had been carrying at the time of accident.

Shweta carefully unzipped it. It had a bottle of water, a pack of biscuits, a new bedsheet, a golden gift wrap. The bag had no papers, no cards of any sort, no wallet which could spring her a blissful surprise. A crushed and crumpled train ticket she opened with crippling optimism sadly bore no name. Male, 27 years, Sangam Express, G3 coach, 23.12.1993 was all it had to reveal. A little peeved, she frisked the pockets again only to detect something in the shape of a book. Disheartened, she took it out just for the sake of psychological satisfaction.

A diary it was, in burgundy cover, with the year 1993 printed in gold. A hesitant pause followed; it was something too personal, a possession not intended for sharing, urged her conscience. She resisted any temptation, unwilling to be privy to the contents of a 'man's' diary and she zipped it back, relieved that she had committed no impropriety.

'Sorry Mamaji, found nothing in the bag,' she said and then suddenly said 'Wait.'

A split second decision it had been, that she was indeed searching for personal information to help the man and no one could ascribe any other motive, if she just checked the first page. With a pinch of guilt she warily turned the cover over. Three seconds of eternity she experienced as the entries blasted through to her brain. Her eyes remained wide open and then were fogged; her mind rendered a muddle, as her emotions slid on a slippery ramp.

Name- U Joshi.

Father's name – S. Joshi.

Permanent Address- HN 1215.........

Present address- HN 135, C/o K Negi, Mussoorie

Her heart skipped many a beat as she turned the next few pages together. What a strange coincidence. She stared at the man on the bed and then began turning the pages frantically again.

The handwriting was definitely his, the same style of writing S in a fancy way. Then she turned to the last page. It contained something that ruled out any possibility of a coincidence over names and numbers.

Could a miracle like this happen? Had their silent prayers been answered? She began to shiver as the two open pages had the poem she had come across in his old diary. Those pages too lay open in front of her eyes. She repeated like an excited child.

My Life's Rugged Terrain

Laugh and the world laughs with you,
Weep and you weep alone, they say,
Alas, I laugh alone,
I weep alone,
Come on my world,
Give me a shoulder to cry upon.
Is it my fault then,
That I want to be loved?
That I want to be hugged?
Come on, it's not too late,
I promise,
I will forgive you.
Let your affection overflow,
Let me be drenched with emotions,
Let me swim in hope,
Let my fears drown,
Before it is too late!
How long will I ride on Granny's plough?
Hoping that some seeds of love,
Lying buried,
Will spring to life?
How long?
How long?
Thanks my dear Granny…
(Udit, The poet)

The name in the brackets left no room for any doubt. Right now, she had to search for her words, as speech had deserted her. She had been rendered speechless in sheer joy and astonishment. The proclamation could wait but she could not. Springing up on her feet she dashed towards the bed and on reaching, stopped abruptly to let out an earth-shattering scream, 'Papa, Mama, it's Bhaiya.

Udit Bhaiya has come home. It's a miracle Mamaji, our prayers have been answered!'

Bina and Shashank were in a daze. How could two miracles happen at the same time? Bina caught hold of Shashank's hand as they walked towards the other side of the bed to hug him.

That night, at the Joshi home, the Johris were there to celebrate. Arvind's efforts had borne fruit and today he felt the same joy that he had experienced years ago when an year old Madhur had walked on his own from one corner of the room to the other.

The celebrations continued as the whole family remained huddled together in the bedroom. And while Shashank was still waiting for the operator to call for the trunk call he had booked to US, Sonam called.

'Hello! Sonam, we have found Udit, We have found Udit today dear,' Shashank said.

'Daddy, are you alright?'

'Yes you don't believe me, do you. Wait I will call Ma! No wait, I will call Udit. You speak to him beta. I have one more good news beta. Oh God, our Shweta has walked on her own today!'

Udit took the phone and said only one word, 'Sonam di …' after which he was so overcome with tears that he handed over the phone to his dad.

Sonam couldn't believe it could be true. She was so overwhelmed with the news that she could hardly speak. It was her husband Anoop who took the phone and talked. He also promised that they would come home on a short trip as early as possible.

And when everyone went to bed in the wee hours of the morning, Udit stole a laddoo from the fridge and sat at his dad's table with his diary. He was eager to put a full stop now in his life and he quickly penned down the concluding verses of the poem he had left unfinished for years!!

Thanks my dear Granny
Where ever you are,
You kept my hopes alive,
Throughout the drought,
Had it not been your love,
I doubt I would have been drawn again,
Towards my native land,
Now full of tender saplings of love,
And now I know
That this harvest of love,
Will be eternal,
Will be eternal.
The fault I know was mine,
And I have suffered enough,
For harbouring those thoughts
But I know I will be forgiven,
By the people who love me today,
And who will love me forever.

By the people who love me today,
And who will love me forever.
……!!